THE FUTURE IS WRITTEN

J O N A S S A U L

THE FUTURE IS WRITTEN:
A SARAH ROBERTS STORY

ADAPTIVE BOOKS

AN IMPRINT OF ADAPTIVE STUDIOS • CULVER CITY, CA

Visit us on the web at www.adaptivestudios.com

Library of Congress Cataloging in Publication Number: 2017941659
B&N ISBN: 978-1-945293-34-4
Ebook ISBN: 978-1-945293-46-7
Printed in the United States of America.

Interior design by Elyse J. Strongin, NeuwirthAssociates, Inc.

Adaptive Books
3578 Hayden Avenue, Suite 6
Culver City, CA 90232

10 9 8 7 6 5 4 3 2 1

This book is dedicated to the readers for all their support over the years. Your love of Sarah has inspired me to continue this series for many years to come.

Happy reading.
Jonas Saul

PART ONE

1

LIFE AND DEATH came down to a choice, a moment of indecision. The snare was set, gripping, pulling, but would she be strong enough when the time came? Would she be able to save the next one?

Sarah Roberts looked at her watch.

Ten fifteen a.m.

Three minutes until the precognition came true.

She found a few stray hairs above the nape of her neck, then tugged them out. The sharp pain fanned out and soothed her as she lay back on the dirty cement.

Vehicles crossed the bridge above. Maybe next time she would pack a pillow. The slope angled down toward a small river at forty-five degrees. The grass to either side looked more comfortable, but the message had been specific. If there was anything Sarah had learned, it was to follow the instructions with absolute precision.

Sit directly under the St. Elizabeth Bridge. 10:18 a.m. Bring hammer.

The hammer sat beside her on the cement with no apparent purpose.

She checked the time again.

Ten seventeen a.m.

The few hairs left on her forearm stood as a chill coursed through her. Within one minute something was going to happen.

Sarah picked up the hammer.

Her pulse quickened. She looked down at a pile of cigarette butts and focused on her breathing.

Keep it steady, she thought, exhaling slowly. Just wait for it.

The smell of rotting fish wafted up from the river.

The water lapped gently at the shore. At any other time the sound would have been soothing.

Cars continued to cruise over the bridge. Something louder, a semitruck maybe, came and went.

She glanced at her watch one last time.

Ten eighteen a.m.

A tire screeched. A horn blared. The sound of metal hitting metal made her jump. She involuntarily covered her head with her arms. Another set of tires squealed before the sound of splintering wood signaled the guardrail had been hit.

A vehicle came into view at an impossible angle. It fell toward the river, followed by shards of the guardrail. The car hit the water roof first and wallowed upside down, the passenger side canted slightly upward.

Sarah grabbed the hammer and scrambled down the embankment. She reached the car in seconds. A woman who looked to be in her twenties was trapped in the driver's side seat belt, her arms dangling toward the water that was seeping in. A small line of blood trickled down her forehead into her hairline. She appeared to be unconscious. There were no other passengers.

The river was quite shallow this close to land—it rushed by just below Sarah's knees—but it was high enough to cover the driver's head. An odd thought struck her. *How come the precognition didn't mention proper footwear? Mom's going to be pissed that I soaked my new shoes.*

Sarah grabbed the handle and tried to open the door. It didn't budge. She tried the back door. It was also stuck, or locked. She looked across to the other side of the car. The doors on that side were bent inward from the crash.

Her stomach churned when she looked at the woman. The water had risen to her hairline and was swirling around the top of her head.

Time was running out.

People yelled down from the bridge, asking if everyone was okay.

Water was now touching the woman's eyebrows.

The hammer.

She looked at the hammer in her hand. If she bashed in the driver's side window, it would shatter and could hurt the woman. She would have to enter through the back-door window.

She raised the hammer and whacked the pane.

Nothing happened.

She snuck a peek at the woman. Her eyes were submerged now. Sarah guessed she had less than a minute.

She swung back farther, twisting with her hips, and shouted as she struck the window again. The back pane shattered and blew inward. She used the hammer to remove stray pieces of glass still attached to the doorframe.

The cold water made her gasp when she dropped down on all fours. She crawled as fast as she could into the backseat while trying to keep from being cut by the floating shards of glass.

From the back, she angled herself between the front seats and lifted the woman's head just as the water brushed her nostrils.

That was where she stopped.

It would be difficult to undo the seat belt that suspended the driver. How could she push or drag her from the car? It would be impossible for Sarah alone, especially since she couldn't go through the driver's side door.

She would have to remain leaning on her side, holding the woman's head up against her shoulder. She used her free hand to cling to the steering wheel.

The water level stopped rising as the car settled on the river bottom. Until help arrived, she had done all she could do. It was over.

Minutes later, sirens wailed in the distance.

And not soon enough, she thought.

Her adrenaline began to ebb, and the shivering took hold. Though she was losing strength, Sarah held the woman's head above the water until the firemen reached the river. They cut the driver's side door off and removed the woman's seat belt, lifting the driver out.

Another fireman helped Sarah from the car and up to the top of the bridge. A paramedic handed her a blanket. She sat on the bumper of an ambulance as an officer fired questions at her. Had she been a passenger? Did she see the accident? How was she involved? As always, she was evasive. She hated cops. She told the police officer she would answer his questions after she warmed up.

Paramedics were fitting a neck brace on a man in a minivan as his family looked on. A garbage truck had lost one of its wheels, which caused the accident.

In the confusion, Sarah dropped the blanket and disappeared behind the ambulance. She adjusted the red bandanna she wore to cover her missing hair. She didn't want to be remembered as the girl with no eyebrows and hardly any hair on her head. Without the bandanna she would draw a lot more attention.

She started running. She had to get home before her mother asked too many questions.

She hated having to lie to her.

2

THE NEXT MORNING, Sarah awoke to a new mission. A note on the floor of her bedroom read: *Dolan. Save yourself.* On the back of the note were instructions to go to the Psychic Fair in town to find him.

Save yourself.

Was this meant for her, or was she supposed to tell Dolan to save himself?

Sarah paid her fee at the main desk and entered the Psychic Fair. The room was packed, people waiting their turn at several tables. Dozens of psychics and fortune-tellers were lined up throughout the room in rows. Some of the psychic peddlers were seated in actual booths; others merely had a table with a crystal ball resting on an intricately designed base with two chairs tucked underneath.

Why am I here?

She clutched her notebook against her chest. Within four strides she was around an aisle corner and hustling through a throng of people.

She smelled something strange. Soft music, trancelike, issued from small speakers on a table to her left. She moved on with no direction, only vague purpose.

Sarah tightened her bandanna. She couldn't risk it falling off in public; people would be horrified by all her missing hair. Six months earlier, the doctor had diagnosed her with a condition called trichotillomania. It was an impulse control disorder where Sarah felt the need to pull out her own hair. Her mother lost it when she realized that the missing hair was Sarah's fault—she doubted her mother even heard the doctor's consolation: *"At least she's not self-mutilating with razor blades."*

The stench of incense clogged Sarah's nose. She moved down the aisle, anxiety twisting her insides. There were men everywhere. She couldn't just ask each one if his name was Dolan. It would draw too much attention.

Why do I get these messages anyway?

A bell sounded somewhere in the building. She felt people staring. Maybe it was her missing eyebrows.

Why am I here? she thought again. *I am nothing like these people. I'm different. I'm real.*

She turned to leave and made it three steps before someone grabbed her arm.

"Young lady, please wait."

"What?" she asked, her tone more angry than she intended.

"I know *what* you are."

The old woman had the classic look of a fortune-teller, with wizened skin and the headband of a gypsy. Her gaze was steady; this was a woman who had spent many years offering glimpses of the future.

"What do you write in that notebook?" the woman asked.

"What are you talking about?" Sarah stepped back and clutched her notebook tighter. She allowed no one access to it.

"Come back to my booth so we can talk."

"Forget it." Sarah shook her head and turned away. An idea struck her. She looked back at the old woman. "What did you mean when you said you know *what* I am?"

"Come back to my booth." The old woman beckoned. "I have a message for you."

A message?

Sarah hesitated for no more than a second, then followed. It was rare for someone not to stare at her missing eyebrows. This woman hadn't even flinched when she looked at Sarah.

The old woman shooed away several people huddling near her booth and gestured for Sarah to sit. In the center of the woman's table sat a crystal ball. Anyone could eavesdrop on their conversation. Luckily most people did not care to listen in on the possible future of others.

Sarah did her best to resume control of the situation. "Before we talk I want to know how much you'll charge, since *you* invited *me*."

"No charge." The woman raised her hand in protest. "My name is Esmerelda. I know what you are, and you must stop."

"What am I?" Sarah pretended to be bored.

"You write things in that notebook. Whatever it is, you act on it, or alter your routine, because of it."

How could this woman know that? Was she a real psychic?

Sarah bent forward as her stomach knotted. The fear she felt when answering her precognitions was nothing compared to the fear of being found out. She hadn't come here to be discovered.

"I want to see your notebook." The old woman held out her hand.

Sarah tightened her grip on the sacred journal. Her palms were sweaty, just like every other time she felt a blackout coming on.

"No one sees what's in here." She leaned back in her chair. She needed to leave, but she wanted to know if this woman could help her.

"Do you know a man named Dolan?" Sarah moved to the edge of her seat.

Esmerelda's eyes narrowed. "Why did you say that name? Is it in your notebook? I can tell you're in a lot of danger. I might be able to help."

It came out so easily—the warning.

"What kind of danger?" Sarah asked.

The woman leaned forward in her chair. Her red earrings dangled down to her shoulders, the earlobes stretched long from the weight.

"You are in danger. It'll happen within twenty-four hours. I've seen your kind before." The old woman was standing now, her face turning nearly the same shade as her earrings. "You're an automatic writer, just like me. You receive messages from the Other Side. That's why I need to see what's in your notebook. I wrote down that I'd meet you here, today. I wrote that I would meet one of my kind and she would look just like you."

"What are you talking about?" Sarah asked, feigning surprise.

"You have a gift," the woman said. "Use it wisely."

"Wait. When you say danger, are you threatening me, or talking about my *gift*?"

"Sarah, whatever is in your notebook, I think it's a message for you. I think you need to save yourself."

Sarah shuddered. *Save yourself. And how does this woman know my name?*

Fear coursed through her. She looked down at her hand. It started to twitch.

Oh no. Not here.

Her hand twitched again, this time with more urgency. Breathing became an effort.

She stood, hopped over the railing on her right, and ran through the crowd toward the main doors.

When she looked back, no one was following her.

If what that woman had said was true, then trouble was coming and it would be here soon.

Two men stood in her way at the doors. She wasn't able to get around them fast enough. Her balance lost, she tumbled and hit the floor.

The familiar signs of a full blackout came over her, and her vision closed down.

Someone asked if she was okay. She opened her eyes and immediately felt for her notebook, but it was gone.

Only her pen rested on the floor beside her.

She made to get to her feet, her eyes scanning the ground in a panic.

"I was asking if you were okay."

An older, distinguished-looking man stared down at her.

"I'm fine," Sarah said as she picked up her pen.

"You appeared to black out. You scribbled in your notebook and then . . . are you sure you're okay?"

The man glared at her. For some reason, he sounded upset. Some of her resolve came back. She regained her footing.

"I'm fine," Sarah repeated, more harshly. "Where's my notebook?"

"Let me introduce myself. I'm the president of the Psychic Fair. My name is Dolan Ryan."

Dolan.

She couldn't believe it. Here he was, the man she was supposed to see, and her notebook was gone.

"Do you have my notebook?"

"No. I was talking to my assistant when you bumped into us and fell down. I saw you writing in it. Then you got up. I'm sorry, but I don't see it anymore."

Sarah didn't want to think about what would happen if her notebook fell into the wrong hands, or the hands of *anyone* for that matter. It held information about the last six months of precognitions: a beating, the kidnapping of Mary Bennett, car accidents.

The pavilion suddenly felt darker, smaller.

Was this the danger she was in? Would the police find her notebook and track her down?

She backed away from Dolan. With a glance to her right, she saw the old woman, Esmerelda, watching her.

"Sarah, there you are." Her parents walked up. "Are you done yet?"

She could have hugged her mother. The look of relief must have been apparent.

"Honey, what's wrong? Are you okay?"

Sarah nodded briefly and turned back toward Dolan.

Speaking loud enough for only Dolan to hear, she said, "I was sent here to give you a message: Save yourself."

A minute later, heading away from Dolan toward the open pavilion doors, her mother asked, "What was that all about? Who were those people?"

"I'll tell you on the way home," Sarah said. Her hands felt empty without the notebook.

Her parents trailed behind her on their way out of the building, her father strangely quiet.

As Sarah left the Psychic Fair, she wondered again who the message *save yourself* was meant for.

3

IT WAS CLEAR that Sarah shouldn't have come.

The fair had just closed for the evening. The pavilion was dark except for a few random lights. There was just enough illumination for her to find her trailer in the back parking lot.

She picked up her crystal ball. It was the prop she hated most. It was all for show; everything was for show. That was the way the public had to see it, as per Dolan.

"Esmerelda."

She jumped, almost dropping the orb. She set it gently back down on the table and turned.

"What do you want?"

"You look jittery," Dolan said, a half smile playing across his lips. "If I had to guess, I'd say something's bothering you."

Esmerelda put her hands up, palms facing him. "Stay out of my head, Dolan."

"You know my rules. I never use my gifts on fellow psychics." Dolan took a seat in the customer's chair. "I wanted to talk to you about a customer you had today. I would've come sooner, but I had to get rid of all the naggers."

"Naggers?" Esmerelda didn't sit. She leaned back against a steel post.

"The desperate stragglers. They remind me of the paparazzi."

"Who can resist you?" she asked, failing to stifle the sarcasm.

"Esmerelda, you've been with the fair for a long time. We've known each other for over twenty years. Why such bitterness in your voice?"

Esmerelda looked away. Dolan was right. Why was she feeling disrupted? Maybe because Sarah was so young, playing a game but not yet aware of its rules. She should have taken her by the arm and told her exactly how much danger she was in. She should have told her to stop listening to the messages.

"I'm sorry, Dolan. You're right. It's been a long day."

"Do you remember the young girl with the missing hair? Quite a distinguishing feature, wouldn't you say?"

"I remember. Why do you ask?"

"I bumped into her after she left your booth."

Esmerelda nodded. "I saw the incident. If you're looking to apologize to her, it's too late. I don't keep personal records of my clients. I didn't even get the chance to do a reading." Esmerelda met Dolan's eyes. "Is there something you're not telling me?"

"Look, Esmerelda. I'm not sure what it is myself. I felt some kind of a spark with that girl. She had a message in her notebook. I have no idea what it means, but it's quite unsettling."

Dolan lowered his head. Esmerelda waited for him to continue.

In the silence between them, she heard someone walking nearby. She peeked around her booth and looked down the aisle just in time to see a suit jacket flutter past. A black jacket. The same type worn by Alex, Dolan's assistant. Was Alex listening in? She lifted her nose and took in a deep breath to see if she could detect his cologne.

"Did you hear that?" she asked.

"Hear what?"

Esmerelda brushed it off and gestured for Dolan to continue. "You said there was something else?"

"Yes."

He rose from the chair and looked down at Esmerelda. She was almost two feet shorter than him.

"She had a notebook with her. When she fell to the floor it popped open. I went to help her up, but she fell into a trance and wrote something down. Then she snapped out of it."

Esmerelda waited. In the darkened pavilion she hadn't noticed how anxious he looked.

"I saw *my* name in her notebook. She had circled it several times before getting to her feet."

"Having your name in her notebook shouldn't worry you. You're the one that makes this Psychic Fair popular. Everyone comes to see you. After all the help you've given the police with missing person cases, you're a celebrity."

Dolan shook his head. "Next to my name it said two words: *save yourself.*"

Esmerelda plunked down in her chair. "Sarah is an automatic writer. She receives precognitions about people in need of help and then attempts to help them."

"How do you know? You read that much?"

"No, I recognized her from the news. She saved a woman from drowning under the St. Elizabeth Bridge. That anchorwoman who crashed into the water when a garbage truck lost its wheel."

"That was Sarah?"

"Yes. And she's in trouble. Something's coming, but I can't tell what. As soon as I warned her, she bolted. I wish I could do more, but I fear that within twenty-four hours Sarah will become a victim of whatever incident she's trying to prevent."

4

SARAH LAY ON her bed, not sure what to do next. Yesterday, Esmerelda had given her a warning at the Psychic Fair. And then her parents argued most of the night about her.

She felt a mounting pressure as she thought of the danger yet to come. Maybe it had to do with her notebook. If the police ever got their hands on it, she would have some explaining to do—the kind of explaining that got you locked up with a nice white jacket.

Automatic writer? She had no idea what that was, but based on the short conversation she had with Esmerelda, she could come to only one conclusion.

Someone or something from the Other Side was using her as a tool.

She needed to get her notebook back. She wanted to reread all the entries and then destroy it.

She couldn't turn to her parents. It would only fuel their arguments. She felt guilty enough about that. They wouldn't listen anyway. Even at eighteen, they still treated her like a child. Some of it was her fault. She hadn't moved out, and there was no indication that she would anytime soon.

She had no real friends to speak of. She had no boyfriend. Adding one to her mixed-up situation was the last thing she needed.

She could think of only one thing to do. She would have to see Esmerelda again and get a proper definition of what automatic writing was.

She kicked her legs over the edge of her bed and sat up.

What could she do about Dolan? Could she help him somehow? *Should* she help? Without specific information, she had no clue what kind of trouble he might face.

Sarah picked up her bedroom phone. After dialing information, she was connected to the Psychic Fair's number. On the third ring, a woman picked up.

Her hand shook as she held the phone to her ear. Surely she had been in more dangerous situations in the last six months. But this felt personal.

She asked to speak to Esmerelda and learned that she was in a session. Sarah left her name and telephone number, and hung up.

She grabbed her address book and opened it to an entry she had made months ago. Mary Bennett, the daughter of a wealthy family. There had been an attempted kidnapping, and at the right moment, Sarah had stepped in to stop it. Afterward, Sarah had tried to slink away undetected, but Mary had grabbed her and told Sarah to call if she ever needed anything. Anything at all.

Sarah dialed the number Mary had given her all those months ago. A male answered and told Sarah to hold.

A moment later Mary came on the line.

"Hello, who's this?"

Sarah took a deep breath. She would never forget that voice. Mary had been her first save.

"It's Sarah," she whispered.

"Sarah? I don't know a Sarah . . . . Oh, wait. Is it you? The one who was by the trash bin that night?"

"Yes."

"Hold on."

Sarah heard the phone drop. A door slammed; then Mary was back.

"Why haven't you called sooner? I have so many questions."

"I don't make it a practice to get to know the people I help."

"Are you saying that I'm not the only one?"

Sarah got up and walked over to her bedroom window. Her parents were still out. "Listen, I didn't call to talk about that. I need to ask for your help."

"Help? Whatever it is, I'll give it my best."

"I need you to do two simple tasks for me. They involve my father and a woman named Esmerelda."

5

ESMERELDA SPENT PART of the next day trying to figure out what was bothering her. Could she be *that* concerned about Sarah, a girl she had just met? Or was it what Dolan had said last night?

She flipped around the closed sign. She was done for the day. No more clients, no more brooding.

"Closing early?"

The voice startled her. Dolan's assistant stepped into view. She should have sniffed him out. Alex was always doused in cologne.

"Yes. I'm not feeling well."

"But it's only the lunch hour. Do you think Dolan will approve of his top psychic taking off early?"

"I don't care whether Dolan approves. I should've retired years ago. I do this because I want to. I don't work for you or Dolan."

"All right, all right, you needn't get so defensive. I was merely concerned."

Yeah, right, she thought. Why did she always feel the need to explain herself to Alex? Not many of the employees got along with him. Everyone wondered why Dolan kept him on.

"I'm leaving, Alex. I'll be back tomorrow."

"Where are you going?"

"It's none of your business. But if you must know, I'm going to my trailer for a siesta."

Esmerelda edged her way around the booth's table. The closer she got to Alex, the more intense his cologne was. Suffocating, like it replaced all of the oxygen in the air.

It was a slow day at the fair anyway. She'd only had a few people to read for this morning, and as she walked through the pavilion she saw it was half empty.

She stopped at the back exit when she saw Dolan.

"Where're you going, Esmerelda?" he asked.

"To my trailer, Dolan."

He moved in front of her, arms crossed.

"I want to talk to you about that girl."

"Again? We discussed it last night. I know nothing more."

"Ah, but I think you do. Come with me."

She moved to go around him, but Dolan reached out and gripped her arm above the elbow. He led her away from the back door.

"What are you doing? Let go."

"We need to talk."

It was so unlike Dolan to act this way. Maybe her precognition of danger had come true and Sarah's parents were here demanding answers.

Minutes later they were under a secluded staircase that led to offices upstairs.

"Alex and I were having a conversation yesterday when we bumped into Sarah," Dolan started. "You already know what I saw in her notebook. You said Sarah could end up a victim of one of her own precognitions. So, tell me, should I be worried?" Dolan ran a hand through his hair. "Yesterday, she whispers that I need to save myself. But then you tell me she's a victim. Is Sarah in danger, or am I?"

"I told you yesterday, I didn't get a chance to do a full reading." This was so unlike Dolan. She saw something in his eyes that didn't seem right.

Esmerelda continued. "I'm sorry, Dolan, but as far as I'm concerned, my conversation with Sarah has nothing to do with you. The reading was for Sarah and Sarah alone. I can't tell you about the danger because I don't know what it is."

"Esmerelda, how long have we been at this together, doing readings, helping people find love, marriage, peace? All I want is to make a little more money. Then I'm done. I want obscurity. Please, just tell me what's going on."

She studied his face. "What's happening to you, Dolan? I've never seen you like this."

"I need to know how I'm connected to this girl."

Esmerelda remained quiet.

"Esmerelda?"

She felt his anger, his desperation.

She turned and strode away in a half jog. The truth was, she really didn't know what form this danger would take. One thing she knew for certain was that it did have something to do with the Psychic Fair, and she wanted no part of it.

On her way out the back door she saw Alex again. He was perched on the table in her booth, watching her.

6

SARAH TOOK A seat near the rear of the city bus. It was empty but for a few teenagers. The doors rattled shut and the bus lumbered forward.

Sarah worried she had made a mistake trusting Mary Bennett. She knew better. Still, they seemed to have made a connection over the phone, and Mary insisted on helping. Sarah had saved her from a kidnapping, and Mary felt trapped in her boring life. She eagerly wanted to help the next time Sarah went to stop a crime.

The familiar *ding* of the "next stop" button woke her from her reverie just in time. She was a block away from the Psychic Fair.

Once off the bus, she headed to the front entrance and halted when she saw the registration table with two women sitting behind it.

She realized too late that she did not have enough money to cover the entry fee. She thought about asking if a notebook had been returned to lost and found, but then thought better of it.

Talk to Esmerelda first.

She approached the table. "I'd like to get a message to Esmerelda. She's one of the readers here at the fair."

One of the women smiled wide, showing all her teeth and some of her gums. "What message would you like to pass along?"

"Could you tell her that Sarah Roberts is out front? Tell her that it concerns the reading she did for me yesterday."

"I can try, but I don't think she'd be able to drop what she's doing. She's one of the most popular psychics we have here. But I'll make sure she gets the message."

"Thank you." Sarah grabbed a pen and paper from the table. She wrote down her home phone number. If she couldn't meet with her, at least Esmerelda could call.

She set the paper on the table along with the pen. Both women ignored her and continued chatting. Neither attempted to deliver her note.

She needed to find another way in.

Sarah stepped outside and rounded the corner of the building. She found the back lot fenced in with a security shack. The lot was cluttered with roughly a dozen trailers and rigs. *The psychics must live in these while they're on the road.*

The sun shone brightly, bouncing off the pavement in a wave of heat. She backhanded sweat from her brow and started for the fence. It looked like her only way in.

The security shack was manned, but the guard had his head down, as if he was reading something.

Sarah crept closer. A quick glance at the guard shack confirmed the guard's head was still down.

She began to climb. It took her less than ten seconds to reach the top. Straddling the bar, she adjusted her weight and began her descent down the other side. With three feet to go, she hopped off and looked over. The security guard hadn't seen a thing. She tightened her bandanna, adjusted her clothes, and started toward the trailers.

"Hey! You there!"

Sarah swung to the right and saw a man in a sports jacket coming her way. She looked back at the guard's shack and saw the guard come out with a scowl on his face.

Then her hand twitched. *Oh no, not now.*

She blacked out and fell to the pavement. When she came to, the man in the sports jacket was kneeling beside her, trying to pry her new notepad out of her hands. She held tight, twisting her body away for leverage. The notepad popped out of the guy's grip.

The security guard called out that the police were around the corner.

Sarah opened the pad and turned away so no one could see.

A new precognition was on the first page.

"The police?" Sarah asked, turning around to face the security guard.

"Yes," the man with the sports jacket said. "You're trespassing. But I'd be willing to drop the charges if you tell me what you wrote in that notepad."

Sarah slid the pad into her back pocket. She looked away without a word and walked toward the guard shack, where the guard was busy unlocking the padlock to the gate.

"I need to speak to Esmerelda."

The guard looked past her to the man in the sports jacket, and spoke. "All readings are done in the pavilion. This is breaking and entering. You can discuss it with the cops."

The cruiser pulled up outside the fence, and her stomach dropped.

The gate rolled open, and Sports Jacket was now talking to the police.

Minutes later, Sarah was put into the backseat of the cruiser. She detested cops.

She looked out the back window as they exited the lot. Esmerelda was running up to the gate. Maybe this was the danger Esmerelda had foretold?

The officer asked where she lived and headed in that direction. This would be a warning. The next time she was found trespassing, she would be charged.

In the backseat, Sarah found a few stray hairs on her forearm and yanked them out, hard. The rush was instant, cooling, calming her.

When they got to her house, her mother came out to meet them. The police gave her a quick rundown and let Sarah out of the backseat, into *the custody of her parents*, as they put it.

Her mother was furious, but Sarah ignored her and ran to her bedroom. She retrieved her notepad from her back pocket and read it over. This time, there were two messages.

The first revealed more about Dolan and what she needed to do for him. The second entry read: *Tonight. 9:23 p.m. Birk Street. North Face. Kidnapping.*

When she was done with the first task for Dolan, she sat on her bed, tingling with excitement. What would he think when he found the note she was leaving for him?

This was the first time real names had come through in the messages.

It was especially unsettling since it involved crimes, not accidents. *What would the police do with information like this?*

She just hoped she could count on Mary Bennett to come through for her.

7

HER MOTHER'S FOOTSTEPS pounded down the hall. Sarah fumbled with the notepad. She got it tucked into her back pocket just as her bedroom door flew open.

"What the hell was that all about?" her mother asked. "They found you trespassing at the Psychic Fair? What's going on, Sarah? You didn't even seem like you wanted to be there yesterday. Why would you go back?"

Sarah kept her eyes aimed at the carpet.

"Sarah, I won't ask you again."

She looked up and saw her mother in the doorway, arms crossed, both anger and worry clear on her face.

"I went to see Esmerelda—"

"Why? And where did you get the money? Don't tell me this has anything to do with your blackouts. Just look at your hair, or what's left of it."

Already her mother had turned to insults. She clenched her fists and waited for it to be over.

"I'm sorry, that was uncalled for." Her mother uncrossed her arms and sighed. "Look, I want your notebook."

Sarah's heart sank. Her mother had never wanted anything to do with it before. What had changed? She tried hard to keep her eyes downcast, because her mother knew how to read her.

"I said I want your notebook, and I want it now." She marched toward the bed.

Sarah flinched away. "I don't have it."

"What do you mean, you don't have it? You're lying to me."

Her mother's eyes narrowed.

"You are going to give me your notebook. This is not open for discussion. Do you understand me?"

Sarah nodded. She didn't want to provoke her in any way. She hated it when her mother flew off the handle.

"Get off that bed and get me your notebook. It's never out of your sight for long. If you've lost it, find it. Now!"

Sarah got up and moved to her night table. She opened drawers, looked under her pillow, opened her closet, and moved clothes around.

"Why do you want it anyway?" Sarah asked. "You never showed interest before."

"I talked to Mary," her mother said.

Sarah's stomach dropped further. Her right hand reached up to the back of her neck and grabbed hair. She pulled. The pain was quick and intense. Adrenaline filled her stomach, warming her.

Why would they talk?

"She called me. I hung up just before the police pulled up."

"What did she tell you?" Sarah asked.

"Everything."

Her mother was being evasive. Sarah guessed she didn't know much at all. This was a fishing expedition.

"What's everything?" Sarah asked. She felt her face heat up and turn red.

"Find your notebook. I know that Mary will be in one of your entries."

Her mother knew more than she was letting on. It had been a mistake to rely on Mary.

Sarah felt light-headed, her knees weak. There was no way she could give the notebook up even if she still had it.

But how was she going to handle her mom? She continued to pretend to search. She opened more drawers, looked under clothes, and even lifted the top mattress to look between the two. She felt the pit in her stomach get heavier.

There was another kidnap victim she had to help tonight. Nothing would stop her from being there.

The police are useless. It always has to be me.

She had never forgiven herself for letting Kim Wepps get taken after her kidnapping details appeared in the notebook. She had read about Kim in the newspaper the day after she hadn't helped her.

"I'd give it to you if I could. I was looking for it this morning and haven't seen it since."

It was a weak excuse. She wondered if her mother would hear the crack in her voice.

"Come on, Sarah. That little book is never far from your grasp."

Sarah crossed her arms when she looked at her mother. "Tell me what Mary said to you."

"She wanted to know where you were. She asked if you were the one who saved that television woman."

"What television woman?" she asked, shrugging.

"You know, when the anchorwoman for NBC was hit by a truck and knocked off a bridge. Her car landed upside down in a river. Apparently, a girl jumped in and saved her from drowning while she was still unconscious. Then the teenager disappeared. After I talked to Mary, I went down to your dad's toolbox and I couldn't find his hammer."

"Why would you look for Dad's hammer?" Sarah asked, trying her best to act like she had no idea what her mother was talking about.

"The news said the teenage girl broke the back window of the woman's car with a hammer. The police are looking for her. I told Mary it was impossible you were involved, but she went on about your notebook and how you saved her from a kidnapping. She said you called her earlier. To tell you the truth, Mary was surprised that I had no idea what she was talking about. I need to know what's in your notebook now."

Sarah tried to deflect. "That doesn't make sense. Why would I have anything to do with *kidnappings?*"

The shrill ring of the phone made her jump.

"Are you expecting a call?" her mother asked.

Sarah shook her head.

She followed her mother into the den, her pulse racing.

"Hello?" She looked up at Sarah. "Yes, she's here. Hold on, please." Putting her palm over the mouthpiece, she whispered, "It's someone from the Psychic Fair."

Sarah lunged for the phone. Her mother pulled it away.

She scowled down at Sarah. "How did this man get our number? And why is he calling for you?"

"I have no idea," Sarah said as she reached for the phone again, this time snatching it from her mother's grasp.

"Hello," Sarah said as she turned away from her mother.

"I saw you today at the Psychic Fair," a man said, his voice deep. "I want to help. But before I can do that, I need to meet with you. Bring your notebook."

Focus, she thought. "Yes, I understand," she said.

Her hand twitched. It felt like the beginning of a blackout, yet not strong enough.

"Good. Come back to the fair and ask for . . ."

Pain shot through her hand, starting at the elbow. She fumbled and almost dropped the phone. "Of course. Good-bye." She hung up without hearing his name.

"What was that all about?" her mother asked, arms crossed again.

"I can't tell you." Sarah needed to make a stand.

"*What?* Why not?"

She mustered up every bit of courage she had. "You want to know what your problem is, Mother?" She had never talked to her mother in such a harsh tone. She couldn't even look her in the eyes. "You still think you're having a parent-to-child relationship with me, and that has to change. I'm going to be nineteen soon. We are now in an adult-to-adult relationship." She walked away and shouted over her shoulder. "I'm going to meet Mary."

"I can't believe this," her mother bellowed. "Are you taking lessons from your father? You listen to me. You will tell me what I want to know because I'm your mother—"

Sarah ran down the stairs and out the front door.

The sun faded beyond the tree line as she made her way to Birk Street. She looked over her shoulder often, and watched everyone that passed.

Mary had betrayed her. A strange man had been watching her at the fair. He had called her at home. *And he wants my notebook,* she thought. *Why is everyone so interested in my notebook?*

She ran her hands over her forearms, searching for any remaining hair to pull out.

8

ESMERELDA STUBBED HER foot and almost fell getting into her trailer. She cut herself preparing vegetables. Her forehead still had a goose egg from when she bumped into a cupboard. Anxiety had always made her clumsy.

Why would Sarah break into the Psychic Fair's lot? Why were Dolan and Alex so interested in her?

After the police took Sarah home, Dolan and his assistant questioned Esmerelda for close to an hour. Nothing she said satisfied them. Dolan said Sarah had left a message at the registration desk for her, proof that Esmerelda was involved with this young girl in some way.

Esmerelda eased her heavy frame onto the blanketed chair in the back corner of her trailer. She sipped raspberry tea as she tried to decide what to do next.

She had told no one that Sarah reminded her of her own daughter, Denise. It was uncanny—except for the hair thing. Was it some kind of medical condition, or did she pull it out herself? Why would she do such a thing?

When Esmerelda first saw Sarah, she actually thought she was looking at a younger Denise. It broke her heart. She hadn't talked to her daughter since her husband's death.

John Hall had left everything to Denise—not a penny was willed to Esmerelda. Her little family had not approved of her psychic readings. They thought it was a sin.

Her husband's will was specific. A trust fund was set up for Denise once John's company was dissolved. If Esmerelda managed to access any of it, the fund was to be dispersed to charity.

It was this kind of callousness that drove Esmerelda out of the marriage two years before her husband's death. She joined the Psychic Fair to travel with Dolan. The last conversation she'd had with Denise was when her daughter called to ask why she wasn't at John's funeral.

That was almost twenty years ago.

When Sarah walked into the fair yesterday, Esmerelda couldn't help but stare.

Her husband and daughter were a part of the past. But meeting Sarah was not a coincidence. Something told her she would see her daughter again soon.

Esmerelda grabbed her cell phone and dialed information. Then she stopped, set the phone down, and leaned back in her chair. Maybe it was too late. She would try to contact Denise tomorrow.

She turned on the TV and flipped through channels until she got to the news. The NBC anchor was pleading for the girl who pulled her from the river to come forward. A story followed about the teenager who stopped a kidnapping but disappeared before anyone could talk to her. The story set Esmerelda's thoughts in motion.

She knew that sometimes Dolan helped locate missing people. He had worked with the police countless times, even though he hated it. It wasn't that he didn't like helping children—it was the notoriety it brought. People would swarm him for help finding lost loved ones.

An odd thought struck her. If Dolan could locate kidnap victims, then why couldn't he just tell the police where the kidnappers themselves were?

Esmerelda leaned forward and set her cup on the table before her shaking hands spilled the tea. Could Sarah know something about this? Maybe that's why Dolan's name was in her book. It would explain his sudden interest in her.

Esmerelda had to talk to Sarah.

A thump by the window startled her.

She spun around in her chair just in time to see the edge of a face disappear.

She went to the kitchen and found a rolling pin. The light switch was near the door. To turn it off, she would have to pass the open window.

Hands shaking, she leaned across the hallway, flicked off the lights, and lowered herself back against the door.

After a few moments of silence, she let a breath wheeze out.

The doorknob rattled as someone tried it. Her free hand covered her mouth as a squeak slipped out.

She looked up at the brass knob as it stilled.

Edging away from the door with as much stealth as she could muster, she picked up her cell phone and dialed 911.

9

THE CIGARETTE DROPPED into the ashtray as Denise Hall stubbed it out. She had held it too long. Ashes had fallen into her lap. She tried to brush them off, but ended up smearing them into her red skirt.

Documents lay before her on the desk in disarray. Denise gathered them up and tossed them into a corner tray. She picked up her phone and hit speed dial.

"Any word yet?" she asked.

"No, but I'm down at the motel sizing things up."

"Do whatever's necessary. Just tell me if it'll work or not."

"It looks like a fit. We just need to punch out one wall and set up a secure perimeter. Once the subject is relocated here, we can finish the reconstruction. We can move within a day."

"Call me with confirmation."

She rubbed a palm against her throbbing forehead after hanging up. Pausing long enough to control her breathing, she rose from her chair, grabbed her coat, and flicked off the lights. The lock clicked as she turned the key.

Her mother's face fluttered through her mind as she stood on the doorstep of her office, eyes closed.

Where did that come from?

Maybe it was that silly psychic stuff she always went on about, a message from afar.

She laughed. *Craziness.*

Her mother, Esmerelda, left for the circus many years ago. At least that was what her father called the Psychic Fair. He had liked to ridicule her. He would say that it wasn't "mother knows best" with Esmerelda; it was "mother knows everything."

Rain began to hit the pavement. She lifted her small purse over her head and ran for the car. Once inside, she opened the glove box and pulled out a small silver flask filled with ten-year-old Scotch. She had sworn it off months ago, but had recently felt the need for it again.

The rain sounded like a small machine gun as it pounded the roof. She held still a moment, listening to the rhythm as water seeped down the back of her neck from her wet hair.

Her cell phone chirped. She tossed the flask back into the glove box, slamming the little door hard.

Maybe some other time, she thought as she answered the phone.

"Yeah?"

"It'll work. One hundred percent. Everything measures perfectly."

"Good. Send them in. Get it ready for the delivery. And do it quietly. You know the drill. I want no one to know you're there. Understood?"

"I'm on it."

She hit the "end" button and tossed the phone on the passenger seat.

She found herself staring at the glove box. Her mother came to mind again. She wondered if Esmerelda was still alive. Imagine if her mother knew what she had done with the trust fund.

She reached over and opened the glove box again.

10

PEOPLE USUALLY STARED at her or averted their eyes. But for the past hour, as she walked toward yet another kidnapping, no one had paid her any particular attention. Her sleeves dropped below the elbow. Her bandanna was red, the one she usually wore to do her notebook's bidding.

Sarah watched the passersby. She felt a sense of foreboding. As if, somehow, *she* was being watched.

Maybe it was the call from the fair that was spooking her?

She was a few blocks from downtown, about a thirty-minute walk to Birk Street. She passed by a store and stopped. She needed to know the time, but she had left her watch at home in her hurry to leave. She pried the crumpled piece of paper out and opened it to the message.

Tonight. 9:23 p.m. Birk Street. North Face. Kidnapping.

She slipped the paper back into her pocket. She almost wished she could just call the police and tell them what was going to happen, let them handle it. But there was no way. They would never believe her.

Thinking about that made her want to pull. She stepped into the store, checked the clock mounted on the wall, and stepped back out to the sidewalk.

Eight thirty p.m.

She pushed the red bandanna above her ear. Stray hairs tumbled out. Savoring the moment, she eased them from their roots. She could almost feel the exact moment when the follicles disengaged.

She dropped her hand and stuffed it into her pants pocket. The hairs were entwined through her fingers. She rolled them around, trying to quiet her nervousness.

At a busy intersection, she crossed on the green and continued south.

Her mother had taken her to the doctor when it started. They misdiagnosed the hair loss as alopecia areata. Sarah never let on that she had anything to do with it. She let them think it was a fungal infection. It was easier than explaining the sheer emptiness she felt inside.

Finally, when they failed to see results from medication, her mother found out the truth.

The new doctor prescribed Zoloft, which she refused to take. She enjoyed being alone, depressed. She didn't want to be like everyone else, happy and fake. The dark moods had become a companion, a form of comfort. Like in the song: *Hello, darkness, my old friend.*

At this point, it wasn't like she wanted a lot of friends. She couldn't very well go with them to things like the public pool.

Sarah had never fit in.

In the beginning she tried to only pull hair from parts of her body that were less noticeable. As hair thinned, it became harder to find quality strands. Then her head was fair game.

Sarah slowed up about a block and a half from Birk Street. She considered the note. What did *North Face* mean? Was the victim going to face north, or be on the north side of the street? Then she recalled Birk Street ran east and west, intersecting with the entertainment district.

Within minutes she had walked up to the corner of Birk and Acton Street. A theater on Birk was showing the newest blockbuster movie. To the left she saw a convenience store and a Toppers Pizza.

Maybe *North Face* meant that she should face north. She looked up and down Birk Street. How was she supposed to know who the target was with all these people hanging around?

This precognition seemed to have more unknowns than the others. They were never too clear, but at least in other messages she was given an article of clothing, a hair color, or something specific, like *bring hammer.*

But not this time.

She turned to her right and walked down about half a block. A clock on the inside wall of a closed barbershop read 9:10 p.m.

The barbershop's door sat recessed in such a way that it was hidden from the street. Sarah stepped in to lean against it. From her vantage point she could almost see the whole north side of Birk Street, including the entrance to the theater and the pizza joint where most of the people had converged. She could even smell the pizzas cooking from where she stood.

While she waited, she reread the note.

I'm as prepared as I can be, she thought to herself.

After Esmerelda's warning she wondered what the hell she was even doing here.

She glanced in the barbershop window.

Nine twenty p.m.

In three minutes, someone will be kidnapped on this street.

Not only did Sarah not know *who*; she did not even know *where*.

11

GERT SAT IN the passenger seat, wondering why his brother was being such a dick. They had been staking out the theater for an hour, waiting for their target to show up.

He had done all the hard work on this one—scouting the place, following the girl. He almost got caught watching her house. Gert always obeyed commands because of the respect he had for his older brother. If it hadn't been for Matt, he would probably be in jail.

Matt was the one who handled the boss. He was also the one who always got paid more money.

Enough was enough. Gert wanted more. He wanted to play around a little with the next girl they took.

"So, how about it?" Gert asked his brother.

"No way. The boss would take you out if you were too rough with any of the subjects."

Gert looked at the dash clock and saw it was 9:21 p.m. He shrugged. "Once we take the girl, is the place ready for us?"

"Yes. I talked to the boss earlier, and it looks like it's all set up, or getting set up. Something like that. Either way, we got the go-ahead to move the girl there after we grab her."

Gert looked down at the floorboards. One of these days he was going to do his own thing. There was no reason why he couldn't kidnap a stupid, rich teenager on his own and keep every penny for himself. He was practically doing all of it himself anyway. He could even have his way with the girl for a week or two while she was tied up in a basement or locked in a cage.

Matt smacked his arm and put the car in gear.

"There she is. I'll handle the girl. You keep the boyfriend off our back. Let's do this and be quick about it."

"I still want to fuck her."

12

PEOPLE SWELLED ONTO the street as the movie ended, mixing with the crowd waiting to get in for the late show.

A girl wearing a blue vest with her date hanging off her shoulder walked right by Sarah. The girl looked up and locked eyes with her. Sarah stared as the couple crossed the street to the north side.

There was something about the girl that bothered Sarah. The vest was too warm for a night like this. The streetlights gave off enough light to see the logo on her vest. It was a familiar brand, but Sarah couldn't put her finger on the name.

She stepped back into the recessed doorway.

A black Chrysler pulled away from the curb half a block down and advanced slowly toward the pizza joint.

The North Face. She snapped her fingers. The vest. All the popular girls at her school had loved that brand.

So she *did* have an identifier for the intended victim, and she had missed it. The girl had been right beside her, and now she was across the street and moving away.

Sarah stepped out. She had to get to the other side of Birk Street. She had to warn the girl to take cover, get away, hide.

Sarah was pretty sure it was 9:23 p.m.

She began to cross the road. Her heart skipped a beat. She caught her breath when she looked into the windshield of the Chrysler moving her way. Both men were staring at the North Face girl as they eased along.

She looked closer at the man sitting in the passenger seat of the car.

Sarah recognized him.

It was the same guy from six months ago—the one who tried to kidnap Mary Bennett. That night, Mary had turned and run back to her dad's car when Sarah warned her she was in danger. This guy had been in a van that night, the side door open, ready to pull Mary in. Sarah remembered how he had grabbed at her for interfering. Her bandanna got ripped off her head, and the man reeled back at the sight of her scalp, bald in places. That was the only reason she escaped.

It was one of her most dangerous exploits to date. She would never forget his face.

The men in the car hadn't spotted her yet. She still had time to get away. But what about the girl? Sarah thought of what Esmerelda said and hesitated. Could she live with herself if she didn't *try* to stop this?

She put one foot in front of the other, moving forward. Time seemed to stand still. The night air cooled her clammy skin.

Indecision wasn't an option.

The two men had pulled to a stop just a few feet from the girl.

For some reason, Sarah had been chosen. She was being given these messages for a reason. She had no idea why. What she did know was that she could do something about it.

She made it to the other side of Birk just as the two men came out of their car. They had parked but left the engine on, ready for a quick escape.

She looked back at the victim. The girl was too far away from her.

The kidnappers would get there first.

She had to think of something.

Both men reached into their inner suit jacket pockets in unison. Everything seemed to slow down. The girl and her boyfriend were standing by themselves in front of the theater doors. Sarah was close enough to hear the two men from the Chrysler say they were police officers. Both men were showing badges of some sort.

Their car. She had to get rid of their car.

She turned and headed toward the idling vehicle. Her legs shook, and she glanced sideways when she was halfway across the street.

They were looking right at her.

Oh, shit.

Sarah bolted toward the car.

One look over her shoulder told her everything she needed to know. She would never get to the car, reach in, pull the keys out, and escape in time.

Footsteps pounded hard behind her.

Without thinking, she dove into the front seat. She grabbed the driver's side door and pulled hard. Her pursuer jammed his hand in to keep the door open, but yanked his fingers out at the last second before Sarah closed and locked it.

She gulped at the air in her panic. The man banged on the window with one hand. She looked up at him. His other hand was pulling keys out of his pocket.

Spare keys with a key fob.

Sarah grabbed the gear shifter beside her leg and tried to push the car into gear.

It wouldn't move. Then her index finger felt a button on the underside of the stick. She put her foot on the brake, depressed the button, and dropped the car into gear.

The doors clicked and unlocked.

She didn't know when she started to scream.

Everything was going wrong.

The door was pulled away from her.

He was in.

She stomped on the accelerator, lurching forward. The man was knocked off his feet. He held on to the car door and was dragged along.

Sarah looked through the windshield and saw his partner standing in her way.

"Stop, you bitch," the man beside her screamed.

He reached up and found a small batch of hair sticking out from under the bandanna and pulled. She would have laughed at the irony, but that many hairs at once, pulled by someone else, stung like a bitch. Her eyes watered and her vision wavered from the tears.

Then the man let go of the door and rolled away from the car.

She tried to gain control of the vehicle once again, but swerved as she overcorrected. The corner of the car clipped the man's partner.

His head bounced against the hood like a basketball. Then he disappeared from Sarah's view. She hit the brake and stopped the car.

She couldn't stop shaking. A part of her reasoned she would be safe now. No one would try to hurt her with all these witnesses. It was over. The girl was saved.

Something dripped onto her shoulder. She touched where the hair had been ripped from her head. She looked down to see blood on her hand.

THE FUTURE IS WRITTEN

The kidnapper stumbled past, his face a mask of shock.

Sarah eased out of the car. People had stopped their vehicles. Pedestrians were coming off the sidewalks to get a closer look. Someone yelled for someone else to call an ambulance.

Sarah came around to the front of the car, holding her head where her hair had come out, her vision still blurred.

The man she hit was lying on the ground, his eyes open wide in a dead stare.

She felt light-headed. A man was dead because of her. She doubled over, nausea coursing through her.

Someone materialized next to her. She tried to focus.

He was holding a gun. Someone in the crowd gasped.

"Who *are* you?" the man asked.

Sarah couldn't answer. She leaned on the car.

"Where did you come from? Why did you show up again? Who the *fuck* are you?" He was shouting now.

He walked around his partner's body, knelt down, and felt for a pulse, the whole time keeping his gun trained on Sarah.

"Whoever you are, you will die for killing my brother." He stepped closer.

His eyes were wide, swishing back and forth in their sockets.

"This gun is loaded with hollowed-out bullets. They will leave a small entry in your cheek, and half your brains on the street. Now get in the car."

Sarah couldn't move. Her feet felt rooted to the ground.

The gun was a foot from her face. It moved a little to the right and discharged. Her body jerked, the loud report ringing in her ear. Someone was screaming.

The world had gone crazy.

"I won't waste another bullet," the man shouted. "Get in the car."

Sarah tried to move, but still felt too weak.

Then darkness set in and she fell to the ground in a heap.

13

ESMERELDA HUNCHED DOWN against the kitchen cupboards while she waited for the police to arrive, rolling pin in hand. After ten minutes she heard people talking outside. It sounded like the security guard. The police had shown up.

She opened the door to see two officers talking with the guard. After she told them what had happened, the officers walked around her trailer, inspecting it for signs of attempted entry or damage. After finding nothing amiss, they told her they would swing by on an hourly basis for the rest of the night.

An hour passed. The police had come and gone. Esmerelda fixed herself another cup of tea and checked the windows to make sure all the curtains were pulled shut. She took a sip from her mug and wondered if she should call Sarah right then or tomorrow. She had probably gotten into trouble when she arrived home in a police cruiser.

Esmerelda wanted to help explain the incident to Sarah's parents as a misunderstanding. She would tell them it was a case of overzealous security.

She also wanted to talk to Sarah.

She picked up the note with Sarah's phone number on it. Someone answered on the third ring.

"Hello?"

"Could I speak to Sarah, please?" Esmerelda tried to sound calm.

"Who is this?" It was Sarah's mother.

"My name is Esmerelda. I saw you yesterday at the Psychic Fair when you came to pick up your daughter."

"Esmerelda? Why do you people keep calling for Sarah? I don't want to be rude, but this is the second call today."

"Someone else called looking for Sarah?" Esmerelda asked.

"Yes. A man. As soon as he called, Sarah ran out of the house."

"Did he give a name?"

"No. He just said he was from the fair."

"Would you be able to describe his voice for me?"

"What's this all about? Why all the sudden interest in my daughter?" Her voice rose a notch.

Esmerelda switched the phone to her other ear. "I'm as puzzled as you are." She cleared her throat. Raspberry scents drifted from her mug beside her. She took a deep breath and tried to relax. "I'm talking to her mother, yes?"

"Yes. My name is Amelia."

Time for some honesty.

"Amelia, I think Sarah may be in trouble."

"Trouble?" Amelia asked.

"How long has she been gone?"

"All afternoon and evening. Why?"

"I think it would be best if you call the police and report your daughter as a missing person."

Esmerelda heard a gasp over the line.

"What're you talking about?" Amelia shrieked now. "Why would you think that?"

Esmerelda heard something scrape on the floor, like Sarah's mother had planted herself in a kitchen chair.

"What do you know about my daughter?"

"When I met Sarah, I saw her gift. I also saw its drawbacks."

"Gift? Drawbacks? You're not making sense. Are you talking about the news anchor in the river? Do you know what's happening to my daughter?"

"All I know is she's probably in trouble. I tried to warn her."

"If I call the police, I'll tell them to pay *you* a visit. You have to understand how crazy this sounds. Yesterday Sarah goes to the Psychic Fair; today my daughter comes home in a police car, accused of trespassing; and then we get two mysterious phone calls. The first one sends her out the door; now you tell me she's in trouble—"

"I know how this must look, but my ability isn't absolute. I can't just ask questions and get answers. Psychic ability is more of a feeling, an intuition."

"I'm calling the police. Good-bye, Esmerelda."

The line went dead. Esmerelda replaced the phone and got to her feet. She had only done more harm. She entered her kitchen and got another pot of tea brewing. It was going to be a long night indeed.

She picked up the remote and turned on her little twenty-inch TV. The news was covering a hit-and-run in front of a pizza place on Birk Street. Television crews were on site, and witnesses were being paraded in front of the cameras.

A young man, about seventeen years old, said he had seen a Chrysler hit and kill a man. It was driven by a young woman wearing a red bandanna. Another man had grabbed the girl, shoved her into the trunk of the car, and sped off.

Another teenager said she would recognize that face anywhere. She knew the girl in the red bandanna. They had gone to the same high school.

Sarah Roberts.

The news capped the story by saying that the police were now looking for eighteen-year-old Sarah Roberts for questioning in the hit-and-run murder of an as-yet-unidentified male.

14

AMELIA HEARD HER husband enter the house.

Their love had died years ago with their firstborn, Vivian.

Not a day went by that Amelia didn't think of her. Sometimes she wondered if Caleb ever did.

She sat in the living room trying to work on a piece of pie.

"You're home late." She put her fork down. "We need to talk." She didn't wait for a response. "Sarah's missing."

Caleb had removed his overcoat and was sorting through a pile of mail on the small stand by the front door. For a long moment he acted as if he hadn't heard her.

"What do you mean, *missing?*"

"She left the house and hasn't returned. It's not like her to come home this late."

Amelia picked up her fork and fiddled with the crust of the pie.

"That doesn't qualify as missing. Is there something else?"

"I got a call from that psychic Sarah talked about yesterday. Apparently, she warned Sarah about some kind of trouble she would be in."

Caleb dropped the envelopes on the coffee table. He settled himself in the La-Z-Boy opposite the couch. "What psychic? From the fair?"

"The one from yesterday who gave Sarah a reading."

"You've got to be kidding," Caleb said. He stared up at the ceiling. "If this psychic really thought Sarah was in trouble, why not tell us?" He raised his hands in the air. "You know why? Because there are no psychics. It's all a crock."

"She advised me to call the police."

Caleb put his hands on either side of his head. "The psychic called here? How did she get our number?"

Amelia ignored the question. "That's not all. A man called just before Sarah left. He said he was from the fair, too. He didn't give a name."

"I knew that fair was a mistake from the beginning."

Amelia got up and faced Caleb.

"Sarah tried to break into the Psychic Fair grounds today. Security caught her and sent her home with the police. They gave her a stern warning but didn't charge her with anything."

Caleb put his hand up for her to stop. "Amelia, this must be a mistake. I've already lost one daughter. I'm not about to lose another."

"Correction. *We've* lost one daughter."

"You know what I mean."

"No, I don't. Tell me what you mean, Caleb." Amelia raised her voice. "I know you blame me for losing Vivian that day. You refer to Vivian as if she was only your daughter. She was mine, too." Amelia touched her chest with her hand.

Caleb dropped his head. "I'm sorry. You're right." He fiddled with a fingernail. "I think about her as my little girl. Since we decided to not tell Sarah about her sister until she was older, we can't even talk about Vivian in the house. I wonder if we made the right decision. It's almost as if Sarah senses something's missing."

Amelia stepped away from the couch and crossed her arms. "I don't want to tell Sarah yet. She has enough problems with that notebook business and her hair pulling. We only recently started helping her out of her depression. I think we should wait a couple of years. I know she's eighteen, but she acts so much younger."

"If we keep waiting, she won't forgive us for keeping such a secret from her. I'm beginning to wonder if we made the right choice in the first place. We could've told her about her sister, just not how she was killed. And now Sarah isn't home and we're panicking. This is insane."

Amelia walked back around and sat down on the couch. "Should we call the police?"

Caleb frowned and rubbed his chin. "She's only been gone a few hours—"

He was interrupted by a familiar beeping from his suit jacket. Amelia watched as he grabbed his cell phone from the inside pocket.

He clicked a few buttons and then read out loud. "Hi, Dad, it's Sarah. I thought I'd let you know that I'm staying at Mary's house tonight. Don't worry. Mom knows who she is. See you in the morning. Love, Sarah." Caleb stopped reading and looked up. "Who's Mary?"

THE FUTURE IS WRITTEN

"We talked on the phone earlier today. She called before Sarah arrived home in a police car."

"What did she want?"

"She told me some interesting things. She claims that Sarah writes prophecies in her notebook. Then she goes out and saves people. According to her, Mary is someone Sarah saved from a kidnapping six months ago."

"That's ridiculous. Are you talking about our Sarah?"

Amelia nodded. "Come to think of it, Sarah said she was going to meet Mary when she ran out."

"Do you have Mary's phone number?"

"I think so. It should be on caller ID."

"I'm going to call her," Caleb said. "We'll straighten this out right now."

15

SARAH WOKE TO darkness. She quickly realized she was in the trunk of a car, her confined space whirring with the subtle susurrations of the engine. A soft red glow emanated from the taillights.

She tried to move her hands, but they were tied behind her back. Her wrists were numb and shrieked with pain each time she moved. Her head pounded where the hair had been pulled out.

She tried to push her feet back and forth, but her ankles were bound, too. When her head moved, the dried and crusty blood on the back of her neck tightened.

She opened her mouth to scream.

Stupid asshole, she thought. *He didn't gag me.*

"Help!" she yelled. Her lungs ached for lack of air. Panting and gasping, she struggled harder and tried to scream again. Nothing much higher than a nasal screech came out.

She grew light-headed and set her head down to slow her breathing.

What did I get myself into?

Deeper breathing kept her awake. She had to stay alert.

The car hit a bump in the road. Her shoulder flared up in pain.

She wished she could pull. Find some hair in a sensitive spot and drag it out slowly. She needed to get untied.

The car slowed. Either the driver was approaching a traffic light or he was stopping.

A bead of sweat rolled into her eye. She shook it away and the headache flared.

She heard what sounded like gravel crunching under the tires as the car came to a halt. She struggled to hold her breath so she could listen. The car door opened and the driver got out. For a moment all she could hear was her own frantic heartbeat.

The trunk lid popped open. The man clicked a flashlight on, instantly blinding her.

"Never try to scream again. There are painful ways to die. You don't want that, trust me." He lashed out, hard and fast. Lightning flared in her vision as she was hit with something like a brick. The pain was unbearable.

A coppery taste filled her mouth.

"Rules," he said. "That's one thing my brother taught me. Follow the rules."

His rough hands grabbed her shirt and lifted her up. Her bound arms and legs screamed in protest. She couldn't suppress a moan.

His face was inches from hers now.

"I've broken a few rules for you already today. You weren't the intended target. So I expect you to follow the rules I set. Rule number one: no screaming. The next time you scream for anybody, I'll teach you what screaming really is."

He shoved her backward. Her head smacked down right where he had removed the clump of hair. She landed awkwardly on her arms, twisting her left elbow. By the time she could think to right herself, the trunk lid was shut, closing her off into darkness again.

An odd thought struck her as she tried to get comfortable. *What is rule number two?*

She heard a cell phone ringing. She closed her eyes and focused on her breathing. Through the trunk's lid, she heard him answer.

"Hello?"

She waited, straining to hear more.

"Matt's dead . . . I know, but I got that girl from six months ago . . . I have no idea why she was there . . . this is so fucked up . . . what am I going to do without Matt?"

He moved farther away.

"That's just it . . . where do you want me to dump her body?"

Then he was too far away to hear any more.

She curled into a ball as the tears finally came. Mary would've texted her dad by now. No one would even start looking for her until tomorrow or even the day after. She was on her own.

The car door slammed shut moments later, and they were moving again.

Sarah wept in the darkness until she fell asleep.

Before losing consciousness, she realized that the danger Esmerelda had warned her about had become a reality.

16

DENISE HALL ORDERED a glass of brandy. She wanted her nerves calm for the meeting. The pub she was waiting in reeked, but it would be closing soon. She was thirty minutes early for the meeting.

You did not want to be late for Mr. Ward.

She thought about all the deals she had done in the past. This one was going to be her most lucrative, for her richest and most notorious contact.

Her stomach lurched at the smell of greasy food. Something unidentifiable was burning in the back. She took a long swig of her drink.

The front door opened, and two large men dressed in suits and matching crew cuts entered the pub. They locked eyes on Denise, then continued scanning, taking it all in.

A waitress approached them only to be waved off.

Denise took another long sip as they took position on either side of the door. It looked rather odd—two sentries guarding the inside of a shitty bar.

She had dealt with Mr. Ward on a number of other arrangements in the past. She knew she was safe. She also understood the routine.

She didn't have to *like* it; she just had to play along.

He was the kind of man the Mafia respected.

Maybe I'm being too kind, she thought.

Mr. Ward was short, no more than five feet tall, with a large net worth—the kind that required more security than the president.

Sometimes Denise wondered how she got here. What was the point? Look out for number one and in the end you die. There was nothing else. Maybe that was why she no longer talked to her mother.

She took another sip from her glass as one of the men answered his cell phone. He put it away and nodded to the other. They walked to Denise's table.

"Come with us," the taller one grunted.

It was always the same.

"Let me finish my drink."

"Now."

Again, just like before. She wouldn't let them push her around. It was only a business transaction. She put the glass to her lips.

One of the men reached under her arm, half-lifting her to her feet. She was almost carried to the door and taken outside into the cool July evening, her drink still in her hand.

Mr. Ward's car was not there. No surprise. The trio turned right and then into an alleyway. Another, larger man stood by the back door of a Chinese restaurant. They guided her in and down a dark set of stairs.

So Hollywood, she thought wryly.

They entered a dank basement. Single bulbs hung from the ceiling. Either the walls were painted black or they were covered in mold. It was too dim to see for sure.

Mr. Ward sat alone behind a table near the far wall. He watched her approach. If she hadn't dealt with him before, this would be intimidating. It certainly had been the first time.

"Sit," he said, gesturing toward the wooden grade-school chair in front of the table.

The apes on either side of her fell away. She set the brandy glass on the table.

"Do you have the package?" Mr. Ward asked.

He was one of those men who always spoke with a smile, like he was the only one who knew the inside joke.

"I got confirmation earlier. That's why I called."

He stared at her through dark sunglasses.

Denise knew the tough guy thing was all an act. He had to make sure his employees never forgot who the boss was.

"How am I to expect delivery?"

"I'm having a discreet location renovated to keep your package safe. The renovations will be completed today, and the package will arrive tomorrow. I'll call with the arrangements."

"The money will be wired to your usual account. When I confirm possession of the package, the money will transfer, as usual."

Denise nodded. She stood to leave.

"May I go now?" she asked.

Mr. Ward nodded.

This time, unaided by the gorillas, she walked toward the stairs. When she reached them, she looked back at Mr. Ward. He hadn't moved an inch.

"This package is different. It has caused me a lot of trouble. I hope you're going to be happy with it."

"That's not your concern," Mr. Ward said with his trademark smile.

Denise climbed the stairs, trailing the smell of chicken fried rice, her stomach in knots.

17

THE RHYTHMS OF the car had a soothing quality. Every breath she took, every second that went by, was another second she was alive. She desperately had to pee, but she was trying hard to ignore it.

She knew the driver recognized her from Mary's attempted kidnapping. She suspected it was the reason she wasn't dead yet. With a shudder, she considered what he might do to extract information from her.

She felt the brakes being applied. The car turned onto a gravel road—her bladder felt like it was about to burst. She could hear rocks bouncing off the wheel well by her head. The car turned again and then came to a stop. Silence.

The trunk lid sprang open. It was dark outside. There was a single light high above.

He yanked her out of the trunk and dropped her to the gravel. Her arms and legs felt rubbery. She just wanted to lie there and rest, maybe with a nice morphine drip.

She saw the glint of a blade in the light. Its downward arc came quickly.

The rope on her ankles fell away. She twisted her head away as he came toward her face. She felt a slight tug and then her hands came free.

The driver stepped back and walked away. He got to the front of a cabin, fidgeted with the door, and opened it. He flicked a light on inside and turned to face her from the porch.

"If you're thinking about running, there's no place to go. Scream if you like. No one will hear you. I wouldn't, though. That would break rule number one."

He seemed to be enjoying himself.

"You should make yourself comfortable while you still can. There isn't much time left."

If he wanted to kill me, he would have done it.

"I'll give you one minute to get in here," he said, and then disappeared inside the cabin.

Trees loomed on every side. She eyed the road. It turned away and was lost to darkness. In the distance, what sounded like transport trucks raced along a highway.

She looked back at the cabin. He was watching her from a window.

She tried to get to her feet. They worked, but with pins and needles. She stood using the back of the car for support. The effort caused pain to flare up where he had hit her.

She knew she could not outrun him. No point in testing him too early.

She started across the gravel for the cabin door. How could her precognition have put her in such danger? Why was she here?

She had never felt so small or unsure of herself.

After all the people she had saved, who was going to save her?

18

"I CAN'T GET an answer. No one's picking up the phone." Amelia replaced the receiver. "It's been an hour since we got the text from that number."

Caleb paced the room, thinking. "I can't just sit around. Sarah isn't home, and it's past midnight."

Amelia grabbed the phone again. "I'm calling the police."

The phone rang in her hand. She jumped and swung around to look at Caleb. He motioned for her to answer it. She shook her head and handed the phone to him.

"Hello?" Caleb said.

"My name is Jack Bennett. I'm sorry if I've disturbed you at such an hour. I'm calling every number on my daughter's phone to see if I can find her."

"*Your* daughter is missing?" Caleb asked.

"She snuck out of her bedroom. I'm calling around to see if anyone can tell me where she is."

"What's your daughter's name?"

"Mary Bennett. Have you spoken to her?"

Caleb talked with Jack for a few minutes. It was assumed that both girls were probably together. They agreed that if one of the daughters contacted either of them, they would phone each other.

Caleb said good-bye and hung up. He didn't think to ask why Jack hadn't picked up the phone any of the times they'd called his house in the past hour.

Caleb tried to talk Amelia into getting some rest, but she refused to sleep until Sarah came home. She turned on the television and sat staring at a game show rerun.

A half hour later he stepped into the living room to find her asleep, sitting crooked on the couch, her head dangling to the side.

He breathed a sigh of relief. He had a phone call he wanted to make in private. There was someone who might know where Sarah could be.

He made his way to the basement and dialed the number.

19

ESMERELDA ROLLED OFF her bed and knelt down beside it. She stared along the narrow hallway of her trailer. She had heard something.

Then it came again—a soft rapping on the trailer door. A man called her name. She looked over at the digital alarm clock.

Three fourteen a.m.

Who could be at my door at this hour?

She walked down the hall and parted the curtains.

It was the security guard from the gate. He had a teenage girl with him.

He knocked again.

Esmerelda opened the door. "Are you aware of the hour?"

"I know, and I'm sorry to bother you. It's just . . . this girl." The guard shook his head. "Mary here says that she has information for you about your daughter. She says it's urgent."

Esmerelda looked at the girl shifting from foot to foot on her doorstep. "How do you know my daughter?"

"Maybe we should talk in your trailer."

Esmerelda shook her head. "Whatever you have to say, you can say it out here."

"Sarah sent me," Mary blurted out. "She told me to talk to you about Denise Hall."

Esmerelda stepped back. Her fingers gripped the doorframe. No one knew her daughter's name. Most weren't even aware she had a daughter.

The security guard turned to Mary. "Wait a second. You mean the same Sarah who broke in here this afternoon?"

Esmerelda cut in. "It's okay." She edged past the guard and softly gripped Mary's arm. "Come on inside so we can talk."

Before shutting the door, she thanked the security guard and bade him good night.

Esmerelda motioned for Mary to take a seat. She flicked on a lamp beside the couch and looked back at her guest.

"Can I get you anything?"

"No, thank you."

Esmerelda came around and sat in her armchair, opposite Mary. "What's wrong?"

"I think Sarah's in trouble."

Esmerelda rubbed the sleep from her eyes. "I know that. I tried to warn her earlier."

"It's not just her, though. She said that Denise might get hurt, too."

Esmerelda leaned back in her chair. "How could my daughter be involved with Sarah?"

"I'm not exactly sure how it works. All I know is, she gets told things. It's usually bad stuff. Things she has a chance to fix. She saved me from being kidnapped."

Esmerelda sprang forward. "Are you saying she gets these messages and changes the future?"

Mary nodded and went on. "Sarah was on her way to stop another kidnapping tonight. She asked me to text her parents saying she was sleeping over."

"Did you send the text?" Esmerelda asked.

Mary nodded.

Esmerelda grabbed the phone. "We have to call the police. We've got to tell them what we know."

"No! Sarah explicitly asked me not to involve the police."

Esmerelda's thumb hovered over her phone. "They're already investigating a hit-and-run on Birk Street. A witness said it was Sarah Roberts who drove the car. It was on the news a few hours ago."

"That's not good. Sarah was worried her identity would be revealed. This has given her purpose after years of depression. She doesn't want to stop, but if the police find out what she's doing, she might have to."

"It seems that she's told you a lot."

"I guess she never really trusted anyone before, but lately she's been nervous about her own safety. She said you might be able to help. She also asked me to tell you that your daughter will be shot either today or tomorrow."

20

SARAH REGAINED CONSCIOUSNESS, slowly and painfully. Everything ached. Her wrists and ankles were shackled to a heavy iron bedframe in one of the two rooms inside the cabin. She had spent the night falling in and out of sleep on the hardwood floor.

Sunlight streamed through the room's storm window. She guessed it was early morning by the low angle of the sun.

The cabin was silent. She shifted but couldn't find even a moderately comfortable position.

In the corner by the window sat an old desk and a wooden chair. On top of the desk was a small stack of paperbacks. She leaned forward and slid the handcuffs to the top of the iron rod.

Something sparkled in the sunlight on the window ledge. She pushed against her restraints to get a better look. A screwdriver sat nestled on the windowsill, a couple of screws beside it.

Her captor had planned on keeping his intended victim here. He hadn't just nailed the windows shut; he had screwed them down.

She needed to get her hands on that screwdriver.

The strain on her wrists was becoming more than she could bear. She dropped back to her knees and rolled onto her side.

The door to her room banged open.

"What're you doing?" her captor asked.

Sarah didn't say a word. He was unshaven and his eyes were bloodshot. She was sure at any moment he would start foaming at the mouth.

"You think you're smart?" he asked. "Moving around, trying to get those restraints undone? Well, let me help you."

He rushed over, dropped down, and produced a key. In seconds, Sarah was free. She scooted on her butt up against the wall by the window. She wanted to show fear. She also wanted to grab the screwdriver when he looked away. Maybe he would give her enough time to drive it into his back.

"You need to use the bathroom and eat. Then you're tied up in the trunk again. We're on the move. If you hear me tell you to stay quiet, then you do it. If you try to signal anyone, you'll cost them *their* life. Do I make myself clear?"

Sarah nodded.

"Answer me!" he shouted. *"Do I make myself clear?"*

Startled by his outburst, she stuttered her compliance.

She was pulling again. It had become an unconscious activity.

He looked at her, bewildered. "What is the matter with you? You got cancer or something?"

She shook her head.

He walked over to her. "Go to the bathroom. Last chance for a civilized rest stop." He pointed at the door.

She had no chance to grab the screwdriver now. He hadn't taken his eyes off her the whole time.

Ten minutes later, after cleaning the caked blood off the back of her neck and readjusting her bandanna, she was eating sandwiches at a wooden table in the kitchen.

Her captor watched her intently. After what seemed like an hour, he told her he was going to make a phone call and that he would be right outside the cabin door. When he finished, they would be leaving.

She had to grab the screwdriver, hide it somewhere, and get back to the table before he noticed.

He stepped out and secured the door behind him. She jumped from her chair and bolted back to the room, even as pain shot through her legs. She rushed through the door, ran to the window, and grabbed the screwdriver, holding it to her chest.

She had to get her breathing under control.

Then the cabin door banged open.

Shit!

She started to move, to hide, but stopped. The screwdriver was still in her hand.

He yelled for her.

She spun into a corner of the room and jammed the tool in the right front pocket of her jeans. Before her hand came out, the screwdriver nicked the inside of her palm.

She knelt down, leaning against the wall.

He entered the room fast, a gun in his hand.

Sarah ducked her head and covered it with her arms.

"What're you doing in here?" he asked.

He crossed the room and checked the window. He turned to her and placed the gun against the skin of her temple.

"Are you fucking thick? You have a death wish?"

Sarah looked away.

"Get up," he ordered.

She remained on her knees. She didn't want to stand up for fear he would see the impression the screwdriver made on her jeans.

"I said, get up."

She shook her head. He lifted her by the back of her shirt and shoved her through the bedroom door.

She fell hard, landing on her stomach before she could get her hands out in front to absorb the fall. She grunted as the tool in her pocket jabbed hard just below her hips.

"I can see you'll need to be taught a few lessons. When I say something, you do it or you get hurt. Understood?"

She nodded.

"Now, get up."

With a struggle, she got to her knees and then to her feet, keeping the pocket with the screwdriver out of his direct line of sight.

"Now walk. Go to the car and stand in front of the trunk."

When she got outside, he popped the trunk and motioned for Sarah to get in. She tried angling herself to avoid the tool in her pocket doing any further damage.

She felt his hands on her back. He shoved her hard and fast.

She had time to duck her head, but banged her shoulder against the top of the trunk, making her cry out in pain.

The trunk lid came down, but not before she saw him smiling.

Evidently my pain pleases him.

In the chaos, he had forgotten to tie her up.

She twisted until she managed to pull the screwdriver out of her pocket.

Then she began planning her escape.

21

CALEB STARTED FOR the door. If he was going to get his daughter back, he was going to have to do it his way. The police had done nothing for Vivian years ago, and he was convinced they wouldn't be of much help this time either.

He paused at the door. Did he really want to do this without Amelia? Would she understand what he was about to do? Could he tell her about the phone calls he received and the one he had made? Lately it had always been a fight with her. She had to do it her way. If he told her what the caller said about Sarah this morning, she would be hysterical.

But maybe she *should* be let in on this.

He turned around and headed for the living room. His wife lay sprawled at a crooked angle on the couch, her neck twisted on the armrest.

"Amelia, wake up. It's nine thirty in the morning. Sarah's still not home."

She grunted a reply and turned to ease the pressure on her neck. She massaged below her jaw, wincing.

"What time is it?" she asked.

"Nine thirty."

Amelia rolled her head back and forth.

"I've got a splitting headache. Can you get me some Advil?"

Caleb was back a minute later with the pills and some water. "Here. Have a shower, and then we'll talk about what to do. I've called the plant and told them I wouldn't be in for a few days."

"Do you have coffee on?"

He looked at his watch. Every minute was important. He couldn't wait.

"It's in the kitchen. Look, why don't you wake up, have a shower, and get dressed, and I'll be back before you know it."

"Where're you going?" she asked.

The doorbell interrupted them.

"Stay here," Caleb said. "I'll get it."

He rushed to the door and saw two clean-cut men through the peephole. They looked like detectives. One of them sported a goatee.

Caleb opened the door and lifted his hand to ward off the morning sun.

Goatee flipped through a notepad and asked, "Are you Caleb Roberts?"

Caleb nodded. "Yes. Can I help you?"

Have they found Sarah? Is she hurt? Or worse?

Both men flashed their badges. "Would your daughter, Sarah Roberts, be home?"

"Not right now. Is there something I can help you with?"

Goatee looked at his partner and then back to Caleb.

"There was an incident downtown in the Entertainment District. A man was killed in a hit-and-run. There were witnesses who put your daughter at the scene. If you know where Sarah is, it's in her best interest to meet with us so we can talk to her."

"A man was killed?" Caleb asked, stunned. Maybe that's why she didn't come home. "There must be a mistake. My daughter slept at a friend's house last night. I've got the text to prove it on my cell phone."

What had Sarah gotten herself into?

"Can we come in?" Goatee asked, and took a step forward.

Caleb blocked his way. "Right now wouldn't be the best time."

"Why is that, Mr. Roberts?"

"It's my wife. She's not feeling well."

He had decided earlier that he would not involve the police, and he was prepared to stand firm on that. If anything, they would just bungle shit up. Caleb had left a message for Dolan last night. He had refused to help locate Sarah, even though that was *what he did*. Caleb knew he was renowned for his success rate in finding missing children.

The other call he had received was from the kidnappers. They told him not to involve the police or Sarah would die.

"I'm afraid that finding your daughter is a priority," Goatee continued, "and we would rather do that *with* your cooperation. So I need to ask if you're hiding Sarah."

"Look, I understand I may appear a little apprehensive. It's just . . . she's such a shy, introverted girl that I can't really believe this is true. What you are saying she's done is extremely unlikely. I'll talk to my wife. We'll make some calls. Leave me a number where I can reach you, and when we talk to our daughter, I'll get to the bottom of this and then we'll contact you."

Goatee said, "It's not that simple. There's more to this than a car accident."

"What else is there?"

"We found several handwritten notes at the scene. We figure they fell out of Sarah's pocket."

Goatee put a hand out. His partner placed a notebook in it.

"Do you recognize this?" Goatee asked.

Caleb nodded. He would recognize Sarah's notebook anywhere.

"We scanned through it and found references to kidnappings, accidents, and crime scenes." Goatee looked at Caleb, his face serious. "Information that only investigating officers would know. In some cases, Mr. Roberts, the author of these notes appears to know what is going to happen and when, *before* it happens. She's either psychic or she plans the accidents and then tries to save people. We don't know what to believe. Help us out."

Caleb couldn't control the waver in his voice. "What're you saying?"

"There are references to Kim Wepps, a girl who was kidnapped and held for ten days not far from here. We're starting to believe your daughter had some involvement. Do you understand why we have to find her now, before she does further damage?"

Caleb closed his eyes for a moment.

"Tell him the rest," Goatee's partner said.

"We got a call a couple of hours ago from a woman who claims she's from the Psychic Fair in town. She told us that your daughter was in some kind of trouble, which we already knew. The odd thing was, she received a warning about *her* daughter, too. It looks like Sarah's planning something new. We need to find her soon, Mr. Roberts."

Goatee had opened the notebook to the last page of writing. Caleb saw *Dolan* circled several times in ink. *Save yourself* was written beside it.

Somehow, this whole thing had to do with the Psychic Fair. There was no doubt about it.

He gritted his teeth.

Dolan wouldn't even see him coming.

22

SARAH HELD ON to the screwdriver as she shifted her position in the trunk. Her hands slid along the smooth, velvety surface of the trunk liner until she came upon the plastic screws directly behind the brake lights. She was suddenly grateful for her decision to take shop class in school.

She removed all the screws she could feel in the dark and then pulled the liner toward her, exposing the back of the brake light assembly.

Her tiny jail gained a small amount of light from outside. This helped her as she tugged on the brake wires, loosening the bulb.

"You awake back there?" her kidnapper shouted through the backseat.

She jumped and almost dropped the screwdriver when he called out from the front of the car. She didn't answer him. She had no idea what difference it would make whether she was sleeping or not.

After a few moments, she heard him talking quietly on the phone. The sound of the highway racing underneath the car was a steady drone that drowned out his words.

With the bulb in her hand, she looked through the small hole where the brake wire had been. The red plastic cover was all she could see. The hole was too small to accommodate her hand. All her efforts were useless.

A dead end. A small hole to nothing.

With the little light coming into the trunk, she started working on the lock mechanism with the screwdriver.

After at least five minutes, with nothing but sore hands, she gave up.

What can I do if I pop the trunk lid open while we're going sixty miles an hour on the open highway?

The next time her kidnapper went to let her out he would see what she had done to the brake light, unless she could replace everything exactly as it was.

The road got bumpier. The car hit a couple of small potholes.

She took the end of the screwdriver and slid it through the hole where the brake light bulb had been. She applied pressure to the top corner of the outside red cover, in an attempt to break it off.

More bumps hit the wheels. She rolled around for a better position and pushed harder. The floor of the trunk was merciless, her right shoulder on fire.

One corner of the brake light cover popped loose, followed by the other. From her limited view of the outside she could see they were on a two-lane highway, with little to no traffic.

They hit what felt like speed bumps in the road, big enough to jar her. The screwdriver got knocked from her hand just as the brake cover gave way. The screwdriver fell to the pavement below, clanged onto the road, and disappeared from view.

Shit, that was my only weapon.

Sarah angled herself to get a better look outside.

She could not believe her luck when she spied a police cruiser following them. She could only hope he pulled them over for a missing taillight. As much as she hated cops, this might be her chance to get away.

"What're you doing back there?" her captor asked.

Her stomach did a flip. She turned and looked at the underside of the trunk lid.

Gravel kicked the wheel wells as the driver pulled onto the shoulder. Sarah dropped her head back to the hole and saw the police car had its lights on.

The cop was pulling them over.

Here was her chance. This would all be over in minutes.

"I know you can hear me," he shouted. "Listen and believe me when I say that I can make you die slowly. And I will take out all of my sexual fantasies on you first."

She heard his car door open as he got out.

"What can I do for you, Officer?"

"I saw your brake light cover fly off. Thought I'd pull you over to let you know you also lost what looked like a screwdriver a little ways back there."

Sweat ran into Sarah's eyes. She raised her hand to wipe it away. Should she scream and take her chances? She barely breathed as she waited to see what would come next.

"Yeah, I knew it was loose. One of my errands in town was to get that fixed."

"Your plates say you're from Florida. That's a long way to head into town up here in Alabama."

Silence. Sarah began to shake when she heard the officer speak again.

"Open up your trunk. I want to get a look at that bulb."

23

CALEB FINISHED WITH the two detectives, locked the front door, and walked back into the living room. Amelia had not moved an inch. How would she make it through the loss of another child? Could he count on her to be strong?

He studied her with genuine concern.

"Who was at the door?" she asked.

"Jehovah's Witnesses. It was hard to get them off the porch. Two guys with all these questions about religion."

"Is there anything new about Sarah? Has she called from Mary's?"

"Nothing yet, but I'm going to jump in the car and go find her."

Amelia sat up. "Where're you going to go?"

"I'm not sure yet," Caleb lied. Then he thought better of it. "I think I'll give that Psychic Fair a visit."

Amelia shook her head. "Sarah wouldn't be there."

"What are you going to do?" Caleb asked.

Amelia picked up the remote control and flipped the television on. Caleb watched as she turned the volume down low and searched for the local news.

"I'm going to get rid of this headache and start making phone calls. I'll start with Mary's dad and then work through the few friends Sarah has."

"Why don't you call hospitals? Maybe she was admitted somewhere last night."

He looked away as Amelia glared at him. "You seem full of all the answers this morning. Why don't you call the hospitals?"

"Because I'll be in the car, driving around."

"Are you okay, Caleb?"

"What do you think?"

"I look at your hands and they're shaking. You're fidgety, moving around like you can't stand still. It's okay, you know. We'll get our Sarah back."

"How can you be so sure?" Caleb asked.

"I just don't want to overreact. I need the first hour of the day to be calm for the sake of this splitting headache."

Caleb couldn't hold it in much longer. How could she be so selfish?

He didn't want to think about the other call he received from the kidnappers earlier. He wanted to weep at how unfair life was. How could both his daughters have been taken from him?

He needed to leave as soon as he could. Every second counted.

"You're not yourself," Amelia said. She set the TV remote down. "I think the first phone call I'll make is to the police department, to see if they heard anything about Sarah."

"No!" he shouted, his voice louder than he intended. "Don't do that. I'm stopping there first. It's only seven blocks away. You and I both know the amount of paperwork we have to fill out on a missing person, and it can't be done over the phone."

"Then I'll join you," Amelia said, as she rose from the couch.

"No. You stay home."

Amelia stopped. She rubbed her temples in circles. "Why's that?"

"In case Sarah or someone else calls. Just promise me one thing." Caleb walked over and grabbed her arms. He stared into her eyes. "Promise me you won't involve the police yet. You remember how badly they handled the case with Vivian. Let me handle them for now. Okay?"

Amelia nodded.

Caleb grabbed his car keys and ran for the door.

24

AN UNBEARABLE SILENCE filled the trunk as she waited for the lid to open. A car whooshed by on the highway. The heat seemed to be rising, making it even harder to breathe.

She braced herself as she heard a key slide into the lock.

There was a soft thumping sound.

"Ah, man. When I looked at that car go by I must've turned. The key broke in the fuckin' lock."

"Step aside," the cop said.

"You don't have to get uptight. I just broke my key."

Sarah heard the agitation in her captor's voice. Something was about to happen. She pushed herself to the back of the trunk and closed her eyes.

"Wait for me here. I've got pliers in my cruiser."

Another car whooshed by.

Moments later, she heard the pliers at work. Metal protested as she listened to one of them working on the broken key. Not ten seconds later a horizontal light creased what little darkness was left in the trunk. A soft blast of cooler air brushed her face as the trunk opened.

She looked up. No one was there. She pushed the trunk lid all the way open and sat up. She had to rub her eyes and squint.

The men were fighting on the shoulder of the highway. It looked to Sarah like they were struggling for the gun that was now out of the cop's holster.

She climbed out of the trunk and fell to the ground. Her legs weren't ready for the weight.

A shot rang out. Sarah instinctively ducked.

She wanted to help the officer but was in no shape to do so.

She looked around to see if she could get someone's attention. Up and down the highway she saw only one car, and it was traveling away from them.

She glanced up at the police cruiser. It would have a radio and possibly another weapon.

She hobbled toward the cruiser. The driver's door was unlocked. She swung it open and pushed herself into the seat.

A laptop sat on the passenger seat, a shotgun bolted into the dash. She decided the radio would be her best bet. Sarah locked herself in the police car and started pushing the radio buttons.

Something hit the windshield. Sarah jumped backward and smacked her head on the headrest.

There was a bullet hole in the glass. Her captor was standing in front of the car, aiming the gun at her.

"Get out," he said. "Or the next one goes in your head."

Sarah unlocked the door slowly and eased it open. She got out with caution and stood beside the cruiser on shaky legs.

"Now get in the backseat."

She moved toward the back of the car with the open trunk.

"No," he shouted, waving the gun at her. "The backseat of the cruiser, you *fuck*."

She turned around and got in the back of the cop car. The front door still sat ajar. She heard him ask the cop for his car keys. She couldn't see the officer from the backseat.

She leaned back. There had to be another way out of this. She had been so close.

She could barely hear the cop ask, "What about me?"

Her captor shrugged. "Wrong place at the wrong time."

Sarah reached for the door handle. She had to make a run for it.

Then the gun went off.

25

BY THE TIME Caleb made it to the Psychic Fair's parking lot, he was fuming. To remain calm he had been reciting his new mantra, *no police, no police.*

People gathered near the entrance doors. The fair looked busier than when he had come to pick up Sarah. He wondered if he would get a chance to speak with Dolan. Then he smiled. Of course he would. Dolan would not be able to refuse him, not after he found out his name was in Sarah's notebook.

He got in behind a small crowd and waited in line. Once he got to the ticket table, he bought a pass, and swung the doors open to the fair.

He saw Esmerelda right away. A girl about Sarah's age stood talking to her. Neither one saw him as they turned away and started down the aisle in the other direction.

Halfway down he caught up with them and called out Esmerelda's name.

"Tell me what's happened to Sarah." He crossed his arms.

Esmerelda turned to face him. "If I knew where your daughter was, I wouldn't just tell you; I'd inform the police, too."

"We don't want the police involved," Caleb said, a stern tone to his voice.

Esmerelda looked at the girl. Caleb turned his attention to her. "Who are you?"

"My name is Mary Bennett."

Caleb unfolded his arms and pointed a finger at her.

"You sent me a text last night."

Mary looked at Esmerelda, then back to Caleb. She nodded.

"What is going on here?" he shouted. "What have you people done? I want answers." Spittle shot from his mouth.

Both women backed away. It looked to Caleb like Esmerelda wanted to say something.

"Tell me where Sarah is," he pleaded.

People stopped what they were doing to watch.

Esmerelda looked past his shoulder. Caleb spun around to see two security guards approaching.

"Look, I just want my daughter back. What is it? Money? Tell me what you want."

"I'm on your side," Esmerelda said. "I don't know who took Sarah."

"Then explain the text I received. Why would you send it?" he asked, looking at Mary.

Someone grabbed his arm. He twisted violently to release the grip.

"Don't touch me," he snarled.

"Okay, mister, just calm down," the guard said.

People seemed to be everywhere, edging closer. He saw two different teenagers with cell phones pointed at him, no doubt recording this for YouTube.

"My daughter was kidnapped last night. She knows something." He pointed at Esmerelda. "And I received a text from her." He pointed at Mary. "But they won't tell me where she is."

The guard stepped forward, halfway between Caleb and the two women.

"I'm sure there's an explanation. Why don't we go in the office and sit down? We can all talk about it there."

"I'm not going anywhere with you people. I want to know where Sarah is right now."

Esmerelda stepped forward. "I already told you. I have no idea. No one here does."

"Okay, mister. Let's go."

Both guards tried to manhandle him. Caleb wasn't as agile as he used to be, but he managed to get out of their grip. He planted a foot, and used his shoulder to knock the guard on his right off-balance. Then, staying low, he whirled around and knocked the other guy off his feet. He hit him square in the stomach.

"Leave me the *fuck* alone. I came here to find my daughter."

The one guard tried to catch his breath while the other held both hands in the air, chest high. He nodded. "Okay, okay, take it easy," he said.

"What is going on here?"

"Who're you?" Caleb snapped at the man approaching from behind Esmerelda.

"My name is Dolan Ryan. I run this fair."

"Then you're the one I want to talk to," Caleb said. He pointed at Esmerelda. "Your psychic here is somehow involved in the disappearance of my daughter. She wrote your name down in her notebook. The same notebook the police have in their possession."

"Why don't we go to my office?"

There were too many people surrounding them. Maybe Dolan and Esmerelda would say more behind closed doors. Caleb nodded.

Dolan led the way to a small office in the back. One of the two guards came inside, and before shutting the door behind him, Esmerelda and Mary crowded in.

As Caleb and Dolan listened, Esmerelda told them about Sarah's appearance on the news, and Mary explained why she sent the text and how she knew Sarah.

Caleb was dumbfounded. He had no idea who his daughter had become. He told them about the police coming to his door that morning looking for Sarah.

"How do you explain your name in her notebook?" Caleb asked Dolan.

"We bumped into each other here at the fair. I saw my name in her book, too. It doesn't make sense, because she claimed that her notebook was missing."

"If my daughter writes down prophecies and then acts on them, it would make sense that you're involved in some way. Your name was circled several times."

Everyone was silent for a few heartbeats. Caleb wondered if it had anything to do with Vivian. Maybe he closed down emotionally and hadn't been available for Sarah. Maybe, in the end, he had let her down.

And now his daughter was missing and he was in a room with self-professed psychics.

He turned to Dolan. "Why don't you help? You've done this sort of thing before. There has to be a reason Sarah wrote your name down. Maybe it was a cry for help. Can't you use some psychic power and figure out where Sarah might be?"

Dolan shook his head. "It's not that simple. I know it's not what you want to hear, but I'm not the police."

"That's ridiculous. Listen to yourself. My daughter is missing and you won't help, especially after it started here."

"What started here?" Dolan asked. "What *exactly* started here?"

The office door swung open, hitting the guard who still stood in front of it. He moved out of the way as a man walked in, followed by two uniformed police officers.

No police.

Dolan spoke first. "Alex, what's this?"

"Your security guard called them."

"Hey, look," Caleb said, raising his hands. "I'm dealing with this amicably now."

"Doesn't matter. You still assaulted two security guards."

"They grabbed *me*," Caleb said, exasperated.

One of the cops stepped closer to Caleb and nodded at Dolan. Evidently, the two men knew each other.

"Come with us," the cop said, motioning to Caleb.

Caleb wanted to run. If whoever had Sarah saw him with the police, it would be all over.

"No," he said.

The air thickened.

"There's the easy way or the hard way," the cop said.

"I pick the hard way," Caleb said. For Sarah.

26

AMELIA LIFTED THE phone. It had been thirty minutes, and she had gotten nowhere. One more hospital to call, then she would call the police. She refused to wait any longer.

The doorbell rang.

She walked to the door like a zombie, the remnants of her headache an echo in her skull. When she got to the door she straightened her shirt, pulled her shoulders back, and opened it.

"Can I help you?" she asked. A dark blue sedan sat parked in her driveway. She could spot an undercover cruiser anywhere.

The tall man cleared his throat. "My name is Sam Johnson. I'm the lead investigator in last night's hit-and-run fatality. I'm sorry to intrude, but would you be able to provide a current picture of your daughter?"

Amelia stepped back and frowned, her stomach performing flips. Her knees got weak and she felt light-headed.

Fatality? Hit-and-run? What is he talking about?

"I'm not sure I understand what you're talking about." She cleared her throat. "Is Sarah hurt?"

The officer raised his eyebrows. He took a step back and looked at the number on the house. "Are you Amelia Roberts?"

Amelia nodded.

"I had two officers come by here earlier to explain what happened. It seems the witnesses' descriptions have been inconsistent. If you could just give me a picture, that would be very helpful."

Amelia wavered on her feet, grabbing the door handle for support.

"Is everything okay, ma'am?" the cop asked.

"Is Sarah . . . dead?"

The officer tilted his head to the side. "Not that we're aware of."

"You said fatality."

"A man was run down by a vehicle on Birk Street. Witnesses said the driver was your daughter. We went over this with your husband. He didn't tell you?"

Amelia shook her head hard enough to welcome the headache back. "He said it was Jehovah's Witnesses at the door."

"I'm sorry to hear that." He looked at his partner, who stood out on the lawn, and then back at Amelia. "Why would he lie to you, Mrs. Roberts?"

"He didn't say anything about police." Amelia raised a hand to her forehead. "I need to sit down. Come in." She left the door open and made her way to the couch in the living room.

"Is there anything I can do?" the cop said behind her. "Would you like me to get you some water?"

"No. Just tell me what your men told my husband."

She sat back while the detective walked her through what he knew about last night.

"And Caleb knows all this?"

"Yes. They even showed him your daughter's notebook. Can you tell me anything about this notebook? Was Sarah in and out at odd hours? Did she ever talk to you about it?"

Amelia put her elbows on her knees and massaged her temples. "I just can't believe this. There's no way Sarah's involved in any sort of criminal activity."

"First we need to locate her. You have to understand, Mrs. Roberts —from our point of view, that notebook has certain details that . . . well, I don't want to jump to conclusions, but . . ." He left it hanging.

Amelia looked up. "Don't, then. Don't jump to conclusions. Sarah is not involved in any crimes."

"We can't confirm that until we talk to your daughter. Although it could be that she *was* helping people. There have been a few cases where an individual saved a life and then disappeared. There's a possibility it was your daughter, ma'am."

Amelia's thoughts wandered. "I thought . . . my husband told me he was going to the police station. He said a missing person's report would be easier to file in person." She stood, not knowing what to do next.

The cop stared at her. "A picture would really help."

"Right. Of course."

Amelia went to her photo albums and withdrew a picture from a few years back. Since Sarah had lost her hair, she had refused to have any pictures taken. Amelia had snapped one while they were on a four-day mini-vacation in Florida. Sarah had only started on her forearm hair and eyebrows at that time.

She walked back to the living room and gave the picture to the cop. She wiped away tears and sat on the couch.

The detective studied the picture for a moment and then slipped it in his jacket pocket. "I'd like to monitor your phones. If she *is* in trouble, and gets a chance to call, at least my guys might be able to trace it. Would you mind if I had a couple of technicians come in to set up a tap?"

Amelia closed her eyes and nodded.

Why did Caleb lie? What is happening to my family?

The detective cleared his throat. "They should be here within a half hour. I'll have a little paperwork for you to sign."

The house phone rang.

Amelia grabbed at it. She answered before the cop could stop her.

"Hello, hello, Sarah?"

"No, I'm sorry. My name is Dolan Ryan. I'm with the Psychic Fair."

Amelia almost hung up. She'd had enough of these people from the fair. "This isn't a good time."

"I understand."

"You do? How's that?" She looked up at the cop.

"Your husband was just here," Dolan said. "He explained everything. I thought the least I could do was give you a call to tell you that—"

"Is my husband still there with you?"

"That's why I'm calling. Your husband isn't here. He was taken away by the police."

27

GERT TAPPED THE steering wheel with his fingers.

This isn't going to work. It's not supposed to be this way.

He looked in the rearview mirror.

Every cop in the state will be looking for this police car soon.

He would have to make her pay. He had promised himself he would have a little fun with the next girl they took, but not with this one. He couldn't get past all the missing hair. She looked like a nuclear bomb survivor.

"What happened to you anyway?"

She didn't answer him. He looked in the rearview mirror.

"I asked you a question. What happened to your hair?"

She continued to look out the side window.

"Fuck you, then."

"It's a disease," Sarah said. "It's contagious."

He shook his head. *Yeah right.*

Doubt ate away at him. He realized that he probably wouldn't be able to pull this thing off. His brother was the one who handled the details. He didn't know what to do next. Where would he go? Where would the ransom money come from?

A cop was dead, and here he was, driving through the town where the officer probably patrolled.

He swore out loud, smashed his hand against the steering wheel, and dropped lower in the seat. He was making too many mistakes. The boss hated mistakes. He should have loaded the cop's body in the trunk. It would have delayed things a little.

Too late now, he thought, angry with himself.

He needed to think things through better.

Number one priority: ditch the cop car. He thought about killing her, but decided to keep her alive for now. He may need her to get out of this situation. Maybe he could use her against the boss. Blackmail him to pay hush money or have the girl go to the cops with all the information needed to put the boss away for a long time.

There, a plan was forming. Maybe he could clean this mess up after all.

He breathed a sigh of relief as they left the small town. He looked in the mirror and spotted the girl scrunched up in the backseat, her knees drawn to her chest.

"This is your fault," he said. "Things would have been easier if you had minded your own business. Who sent you anyway? How did you know about our plans?"

She didn't respond.

"When this is over, you die. You know that, right?"

He rounded a corner and saw what looked like an old motel. From what he could see, the place appeared to be abandoned. He pulled off the two-lane highway and stopped in front of the run-down building. A sign said the area was slated for demolition. That would explain some of the construction equipment and the small white trailer on the side.

He pulled away from the front and drove around back, parking the police cruiser out of view of the highway.

The back of the motel looked like it had some work done to it recently.

That's strange, he thought. *Why renovate this dump when they're going to demolish it?*

He stepped out of the cruiser and scanned the muddy driveway. There were no recent tire tracks or footprints—at least none since the previous rainfall.

The last place to look was the construction trailer. He strode toward the trailer with authority. If someone saw him they might assume he was undercover.

The door to the trailer was locked. He looked in a window. No one in sight.

Perfect.

He could use one of the abandoned rooms to keep the girl for a day or two. Since it was a Friday night, he figured no one from the demolition crew would come back to work until at least Monday. He would be long gone by then. *Long gone.*

He jogged back to the cruiser. Fifteen feet from the cop car was the edge of a steep hill. It fell off into a small lake.

Things were looking up.

He opened the back door and pulled the girl out. She sat on the grass and stared off into space, her face blank. Her right hand was at the nape of her neck. He leaned over to see what she was doing. Her thumb and index finger were yanking on a small clump of hair. He twisted his face in disgust and stepped away from her.

Her fingers fluttered behind her head, hair dropping from them.

He shook his head. *Fuckin' weird.*

He shifted the cruiser into neutral. Then he began to push. The vehicle crested the top of the hill and started its descent. On the way down it bottomed out a few times, scraping against large stones and gouging small holes into the earth.

It hit the bottom of the hill and splashed into the water. Then it started a slow descent to the bottom of the lake.

He turned back to the girl on the grass.

She was gone.

28

AMELIA HEARD THE detective summoning her from the den.

"Mrs. Roberts, I think you'd better come listen to this."

After talking to Dolan, she needed a few minutes before she told the cops that her husband was at their police station.

The sun shone through the blinds covering the front window. Amelia stared at the floor where the light made curious straight lines. Could she handle it if something happened to Sarah?

Within the span of one day my family has fallen apart.

"Mrs. Roberts?" The detective stood in the doorway.

Amelia acknowledged him with a nod and started down the hall.

They entered Caleb's den, where two plainclothes officers were setting up wires and listening devices. She had already forgotten their names.

"We noticed messages on the machine and decided to listen in case your daughter had called in."

"Okay." Amelia took a step back and leaned against the wall.

"How much do you trust your husband?"

"What kind of question is that?"

The detective looked over at his technicians, made a gesture, and turned back to Amelia. Both men stepped out of the room, closing the door behind them.

"What's going on here, Detective?"

"Sam. I would prefer it if you called me Sam. We're going to be spending a little time together, so it would be easier if you'd use my first name."

"What did you hear on the answering machine?"

"I don't want to alarm you. Maybe you should be sitting down for this."

She dropped to the cushions on the couch.

"Just tell me."

The machine clicked and a message started.

Amelia identified her husband's voice immediately. The machine had picked up at the same time as Caleb did, and inadvertently recorded the conversation she was about to hear.

"Hello," Caleb said, his voice rushed.

A whispered response followed. *"I have your daughter. I want five hundred thousand delivered to a location I will reveal in ten days."*

Amelia gasped. Sarah had been kidnapped. It was official now. Her baby had been taken. And her husband knew about it. Why hadn't he told her? Why hide it?

"Who are you?" Caleb shouted. *"How do I know you've got her?"*

"You've got ten days. No police, or she dies. No police."

Amelia heard a click, and the answering machine stopped. She let out a breath and raised a hand to cover her open mouth.

"Mrs. Roberts? Do you need a moment?"

Amelia shook her head. *I have to be strong.* She adjusted her shirt, wiped her face, and addressed the detective.

"What time was that call recorded?" she asked, her voice shaky.

"The machine time-stamped the message at seven thirty-four a.m. Your husband took the call before my officers came to your door this morning."

"Why wouldn't he tell me?" She drifted off. "Maybe because he was headed to the Psychic Fair. We've argued over the past week."

"What did you argue about?" the detective asked.

"I wanted to take my daughter there and he didn't. Caleb doesn't believe in psychics of any kind. He probably went to see who was involved with Sarah's kidnapping because of the warning Esmerelda gave her."

"What warning?" the detective asked. "Who's Esmerelda?"

"When Sarah attended the fair, a psychic warned her that she was in danger. That's why the police took Caleb away. He probably went there thinking they had something to do with this."

The possibility of never seeing Sarah alive again hit her. She felt sick. On the table beside the couch was a Kleenex box, which she fumbled with until one came loose. She blew her nose and tried to compose herself.

"Mrs. Roberts, when you said the police took your husband away, what did you mean?"

She looked at the cop. He was standing by the phone.

How did my life come to this?

She hugged herself. She knew she would lose her mind if she had to bury another child.

It wouldn't be only Sarah dying. It would be a family.

29

"I'VE DONE ALL that I'm going to do," Dolan said as he walked away from Esmerelda.

"Which is not nearly enough." Esmerelda hurried to keep up. "We've known each other a long time. I've never seen you shrug off a kidnapping. Why, Dolan?"

"Too much is at risk."

They were walking through the back corridor leading to the employee parking lot. When Dolan got to his car he would be leaving.

"Look me in the eye." She stopped to catch her breath. "And tell me you are absolutely certain that helping Sarah will do more harm than good."

He turned to face her. She leaned against the wall, panting, a hand on her chest.

"Esmerelda, you know as well as I do that I can't save everybody. More than that, you know that I shouldn't."

He stopped talking as a few employees passed. He looked back at Esmerelda. "There are people who should live the path they're on without interference. Changing fate is a dangerous game. You of all people know that."

"I think there's another reason. I think you're being selfish." She pushed off the wall and stood to her full height, all four feet, eleven inches. "One more teenage girl won't change your life, but it'll change hers."

He turned and started for the parking lot again. She followed close behind as they stepped out onto the asphalt.

"Dolan, listen to me," Esmerelda pleaded. "I don't want to say this, but if you don't at least try to help Sarah, I will leave this fair. Do you hear me? I will quit."

He stopped walking.

"Esmerelda, you are being most difficult. Trust me when I say my lack of interference isn't personal. It's just . . . "

"What? What's stopping you? Tell me."

"I feel someone close to me is either directly or indirectly involved. I don't know how or why, or who this individual is. All I do know is if I *don't* help Sarah, this person will live. If I get involved, they die." He faced her. "I can't aid in Sarah's kidnapping case because I refuse to cause the death of someone I love."

30

SARAH CROUCHED LOW.

She knew he would have seen her if she had gone for the highway. It was too wide open. The woods on either side would have given ample shelter, but getting to them posed the same problem: too far.

So she had run through the open back door of the motel. Maybe she could find a way to get to the front, and then run for the highway. She had tried the dusty pay phone by the front counter, but it was dead.

When the motel owners abandoned the building, they took everything with them, leaving Sarah nothing that could be used as a weapon.

She stayed low, hiding under a window that looked out to the back. She watched as her captor realized he was standing on the brown grass alone, then he turned and ran to the edge of the building, where he disappeared from sight.

If the guy stayed in the front, searching for her near the highway or in the woods, maybe she could get below the edge of the hill and be gone.

Glass broke in a room next to her. She jerked and covered her mouth. He sounded angry.

Her back hunched, she ran for the door that led outside. Just before she reached it, a large shadow filled the door. Sarah came to an abrupt stop. Sweat broke out on her neck and back. A lone drop of moisture glided gently down her spine.

The stranger had some kind of automatic weapon in his hand. She heard more glass breaking behind her, followed by a man screaming.

"He kidnapped me," Sarah whispered. "Can you help me?"

The brute reached in and grabbed her. He spun Sarah into him, almost enveloping her with his size. Her small struggle was futile, her verbal protest quieted by his large hand.

He pulled her outside with him. Half dragging, half lifting, he guided her to the construction trailer. Seconds later they were inside, the door locked behind them.

"Can I use your phone?"

When he clamped his hand over her mouth, it was so large that it covered her nose, too. Her lungs fought for air as she scratched at the hand covering her face.

After a moment, he let her catch one breath and then sealed his hand on her mouth again. Using his teeth, he pulled off a small strip of duct tape. Air rushed to her lungs when his hand left her face, just before the man took the strip of duct tape and covered her mouth. He laid her down and worked on her ankles and wrists until she was secured with the tape.

He nudged her hips with his foot to get her against a wall. Breathing fast through her flared nostrils, she watched him grab a blanket. He came back and covered her with it.

The world turned a soft green. She struggled and twisted, but the blanket remained. It lifted and dropped with her breathing. She couldn't hear much of what he was doing. Her pulse pounded in her head.

A dark urge grew inside her—the need to pull. It blossomed into something uncontrollable, making her moan and writhe. The need was always there. Sometimes it was soft and delicate, other times desirable, a pleasure. But this urge was a demand, one that she couldn't answer.

With the muscles in her arms straining, she wrapped her fingers around, testing the bonds of tape on her wrists. It was no use. She would not be able to pull until someone undid her.

Her mind slipped. She felt a subtle kind of letting go. There was freedom in the pain. There were also tears. One rolled down her cheek and fell into the recess of her ear, cooling as it settled.

She pinched a small piece of skin on the back of her hand. She pinched harder, hoping to calm herself.

Her moans increased.

Something hard hit her in the side of the head.

Consciousness swam away.

31

THOUGHTS ABOUT TOMORROW kept running around in Denise's head. Was everything worked out? Did they have all the precautions in place? Would Mr. Ward be a problem?

She hated dealing with people like Mr. Ward. With him, everything was a pretense. But he was the man with the money. And if all went well, this would be the last deal she made in this business.

She swiveled in her office chair and opened the bottom desk drawer. In it, a dusty photo of her mother sat faceup. It had been taken a year before her father died. The same year they stopped talking.

Her mother had been quite upset with Denise's decision to sell off the family heirlooms. A couple of generations of artwork left to Denise in her father's will. Various collectors snooped around after he passed away.

Denise sold it piecemeal, living off the smaller, less expensive items for the first five years. Then she met Mr. Ward. He paid her top dollar for some of her father's collection. In the last fifteen years, Denise had sold almost everything.

It was rumored that the Rothko painting, *White Center*, would fetch millions at Sotheby's if she had wanted to auction it. It was completed in 1950, and by the late fifties her father had bought it for under a hundred thousand dollars.

The large, seven-foot canvas had not been easy to transport without damage. Fortunately, she had succeeded in the safe relocation. Now it sat in the secured and renovated shell of the Sky Blue Motel, guarded twenty-four hours a day by armed security—the best money could buy. There were reasons for it: the recent break-ins at Sotheby's, plus two other serious art dealers so keen to secure this painting that they had sent men to threaten and intimidate Denise.

Her storage facilities had been broken into as well. She was never talented at being discreet, or security-conscious. It had seemed better for her to keep the higher-priced stuff in warehouses and storage units than just keeping it at home. The threats and attempted thefts had helped to change her ideas on security.

This was her last big piece, her ticket back to normalcy. Once it was gone, she would have nothing left for collectors to hound her for. Museums could take the rest. What did she care? Mr. Ward had made her a generous offer, one that would keep the painting out of an auction house and her out of the poorhouse.

Staring at her mother's picture brought back a lot of memories. Maybe when this was all over, she would try to find her.

"Esmerelda," Denise said out loud.

She jumped when the phone rang.

"Yeah?"

"We got a problem."

"What problem?"

"A cop was just here."

"A cop? What are the police doing there?"

"He pulled in and dumped the car. I've got the girl."

She wondered where these guys got their smarts. She stood and turned to look out her office window. It opened to a garden surrounded by trees. *Calm,* she thought. *Stay calm.*

"What do you mean by 'I've got the girl'? And why would a cop dump his car?"

"The girl he was traveling with. She ran into the motel. Jenkins and I scanned the perimeter, but the cop is gone. He just disappeared."

"Cops don't dump cars and disappear. Could it be he wasn't a cop?" She put a hand on her forehead. This was not good. Mr. Ward wouldn't do business with her if he knew the police were snooping around. It didn't matter whether it was a real cop or not; this could be bad.

"He disappeared. I would know if he was still here. I've tracked people before."

"Then ask the girl who he was and why they came to the motel."

"I can't."

Her frustration hit new levels.

"Why can't you?"

"She's unconscious."

"Why is she unconscious?"

"I knocked her out to keep her quiet."

Great.

"Look, I can't be there until the transaction happens tomorrow morning. Keep the girl safe, but keep her out of the way until this is done. Can you do that?" A beep came through the line. Someone was calling her. "Hold for a second."

She pulled the phone from her ear to switch over to the other line. "Hello."

"Is something wrong?" Mr. Ward asked.

She must have sounded agitated. She collected herself immediately. "Not at all, Mr. Ward. What can I do for you?"

"I was calling to make sure our meeting is still on for tomorrow morning."

"It is. Everything's set. I'll have the account numbers for the wire transfers ready. The package will be prepared for transport."

"Good. I'll see you in the morning," he said, and hung up.

She went back to the other line.

It was dead.

32

THE EDGE OF town was close. Gert checked the signal on his cell phone and saw it had only one bar.

He needed direction. Since his brother was dead, the boss would have to take his place.

He checked his phone again. Two bars.

He dialed the number. He got a machine after five rings. He hit redial and waited. It was answered on the third ring.

"It's two in the morning. Why are you calling now?"

"I got trouble," Gert said. He heard his boss sit up.

"You're fuckin' right you do, Gert. What the hell were you guys thinking?"

"This girl fucked it up. She got in the way. It was the second time in six months she'd been at one of our kidnappings. She was trying to steal our car."

Gert heard his boss swear under his breath. "I figured something was weird with her when I saw her at the fair the other day. With all that hair missing. I called her house and tried to set up a meeting, but she hung up on me."

Gert stopped walking and turned from the shoulder of the highway. An SUV zoomed past.

"I want the money," Gert said.

"You're kidding, right?"

"No. My brother was killed. I won't let him die for nothing."

"Can you hear yourself? We can't do the ransom gig. You don't have the right girl. We know nothing about her parents. Kill this girl and dump the body before every cop in the country is after you."

He shook his head. "No way. Put the money in the account, or I tell the parents who you are."

There was a pause. "You don't want to threaten me. I could give the police your name and location and they'd hunt you down. They wouldn't even ask me how I knew. They'd assume it was my psychic abilities."

He slowed his breathing. Better not lose control. He needed help here, not an enemy.

"She's gone," Gert said.

"What?"

"She's gone. The bitch escaped. I couldn't find her. I looked for an hour and then holed up in an abandoned motel. I fell asleep. I've been walking back toward town ever since."

"You're lying. What motel? Where are you?"

Gert stopped. What if the boss wanted him dead? He couldn't tell him where he was.

His boss continued. "Go back and get her. She can identify you. Once you have her, get her to write something for you."

"What're you talking about, 'write something'?"

"When I saw her at the Psychic Fair, she dropped to the ground and started writing in her notebook. I've worked with a lot of psychics over the years. She's an automatic writer. She's getting messages about the kidnappings. I gave her notebook to Matt. Do you still have it?"

"Are you for real?" Gert asked. "I don't have any fucking little girl's book."

"We need her off the street for good. She can identify us."

"Now I know you're *fucking* with me. Psychics aren't real."

"I saw it. Believe me. That's why she has to be removed."

"Are you sure you don't want this one found safe like the other girls we've taken?"

"She told Esmerelda something important. I may have to remove her, too. Everything is getting out of hand."

Gert pressed the cell phone tighter to his ear as a loud rig passed. "You actually believe this automatic writer shit?"

"The girl has to go. Head back to the motel and find her. After this blows over, we'll take a month off and hit another city. I'll get close to the investigation on my side so I can keep on top of their progress. I'll try to give them something *psychic*."

Gert pressed "end." A fly buzzed his ear. He swatted at it and turned toward town. He needed to steal a car.

He looked at the time on his phone. He could find the girl and be back on the road before the sun came up. His step felt lighter with the knowledge that the bitch named Sarah would die today.

33

AMELIA HEARD THE car approach and looked through the living room window as Caleb strode up to the front door. He walked in and slammed it behind him.

"What's all this?" His eyes were wild, panicked. "Why are you people in my house?"

"Why didn't you tell me about the ransom call?" Amelia asked.

He glared at her. "I didn't want to worry you. You went through enough when we lost Vivian. I wanted to check something out first. Then I was coming home to fill you in."

Amelia stepped back.

Caleb turned away from her. "Okay, everyone," he shouted. "This is my house, and I'm asking you all to leave right now. Gather your things and get out. This is a private affair."

Sam Johnson stepped into the room. "Hello, Caleb. We're here to look for your daughter the right way. Trust me, this is the way to handle this. We've been discreet."

Amelia knew that Detective Johnson's assurances would not win her husband over. After all, Vivian's killer was never caught.

"I don't like it," Caleb said. "I don't want you here, but I won't go so far as to tell you to leave . . . yet. Find my daughter soon, or get out."

Amelia looked at the detective, completely surprised with her husband's tone. Sam nodded and turned away, leaving them alone.

"You said you wanted to check something out," Amelia said.

Caleb took her arm. He led her down the hall and into their bedroom.

"Are they listening in?" he asked.

Amelia shook her head.

"I don't believe in psychics, but I went to talk to Dolan Ryan. The guy who runs the Psychic Fair. If he's really some kind of psychic, then why not help us find Sarah?"

"What did he say?"

"He said he wouldn't help. Then the police took me downtown. I got a cab back to the fair's parking lot to pick up our car. For the last I-don't-know-how-many hours, I've been driving around, hoping to spot Sarah. I know it was stupid, but what else can I do? I feel useless."

The phone rang.

They looked at each other and then left the room. Halfway up the hall, Amelia saw Detective Johnson coming toward them with a phone held out.

Amelia answered on the fourth ring.

"Hello?"

"Is this Mrs. Roberts?"

"Yes. Who's this?" She looked at the cop in the cramped hall. He nodded and rolled his hand in a gesture to keep going.

"This is Dolan Ryan."

"Yes. Go on."

"I know about Sarah's disappearance."

"My husband just came home. He told me about your meeting today."

"Things have changed. I think I know where Sarah is. It's important I speak with you right away."

Amelia fumbled with the phone and then secured it to her ear. "What did you say? If you know where she is, tell me."

"It's not that easy. The location is secluded. I need to debrief the police. They will have to send in a tactical unit. Let me work with them and I'll get you your daughter back."

34

IT WAS AFTER five in the morning and he still had not found a car. The sun would be up soon. The delay complicated things. The girl could be anywhere by now, he thought. She could've hitched a ride, or even walked back to town. But then he convinced himself otherwise; It was stupid to leave the motel. She couldn't have made it far, though. She was weak, tired, and hungry.

He had to go back. He had to be sure.

He made his way to a three-story apartment building. Cars dotted the parking lot. He was hoping to find an SUV or van of some kind. Older model preferred, as car alarms these days were difficult to circumvent.

Headlights cut through the early morning fog. A cop car turned onto the street.

Gert ran and dodged behind a row of trimmed bushes.

He knew they would've found the dead cop back on the highway by now. Anyone found strolling the streets at this early hour would be questioned.

The cruiser moved slowly, drawing closer.

Then he had an idea. Why steal a random vehicle and have to hope he could get past the car's alarm? Why not just take another cop car? He would get more weapons, a police scanner so he could hear what other cops were up to, and he would look like he was transporting a criminal when he got the girl in the backseat.

He searched his pockets to confirm he still had the fake police identification he had used for the girl on Birk Street.

Perfect.

He ran onto the road in front of the cop car. It jolted to a stop.

"Help! My wife is hurt."

The driver's side door opened and the officer got out. He stayed behind the door.

"Put your hands on your head," the cop said.

Gert acted surprised and out of breath. "What? I just told you my wife is hurt. These guys knocked on our door twenty minutes ago and invaded our home. I managed to get away, but I need your help. Come on." He turned away as if to go, then stopped and looked back.

"I said, put your hands on your head," the cop ordered. "Do it now."

He raised his hands, trying to act the part of a distraught husband.

He took a step toward the cruiser. The officer didn't challenge him, but remained standing behind his car door.

"Where do you live?" the cop asked.

Got me, he thought. What was the name of the street he was just on? He racked his mind for a street name. To stall, he cocked his ear and asked the cop to repeat his question.

"Two blocks over," Gert said, pointing behind him.

The officer moved around the door of the car. He kept a hand suspended near his holster. "Step up to the vehicle and put your hands on the hood."

"Are you serious?"

"I said put your hands on the hood."

Gert shook his head and gave the guy his best *I can't believe you* look.

He did as he was told, stepping up to the car and placing his hands on the hood. "You're something else, you know that? My wife could be raped by now. I ran to get help. But now I'm being treated like a suspect."

He talked as the cop drew closer. Then he felt the cop's hands on him. Gert couldn't let the cop pat him down.

He closed his eyes. As the officer frisked him, his hand brushed the gun in Gert's waistband.

With as much speed as he could muster, before the cop had time to react, Gert spun around and jammed his fist into the cop's neck, just below the jawline.

The cop clung to his throat as he gasped for air.

Gert spun the cop around and snatched his gun out of the holster, then shoved him against the hood of the cruiser. The cop bounced off the car and dropped to the ground.

It wasn't a killing blow. A punch in the Adam's apple is an awful feeling, but unless the trachea collapsed, the cop would live. He needed to be careful about random killings.

The cruiser was still idling. Gert slipped behind the wheel and hit the gas. The forward motion slammed the driver's side door closed.

He looked in the rearview mirror. The cop was rolling on the ground, still holding his throat. From this distance it was hard to tell, but it looked like the cop was talking into a handheld microphone suspended on his lapel.

Shit.

He should've ripped that off him. He wasn't thinking fast enough.

Gert dropped the accelerator and raced the car out of town. He increased the volume on the police radio. Dispatchers were sending officers to a domestic and another to a traffic violation for backup.

The clock on the dash read 5:30 a.m. He would be back at the motel in twenty minutes.

It was time to find the girl and try for the state line.

35

THE MORNING SUN shone brightly through her windshield. Even though Denise only had a mile to go, she opened the console between the seats and pulled out her sunglasses.

She would arrive thirty minutes earlier than Mr. Ward. They would transfer the money, load the painting onto his truck, and the deal would be done. As long as everything went as planned, Denise would be free and clear within two hours. Then she would deal with the girl.

She pulled into the Sky Blue Motel. No cars were visible.

Perfect.

She stopped in front of the construction trailer and turned off her SUV. Her stomach was in knots. This was a legitimate sale, nothing illegal, yet she still felt like a criminal.

"It'll be over soon," she said out loud to comfort herself.

She got out of the vehicle and sucked in a deep breath. The smell of the pines made her think of her family's summer cottage.

The wooden steps of the construction trailer creaked under her weight as she fumbled with the keys.

A car on the highway slowed behind her. She turned around to see a dark-colored Cadillac angling into the abandoned motel's parking lot. Two men got out.

"Denise Hall?" the driver asked.

"Who're you?"

"We're the advance team for Mr. Ward. We're here to make sure everything goes smoothly."

The guy had a New York accent.

"I'm sure everything will, but suit yourself. He's not expected for a little while yet."

"You won't even know we're here." The driver smiled.

The men got back in their car. Denise watched as they drove behind the motel.

She had not expected the additional team. She opened the door to the trailer and stepped in. Her head of security, Bruce, stepped out from behind a partition. The partition allowed them to use the trailer at any time without worry of someone looking in through the window.

"Who were those guys in the Caddy?" he asked.

"Mr. Ward's men."

"Early."

"I know. Where's the girl?"

"Over here."

The guard stepped sideways and motioned behind the partition. Denise looked down at the battered girl.

"What the hell is this? What have you done to her?"

"Nothing. She came like that."

The girl was missing clumps of hair. Her forearms were bare. Patches of hair appeared to have been torn out around her head, mostly from the back. She had a couple of bruises, a sizable one on her cheek. Her eyebrows were gone, and in their place, little dots of blood showed where the hair had been torn out.

"Did you give her the bruise on the cheek?"

"No. I knocked her out by the temple."

Denise looked at the girl's wrists. They were raw. Duct tape was balled up on the floor beside her. She fought the urge to look away. This had gone too far.

"Tell me again how she came to be here?"

Before the guard could answer, gunfire cut through the morning stillness. They both ducked, and the guard ran for the door.

More gunfire followed. Someone screamed.

The battered girl woke up.

36

THINGS WERE BAD and getting worse. Gert had pulled into the motel and now saw an SUV parked by the trailer.

He had to hide the cruiser before whoever was in the trailer saw him. He steered for the rear of the motel.

When he got around back, he was greeted by the sight of two large guys in leather jackets standing outside a Cadillac. Right away he could tell these men were professionals. They stared him down, their hands moving for their inner breast pockets.

How stupid, he thought. *I'm driving a police car, and they want to draw on me.*

He stopped the car safely out of view of the construction trailer and the highway. Then he opened the door with his left hand and used his right to pull his gun, which he concealed behind his leg.

"Morning, gentlemen. I'll need to see your driver's license and registration."

The guy on the driver's side of the Cadillac turned and looked like he was about to bend into the car when his partner pulled a weapon.

Gert raised his gun and fired.

A tiny hole formed on the guy's cheek. He fell to his knees. Then, in slow motion, he collapsed face-first into the dirt.

All this happened in the time it took Gert to turn toward the other guy and fire a second shot. This guy had his gun out in record time.

Gert heard the air beside his head part as a bullet passed.

It took Gert three shots before he hit the guy in the chest. The driver of the Cadillac got off two, both going wild.

The driver screamed like a girl as he stared down at the blood bubbling out of his chest. He fell into the side of his car, dropped to the gravel, and then lay flat. Gert stepped closer and used two more bullets to silence him.

Who are these guys?

He wiped the sweat from his face as he frisked the bodies. No wallets, no identification. Just two guys in a Cadillac who shot at cops without provocation.

Man, this is fucked up.

Still hunched down by the second man's body, Gert scanned the bushes, his gun leveled in front of him. Then he stared at the windows of the motel.

Nothing. No movement whatsoever.

His heart raced faster now that the gunplay was over. He hadn't been shot at in years. The morning sun beat down on his back, yet he started to shiver. Swear pasted his shirt to his back. No time to waste. He had to find the girl and get out of the area before more goons showed up.

He headed to the edge of the motel wall, where he peeked around the corner. The SUV was still there.

Staying out of the trailer's line of sight, Gert retreated to the woods behind the motel and started to make his way over.

Within minutes he was standing behind the construction trailer, using a tree stump to remain unseen.

He reloaded his gun and slipped his finger inside the trigger guard as he walked into the open.

It could be that he would find no resistance in the trailer. He hoped that was the case.

With the fake police badge in hand, he knocked on the trailer door and stood to one side.

"Police! Open up!"

37

AMELIA JUMPED WHEN the doorbell rang. Caleb, escorted by Detective Johnson, got up to answer it.

"I'm glad you could come, Dolan," Caleb said after opening the door on Sam's cue.

Greetings were made all around while Amelia stood back, feeling wary. Everyone gravitated toward the dining room. She went to the kitchen to pour a pot of coffee into an urn. She grabbed the cream and sugar and made her way back to the group.

She set the tray down and stared at Dolan.

"Hello, Mrs. Roberts," Dolan said.

She nodded and looked away. There was something about Dolan's eyes. It felt like he could see into her thoughts.

Caleb placed a hand on Amelia's arm.

"I know how hard this must be for you," Dolan said. "I'd be happy to clear up any misunderstandings there may be, but we don't have a lot of time."

"I want my daughter back. That's first and foremost." She forced herself to look at him again. Their eyes locked.

"I understand completely," Dolan said. "I've worked on a number of missing persons cases over the years, and thankfully, many of them turned out well. I think we've got a good chance of locating her today. But we need to act soon."

Her head swam.

"We're all here because you said you knew where my daughter was. I'm willing to look past a number of my concerns about you and your Psychic Fair if I can get my daughter back."

Dolan shifted in his seat. "I met your daughter at the fair. It was brief. We bumped into each other. She lost her balance and fell to the floor, where she jotted something down in her notebook. Before she stood up, I noticed she had written my name. Yet we've never met. Would you know anything about this?"

Amelia looked at Caleb for support. He shook his head.

"When you bumped into Sarah at the fair, why didn't *you* warn her of the danger coming?" Amelia asked.

"I didn't do a reading for her."

"But you claim to be psychic?"

"Yes, I do, and I am."

"Then let's get started," Amelia prompted.

Dolan turned to Detective Johnson. "Sam, have you got a tactical team on standby?"

The detective nodded. He had a pen and pad in his hand, waiting to write down whatever Dolan told him.

Caleb reached for the coffee and poured himself a cup.

"I think Sarah is being held at a cabin on Lake George."

Amelia listened as Dolan gave directions. At one point he looked at her, when the detective asked what he was going to find there. Was Sarah alive? Dolan answered that she was fine, other than some bruising. He said he wasn't getting much more, except they needed to hurry. He felt that her kidnapper was going to move her to a new location, or was moving her as they spoke.

Amelia watched everyone spring into action. Detective Johnson got on a phone and started ordering people to the site. Dolan got up and left the room.

Caleb looked at her. "I'm going with them," he whispered.

"So am I," she said.

Caleb leaned closer. "I think we should follow them in our own car. There's no way they'll let us come along. They'd be worried about the state they find Sarah in."

Amelia nodded. Out of the corner of her eye she saw one of the police technicians beckon to them. Caleb and Amelia got up and followed the tech into the den.

When they were alone, the cop closed the door behind them.

"I think there's something the two of you should know."

"We want all the information we can get," Caleb said.

"It involves Kim Wepps, a girl who was abducted over seven months ago and then found safe in a farmhouse basement not far from here. Kim was taken to an abandoned farm, where Dolan *found* her with his psychic powers. It just seems a little strange to me."

"What are you saying?" Amelia asked.

"I suspect Dolan is involved in some way."

Amelia and Caleb looked at each other. "Go on," Amelia prodded. "Do your superiors feel the same way?"

The tech ignored her question. "The kidnappings look like they're following a geographical pattern, remaining close to Dolan and the Psychic Fair. It just came up recently."

"Are you saying Dolan may be masterminding the kidnappings?" Caleb asked.

Amelia could hear anger in Caleb's voice. She rubbed his shoulder to calm him.

"We've been able to link over a dozen kidnappings to one man or group in the past five years. All of those victims were found by Dolan with his psychic abilities. There are kidnappings happening all over the country, but Dolan only finds the victims of just this one kidnapper with the same MO."

Amelia leaned against the wall, taking her hand from Caleb's shoulder. "Does Dolan know that the police suspect him?"

"Not yet. Detective Johnson doesn't want him knowing anything until Sarah is brought home. If we tip Dolan off, things could go south."

"Okay then, let's go," Caleb said.

"Where're you going?" the cop asked.

"To get our daughter."

38

GERT TOOK A deep breath to steady himself, and then knocked on the trailer again. Rustling sounds came from inside.

He checked behind him. Nothing stirred except the pines. Even the highway was quiet.

He leaned closer, almost touching the door with his ear. It sounded like two people were arguing in a whisper.

He knocked again with the butt of the gun. "Police! Open up!"

The lock clicked. Gert moved back, his gun raised.

The door opened and a woman stepped into view.

"Come out slowly, with your hands up. Is anyone else in there with you?" He winked one eye, batting at a drop of sweat.

"I need to see a badge," the woman said. "I heard shots, and now I'm being ordered out of the trailer at gunpoint. You don't look like a cop."

Gert knew a gun could be trained on him. He needed to play this cool.

What the hell is this place?

If security was tight enough to need those two goons out back, then these people were being extra cautious for a reason. He lowered his gun in a friendly gesture.

"I'm spooked, too, ma'am. I drove around back for a routine visit of these premises and got shot at. Backup is on the way. An officer went missing sometime last night. Witnesses reported seeing his patrol car headed out of town in this direction. We're checking everything out."

Gert loved it when he thought on his feet.

He lifted his fake badge high enough for the woman to see. She leaned forward and squinted in the sun. Only an expert would be able to tell his badge was a fake.

The woman stepped from the trailer. "Is it okay if I keep my hands at my side? I'm not armed."

Gert nodded. "Just no sudden movements. Who are you?"

"My name is Denise Hall. I own this property. I'm planning to clean things up here and then sell it."

"What about the two men out back? Why would they shoot at a cop without provocation?" He loved how official he sounded.

She moved away from him, her head lowered like she was thinking. He heard a cell phone ringing.

"Do you mind if I take this call?" she asked.

He shrugged. "Go ahead."

She pulled out a cell phone and flipped it open.

He took the opportunity to scan the area.

When he turned back to her she had a strange look on her face. He couldn't quite read it.

"Everything okay?" he asked. "You look like you've seen a ghost."

"That was my mother." The woman gaped down at her cell phone. "After over twenty years, she calls me. . . . "

She started shaking her head. She took a few small steps away from Gert, toward the open parking lot.

Something was wrong. Something he didn't understand.

He adjusted his grip on the gun handle.

"Why did you knock on the trailer door?" she asked.

What an odd question. "If you had people shoot at you for no reason, you'd check the area out, too."

"Right. But why not wait for backup?"

She continued to move around until she was on the highway side of him. Now he stood with his back to the trailer.

The woman glared at him. She was stalling.

He raised his gun, fired, and leaped to the right all in one motion. His bullet missed.

The ground was hard, knocking the breath out of him as he landed.

Dust plumed up in a small torrent about his face. Someone was shooting at him.

He rolled toward the trailer. Within seconds he was under the wooden steps.

The woman was running past the SUV parked in the lot. She was going for the highway. He aimed and fired three quick shots. He saw at least one hit her.

He crawled deeper underneath the trailer. Dust filled his nose, and he rolled onto his back. He got his elbows braced in the dirt and edged out from the other side. A solitary window sat directly above him.

The woman he'd shot continued her screaming.

There were only a couple of bullets left in his weapon. He would have to do this right the first time.

He stood and peeked around the edge to get a look at the main door.

No one was visible. The shooter was still inside.

He took a large step toward the door and threw his badge inside the trailer. While the badge was still in flight, he ran back to the window.

He popped his head up and looked in. A large man stood staring out the door with a gun strapped on his shoulder.

Gert put his gun to the screen side of the window. He aimed as best he could and fired all the remaining ammunition into the trailer.

After the noise of gunfire faded, the air had an eerie quiet to it. The woman in the parking lot of the motel only moaned to herself now, her screaming abated.

He ducked down and scurried around the back, where he came to another window. He eased up and looked in. The big guy lay on the floor with his hands clamped around his neck. Blood gushed through his fingers.

Gert was surprised at how little he felt when taking a life. He was growing numb to it.

It was time to go, before people started showing up.

He ran around to the front and up the stairs. His gun was empty, but he kept it raised in a firing position anyway as he entered the trailer.

The big guy wasn't moving now, as blood circled his head.

Gert searched the trailer, end to end. This was his last chance. He hoped the girl was here.

He encountered a flimsy partition and kicked the door five times before it finally buckled and broke open.

And there was his prize. His little automatic writer. He aimed the gun at her, grabbed her by the wrist, and started for the door.

She whimpered and shook her head, dazed.

A new plan formed when he stepped outside. The SUV would be perfect. He opened the back door and pushed the girl inside without too much resistance. She was cradling her head in her hands.

He looked at the steering column. No keys.

He walked out to the woman on the ground, who was sweating and pale, her eyes wide. Blood circled her lower leg and foot.

"Keys," he said, waving his hand in the air. "Give them to me and I won't kill you."

She pointed at the left pocket of her slacks. He bent and fished inside, where he found the keys.

"Good. You tell them the truth of what happened here. Tell the police that I've got the girl and I will kill her if I don't get what I want."

Gert turned to leave and then stopped. There had been so many things wrong about this from the start. There was no way he would be able to go back to any kind of normal life.

Gert knew his boss was lying to him. There would be no other city, no other kidnappings.

He looked down at the woman in the dirt. The blood had slowed its exit from her ankle. She had been trying to staunch the flow. He noticed the sun glinting off something in her hand. Her cell phone.

Good. She probably called for help.

"Whatever you say to the cops will be heard by the man I work for. Tell them that I've decided I will finish this my way."

39

SAM LOOKED THROUGH the windshield of the unmarked cruiser at the passing clouds. Some were dark with rain, others gray and dreary.

"I wonder if the weather's gonna hold," Sam said.

Dolan didn't answer him. They'd been on the side of the highway for ten minutes, waiting for Sergeant McKinley's Emergency Task Force to give them the go-ahead to approach the cabin.

"You okay, Dolan?"

"Sure."

"You seem tense."

Dolan shook his head. "I'm confused on this one. There's something different about this case."

"How's that?" Sam grabbed his coffee from the holder in the dash and took a sip.

"I don't know much yet, but it's coming to me."

"What *do* you know?"

Dolan looked at him. Sam set his coffee back. "I know someone close to me is going to get killed."

"Close to you how? I'm sitting right beside you. That would suck." He smiled and then asked, "What if we get this guy right now?"

"I said we had to work fast because the perp was planning to leave or was leaving at that very moment."

"Are you saying he's gone?"

"Yes, I think so."

"Why would certain information be blocked from you but other pieces come through? Don't you usually get enough of the picture to be right?"

"Usually, but I'm being blocked this time."

"Blocked? How does that happen?"

Dolan shrugged.

Someone whistled outside. Sam looked up as one of McKinley's men waved them in.

He turned the car on and took the left-hand turn onto the cabin's private drive. He parked and the two of them got out.

McKinley walked up to him. "Sam, we're too late. Looks like they were here recently, though. Come inside, I'll show you what we've got."

Sam nodded and looked at Dolan. He was staring off at the trees. Sam followed Dolan's gaze and saw nothing there. A soft rain started to fall.

"You coming in?" he asked.

The psychic shook his head. "Just get it over with. I've got some thinking to do."

DOLAN STOOD UNDER a pine tree watching McKinley's men come and go.

Maybe everything seemed different this time because the person he was trying to locate also had a psychic talent, like repelling magnets.

He didn't want his colleagues to think he was unable to produce results. He knew, however, there would be signs in the cabin to show that Sarah had been there. Signs that would vindicate him as a psychic.

He stepped out and into the light rain. The air held a faint wet-wood smell. It made him think of the Sky Blue Motel.

He stopped halfway to the cabin. *Sky Blue?* He looked up at the gray clouds. *Motel?*

Where did that come from?

He trudged up the steps of the cabin. The men were standing by a small desk with books scattered on it.

McKinley turned to him. "It looks like you are good at what you do. Fingerprints in this room appear to be Sarah's. And we may have found a few strands of her hair. We'll have confirmation shortly. Now, if you could just lead us to where she *is*."

Dolan nodded, turned around, and walked out of the cabin. The rain had subsided to a gentle mist. A soft breeze moved through the trees.

Someone shouted. It looked like McKinley's men had stopped a car from entering.

He recognized Caleb's voice.

What's he doing here?

Dolan hurried up to the road. Sarah's father was standing by his car, animated in his frustration.

Caleb saw him and called him over.

"Did you find Sarah?" Caleb asked. "Is she okay?"

"She's gone. I'm sorry."

Caleb gasped. A small yip came from inside the car.

Dolan realized his mistake.

"I mean she's not here. There is evidence that she was here, but we're too late."

Caleb frowned, holding the open door of his car with both hands. "So she's . . . whoever was here has left already?"

"Yes."

"I thought you were the best. What went wrong?"

"Nothing went wrong. The information isn't absolutely accurate. Only God knows everything." He realized his tone came across harsher than he intended it to be.

"What are you talking about? Either you see things or you don't. These are people's *lives* you're dealing with. You can't send everyone on wild-goose chases."

"It's not that simple," Dolan said. "I wish it was. She was here, but she isn't now."

The officer guarding the access road to the cabin stepped between Dolan and Caleb. He told Caleb he would have to clear the road, to get back in his car and move it to the highway.

Caleb slammed the car door, put it in gear, and started to back up.

Dolan turned toward the cabin to see Sam coming out the front door. He was talking on his cell phone. A moment later he flipped it shut and beckoned Dolan over.

"A woman by the name of Denise Hall is being rushed to Liberty Memorial Hospital with a gunshot wound to her ankle. Emergency crews found her alive along with three dead bodies at an abandoned motel called the Sky Blue."

Dolan stared at him. *Sky Blue Motel.*

"You look surprised."

Dolan realized his mouth was open. "I'm not used to having information given to me this way."

"What way?"

"The name of the motel came to me minutes ago, but that's all. Now you tell me things I should've known. It's all happening too fast."

Sam flipped open a notebook and scanned down the page. "Apparently, this Denise woman owns the motel and was renovating it. The three dead men were security, although word is they were heavily armed and two of the dead may be attached to the Ward family. The bad news is yet to come."

Dolan nodded for Sam to go on.

"It looks like the FBI has an interest in the Ward family. One of the men was an informant. And get this—Denise says a teenage girl with missing hair was taken by the guy who shot her ankle."

Dolan was struck with a thought. "What was the woman's name again?"

"Denise Hall."

Dolan snapped his fingers. "Esmerelda's daughter. Sarah said something to Mary Bennett about her. So Sarah *is* psychic." He said this last part to himself.

"Here's why they called us. They found a cop car at the back of the motel. It was stolen earlier in the morning. Local police knew that we're looking for a guy who killed a cop on the side of the highway and stole *his* car, too. They wanted to give us the heads-up. But they also had a message from this woman, Denise. She said the perp told her to tell the police that he was going to finish things his way now. She also said the guy told her that whatever she tells the police, his boss would hear, too."

Dolan watched Sam as he wiped the edge of his mouth twice.

"What's got me is the message from the kidnapper," Sam continued. "If his boss will hear whatever Denise tells the cops, then that would lead us to believe that his boss is in our ranks. This case is rapidly becoming something much bigger than I anticipated. The FBI may get involved now. Especially if our perp crosses state lines."

Sam stepped away from him to get out of the rain.

Things were going wrong fast.

Dolan wondered how he would survive this and keep his hands clean.

40

SARAH OPENED HER eyes and then snapped them shut. She was baking in the sun. She massaged her temples.

A gentle breeze pushed a newspaper past shards of broken glass. Candy wrappers littered the floor.

She opened her eyes fully, even as the heat from the sun hammered at her head.

She was in what looked like a run-down building. The windows were gaping holes, and graffiti covered the walls.

She moved her legs back and forth and was elated to find them untied. Only her left wrist was tied, with some sort of leather strap that had been bolted together. She rolled onto her back.

When she tugged on her wrist, it caught at the end of its tether in midair. The leather strap was tied with rope to a pipe that protruded from the wall. She tugged again and watched the pipe shift. She yanked harder, causing the pipe to shake more, bits of the wall falling loose.

She was alone. Her head still pounded, but some things were more important—like escape.

In a sitting position, she used both hands to yank on the strap. More of the wall crumbled away, but the pipe stood firm. Coiled as it was, in her weakened state, she found it too difficult to pry off. A smaller lock kept the leather strap secured to her wrist.

Her stomach tightened with hunger pains so intense she felt nauseous. Her tongue moved from side to side, sticking to the insides of her mouth.

With her feet braced against the wall, she yanked again, using all the strength she had left.

It was not enough to break free.

The cooling breeze from the nearest window moved across her face. She heard footsteps. Someone was coming. She turned around and leaned back against the wall.

"You're awake."

Her captor walked over to her and set two bottles of water by her feet. She lunged for one and guzzled almost half the bottle, spilling some down her chin. The water was cool. She felt it hit her stomach, enjoyed the cold feeling in her throat.

I can handle this.

"This will all be over within days." He sat across from her.

She picked up the water bottle and drank from it again, ignoring him. She didn't know when she'd get another chance. Her fingers seized and pulled hard on the hair nestled in the most sensitive spot at the top of her neck. A feeling of relief came over her.

"Why do you pull your hair?" he asked.

She remained quiet. He shrugged and leaned back on his outstretched arms.

"I'm surprised you haven't broken yet. I guess some girls take longer than others."

Sarah watched him from the corner of her eye.

"I've decided I need to kill someone from your family."

She jerked her head around, causing her headache to flare.

He smirked. "Oh, now I've got your attention."

"You can't be serious," she said, her hand tight on the water bottle.

"After you're dead, I will kill your mother. Then we'll be even. I'll use a car to run her down in the road, like you did to my brother." He gave an exaggerated nod.

Sarah used all the leverage she had to swing the water bottle. It made perfect contact with his cheek before bouncing off and sliding away on the floor.

She got in a defensive stance. Her breath came out in pants, matching the throbbing in her head.

"You think you're tough?" he asked. "Is that it?"

She eased back against the wall as he walked away. He pulled out his cell phone and held it up like he was checking for signal strength.

He turned back to her. "You know, humans are at the top of the food chain. We're our own predators."

Sarah opened the other water bottle and drank from it, tuning him out as he paced the room. She wondered what her parents were doing right then. Were they working with the police to find her? She didn't have much faith in that. It was looking more and more like she was going to have to get out of this on her own.

He continued. "Trust me when I say, I will kill you and the world will be a better place for it."

He frowned, rubbed an eyebrow, and turned in a half circle. He lifted his arm, checked the watch on his wrist, and then swore to himself. A moment later he rounded the corner at the end of the room and left her alone.

She grabbed the rope and pulled with renewed fervor.

GERT HIT REDIAL and put the phone to his ear. It rang three times.

"What?" the boss asked.

"Tell me how close the police are. What's my next move?"

"There is no *next move*. You're on your own. Don't call me again."

"Wait! What're you talking about?"

"How many people have we killed over the years?"

"I don't know. Maybe two?"

"Right. As a practice, we let them go, yet you killed three people at that motel, not to mention the cop you killed and left on the side of the road. You've gone too far. As it stands, it looks like they'll be organizing some kind of manhunt. This is the kind of thing you escape by leaving the *fucking country*."

Gert started banging his head lightly on the wall.

"My advice is to find out what this girl can do psychically, and then see if you can use it to your advantage. You should keep her alive until you get somewhere safe. They won't hesitate to shoot you if you're alone, but if they know you have the girl, everyone will be more cautious. That's all I can offer you."

"I've got proof of your involvement. I go down, you go down, too."
Gert flipped his phone shut.

He moved away from the wall. He had to think.

He headed to the SUV for a pen and paper. A minute later, he rejoined his prisoner.

She had been busy. The pipe she was attached to sat askew, bent and sticking halfway out of the wall.

"Write something," he said, tossing the implements at her.

He used a key from his pocket to undo the lock on her leather strap. It took him a long, frustrating minute to get it all undone.

Sarah looked up at him. "What happened to your forehead?"

"Write something!" he shouted.

She jumped back. Fumbling with the pad, she opened it and got her pen ready.

"What do you want me to write?" she asked in a whisper.

"Whatever your abilities tell you to write."

"It doesn't work like that," she said.

"Today it does."

Gert lunged forward and grabbed her neck. He tightened his grip enough to close her windpipe. She slumped down, gasping for air. She was trying to speak, but nothing came out.

"What'd you say?" he asked.

He released her enough to talk.

"Only . . . when I . . . black out . . . can I get a . . . message. . . ."

"I can help that along."

He let go of her neck and yanked his gun from his waistband.

"No," she stammered. "Not knocked unconscious. Involuntary blackouts." She struggled to sit upright, holding her neck. He forced her back down.

"The blackouts come and go," she continued. "Sometimes once a week, sometimes more. I never know until I look in my notebook and see a message there. If you'll let me keep this pen and paper, I'll be able to write something when the next blackout comes."

"I'm not going to give you much time." He stood and scanned the room. "Make me happy, Sarah. I'm not a lot of fun to be around when I'm angry."

Most people escaped their nightmares by waking up.

Sarah escaped hers by going to sleep.

41

DOLAN SAT QUIETLY as Sam pulled the car up alongside Sarah's parents. Caleb rolled his window down.

"You guys hanging in?" Sam asked.

Caleb shook his head. "We put too much stock in Dolan coming up with this location so fast." Dolan flashed back to the note he had found when wandering the Robertses' house, looking for something to attach himself to, something to get his gift into action. He had come across an envelope under Sarah's pillow. His name was written on the outside.

Sarah said she knew something dangerous was working its way toward her, but it was unavoidable. She had to try to stop a kidnapping.

Dolan had folded the note up, intending to share it with everyone, but it had been forgotten in the rush to leave for Lake George. He figured now wasn't the best time.

"We will catch this guy," Sam said. "We're on our way to talk to a woman who saw your daughter just a few hours ago. We've got a description and which direction they were headed in. We know the vehicle and plate number the perp is driving. Hang in there. This may come together faster than you think."

Caleb looked at his wife and then back at Sam. "We're following you to this woman."

"I can't let you do that."

"If this woman was the last known person to see my daughter, then Amelia and I want to talk to her, too."

"Officially I can't agree to that. But I wouldn't be able to stop you if you were to go to Liberty Memorial Hospital to see a woman named Denise Hall."

Sam dropped the cruiser into gear and pulled away. The road was still wet. Sam flipped the wipers on as they came up behind a tractor-trailer.

"Is Sarah gonna make it, Dolan?" Sam asked.

"Can't tell for certain."

"What *can* you tell for certain?"

Dolan detected hostility in Sam's voice.

He was saved by the ring of his cell phone. It was Alex, his assistant. Dolan updated him on the situation and when he was likely to get back to the fair.

If not today, this would probably be over by tomorrow, he told him.

42

SARAH SAT IN the backseat of the SUV. They had been traveling all day. The sun had already gone down.

With the small amount of light from the dash, Sarah leaned forward and read the note in her hand. She had no idea when the blackout had come, but it clearly had happened while she slept. As she read the messages, she found two things unsettling.

After months of getting cryptic messages about people in peril, she had never expected a personal message.

She'd been asleep for a while, and now, when she looked over the seat, the clock on the dash read after one in the morning.

Her captor seemed to be talking to himself, although she couldn't make out what he was saying. He appeared to be coming undone, completely losing touch with reality.

Sarah tried to focus on the note. It came in three parts, with some fading away.

Don't thump, rip, and tear, better to be savage.
Gert's boss will kill him.
Gert's boss works with polic.

The *c* was half written, and the *e* in *police* was missing.

Sarah supposed that her captor was named Gert. She considered how much she wanted him to see. She knew she had to show him something, though.

What if he thought she had made it up?

It would be better to show him all of it, so he could see the mystery of the first riddle. Maybe seen as a package it would lend more credibility to the message.

On the back of the paper she noticed a girl's name: *Vivian Roberts*.
Who the hell is Vivian Roberts?

This was the first message Sarah had written out that pertained to the here and now. Gert had ordered something written, and now he would get it.

What if all of the messages were her subconscious telling her stuff she already knew? Was she psychic, or was someone channeling through her? Someone like Vivian Roberts.

She dismissed the idea a second later. How could she have known to bring a hammer that day at the river? She could be psychic and in the infancy of her gift, but she didn't think that was the case.

She brought her legs up and hugged them. The car was cool, but a sheen of sweat covered her body.

She had to get away from Gert.

She would either have to rely on the Other Side, or handle it herself.

She just hoped she wouldn't have to kill again.

43

AMELIA THOUGHT HER house looked different as they approached it. Sad. Caleb turned off the car, and rested his head back, eyes closed.

It had been an exhausting day. When they finally got to talk to Denise, she was sedated. The relentless interview schedule with different police agencies had worn her out. Amelia and Caleb only got a minute before she fell into a drug-induced sleep. In that minute they learned that Sarah had looked banged up but was otherwise okay.

Amelia got out of the car. Caleb did the same, and they entered their house. It felt foreign with the police officers milling around, sipping coffee. Strangely empty without Sarah.

Amelia stepped away from Caleb. "I need to be alone for a while."

He nodded and turned for the kitchen.

She took the stairs slowly, weighed down by grief. When she entered her bedroom, Amelia collapsed on the bed and looked up at the ceiling. She felt helpless and exhausted. There was nothing she could do but wait. It was beginning to drive her crazy.

She got up and walked into the bathroom. The mirror reminded her she hadn't applied makeup since the morning of the Psychic Fair. These few days had aged her.

She left the bathroom a moment later only to collapse on the bed again, tears streaming down her cheeks.

She would do whatever was necessary to make sure her daughter survived.

44

CALEB WALKED THROUGH the main floor of the house and stopped in the kitchen, where he grabbed a glass and opened a bottle of brandy. After two quick shots, he approached the stereo in the living room. He tuned it to the local rock station and turned up the volume a few notches. He didn't want Amelia to hear what he was about to do.

An officer stood beside a temporary workstation set up by the kitchen phone line, flipping pages back and forth on a clipboard.

"I need answers," Caleb said. "I understand that you're the experts and that you've done all this before, but it's different this time. He's got my daughter, and he's out there killing people."

"Every cop in the state is looking for him now. He shot one of ours. He raised the stakes."

Caleb didn't want to hear anything more, but he couldn't stop talking. "What about Dolan? I thought he could help. I practically begged—"

A knock on the front door silenced him. The cop grabbed his arm.

"You aren't expecting anyone, are you?"

Caleb mouthed the word *no*. They started for the door together, with the officer putting himself against the wall behind it.

Caleb stood a little off center. "Who is it?"

"FBI."

The cop reached past Caleb and looked out through the small window beside the door. Then he unlocked the door and opened it.

Caleb watched as everyone showed identification and stepped inside.

"My name is Special Agent Jill Hanover, and this is my partner, Special Agent Fergus Mant. We're in charge now," she said to the cop. "Your task force is being dismantled. Everyone can pack up and leave. I'll have my own people handle things from here. And turn that music down!"

45

SAM JOLTED AWAKE. Something had awakened him, but he wasn't sure what.

His cell phone rang.

He fumbled in the dark of the shoddy motel room.

His hand found the bedside lamp on the third ring. The phone was on the floor. He snatched it up and flipped it open in one movement.

"Detective Sam Johnson here."

"It's Mike. We've got a problem."

"What is it?"

"FBI is taking over."

"Our task force was commissioned by the FBI. This can't be happening."

"It is. You better get here fast, before this Roberts guy gets arrested. He wants everyone out. The special agent in charge is trying to calm him down."

Sam raised his free hand to his forehead.

"I'm on my way."

Sam slammed his phone on the bed and looked over at the door that separated their rooms. Whatever the problem was, he was sure Dolan was at the root of it.

He knew there was something different about this case. And he knew that difference lay with Dolan.

He walked over to the door. He was about to knock when the door unlocked and flipped open from the other side.

"I'm ready to go," Dolan said.

"It's four thirty in the morning," Sam said. "I thought you'd be sleeping."

"I was, but then I found out the FBI was taking the case from you."

"How did you find out?"

"Come on, Sam, how long have we been doing this? You know I have my ways."

Dolan stepped away from the door and grabbed his duffel bag. He called over his shoulder to meet him in the coffee shop in the lobby when Sam was ready.

Sam shut the adjoining door and started getting dressed, thinking about the questions Dolan was going to have to answer soon.

46

SOMETHING TUGGED AT Sarah's wrists, and then they dropped free of restraint. She rolled her head to the side and guessed the time as early morning. The sun was up, the air cool. Birds flitted past the open windows of the building she sat in.

How many days had it been? How long before it was all over?

A hand wrapped around her arm and lifted her. She was surprised by his strength. She could barely hold herself up. Pain shot from her ankles. She lost her balance and fell headfirst to the dirty wooden floor.

He yanked her up again and forced her to walk. They went down a flight of stairs, around a corner, and out of the building through an old loading dock.

A black van sat idling, its side door gaping. He pushed her in the back and slammed the door. Sarah leaned up on an elbow and massaged her right wrist. The driver's side door opened and Gert got in.

Within minutes they were on the highway. A small wooden bench stretched along the back of the van. She edged over and sat up on it.

He had not restrained her. It was probably clear she had zero energy, and he wasn't afraid of her running.

"I saw what you wrote," he said.

He watched her from the rearview mirror. She looked away, not sure how to respond yet. The last day or so was a blur. She was in a building, then an SUV, and then another building. She hadn't eaten in at least three days.

"You were right, by the way," he added.

"About what?" Sarah asked.

"My boss does work with the police. I have to thank you for the inside tip about him wanting to kill me. I should tell you, though—I already figured that out for myself."

Sarah could see that the message had calmed him. He almost looked happy today.

"That's why you're not tied up right now. I want your hands free to write if you go into another trance. Anything else you want to write would be useful. Like, how to get out of this mess? I will reward you kindly."

"You don't need me for that. Let me go and run for Mexico. You might make it."

Gert drove down an exit ramp and pulled up to a red light. He turned in his seat and faced her. "The only reason I'm talking to you is because of this talent you have. I've provided a pen and paper by the bench there." He pointed to her left. "Write as much as you can in the time we have left. Maybe something will be useful to me."

Sarah picked up the paper and pen. She opened the notepad and flipped through a few of the wire-bound pages.

The light had changed to green. Gert spun back around in his seat and started forward.

"If you try any funny business, you know what'll happen. This isn't over yet, and we're not friends. Are we clear?"

"Yes," Sarah whispered.

She had to get the circulation in her hands and legs going so she could run.

She thought about Dolan. She had left a note for him under her pillow. Could he be Gert's boss?

How would Gert know about my automatic writing abilities unless he talked to Dolan or Esmerelda?

The familiar stirrings in her vision, coupled with the numbness in her left arm, warned her of a blackout.

She slid to the floor of the van and grabbed the pen just as she lost consciousness.

47

FBI-ISSUED VEHICLES LITTERED the front of the Robertses' house as Sam and Dolan pulled into the driveway. The sun was rising. It was just after six in the morning.

Sam looked over at Dolan, who had a resigned look on his face. They hadn't talked much on the way from the motel.

At the front door someone pulled a curtain back.

A woman stepped onto the front porch.

"I'm Special Agent Jill Hanover. You must be Detective Sam Johnson."

Hands were shaken, introductions made. They all stepped inside the house.

Mrs. Roberts sat on a couch in the living room, a Kleenex in her hand. She had been crying. A woman Sam didn't recognize appeared to be consoling her.

"Why are you here?" Sam asked. "My task force was put together years ago. We're handling this case."

"Not anymore," Hanover said in a matter-of-fact tone.

"On what grounds?"

"An officer has been killed and another officer assaulted. A member of the Ward family has been shot. An eighteen-year-old is still out there." She turned away. Sam followed Agent Hanover's eyes. She was looking at Mrs. Roberts. "We will continue this conversation outside," she said.

Sam gritted his teeth and followed her. This was the first time he had ever been removed from a case.

He stepped out onto the back deck behind Hanover. The wind had picked up. It tossed her long blond hair into her face. She had to brush it aside to look at him.

"As I was saying," she continued, "we've got an eighteen-year-old girl out there with this maniac, and you still think this is just a kidnapping case."

"I am quite aware of what's happening. Within a couple of days, this will all be wrapped up. We don't need your interference now."

"Are you aware what the other officers are saying about you and your little psychic friend here?"

Sam glanced at Dolan.

"I asked him to be here. He's helped us tremendously in the past. Without Dolan, there were some girls who may not have made it home."

"It doesn't matter anymore," Hanover said. "You're both off this case. Relinquish all your files to my partner, Special Agent Fergus Mant, and don't even *think* about interfering or you'll be dealing with obstruction charges. All the paperwork is at the front for you to sign when you leave."

Sam stormed off the deck. There was nothing more to argue about. He heard Dolan close behind him.

Mike, his technician, came into view. Sam told him to meet them out front.

Sam paused in the living room and nodded at Mrs. Roberts. When he had started this case he had promised to do whatever he could to bring Sarah home safe.

He was not about to give up now.

48

AMELIA SAT ALONE on the edge of her bed in a room at a Holiday Inn. Caleb had gone to have lunch, and the FBI psychologist had gone back to her own room next door. Apparently, it would be better for the parents to be in a hotel rather than in their own home while the authorities worked the case.

Amelia knew this was only to help control Caleb. Special Agent Hanover wasn't going to have him hanging around the house, getting in the way.

Our house, she thought.

She got up and moved to the window. The wind had died down, the trees only bending slightly in the breeze. In the distance she could see a highway, trucks and cars racing by. She wondered where Sarah was right now. Then she stopped herself. Thinking about Sarah only led to dark thoughts.

She moved away from the window and went back to the bed, where she flopped down. Sarah had saved Mary Bennett from a kidnapping. Why couldn't she save herself?

A part of her felt that she truly knew nothing about her daughter.

The phone in the room rang. She stared at it. The incessant ring came a third time. Amelia picked it up. "Hello?"

At first she heard nothing, then a distant sound. It was like the wind at the end of a tunnel.

A young female voice whispered, *"I'm okay now."*

The hairs on Amelia's neck rose. "Who is this?" she asked.

"Vivian."

She nearly slammed the phone down. What a cruel trick. She could hear someone knocking on the hotel room door.

"Who is this?" she choked. Her eyes were wide, but unseeing.

"Mommy," the soft voice whispered. *"I'm okay. I'm with Sarah."*

"*With* Sarah? Does that mean . . . Sarah's dead?"

She switched the phone to her left hand and pressed it hard against her ear, her other hand over her mouth.

"She's alive."

The voice faded. The knocking on the hotel room door was a hammering now.

"A note will be left for you in a van."

The line went dead.

"Vivian! Vivian! Oh, my baby." Amelia collapsed on the floor, her body shaking with sobs.

The hotel room door flew open. Caleb rushed in.

"What happened?" he asked. "Why were you shouting Vivian's name?"

He knelt and took her in his arms. They held each other.

Amelia looked up at her husband and told him everything. Whether he believed it or not, Amelia knew she had talked to her daughter.

And now she was determined to get out of this hotel room and find a van with a note in it.

49

THE CRAMPS DOUBLED her over. Sarah had known hunger in the past, but not like this. Out of habit, she yanked hair away from inside the bandanna line. She could handle this.

She thought of what she had written down during the last blackout. It made her pull even more.

Who cares anyway?

It didn't matter what she looked like. She had gone way too far. Only stray patches remained on her head.

Getting those prophetic messages and then acting on them, she actually thought she was doing something good.

Look at the mess she was in now.

She leaned back and stretched out across the wooden bench. She placed her hands together on her stomach and shut her eyes. She imagined this was how she would look in her coffin. She didn't want to be the one to let go, give up, but what else was there? If she got a chance to run, she would have to take it.

"You asleep back there or having a blackout?" Gert asked.

She didn't answer him. With her eyes closed, he'd never know the difference. She once heard that the only thing that separated humans from animals was their capacity to hope. She no longer felt sure that she possessed hope, but she had nothing to lose.

"I've got to get gas. I'll pick up some takeout for us. You need to eat."

She kept her eyes closed and didn't move. Once parked, he got out of his seat and made his way back toward her.

There was a moment of silence. She wanted to open her eyes to see what he was doing, but realized the importance of remaining in her exact position.

A knock on the window made her jump. Her heart rate spiked, along with her breathing. She tried hard to remain still.

Did he notice me jolt?

She heard him shuffling to the front of the van. An attendant wanted to know if he could fill up the tank. The door opened.

This was her best chance. She was untied and unwatched. She could not be with Gert any longer. It was too dangerous. Too many people had died already.

This ends now.

She opened her eyes and got up. A Volkswagen van parked ahead of them was getting gas from a young brown-haired guy. He wore a vest with his name sewn into the left breast pocket.

She grabbed the pad of paper Gert had given her and removed the note she had written for her mother during the last blackout. There was a perfect slot between the bench and the side of the van. She left a small corner sticking out. It was just enough for people to see if they were in the back, but not enough for the driver to notice.

She folded the rest of the pad and slipped it in her pocket.

In a crouched position she made her way toward the front of the van. She kept her eyes glued to the windshield, looking for any sign of Gert. It wasn't until she reached the passenger seat that she saw him. He was inside the restaurant at the counter.

She opened the driver's side door and jumped down, her legs wobbly but strong enough to sustain her. She closed the door and crouched low.

The attendant smiled and nodded his head as he lifted the nozzle out of the Volkswagen. She waved her hand for him to come over.

"What can I do for you?" he asked.

He stared at her eyebrows. Her clothes were in disarray, and she probably looked dirty, gaunt.

Her eyes watered as she fought back tears.

What a horrible time to start crying.

"I've been . . . kidnapped. You've got to help me. My name is Sarah Roberts. That man is a murderer. He killed a cop on the highway." She thought of something that would explain her appearance. "Look what he's already done to me. He's torturing me." She tugged on his sleeve. "Please help. Call the police."

"Okay, slow down. I know about this case. I saw it on the cover of today's newspaper."

"He'll be coming back any minute. I have to be gone or he'll kill me."

"Hold on. I'll just pick up a phone and tell him I'm calling the police. He won't do anything crazy in public. You go hide behind a car. Just stay hidden."

"No. No, you can't. Don't you understand?" She darted a glance at the restaurant counter where she had seen him moments before, but he was gone. "He doesn't care. He won't hesitate to kill you, too."

This wasn't working. She told him to call the police as soon as he could. Then she hobbled away. She stumbled on her weak limbs, but managed to maintain her balance.

Exposed, out in the open, she gave it her all. The tree line would provide cover.

Twenty more steps.

She looked to her right. Cars raced by on the highway. People in their own world, completely unaware an eighteen-year-old was running for her life.

She could feel panic set in. Breath hitched in her throat. She felt eyes on her. She anticipated a bullet in the back at any moment.

She didn't waste time to look over her shoulder. If he saw her making a break for it, then he would give chase or shoot.

Something about death seemed desirable, like food. She was so hungry she could taste the smell coming from the gas station's restaurant, her mouth chewing imaginary food.

Leaves and branches brushed her arms as she dropped down a small, three-foot embankment. The cover of trees swallowed her. She stopped about ten feet in to fall to her knees and catch her breath.

She peeked through the branches. The gas attendant was out of sight. Gert was nowhere to be seen.

She made it. She had escaped. A wave of relief washed over her.

She decided to wait in the trees for a few hours. She could wait until the cover of dark or when the police arrived. She could lie down and sleep on a bed of leaves.

Then the gas attendant appeared at the side of the van, pulling the nozzle out and replacing the gas cap. He looked her way once before walking around to the front and heading for the restaurant.

Gert came into view.

She ducked her head down. Not seeing was worse. She pulled on a branch and raised herself up enough to look across the parking lot.

They were talking. Gert was shaking his head.

Sarah started deeper into the thicket. She was determined to put as much geography between her and Gert as she could.

"YOU'RE ALL FILLED up, sir. It came to fifty-eight dollars."

Gert studied the guy. He looked to be around seventeen. Something was wrong with him, though. The kid's eyes shifted past Gert's shoulder, then trained back on Gert, then over to the pumps, and on to a car going by on the highway. Maybe the kid noticed the bulge of the gun under Gert's shirt.

Gert guessed they were about six feet from the van. Could this kid have talked to Sarah?

He kept his eyes on the nervous kid while he stepped over to look in the van's windows. He set the bag of food on the cement and cupped his hands around his eyes to see all the way to the back.

The van was empty. Sarah was gone.

Shit.

He spun around, accidentally kicked the paper bag of greasy burgers, and pulled his gun.

The gas jockey was already running.

He almost made it to the safety of the restaurant.

A LOUD CRACK in the air told Sarah that a gun had been fired.

A high-pitched scream followed.

She stopped running.

Someone had probably called the police by now. But could she trust them? Gert's boss worked with them.

Her priority had to be her mother. Somehow, she had to contact her mother.

But first, she had to see for herself what was going on.

She saved people. *That's* who Sarah was. That's who she wanted to be. Without that, she was better off dead.

· · ·

GERT WALKED TOWARD the attendant, his gun extended in front of him. People were running for cover. A car squealed out of the parking lot behind him.

When he got close to the gas jockey, he saw what looked like a flesh wound on the kid's right calf muscle. He noticed the kid's name tag read *Steve*.

"Where is she?" Gert asked.

Steve lay there with both hands on his wounded leg. Small rivers of blood seeped through his fingers. He responded with only grunts and groans.

Gert got down on his knees and pulled the kid's face close to his. He pressed the gun to the underside of Steve's jaw.

"I won't ask again," Gert said. "Where is she?"

Steve's eyes rolled back in his head as he fainted. Gert let go of him and stood.

There was no sign of Sarah anywhere.

He had lost her again.

Someone yelled inside the restaurant.

Gert gritted his teeth. He raised the gun in the air and fired randomly.

"Sarah! Come out, come out, wherever you are. How many people have to die for you?"

SARAH DUCKED AGAIN. She was close enough to hear Gert yelling.

He was standing halfway between the van and the restaurant. The gas jockey was on the ground, blood pooling below his waist.

This can't be happening.

She leaned sideways against a small tree. Her body was reacting to the stress in new ways: ragged breath, weakness in her stomach and legs, and a heartbeat out of sync.

She had nothing in her stomach to throw up, but it felt like something was coming.

She sat down on the ground, dropped her face into her hands, and lost the last bit of control she had.

GERT RAISED HIS gun and fired through one of the front windows of the restaurant.

He was careful to aim above their heads. He didn't want to be known as a mass murderer. If his brother were alive he would be proud of his restraint.

"That's another one dead," he yelled.

He fired into the roof of the restaurant. "And yet another one bites the dust. How many people have to be shot for your freedom, Sarah?"

Someone was running behind him, footsteps pounding the pavement.

He pivoted on the spot and saw Sarah making a break for the highway. As she hit the shoulder of the road she lost her balance and tumbled forward, rolling directly in front of a large oil tanker.

The truck swerved.

Its horn blared as the driver got his vehicle back under control. Brake lights came on. The oil tanker was stopping, pulling over.

Gert dropped the gun to his side. He started walking to the highway.

This ought to be amusing.

SARAH'S RIGHT SHOULDER screamed. When she lost her footing and fell, the gravel dug in, lacerating her skin.

She scanned the road in both directions. Only two cars were coming, one from either direction. The oil tanker guy was climbing down from his cab.

She looked back at the gas station and saw Gert walking toward her.

Never again, she thought, as she got up and put one foot in front of the other.

She touched the tender area of her shoulder. Her hand came away with blood on it.

Why isn't he shooting me?

A large black car approached. The vehicle wasn't slowing down. She stepped into the middle of the highway. She closed her eyes tight. Her shoulder felt like it was on fire. She focused on the pain and waited.

She could hear the car slowing fast, its tires gripping the hot pavement.

"Are you okay?" the driver of the car asked.

She opened her eyes.

"Help me. Please take me to a hospital. They've tortured me, pulled my hair out."

"What? Hold on."

A large black man opened the door and stepped out.

"What's your name?"

GERT COULDN'T BELIEVE it. Some guy had stopped his car and was talking to her. The oil tanker driver had almost reached her, too.

He couldn't allow a stranger to take Sarah away. He broke into a run.

"Hey!" Gert shouted.

The tall black guy turned and looked at him. Sarah threw herself into the backseat of the car. From fifty yards away he could hear Sarah yelling for the guy to get in and drive.

He raised his gun and fired. The bullet missed. A hole formed beside the black guy in the window of the open driver's door. That was enough to get him moving.

Gert fired again as the driver slammed his door shut. The car lurched forward, away from Gert and the gas station.

It took Gert precious seconds to get back to the van.

By the time he started it and turned toward the highway, the black car had disappeared.

50

SARAH SCRAMBLED AROUND in the backseat and got into a crouched position, favoring her wounded shoulder. She took a quick look out the back window. No sign of Gert's van in pursuit.

"What's going on?" the driver asked. "Why was that guy shooting at us?"

Sarah could detect a slight southern accent. She looked at him in the rearview mirror.

"You okay, girl?" he asked.

"He kidnapped me a few days ago. Please, just get me to a phone, then leave."

"Is that the guy they're searching for? A manhunt, the newspapers called it."

Sarah nodded. The driver mumbled something to himself.

"Don't worry," Sarah said. "You won't be mixed up in this if you just get me to a phone and take off."

"But he killed a cop, and apparently two members of a crime family out of New York."

The driver kept darting his eyes between the road ahead and his mirrors.

There was still no sign of the van behind them. She looked at the back of the driver's head. "He won't let me get away that easy. You need to go faster."

She examined her shoulder. The scattered dirt and small pebbles were easily brushed off. The bleeding was minimal, but it hurt like a bitch.

Asphalt raced by under the car, open, empty fields by the windows. This would never be over until she was home with her parents and Gert was either locked up or dead.

Every mile counted. They crested a rise and saw a small town coming up. The driver swung into a convenience store and gas station on the right.

"You're safe now," he said. "They'll let you use their phone inside."

She mumbled her thanks as she exited the car. He stayed in the parking lot and watched her until she got into the store.

An Asian man stood behind the counter.

"I need to use a phone," Sarah said. "It's an emergency."

She saw the clerk's smile fade and then disappear. She probably looked like she had just walked away from an explosion.

"Please, your phone?"

The door swung open behind her. It was the driver. "The black van is coming."

The driver turned around and flipped the interior thumb lock on the door, locking it from the inside. The Asian man behind the counter protested.

"Get away from the windows," the driver told her. "You too," he said to the clerk.

A vehicle pulled into the parking lot out front. She heard it slide to a stop on the gravel as she ran for the back of the store. On the way she grabbed a handful of Twinkies and a Red Bull from a corner display.

The first door she came to opened into a stockroom. They stepped through it. The driver stood by the door, leaving it ajar as Sarah walked to the back loading area and quietly unlocked it. By this time she had stuffed one full Twinkie in her mouth. It tasted like a gourmet meal.

A gun went off, followed by shattered glass. The driver shut the door and ran for Sarah.

"Open it, open it," he said. "We gotta get outta here."

She pushed down on the bar and yanked open the back door. A loud buzzer sounded. They had set off an alarm. Gert would know she was leaving through the back and be on them in no time.

Back in the sunlight there was no time for indecision. A Dumpster sat twenty feet away on her left.

The driver grabbed her arm. He was clearly panicking. She saw his eyes darting back and forth. Which way to go? Already precious seconds were lost.

The driver freaked and started running. He headed for the open field behind the store.

"No, he'll see you," she called after him.

Sarah bolted for the Dumpster. She grabbed the open lid and swung it shut with a loud bang. Then she turned and ran around the building.

She hoped Gert would waste precious time talking to an empty Dumpster.

Scrunching herself against the wall of the building, she brushed sweat from her eyes as she looked around the corner. Only the black van and the car that brought her here sat out front.

She couldn't believe her luck. The car was idling. She jammed another Twinkie into her mouth and popped open the Red Bull.

Gert was in the back of the building looking for her. In the distance she could hear a police siren. The store owner must have called them. Or maybe they were summoned when the back door's alarm triggered.

She pushed away from her hiding place and ran for the idling car, heart beating in harmony with the pounding of her feet. Her second wind had kicked in. She hadn't felt this alive in days. The Twinkies were at work. She was back in control.

Saving myself.

In seconds Sarah was on the highway, wind caressing her face through the open driver's side window as she finished the Red Bull. She tried to keep the car steady, narrowly missing a station wagon going the other way.

She had limited experience behind the wheel, yet she carefully maneuvered into the little town.

No bullets pursued her.

51

GERT HAD HAD enough. A siren wailed in the distance. He held up his gun and opened the top of the garbage Dumpster.

It was empty.

"Fuck."

He did a complete turn. Nothing but open fields. Maybe he missed them in the store after all. He rushed back in. It was completely empty. Even the clerk had bolted.

The siren was closer.

"Shit."

He had lost Sarah for good this time. The cops were coming. He wasn't going to die in a stupid convenience store on the side of the highway.

He ran for the van. As he did, he noticed the other car was gone. They would be at the police station in no time, giving a description of him and the vehicle he was in.

It was truly over this time.

Sarah had finally gotten away.

That fucking bitch.

Gert pounded the steering wheel as he did a U-turn, and raced up the highway the way he had come. He knew he'd pass the gas station again, but it was better than driving into the small town beyond and possibly getting trapped by some local cops.

After less than a minute, before he lost the convenience store in his rearview mirror, he saw a lone cruiser pull into its parking lot, lights blazing.

Minutes later he drove past the gas station. Police cars were already there, cops swarming the area.

Someone was pointing down the road in the other direction.

No one looked at him as he passed.

He had a head start, with no plan. His brother would know what to do, but his brother was dead.

There was nothing left but to run.

Unless he could get another hostage.

52

SAM JOHNSON GLANCED at Dolan as they listened to the police radio. There had been a shooting at a gas station off the highway. The dispatcher was calling for all units in the area.

Dolan nodded to confirm it was their guy.

Sam threw his coffee out the window and headed toward the gas station.

They had been discussing their next move. Sam didn't want to go against the FBI, but it was too late to give up. He had been the head of the task force for long enough to handle this case until completion.

"Dolan, tell me something."

"What?"

"Why do you think this case is different from all the other kidnappings?"

Sam felt Dolan watching him as he drove.

"How do you mean, different?"

"This is the first time I've seen you come up short. I mean, you didn't get us to the cabin on time. Now you know the perp is involved in the gas station mess, but you didn't mention it—not until it happened."

Dolan rubbed his forehead as he looked out at the passing countryside.

"I don't know. I can only speculate."

"Speculate then," Sam said.

"It could be because I'm involved."

"What do you mean? You're always involved."

"I mean I'm physically in this cruiser. I went to the cabin. Psychics can't read their own future. If I could, I'd be able to pick the next winning lottery numbers."

Dolan's cell rang. Sam watched for the exit to take him east on Interstate 29, while Dolan mumbled into his phone where he was going.

When he flipped it shut Sam looked over. "Who was that? You told the caller about the gas station."

"That was my assistant, Alex. The fair closed down now for two weeks, until we get to the next city and set up. I told him to come and get me. It sounds like this is coming to an end soon anyway. Alex has some talent himself. Since he's not directly involved or helping on this case, maybe he'll have some kind of information for you."

Sam detected sarcasm in Dolan's voice. He couldn't be sure if it was intentional.

"Maybe you'll have more information yourself once you're gone."

"Just drive, Sam. We've worked together too long to fight."

53

GERT KNEW TIME was running out. He had to change vehicles as soon as possible and hole up somewhere safe.

His cell battery had died hours ago. Cash was running low. Using a debit card or credit card would alert anyone looking for him, provided they knew his name at all.

He reminded himself that the cops might not yet know that Sarah wasn't with him anymore. For at least the next hour, they might not shoot on sight.

A long train was crossing the grassy fields ahead, a red light flashing. A BMW SUV sat at the railway crossing. It was the only vehicle. The train moved slowly over the two-lane highway.

He pulled up behind the SUV. Then, with a quick foot, he shot the van forward and slammed the brake hard. It was a perfect hit, just enough to smack the BMW without leaving a broken bumper or worse.

The driver got out at the same time Gert did. It was a lone female with long brown hair, mid-forties, unsteady on high heels.

"What happened?" she asked. "You couldn't see I was stopped?" The woman bent to inspect the damage.

"I'm sorry. My foot slipped. I went to tap the brake but hit the accelerator instead."

"Well, it doesn't look as bad as I thought."

Gert pulled out his weapon.

"Step away from the vehicle."

The woman turned and saw the gun. She tried to step back, but Gert was already grabbing her lapel. He dragged her close to him, the gun now pressed into her abdomen. The expression on her face was pure fear.

"We're going to play a little game," he said. "I'll take your BMW and you drive my van. And then the chase begins."

"What—what chase?"

Her voice cracked. Gert loved her quivering weakness.

"If I catch you, you die. It's that simple. Don't stop for anyone. Don't slow down. Whatever you do, don't let me catch you."

"Why are you doing this?" The woman's voice was weak with fear.

"Because I can. Now get in the van. I left it running."

Gert pushed her away from him. She stumbled to the door of the van.

"Go that way," Gert said, pointing the way he had just come from. "I'll give you a two-minute head start, so drive fast."

He kept the gun pointed at her as she got in the van. He heard the transmission shift into gear. When she looked at him through the windshield, he tapped his wrist.

She turned the van around and started away from him. He raised the gun and fired a warning shot into the back window.

The vehicle skidded and then took off. She must have dropped the pedal all the way down.

Gert hopped into the BMW. When the van was lost to sight and the train had cleared the tracks, he floored it in the opposite direction.

54

IT TOOK SARAH a moment to realize she was alone in the front seat of a car.

She must've blacked out.

She had pulled into another gas station after a cop car passed her with its lights and siren on. She had wanted to stick around to see Gert get arrested. What she saw was the black van drive away unnoticed by the police.

She looked at her right arm while rubbing it. The familiar numbness was there. Did she write something? She looked around for anything she would have been able to write on. A newspaper sat folded beside her. Sketched in the margin was a note:

. . . drive after van . . . twenty minutes left to stop another kill . . . only you can stop Gert's boss . . .

Sarah started the car and got back on the highway, not liking the new message one bit.

She headed out of town as fast as she could without speeding. She looked down and saw a small stash of coins in the ashtray. A pack of gum was in the glove box, which she unwrapped and tossed in her mouth. The taste was incredible.

The note said twenty minutes.

She could just turn the car around and call home. She had won her freedom. But she was too involved now. She couldn't walk away.

Sarah had tried to ignore the messages once. It was after her first blackout, seven months ago.

The next day, she heard that a fifteen-year-old girl got beat up by her father on their front lawn. She learned later that the father was known to police, and a professional alcoholic.

They lived a block away. Sarah could have intervened with a phone call.

After that, Sarah stopped throwing the notes away. She started carrying paper with her everywhere, and eventually upgraded to a notebook.

And when she saved Mary Bennett, she swore to herself that she would act on any message as best as she could. If it was in her power to help someone, she would at least try.

She had been chosen. It made her feel special, powerful. It was like she had an arrangement with God. He would protect her. He would take care of her. This was His deal.

The messages had never been wrong before. If she was the only one who could stop Gert, then she had to try.

At the moment she was wide awake, and feeling strong after the burst of sugar and caffeine.

She passed the gas station where she had last seen Gert. She was going over sixty-five miles an hour. Multiple police vehicles, ambulances, and dark-colored sedans littered the parking lot. She checked her mirrors, but no one was coming after her. No one at the scene would be worried about handing out speeding tickets.

Gert's black van popped up about a mile ahead, coming toward her. Sarah let off the accelerator a little.

Something told her the driver of the van was no longer Gert.

The black van was half a mile away and closing fast. Sarah slowed down and steered the car as far to the right as she could without driving on the shoulder.

When the van got close enough, she saw long hair through the windshield. The driver was female.

Maybe it's just another black van, she thought.

She saw a small hole in the back windshield as the driver raced by her. A bullet hole.

The woman was doing at least eighty miles an hour. That might catch someone's attention at the gas station.

But then what vehicle was Gert in now? She had ten minutes left to find him.

55

SAM SIGNALED AND pulled over onto the shoulder. When the car had come to a complete stop he opened his door and got out.

"What're you doing?" Dolan asked.

"Get out."

Dolan hesitated, then opened his door and stepped away from the car. They looked at each other over the roof.

The last thing Sam wanted for his career was to show up at the crime scene with the *psychic* in tow. Especially not with Agent Hanover there.

"Dolan, you're not leveling with me about something. Call Alex back and get him to pick you up here."

Dolan rested his forearms on the open car door and lowered his head. He adjusted his sunglasses, then looked back up. "I don't know what it is either. Maybe it's because I don't want to do this." A soft breeze moved his hair. "Sam, I can't handle the fanatics anymore."

Sam's jacket rustled in the wind. "So let me get this straight—you agree to help find Sarah, but you're really worried about yourself?"

"Don't be like that. It's true, I don't want to do this anymore. But after talking to Esmerelda, I decided to help one last time."

Sam looked over his shoulder as a rig passed by. Dolan walked around the car to him. "But you know as well as I do, when I agree to take on something, I give it my best." He reached into his back pocket and pulled out a piece of paper. "Here, look at this."

Sam took the note and flipped it over. It was from Sarah. "What's this? How long have you had it?"

"Since I first got to the Robertses' house. Sarah has a gift, too. She knew I'd search her room. She may be the one blocking me, but not intentionally. This is her gig. That's how she saved Mary Bennett and the others over these last six months."

Sam stepped away from him. "Are you trying to tell me that an eighteen-year-old girl thinks she's getting psychic messages and then goes out on vigilante missions?"

"I don't know what Sarah is yet. Not until I talk to her."

Sam looked at the note in his hand. Sam couldn't understand how Sarah would have only partial knowledge of events to come. If she could stop kidnappings, then how did *she* get taken? He believed it went deeper than what her notebook revealed.

"Gun!"

Sam ducked his head as Dolan shouted. He landed on the hood of the cruiser as Dolan made his way around the trunk.

An SUV was passing them, its driver's side window down. A gun protruded out, aimed in their direction. Just as the SUV drew level, a four-door Impala bumped it from behind.

The gun went off, but the Impala's impact had spoiled the shooter's aim. The bullet meant for Sam lodged in the windshield of his cruiser.

The driver of the SUV took another wild shot as he passed. Sam saw the gun hand withdraw into the driver's window. The SUV raced away from them while the Impala slowed down and stopped on the opposite shoulder.

Sam drew his sidearm and stepped toward the Impala, his heart racing.

"Step out of the vehicle, hands where I can see them," he shouted.

The door opened. A frail-looking girl turned in the driver's seat and tried to stand. Sam approached with caution, his internal radar pinging.

"I'm Sarah Roberts. The man who tried to shoot you was my kidnapper. I would've called after I escaped, but I received a message that you would be killed. I guess I got here just in time."

56

SPECIAL AGENT JILL Hanover pulled into one of the last Texaco gas stations in America. She parked her Crown Victoria under the old, weathered sign.

Fergus Mant jumped out of the passenger seat and announced that the FBI would be taking over.

A moment later, Hanover's forensics van pulled in and parked by the restaurant doors.

"I want every shell casing, every fingerprint. I especially want everyone who's still here to give a full statement before they leave. Nothing gets missed."

Two ambulances and five marked police cars littered the parking lot. The immediate area was filled with people contaminating evidence.

She headed for the entrance of the restaurant, where she saw Fergus arguing with a uniformed officer.

"Fergus, find out who showed up on the scene first and get everything you can from them. If the guy bought gas, I want to know about it. If they have any kind of security cameras, I want the footage."

Another agent interrupted her. "Agent Hanover, we just got a call that a black van was pulled over a couple of miles from here. It matches the description of the one reported stolen yesterday."

"Was it our guy? Is Sarah with him?"

"The perp switched vehicles. The driver is a woman who said he was chasing her in *her* BMW. It was some kind of game."

"Did this woman get a good look at the perp?"

"Up close. But here's the good part. The carjacker was alone. He didn't have a girl with him. That jives with what a few of the witnesses are saying here. The girl ran onto the highway and was picked up by a guy driving an Impala. Sarah may have gotten away."

Hanover looked skyward. "Is the helicopter up yet?"

"It'll be in the area in fifteen minutes."

"Okay, put out a call to every law enforcement agency in the state to be on the lookout for this woman's BMW. Inform the pilot to maintain air support at fifteen hundred feet and wait for our call about the location of the perp."

The agent looked down at the report. "There's one more thing. One of the officers who pulled the van over found a piece of paper in the back. It was addressed to Amelia Roberts. It appears to be from her daughter."

Hanover was eager to join the chase, but first she wanted to see to the crime scene.

Mant jogged over moments later.

"You're not going to like what just came through the radio."

"Hit me with it."

"Sam Johnson is in pursuit of the perp as we speak."

"You don't mean the Sam Johnson who ran the task force? The one I took off this case?"

"The very same. But listen, it gets better. Dolan has Sarah Roberts. His assistant is bringing them here." Mant looked at his watch. "In less than twenty minutes."

"Well, this is wrapping up quickly. Get someone to call the Holiday Inn and get Sarah's parents out here. Find out where Sam is, so we can help him stop this lunatic. Update the helicopter pilot, too. Let's move, let's move."

57

GERT PUSHED THE power button on the car phone built into the dash of the BMW, and dialed. The phone was answered on the first ring.

"How do I get out of this?" Gert yelled into the phone. "Tell me what to do."

"Where are you?" his boss asked. "Do you know how many law enforcement agencies are looking for you?"

"I would've never shot those guys behind the motel if you hadn't told me to go back and secure my hostage. It would've been one dead cop on the side of the highway and me long gone. But no, I had to take care of Sarah."

Gert gunned the BMW.

"You lost your bargaining chip. Now they've got Sarah, and she knows about us. Every cop for a thousand miles wants to put a bullet in you."

Gert heard background noise from the other side of the phone. The boss was driving. "Are you going somewhere?"

"I'm in your vicinity."

"What are you doing out here?"

"You've got a tail. A helicopter should be on your ass within a couple of minutes. The police are looking for the BMW you're in. They are not looking for me. I'm your only way out of this."

Gert pulled the phone away from his ear. He hit it on the dash in frustration, then put it back to his ear. "No chance."

"Listen carefully. I will be with Sarah shortly. The famed psychic has her, and he called in his location for a pickup. Tell me where you are and I'll bring them to you. We can finish this right."

Gert relayed the highway number he was on and the name of an exit ramp. He took the ramp and told his boss to look for a BMW

SUV. He would try to find something within a couple of miles from the ramp, on the right side, to hole up in.

"Don't get caught. I'll handle the girl and the psychic. See you soon." Gert clicked off the phone.

The distinctive sound of a helicopter approaching from behind gave him a chill.

58

DOLAN LOOKED UP at the sound of a vehicle approaching. Alex's silver Honda slowed and stopped a few feet away. A soft drizzle started to fall. It felt cleansing, a cool break from the sun.

Dolan opened the back door for Sarah and helped her in. Then he jumped in the front and slammed the door.

"Thanks for coming to get us," Dolan said.

"No problem," Alex said. "I brought some food and a drink for Sarah."

He lifted a lunch bag over the seat and handed it to her, followed by two bottles of water. "That should be good until we can get you to a hospital. How're you feeling? It must've been quite the ordeal."

"I'm okay," Sarah said. "Don't take me to a hospital just yet. Not until we catch up with the asshole that kidnapped me." Sarah tore open the lunch bag. "And what's that smell? Is that cologne?"

Dolan and Alex looked at each other.

"We're not taking her to safety?" Alex asked.

Dolan had worked with Alex for years, but he hadn't seen this edge to him. The man was shaking.

"No, not yet. We need to be there when Gert is arrested. Sarah has information about his boss."

Alex jolted and then adjusted himself in his seat.

"You okay, Alex?" Dolan asked. "Is this too much for you?"

"No, no, I'm fine. I've just never been this close to the action. I'm a little out of my element."

Dolan nodded slowly. Something else was on his assistant's mind.

Alex merged back onto the two-lane highway. Dolan gave him directions to the Texaco station.

Dolan needed to think about what Sarah had told him about her gift as they waited. He had never heard of anyone receiving such specific details from the Other Side. He admired her blind faith in the messages.

Still, he didn't know why he had agreed to let her continue this dangerous search. According to Sarah, she was the only one who could stop the mastermind behind the kidnappings.

Alex said they were approaching the station. Dolan pulled out his cell phone and called Sam. They talked briefly and then he hung up.

"Looks like he followed the guy to an abandoned farmhouse off . . ."

Dolan trailed off when he saw the gun.

"I know where it is," Alex said. "I'd guess we're about five minutes away."

"What are you doing?" Dolan asked.

"This has been a long time coming, Dolan. I've envied you, looked up to you. But you've always treated me like I'm second-class. I could've helped the police, too. But no, you get all the fame and then you whine about it. *Too many people want readings*, you say."

"Look, Alex, I don't think this is the right time to discuss our professional relationship."

"Is that what you think this is all about? I thought you were more insightful than this."

Alex cleared his throat. Dolan kept his eyes on the gun. The Texaco passed by in seconds.

"For the past few years I fed you information on the whereabouts of kidnap victims because I *knew* where they were. I thought you'd think I had great psychic powers myself, but you never did. You just went to the authorities and took the credit."

Dolan kept his hands where Alex could see them. "Are you saying you've been behind all this?"

"You're getting it now." Alex looked sideways at him. "Just wait until everyone hears that your Psychic Fair was involved with these kidnappings. With Sarah dead and the FBI about to kill Gert, I only need to remove you."

"Sarah dead? How do you intend to do that?"

Dolan realized the look he saw in Alex's eyes earlier wasn't fear. It was insanity.

"Pull out your cell phone. Do it slowly."

Dolan did as he was told while Alex tried to keep his eyes on the road and watch him at the same time.

"Now toss it out the window."

Dolan complied. He wanted to sneak a look back at Sarah, but couldn't risk it.

Alex checked his mirror and then applied the brake.

"What're you doing now?" Dolan asked.

"Letting you out."

"I'm not leaving Sarah alone with you."

Alex brought the Honda to a complete stop. "You don't have a choice. Get out."

Dolan folded his arms in defiance.

Sarah's scream followed the echo of the gun. Dolan felt like he had been punched in the side by a sledgehammer. He looked down and saw a red dot on his left side. The dot was spreading fast. He looked up at Alex. Now his eyes held a cool resolve.

"The next bullet goes in your head. Sarah, don't move. I will shoot to kill if you try anything."

Alex lunged across Dolan and opened the passenger door. Dolan felt a numb feeling spread across his midsection. Blood covered his hands. He needed to apply pressure.

Alex pushed him hard and he landed on the side of the highway. He saw Sarah watching him from the backseat, her face pale.

Another shot rang out. Dolan felt it in the ribs.

His breathing became ragged.

Darkness fell as he lost consciousness.

59

AMELIA WORE LARGE sunglasses to cover her swollen eyes. She remembered how Sarah used to call them Mickey Mouse glasses because they were the size of Mickey's ears.

Trees whipped by the Suburban's tinted windows. Caleb sat beside her, head back, eyes closed. The FBI department psychologist sat across from them in a seat that swiveled 180 degrees. She had it turned around to face them.

After the phone incident in the hotel room, the psychologist, Tracy, had been handling her differently, like a porcelain doll.

She felt Caleb's hand creep into hers. She tightened her grip to reassure him she was still there.

"Before we arrive, can we talk about something?" Tracy asked, her voice soft.

Amelia didn't respond right away. She was in no mood for conversation. The woman's fake concern was unnerving. They were mere minutes away from seeing Sarah. What was there to talk about?

Amelia turned her head and looked at Tracy. "Go ahead."

Tracy looked from Caleb to Amelia, then back to Caleb. "Vivian."

Hearing her daughter's name caused a flood of memories. Back to the day she was shopping with Vivian. Losing her in the crowd. Police involvement. Reviewing camera footage in the mall. The FBI coming in on the case when there were sightings of Vivian crossing state lines. An overwhelming feeling of sorrow, guilt, and worry. Holding baby Sarah in her arms and swearing it would never happen to her.

Thirty-four days after she was kidnapped, Vivian was found on a dirt road twenty-two miles from the mall where she had been taken. She had been raped and murdered. The killer was never caught. There was no fresh DNA match. No idle talk in a prison somewhere. No confession from a guilty heart. Nothing. Just her Vivian, dead.

Tracy leaned back in her seat. "Does Sarah know about her sister?"

"What's this got to do with anything?" Caleb asked. "We're about to pick Sarah up. We get our daughter back. Nothing else matters."

"I'm sorry. I do wonder if what Sarah writes is somehow connected to the loss."

"It isn't," Caleb said.

Amelia looked back out the window.

Vivian said on the phone she was with Sarah.

But Sarah wasn't dead and Vivian was.

It just didn't make any sense.

60

GERT DROVE UP on dry, baked earth that hadn't seen farm equipment in years. Dust surrounded the BMW as he slammed on the brakes. He stopped at an angle in front of the steps that led to the broken front door. The unrelenting summer sun had peeled the dirty white paint on the door. It sat askew, held to the frame by the bottom hinge.

Gert forced it back enough for him to enter the dark interior but not enough to break it. He wanted to make it difficult for pursuers to enter.

As his eyes adjusted he could make out old pieces of furniture. It looked like an antique shop that was long abandoned.

He heard the helicopter buzz outside. The rotors were so loud it was all he could hear for a moment.

He entered a room that looked like it had once been a kitchen. Now it was just a pile of wood with outlines of where the cupboards and counter used to be. The paint on the walls was chipped and peeling. Although there was no electricity, he could see well enough from the window in the south wall.

He realized his mistake in holing up in a farmhouse. Soon the cops would storm the place. There was no way he would be able to make it on the run. Prison would kill him.

He looked across the room and saw an archway that opened to another hall. Two entrances to the kitchen and a pile of debris about three feet high in the center of the room made it a great spot for an ambush.

Gert sat under the window, his back against the wall, and listened as the helicopter made another pass.

He pulled out his gun and remaining ammunition, and waited, resolved to meet the end that was before him.

61

SAM DIDN'T WANT to take the kidnapper on alone, but he was the only one at the farmhouse, and the perp didn't know it. After radioing in his position, he was told to stand down. Backup was on the way, with an FBI negotiator and the HRT.

What the hell do they need a negotiator for? Sarah's safe, and no one is talking this asshole out of the farmhouse.

Sam had seen this kind of situation a hundred times. Almost always the perp died, usually by a self-inflicted shot after a few hours of fruitless negotiation. Some idiots chose to come out shooting at officers who were waiting with an arsenal. Others sat it out until the FBI stormed the building. In this case, Sam knew the police would be glad to return fire on a cop killer.

But if Sam could get him in handcuffs in the next five minutes, then he could live to pay for his crimes. Besides, an arrest like this would win Sam some much-needed credibility.

He checked his watch as he approached the broken building from the rear. About three to four minutes was all he could hope for. He had gotten a pretty good look at the place when he watched the BMW pull in. A small copse of trees planted on the north side gave him shelter as he ran up to the wall. At the back of the house a shell of a window long since broken revealed a barren room. With both hands applying pressure on the sill, Sam began to lift himself in.

His peripheral vision caught movement to his right. With one quick motion, he released the sill, dropped his body to the ground, and pulled his gun.

It was Alex, Dolan's assistant. He was holding Sarah by the back of the neck.

Sam kept his gun at the ready.

"What is this?" he whispered.

"This is a problem," Alex said. "You're a problem."

"Are you fucking nuts?"

"Drop your gun, Sam. We don't need another dead cop on our hands."

Alex shifted enough to expose the weapon that he held pointed into the small of Sarah's back. Sam had no idea how Dolan's assistant was involved, but he did what he was told, bending slowly to place his gun in the foot-long grass. When his eyes met Sarah's he was surprised to see a cool confidence. He wondered if she knew something neither one of them did.

"Okay, Sam, here's how it has to work. The FBI will be in the area within a minute or so. I need you to leave us alone, but we're running out of time, so I want you to run, not walk."

"I'm not leaving Sarah alone with you."

"Then you'll die where you stand. Don't be stupid. Turn around and get going."

Alex moved the pistol away from Sarah and aimed it at Sam. Sarah nodded at him.

Sam stepped backward.

He jumped at the sound of a gun being discharged.

Alex had fired but missed.

Sam turned and ran.

The next bullet knocked him to the ground. Sarah's scream was the last thing he heard.

62

ALEX TURNED AND pushed Sarah toward the open window.

"Climb in," he said as he reached down and picked up the cop's gun.

Sarah stumbled and then righted herself. "Why are you doing this?" she asked. "You don't have to. It could end right now."

"Just get in."

Sarah folded her arms across her chest. "I asked you why."

She was stalling for time.

"In a few words, here's what is about to happen. We're going through that window. Then we're going to find Gert. He will be killed with Sam's gun. If Gert returns fire, you'll be in front of me. If he misses, then the cop's gun will be used on you, too. I walk out of here the hero. Or I can shoot you in the face right now. How about it?"

Alex turned at the sound of a vehicle approaching. It was an old blue pickup truck loaded with hay. He looked back at Sarah.

"Everyone will see that I tried to save you," he hissed. "But Gert shot the cop while he was running away in the field and then shot you before I got the chance to get to him. Everyone who knows of my involvement is dead, and I take over the Psychic Fair. Get it?"

"There's only one catch."

"What's that?"

"I'm not going to die today. You are."

Anger coursed through him. He punched the wooden wall of the farmhouse.

"You're going through that window. You've got one second to decide."

"I'll go in. I know that all I've got to do is remember to not thump, rip, and tear. It's better to be savage. At least that's what the note said."

Alex didn't ask for clarification. While she hopped up and through the window he took one final glance at the road and saw FBI vehicles converging in a small dust cloud, headed their way.

Just in time, he thought as he followed Sarah inside and landed on the broken wooden floor of what was once a bedroom.

He grabbed Sarah's arm and began looking for Gert.

They headed for the kitchen.

63

THE TEMPORARY COMMAND post was coming together fast as Agent Hanover briefed the Hostage Rescue Team leader. They took up positions around the perimeter of the farmhouse.

She was interrupted as her earpiece buzzed with the news that Sarah's parents were waiting one hundred yards back on the country road. She told the driver to wait for her signal to approach. They hadn't located Dolan or Sarah yet.

Her tactical team radioed in. There was no sign of Sam Johnson, but his vehicle was found twenty yards from the farmhouse behind a small thicket. The stolen BMW SUV was visible in front of the farmhouse, and a silver Honda was parked in the rear, behind a weathered barn. License plates identified it as belonging to an Alex Stuart.

"Fergus"—Hanover turned to her partner—"find out who this Alex Stuart is. And get me Dolan on the phone. I need to know Sarah's safe before we enter the farmhouse."

Her HRT commander called in that all his crew were in position. Barricaded by the front of a Crown Victoria, her negotiator bellowed on a bullhorn.

Hanover grabbed her cell phone as it vibrated on her waist.

"Speak."

"We've got a problem."

She recognized Agent Mant's voice. "Go ahead."

"Dolan was just picked up by a car five miles from here. He's on the way to the hospital. He's been shot several times."

"What? Where's Sarah?" she asked, her voice rising.

"Dolan has been in and out of consciousness, but he told the driver that Sarah was taken by the shooter—Dolan's assistant, Alex Stuart."

Hanover lowered her phone and looked at the farmhouse. If Alex Stuart's Honda was parked in the rear of the farmhouse, that also meant Sarah was in there with two men. Could they be working together?

The HRT in her earpiece was looking for the go-ahead. The negotiator had tried, but there had been no response from anyone in the building.

She tried to think fast. A couple of guys kidnapping for hire. The girl always comes home, but no perps get arrested. Dolan knew where the victims were, but not the criminals. It would seem likely he's involved.

But then why was he shot?

Fergus spoke to her through her earpiece. Sarah's parents were on the move.

She lifted her wrist to talk into the cuff. "I thought I ordered them to stay back."

"They stepped from the vehicle to stretch their legs. Caleb bolted across the grass. He wasn't seen until . . . well, he should be right behind you."

Special Agent Jill Hanover turned and saw a panting Caleb Roberts approach.

Her radio crackled as the HRT reported an emergency. She listened as one of the team said he found Sam, shot. He was alive but losing blood fast. An ambulance was needed immediately or they would lose another cop.

This operation is falling apart, she thought.

She turned to greet Caleb while she ordered Fergus to get an ambulance here *yesterday.*

Then shots rang out from inside the farmhouse behind her.

64

ALEX HAD JUMPED through the window behind Sarah. They were in a small bedroom. It had to be at least a hundred degrees inside the abandoned building, but she couldn't stop shaking. Maybe her body was finally giving out after days of malnourishment and adrenaline.

Alex seemed more dangerous than Gert, yet she felt no fear of him. She remembered him watching her at the fair, lurking around. She had felt something strange about him then, but it wasn't fear. She felt a small sense of bravado.

Mistakes could happen if she got overconfident. She would have to watch herself, stay alert. Keep a clear mind and seize any opportunity to escape.

Alex stopped fiddling with his weapon and grabbed her arm. He pushed her silently toward the gaping doorway. She knew he was using her to draw fire from Gert. She could not let that happen, but at the moment she felt powerless to stop it.

She wrinkled her nose at the thick smell of mold in the air.

Even though they inched along the hallway, the worn-out boards creaking beneath their feet gave a telltale sign of their approach. She would have to think fast. She needed to figure out what door Gert was behind so she could duck out of Alex's grasp.

She would only get one chance. He could be in the attic, the basement, or even the next room. How could she possibly know?

The hallway opened up on the left to a bright, spacious living room. Sun beat through the broken glass of what had once been a window. One foot in front of her on the right was another opening. It probably led to a kitchen.

A breeze floated through the room, gently cooling her. She could hear someone outside announcing through a loudspeaker that they were looking for a peaceful resolution.

Alex tightened his grip on her arm.

The speaker outside commanded everyone in the farmhouse to come out of the building with their hands raised. Time was short.

Alex motioned for her to continue moving forward. It hit her then that the kitchen would be ideal for an ambush. It was the heart of the building and accessible from two sides.

Alex pushed. As she crossed the threshold of the kitchen, she threw herself forward and half stumbled, half dove for the inside wall on the other side of the doorway, keeping low.

The blasts were deafening. To her right was a mound of broken wood. Studs and pieces of drywall piled three feet high.

As Alex and Gert fired at each other, she crawled to the pile and grabbed a two-by-four with a long nail protruding from the end of it.

She stayed sprawled on the floor until the guns quieted. Alex remained on his feet, bleeding from a wound in his stomach area. She saw Gert with his back against the wall under the kitchen window. There was blood circling two holes in his chest. He had a dazed look on his face as blood gurgled from the corners of his mouth. He sputtered and coughed. She grimaced at the finality of it.

As Alex stepped closer to Gert, Sarah got to her feet and edged around the pile of debris. She got within an arm's length of Alex as he took Sam's gun in his hand and tossed it over his shoulder. He reached for Gert's weapon.

She knew she should just cut and run. But could she get out that window and around the corner before he was on her?

She lifted the wood in her hands in defense, not sure what to do. She wanted to help people. She realized in the same thought that she *was* helping. She was *saving herself*.

Alex was on his knees now, fumbling with Gert's hand to get the gun. With a nail jutting out of the side of the wood in her hands, Sarah swung hard.

But Alex was quicker.

He turned toward her and a flash of lightning erupted from his hand as the nail embedded itself in his shoulder.

Sarah felt something punch her on the left side of the chest, so hard she spun on her feet and fell to her knees. She could see the gun in Alex's hand.

It was just as he had promised. It would look like Gert had killed her and shot Alex, too. Alex would walk out alive, and all evidence of his guilt would die in the farmhouse.

Her mind repeated what she had written down.

Don't thump, rip, and tear, better to be savage. She tightened her grip on the wood and pulled the two-by-four hard to yank the nail out of his flesh. It must have hit bone, because it seemed stuck. Alex screamed and raised the gun again, his hand shaking. She jerked and pulled, dislodging her weapon.

She had enough energy for one last try.

She swung on a smaller arc. Before Alex could fire his weapon, the nail dug into Alex's neck just below his ear. He screamed again and dropped the gun.

He tried to pull the nail out. Before he could, Sarah turned her body away from him, holding the stud in an iron grip. The wood came with her.

The nail pulled itself through the flesh of his cheek, ripping it wide open.

She fell to the floor as he screamed. Blood was everywhere, spilling over his hands as he struggled to keep it in.

Her chest was on fire now. Her breathing became shallow.

Voices came at her from all sides.

She struggled to open her eyes.

She saw men in shiny black helmets and suits carrying what looked like assault rifles.

Then she blacked out.

65

RISING OUT OF a storm, swimming deep, searching for the surface, Sarah fought her way up.

She opened her eyes with a start. Her mouth was so dry it felt like she was massaging sand with her tongue. She was in the hospital. Flowers filled a table by the window. The sun beamed in through the blinds. Her mother was asleep in a padded chair, a book in her lap.

"Mom," she moaned. "Mom?"

Her mother snapped awake and turned to her, blinking rapidly. The paperback dropped to the floor as she jumped from her seat.

"You're awake," she stammered. "Oh, baby, how do you feel?"

"Thirsty."

Her mother grabbed a bottle of water from beside the bed and carefully placed a straw between Sarah's lips. It was painful when she swallowed, and she grasped at the two plastic tubes that worked their way from her nose to the back of her throat.

"What are the . . . tubes for?"

"They go to your stomach. You've been asleep for over two days. I'm so happy you're back."

Sarah sucked on the straw, then rested her head back on the pillow. "Me too."

"We've got a lot to talk about. It seems you've been up to some kind of hero business. I don't know the whole story, but I'd like to hear your version when you feel up to it."

Sarah nodded and looked down at the mound of bandages covering her gunshot wound.

"First, I'd like you to tell me about Vivian Roberts."

PART TWO

66

Four years later . . .

AARON BECK LOWERED his newspaper at the sound of the bus rounding the corner. He folded it under his arm and fished for the proper change in his pocket.

What did buses charge nowadays? He hadn't ridden one since he was a teenager. But with his car in the shop and his wife, Carol, working downtown today, he had no other choice. He refused to pay cab fares.

The bus pulled up and the accordion-like doors slid open. He approached the driver, paid his due, and walked to the back, where it was relatively empty.

He opened his paper and continued reading, so absorbed in the news he barely noticed the girl staring at him. His peripheral vision caught her after a few moments.

She was a young woman in her early twenties, with blond hair layered just past her shoulders. In short, a stunner.

She had a pad of paper nestled in her lap and was scrawling on it with her left hand. Her intensity startled him. He looked down at his newspaper, but couldn't focus. He found himself drawn into her fierce stare, unable to pull away. There was no way he knew this girl.

He was about to speak when she signaled the driver that she wanted off the bus.

Then she walked over and dropped the note into Aaron's lap.

"You don't know me," she said. "You have no reason to believe me. But you've got less than six minutes to save your wife's life. She and three of her friends are about to cross Front Street, downtown. The worker's truck is without a driver, and your wife won't make it." She glanced at her watch. "Call Carol now. There's only five and a half minutes left."

The bus slowed to a stop, and the young girl headed for the door. Aaron watched her leave, mouth agape. This had to be a joke. He looked down at the note and quickly scanned what was written there.

"Hold it!" Aaron shouted. "I need off here, too."

Landing on the sidewalk, Aaron looked both ways. The girl was nowhere in sight.

He pulled out his cell phone. Aaron heard the ringing on the other end. He wondered how much time remained.

Pick up. Don't tell me you left your cell phone in the office. Carol, please pick up.

On the fifth ring Aaron heard the music of his wife's voice.

She was still alive.

"Where are you?" he asked.

"Aaron, is everything all right?"

"Yes! Just tell me where you are."

"Okay, okay. I'm with a few of my girlfriends. We decided to go for a coffee at this Danish pastry shop Marge is always talking about—"

"What street are you on?" Aaron asked. His voice cracked.

"Aaron? You sound—"

"What street?" he shouted into the phone.

Aaron heard her pull the phone away from her ear and ask one of her companions what street they were walking on. "Dwight Street," she said.

"Are you going to pass Front Street?"

"Yes, actually. I'm close enough now to read the sign. Why?"

"Stop! Don't go any farther." Aaron thought he heard her pause.

"Aaron, tell me what's going on." Carol sounded agitated now.

"This girl, on the bus." He was panting now, his heart beating fast. "She told me you'd be dead in six minutes. I'm supposed to stop you from crossing Front Street."

"What girl? What's this about? I'm standing here with my friends. The sun is shining. It's a beautiful day. Everything's fine."

"I've never met her, but she knows us. She wrote about the surgery I had when I was twelve. About how you and I met. She jotted down the year your parents died in that head-on collision. Carol, no one could've known those things." Aaron continued to scan the crowd.

"You aren't pulling my leg, are you? The lights ahead have changed to green. We're supposed to cross Front Street now."

"She told me to stop you from crossing Front Street. If you do, you'll die."

CAROL SAW THAT her girlfriends had started without her. She dropped the phone from her ear and looked both ways. That's when she noticed the dump truck.

Half a block up, road crews were repairing the asphalt.

No one else had noticed the truck picking up speed as it came down Front Street. She didn't see a driver through the windshield.

The truck barreled toward the throng of pedestrians in the middle of the street.

Carol screamed for people to get out of the way.

Only six of the twenty people in the intersection heard her, or chose to pay attention.

SARAH READ THE newspaper the next day. Two people were seriously injured, seven critical. None of the injured were Carol or Carol's friends. They had missed it by inches.

Sarah realized that she needed to work harder. The accident might have been avoided completely if she had stuck around and talked to Carol herself. She also knew that she had to be ready.

She picked up her gun and made sure it was loaded. She had spent the last four years training with guns and martial artists for this day to come. She was ready. Her sister's killer was still out there.

He didn't know she would be meeting him in seven hours.

67

THE WOODS WERE darker this time.

Jack Tate tightened his grip on the terrier's leash, drawing the small dog closer. A soft breeze wafted past his face in the twilight, offering little comfort.

Champ strained toward the trees.

He unclipped the leash from Champ's collar. The terrier bolted away, down the path and around a corner. Jack called after him.

He caressed the rip at the base of his shirt. The two-inch cut had been made with scissors, sliced on an angle near the lowest button. He twirled the edges of the cut through his fingers.

Trees surrounded him on all sides. He called out to the terrier again but received no response. He found Champ digging in the dirt twenty feet away.

"Champ, come here, boy."

The dog continued to dig with his front paws.

With the sunlight fading fast, Jack stepped into the underbrush. Champ didn't look up once. He kept digging as Jack drew closer.

Jack stumbled, then managed to attach the leash clip back onto the dog's collar with just enough light left for him to see what he was doing.

The terrier continued to pull on the leash.

"Come on, Champ."

Impatient, Jack bent to pick up the dog.

Champ had uncovered something in the dirt. Jack stepped back quickly. This time when Champ pulled on the leash, Jack tugged it back in anger.

"Stop it. That's enough."

Minutes later he was on the phone reporting the dead body to the police.

68

JACK TATE SAT on the sawed-off trunk of a dead tree. A cop who identified himself as Winnfield stood over him, flipping notebook pages
back and forth.

"Let me get this straight." The cop raised his pen in the air. "You
were out for a walk. You go into the woods and let your dog run loose.
When you find the terrier digging, you see part of a decomposed face.
Is that your statement?"

Jack nodded and looked down at his shoes. The lights on the three
cruisers rotated ten feet away, flashing in his eyes.

"Something doesn't fit."

Jack looked back up. It was late, and he was tired of talking. He'd
committed no crime.

The cop said, "After the rain, the ground holding the body is soft.
That's probably why your dog would be drawn over by the smell." Officer Winnfield flipped another page in his notebook. "We found your
footprints in the dirt beside your dog's paw prints. But we found no
other recent impressions in the soil."

Jack tried to rise from the tree stump, but Officer Winnfield
touched Jack's shoulder to ease him back down.

"Explain it to me again," the cop said.

Jack groaned in frustration.

"I was walking my dog. He got away from me. When I found him,
he'd dug up the body. Now, I need to get home. Are we done here?"

Officer Winnfield folded the notebook and slid it into the breast
pocket of his uniform.

"You sound angry, Mr. Tate. Please understand, I'm only doing my
job. I have one more question."

Jack sighed and nodded.

"Why is your shirt torn at the base?"

Jack looked down at his fingers as they rolled around the rip. Since
the incident almost twenty years ago, he only wore shirts with this

exact tear. But he wasn't *supposed* to remember what really happened. If he told a cop the truth, he would be arrested.

"I cut it accidentally when removing the shirt tags. What has that got to do with anything?"

"Stay right here," Officer Winnfield said. "Don't move until I come back."

The cop walked over to a man in a suit. People dressed in white were setting up lights around the makeshift grave. Other people were bent over, sifting dirt away to get to the rest of the body.

Jack stroked Champ's head. "This will all be over soon," he said. The terrier lifted his head a notch and then dropped it again, oblivious.

Officer Winnfield walked back over. "You're going to have to come with us."

Jack stood up. "Why's that?"

"Is there someone you could give your dog to?"

"Am I under arrest?"

"Mr. Tate, please listen to me. Is there someone who can take your terrier?"

Jack sat back down on the stump.

Spectators had gathered around the yellow tape.

"Glenda over there," Jack said, and pointed. "She takes Champ when I'm away. She's the one in the white housecoat."

Winnfield took the leash and walked away with Champ.

Jack remained sitting, his knee bobbing up and down. The temperature had dropped to a subtle chill. Jack shivered.

Moments later, Officer Winnfield stood in front of him again.

"Jack Tate, please stand up."

"What's going on here?" Jack asked.

"We're going to continue our questioning at the police station."

"Am I under arrest?"

"Not at this time."

"So, I find a person buried in the ground while walking my dog, call you guys about it, and you make me feel like I'm guilty?"

"We're just trying to figure everything out," Winnfield said as he put a hand on Jack's arm and guided him to a cruiser.

"Why all the suspicion?"

"It's that rip on the bottom of your shirt," Winnfield said.

Jack frowned. "The rip?"

"There's an identical rip, in the exact same spot, on the shirt of the dead body."

69

TWO HOURS PASSED before an officer opened the interview room door and offered Jack a bathroom break.

Minutes later, he retook his seat behind a drab metal table on a hard steel chair. The room was a classic movie setup, complete with a wall of glass and a solitary light hanging from the ceiling.

"Feeling better?" Winnfield asked.

The cop looked refreshed. Jack chose to not answer.

Winnfield adjusted his shirt in front of the two-way mirror and turned back to Jack.

"What can you tell me about the girl?" Winnfield asked.

Jack glared at the cop. "She's dead." His patience had thinned.

Winnfield pulled back in surprise. Jack raised his eyebrows. *Winnfield's new at this.*

The two-hour wait was meant to rattle Jack. Winnfield's swagger and the posturing in front of the mirror was just another show.

"Is that how you want to play it? Sarcasm?" Winnfield asked.

"I already told you everything I know at the crime scene. You've wasted both our time in bringing me here."

Winnfield leaned forward and dropped his hands on the table with a solid thump. "Start by telling me about the rip in the shirt. Why does the girl have the same one?"

Jack looked down at his lap. He had been anticipating this question. He glanced back up, met Winnfield's eyes, but said nothing.

The officer stood to his full height and paced in front of the two-way mirror as he repeated his question.

"Here's what I see happening," Jack said. "You've held me for over two hours to ask me the same question you already asked me back in the woods. Release me or charge me with something, because I have no idea why that girl's shirt was ripped."

Winnfield stopped pacing and leaned against the mirror.

"This could turn into a lot of trouble for you, Mr. Tate."

A buzzer sounded twice. Winnfield opened the door and stepped out. Minutes later the door opened again and two men entered.

"You're free to go, Mr. Tate, but stay local. We may want to speak again." One of the men held the door open for him.

"Someone gonna give me a ride back?" Jack asked.

"As I said, you're free to go, Mr. Tate. You're on your own."

Jack paid for a cab and got home after midnight. When the taxi pulled away he looked over at Glenda's house and debated if it was too late to get Champ. He decided to leave him for the night.

The air calm, Jack breathed in and sighed. He had a lot of work ahead of him.

The ripped shirt meant *they* made a mistake. The fact that the body was found so close to his house was another message. It was so long ago. He couldn't remember the exact details. The bullet had erased part of his memory. He knew that he was lucky to be alive.

As he approached his house, he saw a light flicker past an upstairs window. He stopped and stared, but saw nothing now.

He eased up to the porch quietly and waited, listening, then reached for his keys. He had done this sort of thing before, years ago, when he was a cop.

A creaking noise sounded from just inside the house. He froze. Someone was on the other side of the door.

He stepped back quietly. Cold steel pressed against his neck.

"Don't be stupid," a man said from behind him. "And don't make any noise."

Jack lifted his hands slowly, his house keys falling to the porch.

"Move away from the door and keep your hands where I can see them, but don't raise them too high. It may alert a nosy neighbor."

Jack stepped off the porch and onto the lawn. The man behind him remained close. The front door opened and closed.

"Did you find anything?"

"No," a new voice said.

"Okay, let's move. Jack, do you see the red van on the other side of the street? That's where we're going. Has anyone seen any sign of that fucking girl yet?"

The other guy didn't answer him.

Directly across the road, a slight movement caught Jack's eye.

A tall girl, blond hair flowing past her shoulders from under a red bandanna, stepped out from behind a tree. She lifted her arms in a sleek, precise movement.

The gun glinted in the streetlight and spit out a silenced bullet. The cold steel fell away from Jack's neck. The man grunted as he hit the ground. He held his knee where blood gushed past his fingers.

The girl moved fast. She was already standing beside the second man, gun tip aimed low, telling him to give her his weapons.

Jack stepped aside and leaned against the van, amazed at the girl's efficiency. She was like a panther in the night, as good as any professional mercenary.

She stowed the man's gun in a shoulder holster, kneed him in the groin, and pistol-whipped him unconscious all in one fluid motion.

Then she turned to address Jack.

"My name is Sarah Roberts. You're safe for now, but you need to come with me."

70

SARAH DROVE TO the back of a strip mall and parked behind a Dumpster, keeping a close eye on her new passenger.

Once she parked the car she brought her gun around to aim it at him.

"What's your name?" Her eyes moved to the mirrors to make sure they weren't being watched.

The man leaned his head against the passenger window, gazing absently out the front.

"Your name?" Sarah asked again.

"Jack Tate." He looked sideways at her. "What is this?"

Sarah pushed the gun forward. "Look, you don't get to ask questions." Her jaw clenched when she spoke.

He shrugged. "Okay, okay."

"Who were those men?" she asked. "What did they want?"

Jack motioned with his hands to his mouth, asking if he could talk.

"Don't test my patience. I said, *no questions*. I didn't say you couldn't talk."

"I don't know who they were."

"That van in the street they were taking you to wasn't their vehicle."

Jack turned to her.

"They broke the lock on the back door. Their car was a few houses down. I watched the whole thing."

"I need to ask a question," he said.

Sarah nodded. "Okay, go." She eased the weapon back.

"Why were they taking me to the van?"

"Who knows?"

Jack looked away. "If you know so much about what they were doing, why don't you know who they are? For that matter, why did you save me?"

"I was told to be there."

She had seen his reaction a hundred times. Bewilderment and disbelief.

"Who told you?" he asked. "And why?"

"I'll give you the short answer. I'm looking for a murderer who got away about twenty years ago. Somehow you're connected to him. That's all I know."

Jack leaned his head back and shut his eyes.

"You know anything about what I just said?" Sarah asked.

He opened his eyes and sat up straighter. "I don't."

"Whether you tell me or not, I'll find out eventually."

Jack wrung his hands on his lap. "It's not that I don't want to tell you; it's that I can't."

"Why?"

"I was shot twenty years ago. If you're after a murderer from that time, you're about to be sadly disappointed."

"Why?"

"I tracked down a serial killer. He terrorized and killed young girls throughout the Midwest. I was shot in the head and left for dead. When I woke up, I remembered nothing. It took years to recover enough to live on my own." He glanced at her. "I was a cop. I live on my pension now. I still have horrible nightmares." He shook his head and looked away.

"After I got shot in the head, I was coherent but losing strength. The killer stabbed me, too." Jack pointed below his belly button to where the shirt was ripped. "The knife cut a two-inch slit at the base of my shirt. I couldn't lift the shirt over my bleeding head, but I was able to rip it off. I wrapped it around my head to staunch the blood flow before I passed out. It took almost three hours for them to find me. I would've died if my shirt wasn't stuck to the wound. That's why there's a rip here." He motioned to the bottom of his shirt. "It reminds me of that day."

"You seem to remember a lot for a guy who claims to have had amnesia," Sarah said as she scanned the parking lot. "Tell me why the shirt was ripped on the girl found in the woods."

"I have no idea," Jack said. "Wait a second, how do you know about that?"

Sarah pressed on. "Why would two goons be sent to execute you?"

"Nothing makes sense," Jack said in a daze.

Sarah set the safety on her gun and placed it on her lap. She dropped the car into gear and started moving again.

"What are we going to do?" Jack asked.

"I don't know yet. I'll ask my sister. She'll know."

"Who's your sister? Where is she?"

"My sister's name is Vivian, and she's dead."

71

BLAKE LIGHTLY TOUCHED his wounded crotch.

Who the hell was that girl?

She had knocked him out cold. He touched the side of his head, where blood had already scabbed over. There would be hell to pay for this.

At least I'm not the one who got shot.

He walked over to Marco and touched his neck. A slow and steady pulse. Blood spread out on the cement. Not enough to kill him, but he would need medical treatment soon.

Blake lifted him from under his armpits and dragged him toward Jack Tate's house. Within a minute he was inside the front foyer, winded and out of breath. After setting Marco down, he got a paring knife from the kitchen and trotted back.

Without pausing, Blake jabbed the knife in and out of Marco's inner thigh to sever the femoral artery.

Marco's body jerked as the blood flowed from the new wound.

Blake tossed the knife away and then plugged Marco's nose and covered his mouth. Marco was gone moments later with little more than a whimper.

He washed his hands in Jack's guest bathroom and then stepped back out into the foyer. He looked down at his friend. They had done a lot of jobs in the last year together.

Too bad a girl got the jump on you, old friend.

He pulled out his cell phone and dialed.

"We missed the mark."

"Explain."

"Marco fucked up. This girl came out of nowhere. We were moving toward the van on the street. She shot Marco, pistol-whipped me, and took Tate."

"That doesn't make sense. How could she do all that?"

"Marco had his gun jammed in Tate's neck. Mine was holstered. Look, it won't happen again. I dragged Marco off the street, into Tate's foyer." Blake walked across the hall into the living room. He parted the drapes and looked out at the street, amazed that no one had heard anything. It must've been at least fifteen minutes since the girl showed up, which meant it was time to move.

"What's Marco doing now?"

"Nothing. He's dead."

Blake listened to the breathing on the other end of the phone.

"Good. Now, I want the girl dead. You got anything on her?"

"She had long blond hair and a red bandanna."

"A red bandanna?"

Blake stepped away from the curtains and started for the back door of the house. "Yeah, why?"

"You just met Sarah Roberts."

72

SARAH HAD DECIDED to stay off the road and hide in a motel. She paid cash at the front desk and parked outside the motel room door, backing her Kia up for an easy exit.

Once in the room, she handcuffed Jack to the bathroom sink so he could sleep in the bathtub with one arm dangling out. Tiring of his protests, she made him comfortable with blankets and a pillow, shut the bathroom door, and lay out on the bed to think.

The TV's remote control sat on the night table beside her. She hit the power button and set the volume just high enough to drown out Jack's occasional plea from the bathroom. The motel's courtesy pad and pen sat beside her in bed as she searched the news channels for anything on the guy she shot earlier, but she found nothing.

A half hour later, Jack had fallen quiet. Sarah wondered why Jack Tate was important. She thought she was supposed to meet her sister's murderer, not Jack. Or would Jack lead her to the killer? She had no way of knowing. The message wasn't specific. It just said the street name, the house number, and the man she was to meet. It had also included the word *Vivian*, which meant that this person was connected to her dead sister.

As the adrenaline wore off, sleep settled in.

Then the familiar numbness of a blackout came over her. She welcomed it by grabbing the pen and resting back on the bed, closing her eyes.

Seconds later, she sat up and looked at the pad.

Tate knows more than he's saying.

Sarah jumped from the bed, picked up her gun, and barged into the bathroom. Jack was curled up in the tub in an awkward position, sleeping.

"What happened to you tonight?" Sarah asked.

He jerked in surprise and lifted his head.

"What?"

THE FUTURE IS WRITTEN

"What happened to you? Why were those men trying to kill you?" Sarah shut the toilet lid and sat down.

"I have no idea," Jack said, resting his head back and recounting the night's events.

"Why would the police take you in for questioning if you were just walking your dog and happened upon a body?"

"Again, no idea," he repeated.

"Can you identify the girl you saw tonight?" She lifted the gun so it sat across her thighs. He was lying. His eyes gave him away.

"Who are you?" Jack asked. He turned to see her better. "I should be asking the questions. You're the one who kidnapped me from my home."

"Stop wasting my time. I need to know if you recognized the girl you found buried in the woods."

Jack shook his head. "No, I didn't."

Sarah left the bathroom when she heard her name on the TV. A news anchor was talking about the shooting and stabbing death in the home of Jack Tate. Police were now looking for Mr. Tate and a girl suspected in his abduction, Sarah Roberts.

"*It's unclear how Sarah Roberts is involved,*" the anchor said. "*An anonymous tip said that she shot the man found dead at the scene.*"

Sarah ran back into the bathroom, undid the handcuffs, and ushered Jack out.

"What now?" he asked.

"We have to move. The police know I have you."

"Where are we going?" Jack asked.

Sarah gripped the doorknob, her gun held high in the other hand.

"To get answers."

73

TWO MILES FROM the motel, Sarah grabbed her cell phone and dialed a familiar number. It was after three in the morning. It was picked up immediately.

"Hello?"

"Dolan, I need your help," Sarah said.

"Sarah? What's going on?"

"Can we meet somewhere?"

"Just come to my house."

Sarah hung up and dropped her cell phone in the console. Up ahead she saw another deserted strip mall. She turned right, bounced over a speed bump, and guided the car around to the back alley behind two Dumpsters. She parked and turned to Jack. He'd been quiet since they left the motel.

Sarah had to assume that Jack Tate wasn't her sister's killer. He was important in some way, though. Important enough to keep around for now.

"We have to get a few things clear."

Jack nodded. "Okay, I'm listening."

"I'm hunting my sister's murderer. I won't stop until I find him. Somehow, you're important. Call it a kidnapping if you want. I don't care. If I hadn't shown up when I did, you'd be dead right now."

"I still don't know how I can help." He scratched the back of his head and then folded his arms. He seemed bored.

"We will soon enough. We're going to see someone who may be able to help us. He has a history of investigative work. In the meantime, don't try anything stupid. I need you to stay with me a little while longer. This isn't going to be like in the movies. I'm not going to hold a gun on you the whole time. But if you try to escape, you'll regret it. Are we clear?"

Jack nodded.

"Good. The last four years have been hard. I've been kidnapped, stabbed, shot at, and almost killed quite a few times. It pisses a girl off. Don't add to my list. Be quiet and be cool and everything will work out."

Jack turned and met her eyes. He nodded, then glanced away.

"I've seen a lot of dead girls in my time," he said after a moment. "I've also been shot." He pointed at the scar on his head. "I know how cops think. A lot came back over the years." He turned back to her. "I worked homicide. I might have even worked on your sister's case, but who knows." He paused and then continued reluctantly. "The name Vivian Roberts rings a bell, though."

74

OFFICER PARKMAN SET his coffee down without spilling it. Some days were better than others. Parkman was on his fourth coffee and his seventh toothpick. He figured chewing the little pieces of wood wasn't as bad as smoking cigarettes. Besides, he just couldn't stop.

Sarah Roberts.

He had kept tabs on her over the years since her kidnapping, but she remained elusive. He interviewed her parents, her few friends, and even tried to talk to her directly, but she avoided cops. After everything that had happened, he couldn't blame her.

Sarah had popped up in the news many times since then. She would stop a crime from happening, then disappear. Once she even walked ten people out of a burning building, unscathed. No one knew how she got inside in the first place.

Parkman was there that night. It was a five-story printing press. The company had gone bankrupt in the early nineties, but the main floor was being used by a writers' group. The group was having a Halloween party. The fire spread fast.

Sarah had been waiting on the third floor. She had an ax and used it to chop away at an old, boarded-up window. The folding ladder that she had brought with her was secured to the ledge, and everyone climbed out with minutes to spare.

The authorities had picked her up for questioning after that one. His fellow officers interviewed her, drilled her with questions, but got nowhere. She told them that if she were gifted, she would hardly have allowed herself to be kidnapped, beaten, and almost killed all those years ago. In the end, they let her go.

Parkman's work had suffered because of Sarah Roberts. At one point he worried that his obsession with her would cost him his job. After repeated warnings, Parkman relented.

Yet now her name had resurfaced.

Parkman believed the Tate case had everything to do with Sarah. But if he knew anything about Sarah, he knew she wasn't a criminal. If she truly had shot the guy, there had to be a reason. In his mind, she was a superhero. His colleagues were harsher. Many believed she set accidents up just to save people. He once overheard whispers of occult stuff.

Whatever they believed, Parkman knew he was her only friend inside the police department. He needed to locate her before anyone else did.

He drained the rest of his coffee and headed for his car. He popped a fresh toothpick into his mouth as he stepped outside.

It was six in the morning.

Time to find Sarah Roberts and Jack Tate.

And he knew just the person to talk to.

Sarah's old friend Dolan Ryan.

75

DOLAN SQUINTED IN the morning sun as he opened the door. "Come in, come in. You must be Jack Tate."

Jack looked at him sideways. "How do you know my name?"

"He's psychic," Sarah said.

"I saw it on the news." Dolan looked at Sarah. "Both your names were mentioned."

They filed into Dolan's kitchen.

"Coffee?" he asked.

Jack and Sarah shook their heads in unison. Dolan leaned against the counter and waited as the two of them sat at his kitchen table. He saw that Sarah was cautious around Jack, watching him. There was a bump in her shirt near her belt line where her gun was hidden.

Sarah told Dolan everything that had happened in the last twelve hours, starting with her precognition.

Dolan glanced at Jack. "You don't know who those men were?"

Jack shook his head. "I've got enemies from a few decades ago. But I'm in my mid-sixties now, retired for a long time on a disability pension. I'll die of natural causes soon enough."

Dolan looked at Sarah. Something was happening to her. "Are you okay?"

Sarah grabbed a notebook from her back pocket and then slipped off the chair. She hit the floor, her body limp. Her eyes rolled back in her head. She gripped the pen so tight in her hand, Dolan thought she might snap it in two.

Dolan couldn't see what she was writing. Jack stood in alarm.

A moment later, Sarah gasped and sat up. She used the chair to get herself off the floor.

"What does it say?" Dolan asked, moving closer.

Sarah looked down, her eyes widening. "*Run out the front door . . . they're in the back.*"

"Let's go!" Dolan said as he jumped up. He grabbed Jack's arm and ran.

Dolan got to the front door first and peeked outside. As he gripped the door handle, he heard the soft sound of glass breaking somewhere in the back of the house. He ripped the door open and all three of them tumbled onto Dolan's front porch and right into Officer Parkman.

"Whoa," Parkman said. Dolan saw him flip a toothpick to the other side of his mouth. "Where are you three going so fast?"

"Someone just broke a window in back. We're assuming they're armed."

Parkman flipped open his holster. In a hushed voice, he said, "Quietly make your way across the lawn and get into my cruiser. Stay low. Wait for me there."

Dolan nodded, staying ahead of Jack and Sarah, who followed close behind. He looked back once and saw Parkman talking into a cell phone. Then Parkman lowered into a crouch and entered the house through Dolan's front door. Dolan remembered Parkman from a couple of years ago. He had come to question him about Sarah after the fire at that writers' group building.

The trio made it to the police car and then ran past it.

"Aren't we supposed to wait inside?" Jack asked.

"You go inside that cop car, you'll die," Dolan said.

Sarah nodded. "I'd listen to him."

They ran across the street and behind a black van. From this vantage point they had a secure view of Dolan's house.

Gunfire was heard from inside his house. It always surprised him how much it sounded like firecrackers. Parkman reappeared. He hunched down at the end of the porch behind a lounge chair. Sirens sounded in the distance.

"What do we do now?" Sarah asked.

Dolan looked back at her. "I think you're going to have to trust the police on this one."

Sarah glared back at him. "Not an option."

"You need to think about it."

"Just did."

"Look, you can't help anybody if you're dead."

"I won't be dead. Vivian won't let that happen."

"You almost died four years ago."

Sarah studied the street as the sirens grew closer.

"Come on, Jack, we're leaving." She pulled on Jack's sleeve.

"Where will you go?" Dolan asked.

"Off the grid."

Dolan surrendered. "Be safe and call me if you need me."

Sarah bent low and motioned for Jack to follow. They hustled across the street and into Sarah's car. Dolan watched her do a U-turn and drive north as three cruisers came from the south.

It took ten minutes for the police to clear the house. The shooters were gone, except for the one shot by Officer Parkman. The perp had died in Dolan's main hallway.

Dolan was giving his statement to another officer when Parkman interrupted.

"We found these on the dead guy. Any idea why?"

He pushed photos into Dolan's hand. They were big enough to carry in a breast pocket. Sarah was in the first shot. It was a bad picture of her, taken about four or five years ago when chunks of her hair were still missing. The second shot was of him, also taken about five years ago, when he still ran the psychic fair.

The people in the third, fourth, and fifth photos he didn't recognize.

"Who are these three?" Dolan asked.

"That one there"—Parkman moved closer and pointed—"is the dead girl Jack Tate found last night. The other two we're still trying to identify. How do you think Jack is tied into all this? And how safe is Sarah right now? She shouldn't have run."

"You know as well as I do that Sarah doesn't trust cops."

"We may be her only friends right now. I care about Sarah's safety, whether she knows it or not."

"Sarah knows what she's doing." He handed the pictures back as another plainclothes cop burst in the front door.

"I think we've got the connection to Jack Tate," the cop said.

"And?" Parkman asked.

"The last case Tate worked was a cold case. About twenty years ago."

"So what's the connection?" He pulled the toothpick out of his mouth.

"A girl was raped and murdered. Tate was shot in the head, presumably by the killer."

"And?" Parkman asked.

"The murder victim was Sarah's sister, Vivian Roberts."

76

SARAH DROVE OVER two hours until they reached the next city. It didn't look good to run, but she had no choice. She had somehow drawn the killers to Dolan. She needed to get a handle on what was going on without risking others.

Jack had fallen asleep beside her. She kept the radio on low.

A restaurant to her right offered an all-you-can-eat breakfast. She pulled in, turned off the car, and put her head back to rest.

SHE MUST HAVE fallen asleep. The clock on the dash said she had lost two hours. Jack sat outside on the hood of the Kia.

The door opened with a squeak when she got out to stretch her legs.

"Why didn't you leave when you had the chance?" she asked.

He turned around. "Because I remembered the connection. Vivian Roberts was the last case I worked on before I was shot."

Instantly awake, Sarah walked around the car and stood in front of him.

"That means whoever shot you all those years ago is connected, too. They want to silence you."

Jack nodded.

A large truck lumbered by. Sarah turned to avoid the clouds of dust.

"You're in more trouble than you think," Jack said.

"What about you? Those men were sent to kill *you* last night."

He paused and wiped his face with his hand. "People you know or people you've worked with before are in danger. Look what happened at Dolan's house this morning."

Something didn't add up. Why hadn't Vivian given her more? Whenever her precognitions had something to do with family, the messages were more like riddles. This was the only part of her ability as an automatic writer that she hated, because it came with the potential for personal injury. Still, she knew if this ultimately led to her sister's murderer, she would do whatever was needed.

"Let's get some food and get back on the road," Sarah said.

After they ate, they ordered two large coffees and left the truck stop, heading back into town.

Sarah pulled out her cell phone and tried her parents' home number. She got no answer. If someone was after her and they went to Dolan's, they might try her parents next. Hopefully, they were just away from home.

She called Esmerelda next. The line was picked up on the first ring.

"Esmerelda, is everything okay there?"

"Hello, Sarah. Everything is fine. Is there something I should know?"

She briefly told her what had happened.

"I tried my parents but got no answer. You need to be careful. I don't know who these people are or what they're capable of, but they could be coming after people I know."

"I'll call your mom and dad, too. If I can't reach them, I'll head over to their place."

"Okay, thanks. I'll call you as soon as I hear something on my end."

She hung up and watched the road, then scrolled through her phone book and stopped at Parkman's number. He'd called so often in the past, she had kept his number so she knew when *not* to answer.

She took a long sip of her coffee, then dialed.

"Parkman here."

"It's Sarah."

"Where are you?"

"Out of town."

"Why call me?" Parkman asked.

"You're the only cop I *think* I can trust. And you know I didn't kill anybody last night at Jack Tate's home."

She felt Jack's eyes on her. She watched the road and kept the phone pressed to her ear.

"Sarah, all these years . . . I could've been helping you."

"Parkman, you were harassing me. But you know enough to realize that I'm not responsible for what happened in the last twelve hours. You know I'm clean."

"You're too late."

"What are you talking about?"

"They put me on a desk. I've got a week's worth of paperwork for the shooting at Dolan's. I think they're afraid it's too personal for me."

"Is it?" Sarah asked.

"Yes, I suppose it is. What will you do now? They have your name in every cruiser."

"Can you tell me who was at Jack's place last night, or at Dolan's this morning?"

"Not yet. They didn't give me the ID on the body they pulled from Jack's, and they yanked me before forensics dealt with the scene at Dolan's. I'm out of the loop."

"Okay, call me if you learn anything."

"Have you still got Jack Tate with you?"

"Yes." She snuck a look at him. He was sipping his coffee and staring out the side window.

"Do you know he used to be a cop?"

"Yes."

"His last case was your sister's murder."

"I know."

"That's probably why you showed up at his house last night. Well, I have something else for you."

"What?"

"He was under investigation a couple of times as a police officer for unbecoming conduct. Also, he had an estranged younger brother who was killed four years ago. I think you knew him."

"Who was he?"

"Alex Stuart."

Sarah stole another glance at Jack.

"You're kidding, Parkman. Right?"

"I'm not. Watch yourself, Sarah. He's not the guy you think he is."

77

IT WAS JUST after noon when she pulled onto her parents' street. She parked ten houses away from their house and got out.

Jack took a deep breath. She nodded and together they started up the street. She'd lived here for many years. Her parents almost split up before her kidnapping, but their relationship had recovered by the time she moved out at nineteen. They were still doing well as far as she could tell.

Her cell phone rang. It said *private caller*. Probably the police. She chose to ignore it.

Jack looked like he was a cop again. He stared across the street and scoped the area out as they walked. She couldn't trust him, but for now he might be useful.

She started up the front walkway. The house looked smaller somehow. Perhaps she just missed being here. She glanced at her old bedroom window and longed for a time when things were simpler.

She paused at the front door. Jack continued to watch the street, staring intently at a certain house.

"What's going on, Jack? You see something?"

"I thought I saw someone watching us through those curtains," he said, nodding with his head. "Do you know who lives there?"

"That's the Ellises' house. If they saw me they would've come out and said hello."

Before she could unlock the door, her cell phone rang. Private caller again.

Jack moved up the sidewalk toward her. "Can we go around to the back door?" he asked.

"Sure. Why?"

"Something's wrong across the street. Aren't you going to answer your phone?"

They started around back as Sarah answered her phone.

"Hello?"

"We have a problem," the caller said. "You're in possession of what I need, and I'm in possession of what you need."

"Who is this?" Sarah asked. Jack banged on the back door of the house.

"That's not important. But what is of great *fucking* importance is Jack Tate."

"Why?" Sarah tried to keep her anger in check. She could handle inscrutable messages, but when people *acted* mysterious, it pissed her off.

"Your parents for Jack Tate."

"My parents?" Sarah asked as her stomach dropped. She joined Jack in banging on the back door.

"They're not there. You're wasting your time."

Sarah pulled the phone from her ear and covered the mouthpiece. "Jack, you were right," she whispered. "We're being watched."

They jumped off the porch and raced to the back fence. Before passing through the gate Sarah checked her phone again. The caller had hung up.

She dropped it in her pocket and jumped the fence.

My parents?

How could she live with herself if something happened to them?

"What was that all about?" Jack asked.

"The guy on the phone wants to exchange you for my parents," she said. Tears crept into her vision. She fought them back, not wanting to cry.

"Call the police and tell them what you know. Maybe they can do something about the people in the Ellises' house."

Sarah went to dial 911, but stopped. She called Parkman instead.

"Parkman here."

They emerged from the alley and turned left, walking away from her car. "We have a problem."

"What kind of problem?" Parkman asked.

"Someone's taken my parents. They want Jack in exchange. They're watching us."

"Watching you? Where are you?"

"Just left my parents' house."

"I knew people close to you would be in danger," Parkman said. "Damn it."

"Can we get someone on this? If anything happens to them, I don't know . . . " Sarah choked up before she could finish.

"I'll look into it. But once I pass on the information I'm stuck at my desk."

"Fine, but please do something. I need your help." Sarah hung up.

"What now?" Jack asked. "The cops are looking for both of us. Whoever is behind this sent goons to my house last night to kill me. Then they went after Dolan, and now your parents are missing. That leaves me with one conclusion."

Sarah looked at him as they ran down the street. "What conclusion is that?"

"I'm the one they're after. They think I can identify them. You're just in the way."

"It's deeper than that. You and my family are much more connected than you think."

Jack slowed and looked at her. "What are you talking about?"

"Come on. We can't stop." She tugged his arm and continued down the street.

"How are we connected?" Jack asked.

"Your brother, Alex. He had me kidnapped four years ago. He tried to kill me."

Jack stopped. He raised a hand to the side of his head.

"That must be it."

"What?" She tossed her hands in the air.

"It's a long story, but my family was always on the wrong side of the law. I hated it. So I became a cop. Alex was born twenty years after my sister and me, but to a different father."

"Okay, great story, but tell me more on the way. We have to keep moving."

They jogged a few more blocks and then Jack stopped again.

"When you said Alex kidnapped you, it suddenly hit me."

"Do I have to pull it out of you? Talk, man." It was easy to tell he wasn't used to anyone demanding answers from him.

Well, he'd better get fucking used to it.

A car sped along the street toward them. Sarah pushed Jack back and started away from the sidewalk. The car pulled over, kicking up gravel and dust. The passenger door swung open, and Sarah bent to yank her weapon out.

"Get in!" Esmerelda shouted.

Sarah released the grip she had on the butt of her gun and hopped in the backseat. Jack jumped in beside her.

"You okay?" Esmerelda asked.

Sarah nodded. "Better now. Why are you here?"

Esmerelda looked at her in the rearview mirror as she got the car back on the road. "I told you I'd check in on your parents. When I didn't get an answer, I came over and saw people surveilling their house from across the street. I've been trying to find you. You want to introduce me to your new friend?"

"His name is Jack Tate. He's an ex-cop, and he was just about to tell me something interesting regarding his family history."

Jack appeared dazed. "It started when I left home to join the police force. My mother got mixed up in some sort of voodoo. The man she met was crazy. He got her pregnant and she had Alex. His last name is different than mine."

Esmerelda cut in. "Do you mean Alex Stuart?"

Jack nodded. "After he was born I only visited once in a while. One night I came over unannounced in my cruiser. This would've been when Alex was eight years old or so. They were doing some kind of ritual with candles in the living room. Alex was naked. I arrested Armond, Alex's father, on child abuse charges. He got bail and was home the next day. *I* was told to stay away. My own mother didn't want anything to do with me. But the investigators came up with all kinds of insane stuff Armond was doing."

Sarah turned in her seat. "So what came of it?"

"Armond went to prison until Alex was fifteen years old. My mother disowned me."

"How is this relevant?" Esmerelda asked.

Jack fondled the rip in his shirt. "Alex was really messed up. I wanted to keep tabs on my mother—you know, see how she was doing. Alex was happy his dad was in jail. So we talked. About voodoo dolls and out-of-body experiences. He always smelled of cologne, like he was showering in the stuff."

Esmerelda and Sarah exchanged a look in the rearview mirror.

"Alex was sexually and physically abused," Jack continued. "He was quite sick. The last I heard, he was involved with the Psychic Fair. I later heard Alex was killed in a shoot-out somewhere in the Midwest. Now I know what happened."

Sarah nodded. "I was there."

Jack looked at her, his face twitching. "After Alex died, I decided to see what Armond was up to. All I could gather was that a few teenage girls didn't make it home. They were sexually assaulted and killed. The police attributed those crimes to Alex after he was dead, but they found a voodoo doll with one of the bodies. I told the police about Armond, but they brushed me off. The case was closed." Jack looked down at the rip in his shirt. "Armond is still out there. He'd be about sixty now. It might have been him who shot me. But I have no proof."

"Sarah, here, take this." Esmerelda handed Sarah a notebook and a pen.

"You're going to need that to help us get out of this."

78

DOLAN WATCHED THE glass repairman set a new pane in place. The police had left an hour ago.

"How much longer?" Dolan asked him.

"Five minutes."

Dolan grabbed the kitchen phone and dialed.

"Sam Johnson."

"Sam, it's Dolan."

"Dolan, it's been a long time. Last I heard, you'd retired from the Psychic Fair business."

Dolan sat at the kitchen table. "Sam, I need your help." He paused. "You still there?"

"Yes. You know what happened the last time I helped you? They've had me running the evidence room ever since."

"You were a cop doing your job. Alex shot me, too." Dolan drifted off as he saw the glass repairman look up. "One sec, Sam."

He put a hand on the phone. "Are you done?"

"Yes. I'll just collect my tools."

Dolan nodded and went back to the phone. "Sam, it's about Sarah."

"Oh, and that inspires me to help even more."

"She's mixed up in something and needs our help. After what you did for her four years ago, you're still one of the only people she trusts."

"Look, Dolan, I live an easy life now. I sit in the evidence room all day and go home to a quiet evening by the television. I golf, for Christ's sake. That other stuff isn't my life anymore."

"Sam, Sarah's on the run with an ex-cop named Jack Tate. She showed up here this morning, and we were attacked at my house. That nosy cop, Parkman, showed up at the right time and shot one of the perps. Whoever they are, they know where she'll turn next and who she'll turn to. We need you. Sarah needs you."

"Sorry, Dolan, I can't help."

Dolan bowed his head. He heard the front door shut as the glass repairman left.

"Will you at least call me if you hear anything?"

"I'll call. But the chances of me hearing something are slim to none in the evidence locker."

"Just call me if you hear anything." Dolan hung up without saying good-bye.

79

"WHERE ARE WE going?" Sarah asked.

Esmerelda merged onto a two-lane highway and sped up. She checked her rearview mirror.

"Is everything okay?" Sarah asked as she turned around and looked out the back window. They were going faster and faster.

"I think we're being followed," Esmerelda said.

"What are they driving?" Sarah asked.

"It looked like a black SUV. About eight cars back—oh shit!" Esmerelda smacked the steering wheel.

Sarah looked up ahead. A police officer stepped out onto the road and waved for Esmerelda to pull over. They were still a hundred yards away, but Sarah could already see the radar gun.

"It's okay, Esmerelda. Whoever is following us will get spooked by the cops. The worst we'll get is a speeding ticket."

"I wouldn't be so sure. What if this traffic cop recognizes you two?"

She eased the car over and slowed to a stop. The officer walked up to the driver's side window. Esmerelda rolled it down slowly. Sarah turned around to look through the back window. Car after car passed by, but no SUV.

"Do you know how fast you were going, ma'am?" The cop leaned down to look inside.

"Not really, Officer. I kinda got carried away. We were talking. Sorry about that."

The cop glanced into the backseat.

"I'm going to need to see your driver's license and registration, ma'am."

Esmerelda fumbled in the glove box and produced the documents. He asked her to wait for him as he walked back to the cruiser. Sarah kept an eye on the road. Jack sat beside her, fumbling with the rip in his shirt.

What the hell is with that damn rip?

"There's a problem," Esmerelda said.

"What problem?" Sarah asked.

"He's got another cop with him. They're both in their cruiser talking."

"It's routine. Nothing to worry about," Jack said.

A black SUV slowed down to park on the shoulder about two hundred yards back.

"Esmerelda," Sarah said. "Is that the SUV you saw?"

Esmerelda turned to look out the back window. "Yes."

The cop opened his door and stepped from the cruiser. He placed a hand on his holster as he neared Esmerelda's vehicle.

"We got a plan?" Sarah asked as she reached for her gun.

"I have no clue."

Some of Esmerelda's words were lost as Sarah blacked out.

SHE SWAM BACK to consciousness with no idea how long she'd been out. The pen Esmerelda had given her was locked in her hand. Before reading the message on the notebook, she looked up at the officer shouting through Esmerelda's window.

"I'm asking you to step out of the vehicle," he said.

"Okay," Esmerelda said. "I will, Officer. But I want to know why."

The cop unclipped his holster. His partner came around the front of the vehicle.

"I have reason to believe that you are aiding and abetting two people wanted in connection with a shooting. I need all three of you to exit the vehicle and keep your hands where I can see them."

Esmerelda reached for the door. "You okay, Sarah?"

She got out of the car before Sarah could respond. Jack stood beside the car already, the doors open. A vehicle raced by, the wind softly shaking Esmerelda's car.

"I won't ask you again," the cop said as he leaned down to look at Sarah.

She edged to the door, but remained inside the vehicle. "Officer, can I ask you something?"

"Get out of the vehicle, now."

"Do you know a man named Aaron Beck?"

The cop looked at his partner, then back at Sarah.

"He's a close friend of mine. Why?"

"Did he tell you what happened on Front Street with his wife, Carol, the other day?"

"What are you talking about?"

Sarah placed her feet outside the car on the gravel shoulder and looked up at him. "I'm telling you this because I want you to trust us. That woman there is a renowned psychic. This man here, Jack Tate, is a retired police officer."

The cop cut in. "I know who all of you are. We're supposed to take you in, Sarah. That is your name, right?"

"I'm the girl that spoke to Aaron and told him to call his wife so she wouldn't get killed by that truck."

Something she said hit a nerve. Both cops looked at each other, then back at her.

"Here's why I'm telling you this. If we do not get back on the highway within a few minutes, you and your partner will be killed."

His hand went back to retrieve his pepper spray canister.

"Enough. Get out of the *fucking* car."

Sarah stood slowly and looked back at the idling SUV. It hadn't moved.

She raised her hands above her head, the notebook in her left one. She glanced up at it and started reading.

"Officer Cooper. You've been on the force for eight years. Your wife, Sofia, has asked you to consider changing careers, as she fears for your safety." Sarah stopped to let that sink in. "Mr. Cooper, we are being tailed by highly professional killers who will stop at nothing to get what they want. I know it sounds over the top, but it's true. They kidnapped my parents. There's an SUV parked down the road. Those are the people responsible for the shooting last night and this morning. We also believe those are the people responsible for the dead body Mr. Tate found last night in the woods."

Officer Cooper took a quick look back at the SUV.

"You can tell it to the cop who takes your statement," Cooper said. "My job is to take you in. How do you know all that stuff about me anyway?"

"It's written right here. I'm an automatic writer. I write messages that someone on the Other Side channels through me. When I say that you will be killed if you don't let us go, it's not a threat. It's the truth."

"I'm taking it as a threat. Give me that notebook." He grabbed it from Sarah's hand. "I want all of you down on the ground. Now!"

Esmerelda and Jack started to get down, but Sarah remained standing.

"You're not listening, Officer Cooper. We don't have the time—"

"*You're* not listening. On the ground, now, or I will spray you."

Sarah started to drop, keeping the gun at her back hidden. She glanced behind them and saw the SUV moving. It was merging with traffic, heading their way.

Cooper's partner worked on securing Esmerelda's hands and then stood and started on securing Jack's. Officer Cooper had returned his weapon to his holster.

"That SUV is coming," Sarah said. "Please, pull your gun back out and get behind the vehicle."

He read out loud from the notebook. "*They're like a sect or a cult. They're meaner, more organized, and they enjoy the hunt, the kill. Beware of Armond. He's cunning.* What is this stuff? And who is Armond? Hey, Joe, do you know anyone named Armond?"

The other cop shook his head as he finished with Jack's wrists.

"Get away from that SUV. Now!" Sarah yelled.

Esmerelda started around to the front of her car. Jack didn't move. Cooper and his partner turned to address the SUV as it slowed.

"Move along," Cooper shouted at it.

She heard bullets hitting metal as they embedded themselves into the side of Esmerelda's car. She ducked her head and rolled away.

Doors opened and closed. A large man grabbed her arm and half lifted, half dragged her to the SUV, his grip unforgiving. Esmerelda and Jack were already being tucked inside by other men. Before the last man got back in the SUV, he turned and emptied his weapon into the two policemen who lay on the shoulder of the road.

Cooper's body spasmed as each bullet hit him.

Sarah eased out her gun and aimed. She had two bullets left. Both hit the man in the back of the head. He went down like a heavy bag of rocks.

She addressed the driver, but he had already drawn on her.

"Drop it or die," he said.

Her gun was empty. Should she bluff or drop her weapon?

The driver made the choice for her. He closed one eye, then fired his weapon. Sarah's gun tore out of her hand, landing on the shoulder of the road.

"Now throw out your cell phone."

"I don't have it on me." Sarah was shaken by how close that was.

The driver adjusted his aim until she was staring down the barrel of the gun. "I won't ask again."

She pulled it out slowly and tossed it away. The phone landed in the tall grass.

A plexiglass partition rose up between the driver and the three prisoners. The back window rose simultaneously.

Sarah kicked at the door as the driver pulled back onto the highway.

Esmerelda asked for calm, and told Sarah to save her energy. Wherever they were going, they would need it.

When Sarah glanced back at the three bodies, cars were already pulling over.

Her gun was at the scene with her prints on it. Bullets from her gun were in the dead man who shot the two cops.

Another manhunt would begin. This time, she wondered if she would make it out unscathed.

A feeling of peace came over her. She knew she had killed without hesitation, and she felt a certain kind of pride, knowing that another piece of human scum had been wiped out.

And she had been responsible.

80

DOLAN GOT UP and ran to answer his phone. He'd been waiting for a security guy to come by and give him an estimate on installing an alarm system.

"Hello."

"Dolan, we have a bigger problem than I thought."

"Sam," Dolan said, relieved. "What's going on?"

"Two traffic cops were killed this afternoon. They found an unidentified body nearby. Obviously, a full investigation is under way, but I'm hearing that the John Doe had the same-caliber gun as the guy found in Tate's house last night. But that's not all."

Dolan turned a kitchen chair away from the table and straddled it. "What else?"

"The unidentified guy had two bullets in the back of his head. It looks like they were fired from a gun found at the crime scene. Early ballistics suggests that it's the same gun used last night at Tate's house. My guess is that it's Sarah's weapon."

Dolan ran a hand through his hair.

"There's more."

"More?" Dolan asked.

"Caleb and Amelia, Sarah's parents, have disappeared. From the looks of their house, they've been kidnapped."

Dolan walked to the front door. He looked out into the street.

"How did this happen?"

"I have no idea, but whoever did this will be caught."

"You know as well as I do that if these guys will kill a cop, they won't bat an eye at killing Sarah."

"You mean Sarah and Esmerelda."

"What?" Dolan spun away from the door. "How is Esmerelda mixed up in this?"

"It looks like the cops were doing a routine speed trap. They pulled

Esmerelda's car over. She's missing, too. That's all I got from upstairs when I was on my lunch break."

"Sarah must've called Esmerelda for help. It almost feels like it didn't end four years ago." He paused. "I'm coming over. Get off early. We've got to do something about this."

"There's not much we can do," Sam said.

Dolan climbed the stairs to his bedroom. He ripped open drawers and started to change. "Yes, there is. We can find our friends, Sarah and Esmerelda. Were there any witnesses?"

"Responding officers are on the scene right now interviewing people."

"Okay, do what you can to find out what they're saying. I'll be there inside a half hour."

"Dolan, let me—"

Dolan terminated the call and stomped downstairs.

He went to grab his car keys and was greeted by two men in black jackets.

They were holding guns.

81

SARAH LEANED AGAINST the back of the SUV. When the door opened, she'd be ready.

"Sarah," Jack said. "That cop read something about a sect or cult in your notes. What was that?"

Sarah turned her attention to him. "I don't know exactly. That's how the messages come through. Sometimes they're specific, but sometimes it's more of a riddle." Jack looked concerned. "What is it, Jack? Do you know something?"

"There was a warning about Armond, right?"

Sarah glanced at Esmerelda and then back at Jack. "Go on."

"After he served his time in jail he took his interest in mysticism to the next level. He formed a following. I think what happened to you and those other girls four years ago was Armond's brainchild. He was always trying to find a way to make money from his hallucinations."

"Could Armond be that powerful?" Esmerelda asked.

Jack nodded. "If left unchecked, yes. If he's been at this as long as I suspect with the police staying off his back, then he would have a large following doing his bidding."

The driver pulled off the highway. Sarah looked out the back window but didn't recognize anything. They passed a sign, but all she got was a glimpse of its backside.

"What does this have to do with us?" she asked.

"Probably nothing," Jack said. "Wrong place at the wrong time. You said you got a message that those two men were going to kill me at my house last night?"

Sarah shook her head. "No, I received a message about my sister's murderer. It had your name and address on it. I interfered because you were the only name my sister gave me, and I *assumed* they'd come to kill you. That and the fact they were taking you away at gunpoint."

Jack looked down at his lap. "Your sister, Vivian? She's the one who talks to you, right?"

Sarah nodded. "It started five years ago."

Jack tilted his head and frowned. "Can you tell me how?"

She considered how much to tell him. "I was depressed. I used to be a puller."

"What's a puller?"

"Someone who pulls their hair out strand by strand. It relieved the pain I felt from the depression. After the kidnapping, I felt stronger. I found a way to stop pulling."

"Why would you do that in the first place?" Jack couldn't hide his confusion.

"I didn't do it by choice. It was more I *had* to. It was comforting. But I'm past that now."

The SUV slowed. They were in a wooded area with no visible buildings of any kind. The driver turned onto a dirt road.

Esmerelda asked him where they were going, but got no response.

The SUV pulled into an opening about five hundred yards off the highway and stopped. Two other SUVs were parked in a small clearing, their back doors open. Sarah counted four men, all wearing the same black jackets. They were all holding handcuffs.

Their driver got out.

"Okay, stay calm and do as they say," Sarah said.

The back door unlocked. Men moved toward the truck.

"Easy now," the driver said, and swung the door open so his co-horts could have a clear view. "Sarah, I want you first. Step out slowly and put these on." He tossed handcuffs at her.

Esmerelda nodded. "It'll be okay, Sarah. Take care of yourself. Everything will work out."

"I'm sorry," Sarah said as she dropped to the ground and applied the cuffs to her wrists, keeping both arms in front. One of the men grabbed her by the hair. The pain was instant and fierce. Her knees weakened under his grasp.

"I should fucking kill you right now, you meddling bitch," the man said. "You killed our brother."

"I didn't kill him," Sarah said.

Something hit her cheek and knocked her to the ground. Her face connected with the gravel. A sharp stinging rose in her other cheek.

Someone dragged her up to a standing position.

"Please, she's just a young girl," Esmerelda said. "Leave her alone."

"Shut the fuck up, old lady, or you're next."

Her assailant started dragging her to one of the waiting SUVs. He opened the back door and shoved her in. She anticipated his move and got her legs up and in without banging them.

A long time had passed since she had felt this kind of pain.

He grabbed her again and brought her close. He had a black blindfold in his hand. Just before he wrapped it around her head she saw Esmerelda had been removed from the vehicle. They were walking her to the other SUV. Jack had remained in the backseat.

Then the blindfold was secured over her eyes. He shoved her back and slammed the door. Someone got behind the wheel, and a moment later the vehicle was under way.

She lay back and stretched out, willing the pain away so she could think.

Earlier, when they pulled up close to the four waiting men, Sarah had noticed all their untucked shirts had small rips near the bottom.

The same rip on Jack Tate's shirt.

82

SAM HAD WAITED long enough. He had tried calling Dolan's house again. No answer. He tried Dolan's cell without success.

That was half an hour ago. He tried the house phone one more time as he turned onto Dolan's street. Still nothing.

He stopped in front of Dolan's house. The front door sat ajar, lights on inside. He got out and ran to the front.

"Dolan?" Sam called. "You in there?"

He pushed the door aside and stepped in. Everything looked as it should. He searched each floor quickly. With no sign of Dolan, he left through the front door, secured it, and ran back to his car.

It took him thirty minutes to get to the crime scene on the highway. A temporary tent had been erected. The two-lane highway was reduced to one as officers rerouted traffic around the site.

He showed his ID and pulled to the shoulder, angling his car away from the setting sun. In the shade, he saw the area was populated with FBI agents.

Sam walked over to one of the few officers he recognized.

"Parkman, what're you doing here?"

"I could ask you the same thing. Don't they have you stowed away in the evidence locker?"

"And they have you at a desk. So what are you doing all the way out here? Are you working with the FBI?"

"I was involved with the shooting this morning at Dolan's house, and I have a unique history with Sarah Roberts. Special Agent Jill Hanover asked for my assistance on this case."

"What case? Since when does the FBI get involved in a police shooting this fast?"

"Since today," a woman interjected. Hanover. "Good to see everybody could join the party. What are you doing here, Johnson?"

"I just came from Dolan's house. We were supposed to meet there, but he wasn't home. I thought maybe he would be out here, you know, trying to conjure something up to help you."

"How is Dolan these days?" Hanover asked.

Sam shrugged and glanced at Parkman. "His front door was ajar. There was no sign of a break-in, but I couldn't locate him."

Hanover turned away and spoke into her radio. She was sending an agent over to Dolan's house.

Good, Sam thought. *That was the right move.*

She spun back to Sam. "I think we have all the help we need here."

"And I think I'm coming down with déjà vu. Sarah's kidnapped, I'm looking for her, and you step in to take over the case."

"Correct me if I'm wrong, but weren't you shot for your efforts? Do us all a favor, Johnson, and go home. We got this." Hanover turned and walked away.

"I don't think she likes you," Parkman whispered.

"Nope, but that doesn't matter. What can you tell me, Parkman?"

"The investigation is just getting started."

"Just tell me what you already know." Sam guided him to the side.

"There's the dead guy in Tate's house and the guy I shot at Dolan's. No identities on them yet. I was back at the station filling out paperwork. Half an hour later, I get the call that the FBI has requested my presence. So here I am."

Sam gripped Parkman's arm and pulled him even farther from the makeshift tents.

"I can see it in your face. What else is going on?"

Parkman stared at Hanover as she talked to two other FBI agents for a moment, then turned back to Sam. "They found handwritten notes on the ground."

"What kind of notes?"

"I didn't get a chance to memorize them, but I know there was some personal stuff about one of the cops who was killed here. Stuff about his wife. It looks like it was Sarah who wrote it. That's why I was called in."

"What else do you know?"

"The note said the officers would die. The FBI is taking that as a threat. They found Sarah's fingerprints on the gun that shot the John

Doe in the black jacket. Whichever way this goes down, it looks bad for Sarah."

"They don't know Sarah like we do. You and I both know that Sarah's clean."

"Tell that to the FBI."

Sam shook his head, frustrated. "This is crazy. It will only prove to Sarah that she can't trust us."

"I've tried to reason with them, but there's nothing I can do. Special Agent Hanover is in charge. I'm just along for the ride, although I think it's because they know I'm the only cop Sarah might talk to. I think they had my phone records pulled."

"Phone records? What are you talking about?"

Parkman stepped back to let an officer walk by. When he was out of earshot he turned back to Sam. "Sarah called me this afternoon. She said her parents had been kidnapped and she was being followed."

Sam crossed his arms. "Her parents? What the hell? I'd bet this is all connected to what happened four years ago."

"I just can't figure out how Jack Tate is involved."

Sam dropped his head, then looked up at Parkman. "You'll call me if something comes up? You know how I feel about these people."

"As soon as I can, I'll call." Parkman started back toward Hanover.

Sam ran for his car, feeling Hanover's eyes on him as he pulled away from the crime scene.

83

SARAH WOKE TO a screaming bladder and a headache. The vehicle had slowed down.

She tried to adjust her position. Everything ached. Her shoulders, her scalp, and her pounding jaw.

These people were insane. She had to find out why everyone's shirts were torn at the base like Jack's.

The SUV stopped and the engine died. The driver got out. As the back door of the SUV opened, her blindfold was ripped away. She peered into the dark.

"Come on, get out."

This man was different from the one who had roughed her up earlier.

It was difficult with her hands cuffed, but she managed to hop out. Her new escort held her arm and guided her away from the vehicle.

"Where are you taking me?" she asked.

He didn't respond.

"Where are the people I came with?"

She scanned the area. Ahead, small huts were lined up in a row, like the kind used on a lake when ice fishing. There were at least ten. Some of them were secured with padlocks and chains wrapped around their doors. The other ones had their doors sitting wide open. The sheds sat on cement blocks.

"Is this the jail you plan on keeping me in?"

He pushed her toward one of the open sheds. Before being locked away, she tried to take in as much of the area as she could, but there wasn't much to see except a line of trees and, beyond that, darkness. Lights had been rigged up to shine directly on the door of each shed.

"Why does everyone here have a rip in their shirt?" she asked.

He stepped closer and gestured for Sarah to enter the hut. She used the cement block someone had placed on the ground as a step and entered the dank-smelling room. The door shut behind her. She heard the lock snap into place.

"Where's the bathroom?" she yelled through the door.

A moment later, his footsteps faded away.

It didn't take long to feel her way around the small hut. It was a square room with some kind of linoleum flooring. She found a tiny raised platform in one corner. It was roughly the size of a small school chair, and it had a hole in it. It certainly smelled like an outhouse.

She eased her pants down and hovered over the hole. When she was finished, she felt around for toilet paper but came up empty-handed.

The only opening in the room, other than the padlocked door, was the small hole.

Sarah lowered her head into her arms and wept. She hadn't realized how tired she'd become. Why wouldn't Vivian help now?

Noises from outside came and went. A vehicle passed. She heard footsteps as someone in heavy boots walked by.

Then Esmerelda shouted out in the distance somewhere. Sarah jumped up in the dark. Her body resisted. She felt heavy with sleep.

Then Esmerelda's voice again. "Are you okay?"

"We're fine." It was her father's voice. She had barely been able to hear it.

"Mom! Dad! Can you hear me?" Sarah shouted.

She received no answer.

"Esmerelda!" she tried again.

Nothing. Just the soft rustle of leaves from behind her shed. Even if she was able to figure a way out, everyone she loved was trapped here. She couldn't just leave them behind.

She eased back down to the floor. Her fingers found a few strands of hair on her forearm. New strands had grown in over the past few years. She rolled them between her fingers and tugged softly. The old feeling of pleasure wasn't there. The need, the desire to pull, was gone. She let the hair go and rested flat out on the linoleum floor.

Sleep took her in seconds.

84

SAM JOHNSON FLIPPED through the TV stations without really watching anything. He usually didn't mind a Saturday morning with nothing to do, but not today. He was fidgety, tapping his foot, drumming his fingers.

When he transferred to the evidence room four years ago, he had adjusted well. He golfed, joined a chess club, and felt practically retired.

But now Sarah was in trouble again, along with so many others. It wasn't *just* Sarah this time. That's why he wanted in on this even though his gut said to stay away.

He also knew that whatever was happening wasn't her fault.

His phone rang and he flipped it open.

"Yeah?"

"Sam, it's Parkman."

"What is it?" Sam asked as he sat up on the couch.

"The FBI wants this kept close to them because of how many kidnappings have happened in the last twenty-four hours."

"Of course. Just tell me what you got."

Sam turned off the TV. He headed for the bedroom to get dressed.

"Jack Tate was following a lead the night he got shot twenty years ago. He was after a man named Armond Stuart. You'll remember Alex, Dolan's assistant?"

"I remember him quite well. Fucker shot me."

"Armond is Alex's father."

"What? Jack was after Alex's father twenty years ago?"

"Here's the juicy part. I can't find anything on an Armond Stuart. The guy doesn't exist. No social security number, no address, no nothing."

Sam stopped in the doorway to his bedroom. "Are you sure?"

"Absolutely."

"Then how did Jack come across the name during his investigation?"

"No one knows."

"How is that possible? He must've had a good-enough source to write it in his reports." Sam made it to his closet and started rifling through his dress shirts. He paused as an odd thought struck him. "Unless Jack Tate is Armond himself."

"No one will ever know. After he took a bullet to the head he apparently got amnesia. Been living like a recluse ever since. His neighbors claim they almost never see him."

"Okay, my radar is pinging. After Jack was shot all those years ago, what happened to his investigative work? Who took over his cases?"

"I'm still looking into that. It appears there's a lot missing."

Sam selected a blue-collared shirt and tugged it one-handed off the hanger. "I'm heading out. Can we meet up later?"

"Sure."

"Okay, Parkman, I'll call you." Sam hung up.

He got changed and left the house. He knew Officer Winnfield was the cop who talked to Jack Tate the other night.

Maybe he could shed some light on Tate.

85

THE DOOR TO Sarah's tiny prison opened. It was the same guy who sucker punched her.

"Get up," he said.

She got to her knees, stiff from a night on the hard floor. Her face still ached from the punch.

The man grabbed her arm and pulled her from the little room. Pain flared in her wrists where the cuffs were starting to chafe.

They walked down a path cut between the small sheds. Most of them had their doors sitting open, empty.

By the time they got to the end of the sheds, she had counted at least twenty, ten on each side. Could they be harboring that many victims at any given time? What was this place for?

There was a larger building up ahead, like a small airplane hangar with a barn on the side. So far, she couldn't see any fences or gates. If she made it to the trees, she'd be gone. Although it couldn't be as easy as it looked.

They made it to the entrance of the barn. The brute let go of her arm and stepped back.

The main door opened, and an odd-looking man wearing black-rimmed glasses stepped out.

"Come in, Sarah," he said.

"What's going on?"

Something clicked behind her. She turned to look. The man had a gun aimed at her.

"I want to be the one who kills you," the brute whispered. "Run, try to escape—just do it when I'm watching."

"Blake, stand down. Sarah, come."

Sarah remembered him then. He was the one she had pistol-whipped in front of Jack's house. "What happened to your face?" she asked. "You've got a nasty red mark."

"Ask me that again, bitch," he said, his teeth clenched.

"You sound like you enjoy being tough," Sarah said as the gun inched closer. "I'll remember that, *and* I'll make sure you're one of the first ones *I* kill when this is over."

She turned away even though her legs were shaking. Men like that were the reason she did what she did. Men like that shouldn't and couldn't exist in a civil society where mothers and children also existed.

Inside, the lights had been dimmed. The place was crowded with tables and desks. It looked like a planning station for a war zone.

Crazy Glasses guided her to a corridor that led away from the main room. After twenty steps down the darkened hall, he opened a door and told her to go in and wait.

A table and chair sat in the middle of the room. On it were a pad of paper and a pen.

Glasses shut the door behind her. She walked around the room looking for cameras or peepholes. It appeared to be sealed off. She had only two minutes alone before the door opened. Blake and two other men filed in. Sarah backed up to the corner.

"Sit," one of the men ordered.

"I'd rather stand," Sarah replied.

The man closest to her swung hard. Sarah recognized a strap of some kind as it lashed across her left shoulder and collarbone.

She fell to her knees and held her shoulder as best she could with cuffed wrists. She pushed herself away from the man who still wielded the strap.

"Get away from me," she shouted.

He swung the strap back and forth and then collected it into a ball. "Get up and sit in the chair or I will whip you to a bloody pulp."

He spoke with a British accent.

She got to her feet. Sweat beaded up on her forehead. The pain made her woozy. When she eased the chair out to sit, she saw each man in the room sported a rip in his shirt.

She hunched her back and used her right hand to gingerly reach inside her shirt and feel the wound. Blood had formed on the surface of the skin. Her hand came away crimson.

What the hell is on that whip? Studs?

"Tell us what you do."

"What are you talking about?" she said.

The man unfolded the whip and stepped closer.

"Okay, okay." She glanced back at the table with the pen and paper. "You mean automatic writing?"

The man with the whip nodded. He stepped closer, produced a key, and with deft hands undid her cuffs.

Sarah gently massaged the feeling back into her wrists.

"I have no control over it," she said, keeping an eye on the man with the strap. "It happens when it happens. I black out. For me, it's lost time. When I come to, there's a note of some kind with a message. I follow the instructions. That's it."

No one responded. The three men stood in a semicircle, watching her.

"Is there anything else?"

The man who had removed her cuffs asked, "How can you save all those people from a burning building but you can't save yourself?"

"I have no idea."

Strap Man stepped closer. "What?" Sarah asked. "I really have no idea."

"You're going to sit here and explain until we are content with your answer. You will know we are content when we ask another question."

She leaned against the table. It felt like she'd been burned.

Question Man stepped around behind her. "Who do you think we have here?"

"Esmerelda, Jack Tate, my parents."

"So you don't know who else?"

Sarah turned around to look at him.

"It's okay," he said. "You don't have to answer that last question. In about five minutes it won't matter what you know."

Blake pulled out a revolver.

Question Man continued. "There's one bullet in that gun. You have sixty seconds to write something before my colleague here points the gun at your head and pulls the trigger. Every time you black out and write a prophecy, we move the clock back another sixty seconds. At most, you have five minutes left to live. At the least, one minute."

She instantly felt sick. She wanted to get up and smash his face into the wall, but knew there was no way she could get past all of them.

"Are we clear?" the man said. "The clock starts now."

"Wait—you can't—"

"Sarah, you don't have time to talk." He pointed at the paper on the table. "You need to write something or you will die."

They had to be joking. "That's not how it works!"

"Good-bye, Sarah," Question Man said as he headed for the door.

"It's involuntary! I just pass out."

He stopped at the door, his hand on the knob. "Well then, you had better pass out." He looked at his watch. "Thirty seconds until the first round of Russian roulette."

He stepped out, followed by the other man. Only Blake stayed behind.

"You have to listen to me," she said. "Put the *fucking* gun away. This is ridiculous."

Blake brought the tip of the weapon to her temple and stared at his watch.

"Look, give me time. I always write something eventually." Her heart raced. Something in her soul shouted, *It'll be okay*.

At the one-minute mark, she opened her mouth to protest.

Blake pulled the trigger.

86

SAM HAD RARELY worked a case with so few clues. He had nothing to go on. He parked in his usual spot and walked straight to the second floor, where he found Winnfield at his desk, sipping coffee.

"Winnfield, you got a sec?"

Officer Winnfield set his coffee down and leaned back in his chair. "Sure, Johnson, what do you need?"

"I want to talk to you about Jack Tate."

Winnfield looked around. "I can't talk about that."

Sam frowned. "Why not? What's the problem?"

"The FBI took it over," Winnfield said. "Listen, Sam, let's go across the street and grab a coffee. What do you say?"

Ten minutes later they were seated opposite each other.

"What's going on?" Sam asked.

Winnfield looked around the coffee shop. "I don't even know where to start."

"Come on, Winnfield, just tell me what's up."

"I'd been pushing Parkman for information. The FBI just walked in and took me off the case. Then they let Jack Tate walk."

"I know all this. I talked to Parkman, too."

"Did you know that the dead guy in Jack's foyer also had a rip in his shirt, just like Jack and the dead girl discovered in the woods?"

Sam wasn't sure he heard him right. "How could that be?" He glanced up and watched as three teenagers entered the coffee shop.

Winnfield shook his head. "This is something big. Bigger than Jim Jones or that David guy in Waco."

"What makes you say that?"

Winnfield leaned in close and lowered his voice. "They got a license plate of the retreating vehicle from a witness on the highway. The SUV belonged to a college professor on the other side of the city. A couple of uniforms went over to look into it. Apparently, the professor's plates were lifted off his vehicle two nights ago. But get this: so were ten other license plates in the same neighborhood. Whoever these guys are, it looks like they have at least ten vehicles and they change plates routinely. I've never seen anything like it. Bizarre, really."

Winnfield was so close, Sam could smell the latte on his breath.

"You know," Sam said, "a lot of people have gone missing since last night." He sipped his coffee. "Has anything come in on the dead girl Jack found?"

Winnfield shook his head. "Her fingerprints were burned off and her teeth removed. There's evidence of some kind of sexual abuse, but nothing conclusive until the autopsy report comes back. They've estimated her age to be around sixteen. I'm starting to get the feeling that this has something to do with human trafficking."

A couple more teenagers entered the coffee shop. He watched them for a moment and then looked back at Winnfield.

"What was that?" Sam asked. "Missed some of it."

"I've been ordered to finish my reports and then hand them over to the FBI. Then I'm supposed to let it go."

It was a big case for him to land. To have it ripped out from under him by the Feds was shitty. Sam remembered that Winnfield liked getting noticed for his arrests. This one gave him the wrong kind of attention.

"Winnfield, I gotta run," Sam said. "Thanks for the coffee." He pushed out his chair.

"Hey, Sam, you'll let me know if you find anything, right?"

"Of course, Winnfield. Of course."

Sam patted his shoulder on the way to the door.

87

WETNESS SEEPED THROUGH Sarah's pants. Her bladder had released, surrendering its warmth.

Blake lowered the gun and looked at his watch.

Sarah turned away from Blake and grabbed the pen. She figured she had at least half a minute. There was no way she could reason with these people. She had to beat them another way.

She held the pen tight, rocking back and forth in the chair to the imagined rhythm of seconds on a clock. After a count of twenty, Blake raised the gun again.

Sarah rolled her eyes back as far as she could and slumped in the chair. Her hand worked the paper furiously. She wrote whatever came to mind. After a few moments, she dropped the pen and slipped out of the chair.

Her urine was cool when she hit the floor. She bumped her elbow but kept the groan buried. She hadn't heard the click of the gun.

Blake picked up the paper. She waited while he read it, holding her breath. She had done what they'd asked for.

She writhed on the floor and moaned. Blake moved to the door, the paper in his hand. His gun had been put away. He stood rigid as he stared at her from the door.

She made it up into the chair and sat, trying to look defeated. The smell of urine was intense. She hated being so weak.

Blake moved fast. He pulled his gun out again, but this time he held it backward, the butt of the handle facing her.

"Aren't we done?" she asked, pulling away from him.

"You have a debt to pay," he said.

"What debt?"

"I owe you for the pistol-whipping at Jack's place," Blake said.

He stepped in, his speed incredible. Even though she tried to block his advance, the handle of the gun struck her cheek so hard she rocked violently back into the table, then bounced to the floor.

88

PAIN THROBBED IN her ear. It was like she could hear the ache. Sarah gingerly touched her face where it was swollen and tender.

She rolled to her side. Maybe the blow had cracked the orbital bone around her eye. She felt the floor in the darkness and confirmed she was back in her little prison.

She felt her way to the door and ran her hands across its surface, looking for weaknesses. It was rock solid. On bended knee she felt the edge of the linoleum and traced it for a few feet. It was bonded to the wall in a solid grip.

Without tools of some kind, there was no way out.

Discouraged, she shuffled over to the hole with the raised seat. A faint urine smell wafted up. Her fingers paused on the clasp as she went to undo her pants.

The hole.

Where did it lead? How far down did it go? If she got under the shed, could she find a section of the wall where it would be weak enough to push or kick through?

She measured the hole as best she could. It was about the circumference of a basketball. Her shoulders wouldn't get through. She braced herself, grabbed the edge, and pulled upward in an attempt to break off a piece. Nothing moved. She pulled again, as hard as she could. Still nothing.

She reached through and touched the ground below, trying not to breathe in the stench. Within seconds she found what she was looking for. Rocks and small pebbles were mixed in with the random dirt under the shed. She located the biggest rock she could find, about the size of a baseball.

She had heard nothing from outside. No light emanated from under the shed's door. For her plan to work, she hoped it was early morning.

Sarah lowered her pants and urinated on the rim of the hole, making sure to soak the wood surrounding the area she was going to focus on. When she was finished, she did her pants back up and waited for the urine to work its way in.

With her ear pressed against the wall of the shed, she listened for anyone who might be close, but still heard nothing.

She slid across the linoleum floor and felt the rim again. It was still wet. There would be no way to mask the banging. This was her only chance. If it didn't work, she would be out of options.

She held the rock aloft in her right hand and said a quick prayer. Then she brought it crashing down on the wooden edge of the hole. Again and again she smashed the rock into the wood. She felt the madness of the situation overwhelm her. She grunted in frustration with each downward stroke.

The wood finally cracked under the blows. She stopped and dropped the rock, panting. Her fingers found the split wood. Elated, she picked up the rock and continued.

Another crack resounded throughout the shed. She stopped and listened. It was hard to hear anything outside over the pounding in her ears.

She stood over the hole, grabbed the split rim with both hands, and yanked. It cracked again and broke away. She lost her balance and fell back, but she'd done it. The hole would be big enough for her shoulders.

Someone shouted outside, and a vehicle's engine revved.

They had heard.

She dropped her head down into the hole first. The stench filled her nostrils—rotting earth mixed with human excrement from long ago. She lifted her head back out and took a deep breath.

They were close. At any second her door could burst open.

She took one more deep breath and dropped in. Her shoulders eased into the opening and filled it. With a slight nudge they popped through. She wedged her right hand in ahead and felt her way to the ground, supporting her weight on her forearm and elbow.

Someone was at the shed door behind her. The locks clicked against the chains that secured the tiny prison.

Time had run out.

With her left arm pulled through now, she moved forward into the wet and cool earth under the shed. The linoleum floor of her shed was about two feet above the dirt floor. It was just enough room for her to crawl along on her arms.

The chains that secured her door were being ripped out of their loops. The door would open any second.

She crawled away from the gaping hole, pulling her legs in after her. She pushed away from the opening. A meager light cast down through the hole as the door to her shed opened.

Multiple pairs of boots rushed in. Someone barked out commands.

She moved toward the edge of the space underneath the raised shed. A light shone past her. Someone had stuck his head in the hole with a flashlight.

"I can't breathe in there," a man yelled. "She pissed all over the fucking hole."

"Take another look and confirm whether she's down there or not."

Sarah crawled as far as she could and hit the outer wall. She could go no farther. They would find her trapped like a mouse in a corner.

She grabbed the cool, wet dirt and smeared it on her face, swallowing the bile that crept along her throat.

"Okay, give me a sec," the man above said. "Let me catch a good breath first."

She covered herself with more dirt. As she massaged it on, she bumped her wounded cheek and almost screamed out in pain.

The guard dropped his head in and scoured around in a circle. The flashlight passed by her, but didn't stop. She had buried her face and hair in the ground just in time.

The flashlight holder shuffled back out of the hole. He took large gulps of air.

"Well?" someone else asked.

"She's not . . . she's not down there. She's gone."

Sarah lifted her head out of the dirt and breathed as quietly as possible. She heard footsteps above her and a few curse words muffled by the floor.

"I want the entire area scoured. We cannot let this one get away. Shoot on sight."

"Sir, yes, sir!"

Sarah didn't move for a few minutes. The rank smell eased as she got used to it.

Sarah rolled closer to the broken hole in the floor of the shed. A soft light filtered down. They hadn't closed the main door.

That's right, she thought. *Leave it open.*

She raised her head out of the hole and risked a peek into the room. It was empty.

She gripped the rim and lifted herself out. Her running shoes made no sound as she stood on the linoleum floor, covered in dirt and bits of urine-soaked feces. She crept up to the wall beside the open door.

The sun had started to rise. They didn't think she was inside, but they weren't stupid. Someone would be watching her shed.

She strode back across the floor and slipped effortlessly into the piss hole. Sprawled out on the dirt below, she could swear someone was at the door, looking in.

She froze and listened.

Is that the soft rustle of a jacket?

Sarah rolled across the dirt to the corner again. When she got there, she dipped her face and hands toward the outer wall.

Someone walked across the floor above her.

Then the ground exploded as he fired multiple rounds into the floor.

She almost screamed in shock.

The gun changed direction. The bullets were getting closer. If she made a noise she would die. She pushed herself into the wall as far as she could and buried her face.

When the first bullet hit her arm, she didn't make a sound.

She passed out.

89

SAM JOHNSON PULLED into the truck stop on the edge of town. He spied Parkman's sedan and pulled in beside it.

Sunday morning and the place was packed.

Parkman had found a table in the back corner of the restaurant. He dropped the menu.

"Why meet way out here?" Sam asked.

"One sec." Parkman motioned to the waitress.

After taking an order for a breakfast special and a coffee for Sam, the waitress left.

"Have you learned anything new?" Parkman asked.

Sam shook his head. "Nothing. I talked to other officers, but everyone has been kept out of the loop."

Parkman nodded. "Even me."

"I thought the FBI took you on to help. You know more about Sarah Roberts than anybody."

"They have what I know already. They didn't need me anymore. I had to sign a confidentiality waiver."

The waitress set a coffee down in front of Sam.

When she walked away, Sam said, "Tell me everything."

"There's nothing to tell. I'm supposed to report back to my desk on Monday morning."

Sam clasped his hands together.

"So all we have are ripped shirts and a bunch of license plates stolen from the same neighborhood."

Parkman's head shot up. "Wait. I know of a sixteen-year-old girl who went missing in Utah."

"What's that got to do with this?"

"She was seen here, downtown, two days ago, with three men, by a witness who knows the family in Utah. He figured he had a case of mistaken identity, but when he called the family, he discovered the girl was missing."

Sam raised his eyebrows.

"The witness told the cop who took his statement that the men wore ripped shirts. Why didn't I remember that before? The rip was about two inches long and cut on an angle."

"How would a witness see that kind of detail?" Sam asked.

Sam's cell phone rang. He pulled it out and frowned.

"Hello?"

"Sam Johnson?"

The voice was deep, like the caller was trying to disguise it.

"This is Sam. Who am I talking to?"

"Interested in an exchange?"

Sam looked at Parkman. "What kind of exchange are we talking about?"

"Call it a two-for-one deal."

"I'm going to need a little more than that."

"I will give you Sarah Roberts's parents, Amelia and her husband, Caleb. He has proven to be quite a problem."

Sam felt the color leave his face. This was the closest anyone had gotten to this group.

"In exchange," the caller continued, "I want you."

"Excuse me?"

"I want you. In exchange for the parents. I will give you three seconds to give me a yes or a no."

He spoke before he could do a gut check.

"Yes."

"Good. I'll call back within the hour. Talk to no one about this. We see any problem, the parents die. And get rid of Parkman."

90

WITH HIS COFFEE finished and excuses made, Sam jumped in his car and headed back into town.

How did they know he was with Parkman? And why did they want him?

He had fought in the line of duty before, been shot and almost killed, but he never willingly walked into such certain danger.

His hands shook on the steering wheel. He was duty bound. *Protect and serve.*

A nervous laugh escaped his lips.

He'd done that his entire adult life. His reward was the evidence room.

Two days ago he wouldn't even have contemplated this. Two days ago he was considering what to watch on Netflix for the weekend.

If he were being honest, he had been getting itchy to do something more important.

He drove fast and made it home forty-five minutes after he received the call. Once inside, he opened his gun cabinet. The drop-point knife sat right where it was supposed to be.

Sam lifted it out and unsheathed the blade. It was designed for hunting, with a robust, curved blade of thick steel, which allowed him to remove the skin from an animal with ease. Also good for easy slicing of a combatant, if it came to that.

He strapped the knife to his inner thigh. This was a suicide mission. Once the parents were safe and out of the perp's control, Sam meant to do as much damage as he could.

The cell phone in his jacket rang. At the sound, his stomach dropped.

"This is it," he said, just before he answered the phone.

"Are you listening?" the voice asked.

91

SARAH FLUTTERED HER eyelids as she came to. Something stank. She forced air out of her nostrils and shook her head to clear it. She waited and listened, breathing in and out slowly, remaining quiet.

After a minute, she moved. Her battered muscles protested.

It was pitch black under the shed. She tried to spin her body around while running through what had happened.

Someone had come back in. They shot the floor up. Bullets hit her.

She scoured her body for new injuries. Her left arm was cut badly, and her leg was a bloody mess. She felt a small scab crusted over an area where it looked like a bullet might have just nicked her.

The ache in her left arm was deeper. She felt a gouge near the top of her triceps. She was hit twice, but both bullets only grazed her enough that they could clot on their own. Otherwise, she would have bled out in this shithole and died.

As gently as she could, Sarah moved toward the opening. Her fingers caressed the rim of the broken hole. Carefully, and with great effort, she got herself up and sitting on the edge.

When was the last time she'd eaten? Breakfast with Jack twenty-four hours ago?

Sarah got to her feet and walked to the open door. The darkness was broken by the mounted lights. She couldn't see a single person anywhere.

Earlier, the sun had just been rising. Now, it felt like it was very early in the morning. That meant she had been under the floor for almost twenty-four hours.

How did I lose a day?

With a careful step, Sarah walked out into the open.

She waited for a bullet to hit her or an alarm to sound, but nothing happened as she retreated into the trees behind the line of tiny jails. She rushed headlong into the dimly lit brush, taking deep breaths to rid her nostrils of the horrid smell in her shed. Unfortunately, she brought much of the scent with her.

In minutes she had left the lights of the compound behind. The trees opened up and became sparser as she walked into an open field.

To catch her breath, Sarah slowed and looked back. The compound was completely hidden. No one would see a thing unless they were looking from above.

With no plan but to get as far away as possible, Sarah continued walking.

At least half an hour passed before the sky brightened in the east.

Sarah had traversed hills and small thickets of brush but hadn't crossed a road yet.

Maybe she was walking parallel to one. She turned to the right, which was still heading away from the compound, and continued on.

As the edge of the sun crested the hillside, Sarah saw her first glimpse of civilization. A dirt road was roughly five hundred yards ahead. It led to a small white farmhouse. There were no cars in the driveway, but it didn't look abandoned. As she drew closer, she saw a large aboveground pool in the backyard with a green cover lying across the top.

Cautiously, Sarah crept toward the back door. With a final look around, she opened the screen door and tried the inner door handle. It was locked. She eased the screen door back into place.

When she got around to the front of the house, she glanced in the living room window. The furniture looked new and expensive. She prayed no one was home. She needed to shower, borrow some of their clothes, and contact the authorities.

She tried the front door, but it was locked, too.

She looked horrible, covered in dirt, bloody and bruised, but she really had no choice. She grabbed the knocker and rapped the door three times.

She moved back to the edge of the porch steps. Nothing happened. If these people were home, they had to be asleep.

She tried the knocker again, pounding the door to make sure if anyone was asleep, they'd wake up.

The farmhouse had old storm windows.

She tried the two front ones, but they didn't budge. Being careful to watch for an approaching vehicle, she walked around the house trying all the windows.

When she returned to the back of the house, the window leading into the kitchen lifted with ease. She pushed it up and hefted herself onto the sill. With a slight wince, she swung both legs around and into the kitchen. She hopped off and dropped to the tile floor.

"Damn, that hurts," she muttered under her breath.

She leaned on the counter and took in her surroundings. The place looked lived-in. People had been here recently. Which meant they could be back at any time. She looked for a phone but couldn't find one in the kitchen. She walked into a hallway and then into the living room, being careful to remain quiet. No phones anywhere.

Maybe they didn't have access this far out. She had no idea where she was. She had been blindfolded on the way in.

She needed to be certain the house was empty. The stairs were off the hallway. On each step, she tested for creaks. At the top, three open doors led to bedrooms and another led to a bathroom. After a look in each bedroom, she began to relax. All the beds were made, and no one was home. As long as the occupants didn't come home while she was still inside, everything would go smoothly. Although, on second thought, let them call the police. Maybe that would be the best option.

She entered the bathroom and turned on the shower. Hot water came quickly. She disrobed, removing her filthy, disgusting clothes, and hopped in.

Five minutes later, clean but in pain from the water hitting her wounds, Sarah entered one of the bedrooms and opened a closet door. It was empty except for a few boxes. She went into the other bedroom and couldn't find any clothes there either.

I will not put those shitty clothes on again.

In the master suite, she opened the closet to reveal a large wardrobe of men's clothing.

With a quick check of sizes, she found a slim pair of track pants with a tie strap she could adjust. Next, she selected a clean white undershirt and a collared shirt to go over that. She ran back to the bathroom and grabbed her running shoes, brushing off the remaining dirt and slipping into them. With a final look in the mirror, she was ready to go.

She stopped cold and stared at her reflection. The collared shirt she wore had a rip in it at the base.

She heard a car outside.

She ran to the bedroom that looked out onto the front lawn. Four black SUVs pulled in the driveway.

They'd found her.

She bolted back to the bathroom and gathered up her dirty clothes. She brushed the remaining pieces of dirt under the bathroom carpet. As she raced out of the bathroom, she caught sight of the steam on the mirror from the shower. She turned back and wiped it as fast as she could, then pulled the shower curtain closed.

It took her a few seconds to find the attic door in the roof of the second bedroom. She set her clothes down, brought a night table over, and stood on it to push the wood up into the attic. It lifted with ease. Before thinking about how she could get herself up and in, she tossed her dirty clothes through the hole so at least they were out of the way.

The front door opened below her. Voices of multiple men carried up the staircase.

She climbed down and ran around the bed to the other table. It was better to have two misplaced nightstands than just the one.

She used every last bit of strength she had to lift herself up and into the attic.

Someone ascended the stairs, pounding his footsteps hard.

Now two people were at the top of the stairs. They were discussing a cop—someone who was doing a trade of some kind.

She maneuvered the wooden attic cover and eased it back into place. It dropped with a soft thud.

"What was that?" one of the men asked.

The men in the upstairs hallway ran into the bedroom. She crawled backward, making every effort to be soft and quiet.

"I thought I heard a thump."

"Where?"

"In here."

"There's no one here, John."

"I can see that, asshole. What happened to the end tables?"

"I have no idea. Maybe someone moved them."

Sarah held her breath. *I could really use a break here.*

"Let's just put them back and get changed. We have a long day ahead of us."

Using what little light was available to her, Sarah checked out her new digs. The ceiling had exposed joints and peaked in a V formation above her head. Pink insulation was jammed in between the studs. There was a thick layer of dust covering the floor, but enough room to lay out.

Four moving boxes were piled in a corner. She considered taking a look in them, but decided to wait until the men below were either gone or asleep.

A gentle move to the right got her farther from the trapdoor and her old, dirty clothes. To be back in a confined space, smelling that shit again, was just wrong.

She eased a little farther away and lay down.

She had escaped the compound only to walk right into their home. She had no phone, no way to contact the outside world, and no idea where she was.

There were people walking around on the second floor below her. A toilet flushed. Someone shouted something. Someone else laughed.

Then she heard someone say Sam Johnson's name. She strained to hear more.

The voices were too far away, but she was sure she heard the words *trade* and *kill him.*

92

SAM PARKED IN the spot they told him to.

He took out his cell phone and texted Parkman his whereabouts. It was a risk, but maybe his colleagues would come and check the mall cameras to see what had happened. Still, these people wouldn't have chosen a mall setting if they were worried about security cameras.

The dash clock read 10:01 a.m. He was a minute late.

Sam unclipped his holster and placed it with the gun under the front passenger seat. He touched his leg and felt for the knife. It was exactly where it was supposed to be.

He followed a group of oblivious shoppers into the mall.

His instructions had been simple. Walk to the maintenance doors by the JCPenney and then to the garbage compactor out back. A garbage truck would be there to pick him up.

As if on cue, the truck came into view and lumbered up to him. A single driver wearing a black bandanna and sunglasses nodded at him.

Sam stepped onto the rungs on the passenger side and looked in the open window.

"Get in," the driver said.

"Where are Caleb and Amelia?"

"You get nothing until you get in."

Sam opened the door and sat down in the passenger seat. The garbage truck started moving right away. He waited. A deal was a deal. He just hoped they would honor their part.

The driver swung around and stopped four rows away from Sam's car.

"The parents are over there," the driver said, pointing at a black Suburban.

The doors opened. Amelia, followed by Caleb, stepped out into the sunlight. They looked disheveled and disoriented.

The garbage truck driver reached down and lifted a device from the seat beside him. He looked over and smirked as he pushed a button.

The explosion made the garbage truck sway. Sam shut his eyes and shielded his face. With horror, he wondered if Caleb and Amelia had been fitted with explosives, but when he looked through the windshield he saw that it was his car. It was completely engulfed in flames, along with the two cars on either side.

Caleb and Amelia had taken shelter behind the Suburban.

Sam looked at the driver. "You're insane. Innocents could've gotten hurt."

He shook his head. "How do we know if you have a tracking device on your car? Maybe you left a message in there. Besides, you knew this was a one-way trip when you signed on."

"You keep telling yourself that," Sam muttered.

He looked for Sarah's parents again and saw they had run across the street and were headed into an office building—toward safety.

The driver got under way. Fifteen minutes later they exited the city limits. Flat grassland and the odd batch of trees passed by as they cruised just under the speed limit.

He looked in the rearview mirror. Two black SUVs were following close.

It took them no time at all to pull over and get rid of the garbage truck. Sam was ordered into the second SUV. He and the driver climbed into the backseat. Then they were under way again.

The front passenger pulled out a long strip of black cloth. The driver shook his head. The passenger shrugged and put the cloth away. No blindfold? That wasn't a good start.

It crossed his mind to try to take out as many of these guys as he could and then run for it. He'd already saved Sarah's parents, so now he could take off. But he remained quiet and waited. It was Sarah, Esmerelda, and Dolan that he was after. Then he would find a way to finish this.

Even if it cost him his life.

His eyes felt heavy. No one spoke. One man sat beside him, with two in the front. He needed conversation to stay alert.

"Tell me, does your group have a dress code?"

No one responded.

"You all drive the same black SUV, and you all wear the same black jackets. You all rip the bottoms of your shirts. Why is that?"

The guy beside him ignored him and looked out the window.

They pulled off the highway and started up a winding dirt road. He hadn't seen a house or any sign of life for quite some time.

The SUV pulled up and stopped in front of a barnlike structure that was attached to an airplane hangar. He wondered if they kept a getaway plane.

The men got out and walked around to Sam's door. He stepped out. An older man approached and took off his glasses.

"We will dispense with the niceties," the old man said. "I have paid a steep price to have you join us today. Please, come with me so we can begin." The man turned and gestured with his hands toward the barn doors.

Once inside the barn, he followed the old man down a hallway and into a room. One table and one chair sat in the middle, with a solitary light dangling above the table.

An interrogation room.

The old man waved him in. "My friend Blake and his associate have a few questions for you. After that, you will be made comfortable, provided you answer correctly. I bid you farewell."

The door shut behind him.

Sam addressed the man called Blake. "Would you like to start, or should I?"

Blake reached inside his jacket and pulled out a whip.

"Okay, I'll talk. Fire away," Sam said.

The associate pulled out a gun. "If you insist," he said.

"Wait, wait—"

The gun coughed. Sam felt a tearing below the knee, knocking his leg out from under him. He dropped to the floor.

The pain wasn't what hit him first. It was the shock. He heard his scream start as a frustrated wail, and then turn into something more painful.

Blood oozed out of the wound.

"What the *fuck!*" he screamed.

Blake grinned wide. Something about that guy freaked Sam out. Some men acted the part. Some wanted to be tough. A guy like him, the evil came off him in waves.

"I was willing to talk," Sam managed to say. He tried to calm his breathing and looked at his leg. The bullet had gone right through. A glance at the floor three feet behind him confirmed it. There was a small indent in the floor where the bullet had hit.

When he turned around, the guy with the whip moved toward him. In a flash, he had wrestled Sam to the ground. He had no strength to fight the guy off. The pain became excruciating.

One hit in the face and he passed out.

93

SARAH HADN'T HEARD anything for some time.

She angled her body up so she could crawl. If someone had thought to put a window in the attic, it might not be so hot. Sarah brushed at the sweat on her forehead.

It took her a full three minutes to cross five feet. At the boxes, she unclipped one and took a look inside. Old blankets and what looked like tablecloths.

She moved to her right and opened another box. Inside were school supplies. Empty binders and textbooks. Before closing the lid and moving on to the next box, something caught her eye. A pencil case. She opened the zipper and pulled out a red pencil.

Her arm went numb.

She had a couple of seconds to secure herself before passing out.

What am I going to write on?

PEOPLE WERE IN the room below her as she stirred awake. Something was burning. Maybe they screwed something up in the kitchen.

The pencil wasn't in her hand anymore. She looked around, but it was gone.

What was that smell?

She could see no sign of paper anywhere. Perhaps she didn't write anything this time.

The smell in the attic quickly became unbearable.

Someone pounded down the steps below, yelling something like, *Everyone out.*

She moved with stealth to sit right over the trapdoor. The burning smell grew stronger.

Was the house on fire?

From her new position she had a sidelong view of the boxes. One of them had something on the side of it. She edged closer. The writing was in red pencil.

The words chilled her.

 . . . *hide when wet . . . kill to save a life* . . .

What the hell did that mean?

The burning smell gagged her. She coughed. One last look at the message and she scurried back to the attic door.

She had to get down or she'd be killed by the smoke filling the crawl space.

Being careful to do it quietly, Sarah lifted the attic door and looked down. The room was empty, except for smoke.

She placed both hands palm down, then ducked her head through first and brought her hips to her hands to prepare for an inverted roll. Next, she dropped her butt through the hole, and her legs followed as she unrolled herself into a hanging position. With only three feet to the floor, she let go of the frame and dropped into the room, taking the weight onto her good leg. .

She knelt down to get below the smoke. It was rolling up from downstairs.

At the window in the front bedroom, she saw one black SUV pulling away. It hit the road at the end of the driveway and turned right.

The last SUV still sat in front of the house, but she couldn't see anyone around. She coughed, then coughed again. She heard the flames licking at something downstairs.

The window had a small latch halfway up. She undid the latch and opened it, managing a few gulps of fresh air. She closed her eyes and filled her lungs.

Then the window shattered above her. She jumped back and landed hard on her ass in the center of the room.

Angered voices screamed from below. The remaining driver and passenger must have walked out toward their vehicle to leave and seen her at the window.

Sarah crept closer to the sill and listened.

"She's in the house!"

"We can't go back in now. Leave it. She'll die in the fire."

"Maybe I hit her when I shot at the window."

Sarah muffled a cough with her sleeve. She wanted to hear as much as she could.

"I'm waiting until the house collapses. What if she walks away from this?"

"She won't walk away. I'll call in and tell them we found the girl and that she's going to burn. I'll wait for you in the car."

She got up and rushed from the room. In the bathroom she found a couple of towels draped over the shower curtain. She turned on the shower and ran them under the water, relieved the water still ran.

The note said *hide when wet*, so maybe this was it. Leaving the water running, she wrapped one of the towels around her shoulders and the other she laid atop her head. Cool water dripped into her ears. In a moment's reprieve from the rising heat, she felt a stir of hope.

The bathroom filled with smoke. She could almost feel the heat rising through her shoes. She ran back into the bedroom with the open window.

Without exposing herself, she leaned in close and sucked at the fresh air, coughed, and then sucked some more.

The house shifted under her. This was madness.

Hide when wet.

She was wet and hiding.

Kill to save a life.

She would love to kill the bastard downstairs, but how?

The air coming in from the window was so sweet she didn't want to leave. Allowing herself one last long inhale, Sarah got up and ran to the top of the stairs. It was the only way down.

But it was too late.

The stairs and the entire bottom floor were completely engulfed in flames, the heat unbearable. She had to move back.

There was nowhere to go, no way out.

She screamed at the injustice. She didn't want to die this way.

The floor under the bathroom collapsed with a huge bang.

It would only be a matter of minutes before the hallway fell, too.

Sarah screamed and prayed.

94

PARKMAN STRUGGLED TO contain his anger. The car door stuck. He fumbled with the handle, got it open, and almost fell out.

"Shit!" he yelled.

He had squealed into the mall parking lot with his siren on, and now a small crowd was staring.

The place was already sealed off as a crime scene in two areas. Parkman saw the bomb disposal crew packing up as crime scene detectives went to work and FBI agents stood around in their suits talking.

He spotted Special Agent Jill Hanover as she waved at him. Someone had to be held accountable for these mistakes.

And it was a terrible time to be out of toothpicks.

"Parkman," Hanover said. "You came."

"Wouldn't miss it," he said as he walked up.

"Do you have a problem being here?" She raised an eyebrow.

He stared back at her and gave no response. She took that as her cue to go on.

"We have Caleb and Amelia," Hanover said. "But they won't talk to us."

"I wonder why."

"What's that?" Hanover snapped.

"I said, I wonder why."

Hanover stepped closer.

"I don't like this any more than you do," she hissed. "I didn't ask to be kept out of the loop. Sam did this on his own. Now, I've asked you to come back on the team because the Robertses refuse to talk to us. If you don't want to help, then fuck off!"

She stepped back and crossed her arms.

Parkman turned around to walk away. She grabbed his shoulder and swung him back.

"Where're you going?" Hanover demanded.

"To talk to the Robertses. Isn't that what you want?" He tried hard, but couldn't keep the distaste for Hanover off his face.

Sam could've been killed here today. The Robertses were freed in exchange for a good cop, and no one knew anything about it. Even the mighty FBI was clueless.

This case was fucked from the beginning. Maybe Parkman could've done something to help if he had not been treated like their personal yo-yo.

He turned away from Hanover and walked over to Caleb and Amelia Roberts, who were sitting in a black FBI Suburban. Parkman showed his ID to the agent and stepped in.

"They drag you out to talk to us?" Caleb asked.

"How are you two doing? I can't imagine how tough this has been."

Caleb looked at his wife and then back to Parkman. "We're okay, but this feels like it did four years ago. What is the FBI really doing to get our daughter back?"

Parkman reached for the toothpick in his mouth only to remember that he didn't have one.

"Unfortunately, there are no guarantees. But I assure you, I will do everything I can."

Six bottles of water were stacked neatly in a holder by the door. Parkman gestured, and after Caleb nodded, he grabbed one.

"You know that Sam was the one who was the closest to helping Sarah last time. He's on the inside now."

Caleb frowned and leaned back in the leather seat, crossing his arms.

Parkman glanced at Amelia. She appeared to be tuned out, but he knew better.

"Caleb, Sam and I will do everything we can to get Sarah home safe."

"We were told that if we help the police in any way, Sarah would be the first to die."

"Is that why you won't talk to Agent Hanover or her team?"

Caleb turned to his wife. "Sarah walked into this, as far as I understand. She gets those messages from Vivian. This vigilantism has always bothered us, but Sarah is twenty-two now and we can't stop her." He looked back at Parkman. "If her sister got her into this, then her sister will get her out."

Parkman was still holding the bottle of water. He uncapped it and took a swig. "Is there *anything* you can tell me?"

"They blindfolded us each way. The ride was direct, not too many turns. It lasted at least an hour. That's all I know. We were held in little rooms, like small sheds, until they brought us here. That's it."

Parkman looked at Amelia and then back to Caleb. "I imagine you'll be in custody until this all ends."

"According to Hanover, yes."

"I'll be in touch."

They nodded and Parkman stepped from the Suburban. He headed directly to his car.

Hanover yelled behind him. "Wait up!"

He got to his car and turned around. She was twenty feet back.

"What did they say?" she asked. "You're just going to leave?"

"They said nothing. They're sworn to secrecy or Sarah dies."

He saw doubt on Hanover's face.

"I gotta go," Parkman said, and opened his door.

"Wait. Where are you going?"

"To figure this thing out. To find Sarah and Sam."

"Not without us you aren't."

"Watch me."

Parkman squealed out of the parking lot, knowing he was leaving his job behind.

95

SARAH RUSHED INTO the back bedroom and closed the door behind her in a feeble attempt to keep the smoke out.

The bedroom window opened easily. What little smoke had made it into this room before she shut the door billowed out as she sucked at the air from the outside. This room had a bed, two night tables, and a small desk. She walked over and opened the closet.

Something banged in the house, startling her. The door buckled from the heat, and smoke forced itself under it.

On the shelf above the hangers she spied a man's leather belt. It would have to do. Maybe if she secured it to the window somehow, the few feet it offered would be enough for her to jump without breaking an ankle or a leg.

A moment later she was at the window, belt in hand. She looked out the window and wanted to smack herself for forgetting.

The pool.

It was still filled with water.

How could I have forgotten?

It took her no time at all to crawl onto the windowsill. She wrapped the belt around her right wrist and sat there for a second, judging the distance.

The house shifted again as she hovered in the window.

Hide when wet . . . kill to save a life . . .

That must be what it meant. When she hit the pool she had to hide as the men investigated the noise. The life to save was hers.

That meant it was time to kill some bad guys.

She counted to three and pushed off the sill.

96

SAM HEARD THE smack as much as felt it.

He rose back up to his own nightmare. When he opened his eyes, the gunman was sitting on the table and Blake was standing over him, rubbing the palm of his hand.

Blood still oozed from his leg, but it had slowed.

His leg throbbed where the bullet had punctured it. The strap was wrapped around his leg above the thigh. It had been pulled snug into what looked like a decent tourniquet.

The man with the gun said, "There will be no more first aid."

Blake moved over to the door, and the gunman stood a few feet away by the table. He couldn't rush them without getting hit by another bullet. If he got close enough, his knife would be aimed for the jugular.

"What do the police know about us? Bring us up to speed."

Sam grunted as he rolled over, angling himself to get better access to the knife.

"What *do* the police know?" Sam echoed.

"Don't repeat the questions. Just answer them."

He got into the best position he could find and allowed his wounded leg to rest. Below the hip, he was rapidly becoming numb, which was a good thing. He needed to think clearly.

The gunman stepped closer. "We haven't got all day."

Sam raised a hand. "Okay, okay. Just give me a second."

"Tell us what the police know."

"We know about the kidnappings. The police know that you have Esmerelda, Dolan, and Sarah."

"What else?" The gunman hovered close.

"We know that anyone associated with this group, whoever you are, has a rip at the base of their shirt." Sam looked over at Blake. "Like that one." He pointed.

"I need to know if the FBI has any idea where we are at the moment."

"They believe that your group is responsible for the two dead cops."

"That was unfortunate."

Sam eased his leg to the side and scrunched his face at the pain. "Batches of license plates were stolen from the same neighborhood. We believe those are the plates that you guys use on all your SUVs. Hey, look, could I get some water here?"

The gunman shook his head. "No water."

"Fucking idiot," Sam muttered.

"What was that?"

"I don't work directly with the FBI, but I know Jill Hanover is in charge. I also suspect they know that Jack Tate is involved with you guys. His shirt was ripped, along with the dead girl found by his house. She was his victim, they think."

"No, the dead girl was planted there. The FBI have been getting close to Jack, watching him. He had us plant her to shine less light on him as a suspect. The ripped shirt was an oversight. He was pretty pissed we fucked that up, eh, Blake?"

Blake nodded.

"Why tell me that?" Sam asked. "When I leave here, I'll report what you said."

"Leave here? What else do you have for us?"

Sam sprawled flat out on the floor, getting comfortable. "We know about a recent kidnapping in another state. The girl was spotted here locally. Since you guys are in the area, I think the FBI has put it together that she's been taken by your group." He stopped and looked sideways up at the gunman. "Let me ask you something. What do you call yourselves? Is this all about human trafficking, or is something else going on here?"

The man snickered under his breath. "Human trafficking," he repeated sarcastically.

"I know that whatever is happening, it's crazy. You can't kill cops and not expect a manhunt."

"That's why we're moving shop. We'll be halfway across the country within days. But enough about that. Do you have anything else to tell us?"

"I was working alone on this. Officially, it's not even my case." He moved again to get better access to the knife. The bullet had ripped open his pant leg two inches from the knife. The tourniquet was an inch above that. Sam had no idea how they missed the blade.

"Are you saying you don't know that Sarah Roberts escaped?"

He jerked his head up in surprise. "Sarah escaped? When?"

"That's not important. And now we know the cops don't know much more than we thought. Sarah must've never made it back. It's a long walk."

"What *are* you doing out here?"

The gunman laughed, grating Sam's nerves. "You see, Blake. Our operation isn't in jeopardy. Go take care of the rest of the prisoners. We won't be needing them anymore. Then come back and help me dispose of Sam's body. Reassure our investors that all is well in the nation. Soon we can move the remaining girls to the new compound."

Blake opened the door and stepped out, closing it firmly behind him.

"Girls? New compound?"

"Yes, Sam. Young girls, born to be sluts, really."

The gunman turned away. The magazine in the gun unclipped. He was checking his weapon, getting it ready for use.

Sam said a quick prayer, and yanked the blade free.

The door opened.

"We found Sarah." It was the man with the black glasses. "You won't believe where."

Sam clutched the knife in his right palm, blade angled down along his wrist, keeping it out of sight of both men.

"Tell me," the gunman said.

"In our safe house."

"Did they kill her?"

"They didn't know she was there until they set the house on fire. Luke saw her in a window and shot at her. He's staying behind until he's sure she's dead."

Sam prayed Sarah would make it. A burning building hadn't stopped her before.

"What are the odds she'd show up there?" the gunman said.

"We're all ready to go. Finish up here and we'll leave in less than thirty minutes."

The man with the glasses stepped back out.

"You were saying how this is all about the girls," Sam said. "What were you talking about?"

The gunman looked over at him. Then he nodded. "I've got a few minutes, so I'll humor you. We're an extension of a larger group that brings girls in from all over the world—the US included—for the elite. Some of us have been at this for many years. Armond started the group way back when he was a cop."

"Armond?" Sam asked.

"You know him as Jack Tate. It began as a massage parlor in the seventies and eventually escalated to Armond picking up girls that were specifically requested by clients."

Jack Tate was Armond Stuart. "Requested girls? How does that work?"

"Certain men have a taste that is hard to satisfy. Armond would go all over the States to get what they wanted, at a price. He got rich fast, but he needed help."

"Is Armond his real name?"

"Does that really matter?"

The gunman clipped the weapon's safety off and aimed it at Sam.

Sam said, "So you guys are basically all pimps."

The gun faltered and lowered again.

"No, we offer a service. Some of the richest men in the world pay us to enjoy the benefits of sleeping with a girl at any age they request with complete anonymity. Our only condition is confidentiality. Break that and the price is castration. Break confidentiality twice, death. That's it. Pay your bill, have fun, keep your mouth shut, and walk away clean. Our clients respect that."

"Then why the psychics?" Sam asked. "Why run the risk of kidnapping people you won't use and killing cops, too?"

"Oh, we use psychics all the time. We kidnap at least two to three psychics per year to have on staff. Armond believes they help us to find the right girls and learn when our risk factor is high. When they refuse to help or simply can't anymore, they're disposed of. Sam, the only people who get out of here alive are the ones who pay money to enter. That's it."

"Not if I can help it," Sam said, and stood using the wall. A dizzy spell came and went.

"What do you mean by that?" The gunman stepped closer.

Sam coughed himself into a fit and bent over. He stopped for a second, eyes watering, and leaned back up.

"I want . . . ," Sam tried, and then coughed into his arm.

"Sam, your time is up. Speak your piece, and then I have to go."

Sam raised his empty hand and beckoned. The guard stepped forward.

With as much speed as he could muster, Sam lunged. The blade sliced at least an inch deep into the gunman's throat. His eyes widened in surprise.

Sam let out a sigh of relief as the gun fell to the floor.

In less than a minute, the gunman's body lay still in a pool of blood. He died with his eyes wide open. Sam left them that way.

They can dry right out of your fucking head, asshole.

Sam picked up the gun, feeling the cold steel and weight of the weapon. A rush of adrenaline flowed through him. He limped to the door and looked outside. Deep, regular breaths had dispelled the wooziness.

The hall was empty. He started out in pursuit of Armond.

Today, he gave back to all the people the police couldn't protect.

97

SARAH HIT THE pool cover hard. It collapsed as water seeped in around her. She rolled toward the edge of the pool.

The water was cold but refreshing. She managed to take a deep breath before being completely submerged.

The belt was still wrapped around her right wrist. In the water, on her back, she loosened it and wrapped it around her left wrist, too. Then she brought the belt's ends apart until it was taut.

The perfect garrote.

She looked up through the film of water and saw the house completely aflame.

She estimated she'd been upside down in the pool for half a minute. She released some air from her lungs and gently moved her legs to stay near the bottom. Within ten to fifteen seconds she would have to surface.

A shadow crossed her vision. She stopped. Her lungs' protest deepened.

But she waited.

Hide when wet . . .

The shadow passed the surface of the water again.

Sarah lowered her head, chin touching chest, and looked at the shooter.

The man had his back to her as he stood transfixed by the burning house.

As slow as she could, Sarah eased to the surface.

Chance favors the prepared mind, she thought as the guy backed toward the pool. *If he only knew.* He stopped a couple of feet in front of her.

She took two deep breaths and then held the last one. Sarah brought the belt up and around the guy's throat and yanked him back. Her feet slipped, causing her to fall backward into the pool. The goon fell with her. Normally, a man his size would knock the wind out of her, but the water softened his descent.

He didn't get a chance to gulp a breath before the belt tightened around his throat. As they dropped under the surface of the water, he tried frantically to release its grip.

The water weakened his struggle. His fight slowed until he stopped, floating motionless above her. Sarah's chest burned for air, but she held on to make sure he wasn't bluffing. She pulled on the belt harder still and waited a few more seconds until her chest felt like it was on fire. Convinced he was gone, her lungs about ready to burst, she eased out from under him and stood to breathe.

She glanced back down at the man. He was definitely dead.

She climbed out of the pool. Even though the sun was high and the day warm, she shivered when the air touched her.

The crackling of the fire was louder than she thought it would be.

Not three feet from the pool sat the guy's gun.

She picked it up. A Sig Sauer P226. A military weapon.

What are these guys involved in?

Sarah popped the magazine release. Two bullets were missing out of a full clip. She popped it back in and released the safety.

In the backyard, twenty feet from her, a large rock sat in a tuft of grass. She grabbed it and ran close to the house, watching for pieces of debris that might fall. This side of the house was upwind as the smoke rose away from it, leaving the exterior wall untouched.

At the front corner she took extra care, edging around until the SUV was in view. The driver sat behind the wheel. He was examining something on his lap.

Sarah threw the rock toward the SUV. Then she turned and ran in the opposite direction.

She cleared the back and ran around the pool. On the far side of the house, she held her breath and ran through the smoke, her eyes watering. Having almost completely circled the house, she slowed as the SUV was about to come into view again.

The driver was nowhere in sight. She jogged along the front of the burning house and turned the corner, the Sig raised and ready to fire.

But no one was there.

If the driver had looked in the pool he would have seen his dead partner. She had wanted to lure the driver out, but now she had no idea where he was.

With the amount of smoke the house emitted, someone was bound to see it and call the fire department soon. She had to locate the driver, execute or incapacitate him, and leave. Otherwise she would never find the compound and she would risk losing the only people she cared about.

Something loud crashed behind her as the fire continued its assault. Impulsively she stepped away from the wall. She looked left and right, watching each side in case the driver emerged.

The driver's side door was still open. Like an invitation.

He would want a sure shot. One that was closer. As soon as she figured out he was gone she would move on the open door of an empty SUV. Then he would pounce. That had to be his plan.

Now what?

She ground her teeth as time ran down. Then she clenched her jaw and fired two bullets into the side of the house.

She hoped her ruse would work. Would the driver think his partner had silenced her? Would he come out of hiding?

She waited, gun ready. After a slow, agonizing count to ten, she stepped around the corner of the house and into the open, the weapon held out in front of her.

The driver stood ten feet away, his weapon pointed at the ground.

She stared at him.

He stared back.

Neither said a word.

Fire licked the wall where Sarah had been moments before. The house burned as they waited to see who would move first.

Sarah applied soft pressure to the trigger. The Sig spit in her hand, and a red dot formed on the driver's throat at the base of his neck, dead center.

His hands covered the wound, his gun dropping to the grass. His eyes widened as blood seeped past his fingers and his life ebbed out in a liquid torrent.

He fell to his knees.

Sarah wasted no time. She strode past him, only slowing to grab his gun, and continued on to the SUV.

When she hopped into the driver's seat, the keys were still there.

In seconds she left the burning house, turned to the right, and had the vehicle racing down the same road the other SUV had taken earlier.

98

AN HOUR OUT of town and Parkman was already regretting how he'd handled Agent Hanover. He couldn't be sure if his hunch had led him on the right highway out of town.

The mall was two miles from Route 9, which led into a flatland area. Without overthinking it, Parkman had assumed this was the way the others would have traveled.

But he could drive this road for days and find nothing. Hanover was his lifeline, whether he liked it or not. He pulled into a truck stop and aimed his car at the road. Then he dialed her number and waited.

"Agent Hanover."

"Hanover, it's Parkman."

"Where are you?"

"Hanover, I'm not a rogue cop. I don't think I can, nor do I want to, do this on my own. When Sam traded himself for the Robertses, in my opinion, that was heroic. I admire his decision, and I wouldn't have tried to talk him out of it, but that's not me."

Parkman heard her pull the phone away from her ear.

"Sorry about that," Hanover said. "Listen, Sam pulled a lone ranger stunt. How can I protect him when he does that sort of thing? All I can do is rely on people like you, Parkman. Don't alienate us. I've got nothing to go on. Right now, I need you."

He watched the traffic on the small, two-lane highway. She was right.

"Okay, I'm in until this is finished. When Sarah is home and whoever's responsible is dead or in jail, only then do we part ways. Deal?"

"Deal," Hanover said without hesitation.

"I'm about an hour outside of town. The Robertses said their ride didn't have many turns. I jumped on the closest highway, Route 9, and here I am, mindlessly driving around—looking for what, I don't know."

"Okay, let me call the local cops in that area and see if there have been any disturbances within the last twenty-four hours. If we have

Sam and Sarah out there somewhere, I'm sure they're going to fight their way out of this. I'll call you back as soon as I have something."

"Okay, Hanover. And thanks."

"We're on the same side, Parkman."

The line went dead.

Parkman got out of his car and entered the truck stop.

After searching the store and asking the clerk, Parkman learned they didn't have flavored toothpicks.

99

AFTER TRAVELING THREE miles, Sarah found a driveway that meandered through a patch of trees. She slowed and took the turn. If this gravel road led to the compound, she could be driving into gunfire. The only advantage she had was the SUV—they'd think she was one of theirs.

The sun came at the SUV on an angle, creating a glare on her right side. A pair of sunglasses would help.

Sarah tried to brace herself for what was to come. She was still trying to reconcile with the side of herself that was comfortable with killing. She was afraid she would lose her humanity, but in times like this, she didn't see a choice.

Turning around a final bend, she came to the front yard of a house.

She stopped the SUV and stared at the curtained windows. Children's toys were scattered across the front lawn. A small homemade fort had been built beside a swinging tire near a large oak tree.

The house did not look like that of a ripped-shirted compound member. Could it be a red herring? Were the toys there to discourage a more in-depth inspection by authorities?

Sarah had to be sure. She let her foot off the brake and eased forward, the tires crunching gravel. The driveway led along the side of the house, toward the backyard. More toys littered the yard, together with normal backyard items: a barbecue beside a raised deck, lawn chairs to sit and watch the evening sun go down.

Sure that this house had nothing to do with the compound, Sarah did a three-point turn and eased up past the house again. As she was about to accelerate down the driveway, she slammed on the brakes and turned around to see the curtains in the bay window flutter closed.

She released the brake, got clear of the house, and gunned it for the road.

The compound couldn't be far. When she escaped, the walk that morning took no longer than an hour, which she figured to be about five or so miles.

She would find it.

She had no idea how to break Esmerelda and Dolan out.

All she knew was she had to find a way.

100

SAM HOBBLED UP the small hallway, his leg needing a fresh tourniquet. He briefly considered retying it, but didn't want to waste the time. Or pass out in the process.

He got to the front door and peered out through the small window. There was no one around—the place appeared deserted. Sweat trickled down his gun hand. He gripped the door handle and eased it open, leaving a bloody smear behind.

Outside, he scouted the entire field before him, but it was barren except for the rows of huts, which appeared to be empty.

Something wasn't right. It was too quiet.

The loss of blood was catching up to him. If he didn't get to a phone soon, he could be in serious trouble. He leaned against the building and edged along the wall toward the hangar.

A wave of dizziness enveloped him. He shut his eyes and breathed deeply, trying to remain calm.

"I see you have dispatched my colleague."

He jumped off the wall and spun around.

Whoever had spoken a moment before was inside the hangar door, talking through the screen. Sam lunged and ripped open the screen door. He charged into the hangar, chanting two words to himself: *for Sarah.*

As he met the concrete floor, he lost his balance and fell hard, bringing his gun up.

"That won't be necessary," the voice said. "You're wounded. Let it go. Just let it go."

It was the man with the glasses.

There was a small Cessna in the hangar and one black SUV. Two people were in the backseat of the vehicle. He could barely make out Esmerelda and Dolan.

"Drop your weapon," Glasses said, his mouth twisted up in a sly smile.

The guy's trigger finger moved. At this range, the more competent of the two was the man standing.

Sam lowered his weapon to the cement floor. "Where are the girls?"

"The girls?" Glasses sounded surprised.

"Yeah, the girls. Where are they? Have you already shipped them to your new *recreational* club?"

"Oh, you needn't concern yourself with the welfare of the nubiles. Move the gun away from your person."

Sam slid the weapon away. It came to a stop a few feet from him.

"What were you hoping to achieve?" Glasses asked.

"Just tell me about your captives. You're going to kill me anyway."

"Demanding. Hmm, okay, let's do another trade. You will save me some time if you tell me what happened to my interrogator. Tell me, and I will tell you what you want."

"Your man was careless. No one patted me down. I came here with a knife. I used it to slice open his throat."

Glasses stepped back and looked at the SUV. He tucked his gun into the waistband of his pants.

"The captives are gone. They're on their way to our new community, where business will continue as usual. Now that Sarah Roberts is dead, I will have to milk every bit of psychic ability out of these two. Now, Mr. Johnson, I will be leaving you here, alive. You probably won't last the night, and since our establishment is so well hidden, you won't be found for quite some time. I don't believe in quick deaths."

Glasses started to walk away, but Sam bellowed after him.

"Wait!" Then, after collecting himself, he continued. "Sarah Roberts is dead?"

He could tell that Glasses was enjoying himself. He wasn't going to leave him alive after all. This was just a game for him.

"Oh, I was sure you heard. Sarah escaped and made it to our safe house five miles from here. She burned down with it. Such a promising girl. From what I've heard we could've done great things with her. But alas, she isn't with us anymore."

"I wouldn't be too sure about that. You might want to get some confirmation."

"Oh, but I did." Glasses smiled.

"I still think you're wrong," Sam said as his voice weakened. He rested his head on the cement and closed his eyes. Maybe the end would be welcoming.

He heard the sound of the hammer clicking into place.

As he waited for the bullet, all hell broke loose inside the SUV.

101

PARKMAN'S CELL PHONE rang. He had been watching the road from the truck stop parking lot, gnawing on one of his last toothpicks. When he saw it was Hanover, he answered.

"What do you have?" he asked.

"There was a house fire just off Route 9. No one called it in until a neighbor saw the smoke. Oh, wait, I'm getting another call."

Parkman turned his car on and waited.

Hanover came back on with new urgency. "Parkman, where are you right now?"

"It's called Mackie's Truck and Tow. It has a little restaurant, too."

"Okay, one sec," Hanover said. Then a moment later: "Leave now and head two miles east. You'll come to a side road. Turn right and drive for half a mile."

Parkman put the car in gear and raced out of the parking lot. He hit the highway and brought the cruiser up to eighty before asking, "What am I looking for?"

"There's a parallel road to Route 9 called Martin Road. The house fire is there. The volunteer fire department is still trying to get the fire under control, but they found two bodies. One was in the pool in the backyard, with signs of strangulation, a belt floating nearby. The other was shot in the throat in the front yard. I want you to go to a house that's about two miles farther down."

"Why?"

"One of my people just intercepted a 911 call from a woman who said someone was prowling around her yard."

"How is that connected?" Parkman asked.

"The woman said it was a black SUV. The plates were stolen. Keep your eyes peeled. I gotta go, but call me as soon as you have something."

The phone went dead just as Parkman saw the sign for Martin Road. He turned right, and raced along the dirt road. In under a minute he saw smoke in the distance.

He spotted the driveway and turned into it. The road was long and winding. He flicked on the siren and lights. He needed to come in strong.

A house came into view. He flipped off the sirens but left the lights on. Just as he stopped, a woman in her twenties opened the front door of the house.

Parkman did a quick scan of the area, and stepped toward her.

"Ma'am, did you call in a suspicious vehicle?"

"Yes, it was like they were checking the place out."

"Can you tell me if they went left or right when they exited your property?"

"No, but if I had to guess I would say right."

"Why's that?" Parkman glanced over his shoulder.

"If you go left, it's a dead end about three miles down. The only house down that way is the Renfeld place, and I can see the smoke from here. Going right will take you three miles to the old, abandoned airport hangar, and I . . . "

Parkman leaped back into his car.

At the end of the driveway he turned right and raced down Martin Road.

The lights still flashed, but he kept the siren off. A black SUV was parked on the side of Martin Road. The brake lights were lit. He turned off his lights and eased up about twenty feet from the rear. It was a black Chevy Tahoe with tinted windows.

He dialed Hanover and got her voice mail. He told her where he was and described the Tahoe.

With his gun on safety, he looked in each mirror to make sure this wasn't some kind of trap. He opened the door and stepped out, staying behind it.

"Hey!" he yelled. "Exit the vehicle with your hands in the air."

The Tahoe's door popped open an inch.

"Don't shoot," a female said. "I'm coming out."

"Just make sure your hands are where I can see them," Parkman shouted. He stole a glance behind him. They were still alone.

The driver's side door opened, and a pair of legs in track pants swung out.

Sarah Roberts.

"Take it easy, Parkman."

"Is there anyone else in the vehicle with you?" he asked.

"No one," she said as she hopped out.

Parkman lowered his weapon and stepped out from behind his car door. He hurried over to the SUV and peeked inside. The Tahoe was empty.

He holstered his weapon. "What the hell happened to you?"

Sarah lowered her hands. "It's a long story. One that I can tell you as soon as we get everyone to safety. I suspect the people you're looking for are down this road."

"Tell me what you can," Parkman said as he walked back to his cruiser. "I have to call this in while you talk. Were you the prowler call we got from a house a few miles up the road?"

"Yes. But we're running out of time. We can't wait for backup. You're it. You and me. I'm going in. I hope you're coming, too."

"Sarah, wait one minute. Let me call this in first."

Sarah hopped back to the Tahoe. He watched her get in the driver's seat while he tried to raise Hanover on the phone. This time she answered. He gave her a quick update and then hung up.

Parkman headed back over to the Tahoe.

"I was taken with Esmerelda," Sarah said. "I know they have Dolan and my parents—"

"Correction. They *had* your parents."

"What?"

"Your parents are safe. Earlier today they were given up in exchange for Sam Johnson."

She shook her head in disbelief.

"Sarah, what happened to your arm?"

"I was shot, twice. Once in the arm and once in the leg, but the bullets just grazed me. Listen, that's not important. Are you coming?"

Parkman nodded and walked around to the passenger side to get in. Sarah started up the access road to the hangar. A line of small buildings came into view.

Sarah pointed. "Those are the huts they kept us in. Behind them is a large building where they do the interrogations and torture."

Parkman nodded. "Stop here and let me out. The doors are all open. They look empty. If anyone's still here, they'll be in the hangar. I'll snake along behind those buildings."

Sarah stopped and Parkman jumped out. He turned to her. "Watch your back."

Sarah hit the gas and pulled away so fast the door slammed shut on its own.

Alone now, Parkman checked out a few structures and continued toward the hangar. Up ahead, Sarah parked to the far right of the barn.

The only sound was the soft wind. The place had a deserted feel to it. He didn't want to admit it to himself, but they might be too late.

Sarah motioned to him that she was going in the back of the hangar. He nodded and pointed at himself, and then the front, indicating his direction.

If there were still hostiles in the building he wanted to be the first one in. He bolted for the hangar door, swung it open with one swift pull, and jumped in low, his weapon out.

Sam Johnson lay on the floor, his leg covered in blood, with a strap wrapped around it like a tourniquet. His eyes were closed. If Parkman hadn't seen the slight movement of Sam's chest, he would've assumed the man was dead.

Three people were near another black Tahoe. He recognized Dolan and Esmerelda right away. The third person was a man holding a large gun.

"Drop it!" Parkman shouted.

The man lowered himself behind Esmerelda. He locked a hand on her throat and raised his gun to her temple.

"*You* drop *your* weapon!"

Parkman held fast for a moment, then lowered his weapon to the side.

"Throw it away," the guy yelled.

As soon as the gun was down, the guy would shoot. He knew it.

Sarah stepped out from behind the nose of the Cessna, close enough to punch the man holding Esmerelda. Without saying a word, she fired her weapon and swiped at his gun with her free hand. His leg burst in a shower of red.

Dolan grabbed Esmerelda and pulled her away so forcefully that the two of them slid across the floor.

A scream echoed throughout the building as the man grabbed at his bleeding leg.

Parkman holstered his gun and bent to check on Sam. His pulse was weak, but he was still alive.

When he looked up again, Sarah was gone.

He ran outside. The man was wounded, and Dolan was more than capable of dealing with him now. Parkman needed to find Sarah before she got away.

The black Tahoe she had been driving was gone.

Sarah had disappeared.

102

SARAH DROVE FOR at least an hour before pulling into a mall parking lot. It took her five minutes to find a dark corner with another SUV like hers. She angled the Tahoe into a spot that blocked the view from the mall itself. Then, wasting no time, she searched the vehicle.

She found a quarter and used that to unscrew the license plate from the black Chevy Suburban. Careful to keep a watchful eye out for curious onlookers, she switched the plates and got back in the Tahoe.

Two miles away she filled the gas tank. While in the gas station, she bought a notepad and a couple of pens, along with two Red Bulls and an armful of snacks. Using her credit card would probably tell the authorities where she was, but she had no choice. From the bank machine in the corner she took out five hundred as a cash advance to avoid using the card again. When the police arrived at the gas station to pull the camera feeds, they would see the new plates. She would have to change either the plates or the vehicle again soon.

She used the restroom and got back in the SUV.

Dolan and Esmerelda were safe. She knew her parents were in protective custody. Now it was just her against them. This had become personal. They had packed up and left—to where, she had no idea, but she figured Vivian knew and would tell her soon.

It concerned Jack Tate somehow. Her sister had led her to him. He was the key.

But why hadn't Vivian warned her about the rest of it?

Sarah drove on into the afternoon with no destination in mind. She had a credit card with a few thousand still available on it, but couldn't use it. Five hundred in cash, and a full tank of gas in a stolen vehicle with stolen plates. Half the state police and the FBI would be on her tail soon while she hunted down her elusive prey.

How many people had been held in that compound? Where were they now? Time was a luxury Sarah did not have.

Somewhere out there, a man named Jack Tate was connected to the murder of her sister.

One thing she was pretty sure of was that he was part of a bigger movement.

A movement that Sarah intended to bring down.

103

ARMOND TRIED THE cell number again. It went directly to voice mail.

"Fuck! Where is everybody?"

Jeffries turned around in the front passenger seat. "Armond, we are safely away. Once we are secure in the new compound we can take care of these people."

Armond glared at him. "That is precisely the problem. I only have four guards left. We have eighteen girls in that bus. You know how this is done. There are always two with me and two with the girls."

"I understand." Jeffries looked at his watch. "We will be in Arizona in six hours. Surely some of Tom's security could stand in while Kent and I take care of Sarah Roberts. She's just a girl. It will be our pleasure."

Armond shook his head. "It's too risky. I have something else in mind for Sarah. Just get us to Arizona."

He looked down at his cell phone and dialed Tom Jacobs's private line. Tom answered on the fourth ring, slightly out of breath.

"Tom, it's Armond. What's happening there?"

"We are preparing for your arrival. The short notice has my select few working extra hard to accommodate your group."

"And sleeping arrangements?"

"Yes, Armond. I have decided to put the girls on the top floor of the temple. That's where they will be the most secure. We already have beds up there for other church business, so I've had my men carry up the rest to accommodate your needs."

"Good. There are a few other things I'm going to need," Armond said as he stared out the tinted window of the Tahoe.

The countryside raced by. Hearing that Sarah was alive and his two men were dead nearly drove him over the edge. He only hoped Dolan and Esmerelda had been killed. Since he'd lost contact with the remaining crew member at the hangar, he could only assume the worst.

"I need you to call that local marshall, the believer, and ask him to give you a location on one of my SUVs." Armond read the vehicle identification number to Tom. "I need him to search for it as privately as he can, as soon as possible. Can you do this?"

"It will be handled. As soon as he gets an ID on its location, I'll contact you."

"We are about six hours away. You will be ready for us?"

"Of course."

Armond hit the "end" button and turned back to the window to look at the bus following them. It had blacked-out windows and was labeled with church insignia. Armond had always been friendly with fundamentalist Mormons. They believed, in certain excommunicated groups, that it was right to arrange marriages for preteens. Armond himself had left the Texas compound just a few days before the early April 2008 raids on Warren Jeffs's outfit.

He didn't believe in their doctrines. But these people gave him a place to hide when he needed one.

He scrolled through his cell and dialed. This line was answered instantly.

"I need a job handled," Armond said.

"Go on."

"There's a girl that needs to be dealt with. Her name is Sarah Roberts. I don't know where she is at the moment, but I may know within the hour. Can you do this?"

"Yes. Call me back when you know where she is."

"You should know this girl is quite good," Armond said. He couldn't allow any more mistakes with Sarah. "I have to warn you to be careful. She has been trained very well."

"I understand. I will be prepared and waiting to move out at your call. This will cost you."

"Do the job well and I will pay you accordingly."

Armond disconnected the call and leaned his head back on the seat. The ex-marine he had just spoken with had come back from his tour of duty with PTSD and turned into one of the best hit men Armond had ever known. It was thanks to people like him that the few people who had crossed Armond had disappeared without a trace.

Sarah Roberts would finally be taken care of the right way. The only sour note was that he wouldn't get the pleasure of doing it himself.

His phone rang. *Private.*

"Yeah."

"It's Tom. The marshall called me back. The vehicle is traveling south on Eighty-Four, going toward Salt Lake City. It could be at our compound in five to six hours, if that's where it's headed."

"Keep me posted when it stops. I've got someone meeting it."

"Understood."

Armond terminated the call and dialed his man back.

"She's traveling on Eighty-Four, heading south toward Salt Lake City. Start now and I'll call you when she stops for the night."

"Anything else?"

"Do not underestimate her."

104

SARAH CLUTCHED THE piece of paper.

Fredonia, Arizona.

She knew every mile was a blessing. In a stolen SUV with a trail of dead cops and dead goons, every cop in the state was looking for her. It was all thanks to Parkman. No other cop knew her like he did. No other cop would've trusted her like he did.

She flipped on the radio to see if she could catch anything on the news.

There was no way she was going to try to make it to Fredonia in this vehicle. She would have to change cars somewhere in Salt Lake City.

She sat up straighter as an idea formed. Four years ago, Gert had taught her an effective way to get a car. All she needed was a cheap motel that accepted cash and no names.

After Sarah fled the airplane hangar and gassed up, she had pulled over to relieve herself in some bushes by the side of the road. When she got back in the driver's seat, her arm went numb. The familiar pull from the Other Side caused her to grab the pen before passing out.

Minutes later, pen held rigid in her hand, she woke to two messages. One said, *Fredonia, Arizona*, and the other said, *10:18 p.m., get a drink.*

That was it. She was scared and chasing murderers, and her sister wasn't helping.

She passed a sign for Salt Lake City. She'd be on the outskirts in less than an hour.

Her eyelids were getting heavy. She wanted a long, hot bath and a warm bed.

"If something really bad is coming at ten eighteen tonight, then why not just tell me?" she asked out loud. "I might not listen to this message, you know. Let's see what happens then."

She slammed the steering wheel, then flipped the radio stations around until she heard the Rolling Stones singing "Emotional Rescue." Sarah sang along.

"Why?" she shouted at the windshield. No answer came. No one spoke from the Other Side. Her arm didn't go numb. She was alone in a stolen SUV with no help. No one knew where she was.

She drove on, knowing it was the right thing to do, knowing she had no choice.

She drove on, alone.

105

PARKMAN STARED THROUGH his windshield, trying to figure out why Sarah had run.

The FBI had shown up. He was no longer needed here. Dolan and Esmerelda were safe, and the guy Sarah shot was being treated before his interrogation.

So far, the man said he had no idea where his colleagues were relocating to, but he did admit they had at least a dozen young girls in a Mormon church bus.

Armond Stuart—also known as Jack Tate, a former police officer, brother to Alex Stuart—was the head of the organization.

Parkman had missed Armond by an hour. He called Hanover before she arrived at the hangar and asked her to see if they could get a record of Sarah's credit card and debit card purchases. Sarah wouldn't get far without money. Then he took the highway heading south toward the Mormon capital, Salt Lake City. If they were in a bus trying to pass off as a church group, then perhaps they'd be heading that way.

He answered his cell as it rang, moving his last toothpick to the other side of his mouth.

"You got anything?" he asked.

"Her credit card paid for gas and a five-hundred-dollar cash advance at a Chevron about forty miles south of the hangar. How close are you to that area?"

"I'm coming up on it soon. I'll get back to you when I have something. Call me if there are any more pings on her cards." Parkman disconnected.

He pushed the cruiser harder, bringing his speed up to eighty miles an hour, and flipped the light on his dash.

Within ten minutes a Chevron came into view. In a slew of dust, Parkman pulled in and stopped by the gas pumps.

He spit out his toothpick and headed for the store.

The door banged shut behind him. "I need to speak to the manager," he said, pulling out his badge.

The young clerk behind the counter lost all color in his face. "I'm sorry . . . ah, he's not here. Is there anything I can help you with?"

"A blond girl, twenty-two years old, came through here in a black Tahoe with tinted windows roughly thirty minutes ago. She wore track pants, a collared shirt. Does this ring a bell?"

The clerk frowned, thinking.

"Look," Parkman continued. "I need access to your cameras. Can you do this for me?"

The door chimed as a woman came in to pay for her gas. She walked to the counter, edged around Parkman, and tossed a twenty at the clerk. "That's for pump three."

The clerk nodded and the woman walked out.

"So?" Parkman tried again.

"Sure, I guess. Come around the counter."

Parkman sat in the clerk's chair as the clerk rewound the digital camera to a half hour before.

Within five minutes, Parkman saw what he was looking for. A black Tahoe pulled in and Sarah Roberts got out.

"This is it. I need a pen and paper."

The clerk handed it to him. Some of the color had returned to the clerk's face.

"What's your name, kid?"

"Samuel."

"I know a good cop named Sam. Listen, I need gas. While I finish here, go out and gas up my cruiser."

"I, ah . . . I'm not supposed to leave the counter."

"What, do you think someone is going to steal from you when you have a cop standing here? Oh, and you guys sell toothpicks, right? I have to have toothpicks."

The clerk nodded, pointed at the rack with the toothpicks, and stepped outside.

Parkman looked back at the small TV screen and pushed "play." He watched as Sarah came onto the store's interior camera to pay for snacks. He saw two Red Bulls in her hand. She used the cash machine in the corner and then left the store. He wrote down the Tahoe's license plate number before she sped off camera.

The clerk showed back up and handed him a box of toothpicks.

"Thanks. I've got what I needed. How much do I owe you?"

"Forty-eight even," the clerk said.

Parkman nodded, paid, and thanked him before running out the door.

He called Hanover and gave her the plate number. It belonged to a man who lived ten minutes from where Parkman was.

"Sarah knew we'd be looking for her," Parkman said. "She changed plates already."

"Things are looking worse every minute, Parkman. Is she still the girl you know, or has she lost it?"

"She saved my life in that airplane hangar. That guy had Esmerelda and Dolan. Without her, we'd be dead."

"Fair enough, but rein her in. She's not a cop. We can't have vigilantes running around."

Parkman ended the call and grabbed the new toothpicks.

He felt good knowing he was on Sarah's tail.

Better me than some other cop.

For the umpteenth time that day, Parkman hit the gas hard, flipped his lights on, and raced after Sarah Roberts.

106

SARAH WATCHED FOR motels as soon as she could see the lights of Salt Lake City. Nothing looked secluded enough, but she was getting tired and those two Red Bulls had run their course. Either she found a motel soon or she slept in the Tahoe.

She decided to try the other side of the city. On the south side now, she turned off on Highland Drive and pulled into a Motel 6.

The sign out front flashed "Vacancy." She parked near the front desk and headed in. The clerk was a young man wearing a blue jacket.

"Can I help you?" he asked.

He studied her bruised face and the odd choice in clothes. She looked at his name tag.

"Cliff," she whispered, and then looked back at the door. "I'm in a little trouble. I wonder if you could help me out?"

"I can certainly try. What can I do for you?"

Sarah looked back at the door one more time. The clerk followed her gaze.

"My boyfriend gets pretty violent." She brought her hands to her face to touch a bruise. "If he comes looking for me, I'm afraid he'll kill me."

"Why don't you just call the police?" Cliff asked, looking unsettled.

"Oh, no," Sarah said. "The last time I did that I was in the hospital for weeks. Look, all you need to do is let me park my SUV in the back and rent me two rooms. One will stay empty with my name on it, and I'll sleep in the other. I'll pay you for both; just don't tell anyone. In the morning, I'm gone, forever. That's all I'm asking."

The clerk looked around the lobby, then focused back on Sarah. "So you'll pay for two rooms, stay the night, and leave? That's it?"

"Yes, I just don't want to use a credit card."

"Fine with me. But I'll need a cash deposit."

Cliff booked room 104 under her name, then gave her the key to room 107. She moved the SUV to the back and found the door to 107.

After using her key, she entered the small room with one bed. The dresser had a television on it, and there was an open door at the back that led to the bathroom.

She grabbed the chair from the desk area and jammed it under the door handle. As she headed for the bed she took out the papers with Vivian's messages and tossed them into the wastebasket. She checked her gun to make sure the safety was on.

Intent on resting for a few minutes, Sarah flopped down on the bed, arms spread, gun by the pillow, and moaned. She couldn't find the strength to turn off the lamp by the bed. Her eyes barely functioned when she looked at the alarm clock. It read 7:32 p.m. She had over two and a half hours until she needed to go for a drink, according to her sister.

A dilemma for another time, Sarah thought as she drifted off to sleep.

107

ELSON PULLED INTO the motel parking lot around ten in the evening. He checked that his gun and hunting knife were secure and got out of his car. The parking lot was full of pickup trucks, Saturns, an old Volvo, and a beat-up Chrysler, but no black Tahoe.

It had to be here. Armond said it would be.

Elson had parked in the far corner by the back entrance.

He circled the motel and found the Tahoe in back. He checked that the doors were secure and walked around to the rear. Sure that no one was watching, he dropped to the ground and slithered under the chassis. From inside his breast pocket he pulled out a small explosive device. He set the timer for 10:18 p.m.

That would give him enough time to deal with the clerk, find Sarah, execute her, and leave. With the SUV in ruins, the police would have little to go on.

He sauntered away from the vehicle as if he didn't have a care in the world.

In the lobby, Elson rang the silver bell on the counter.

A young man walked out from the back office.

"How can I help you?" he asked.

"Actually, I'm looking for my sister. We're supposed to meet here. She would've checked in about two to three hours ago. Younger than me, about twenty-two years old. Her name is Sarah Roberts."

The clerk took a step back. He looked down at the registry, then stared at Elson.

"I'm sorry, but I can't give out that kind of information. That's confidential." He tapped his fingers on the counter. "Although, come to think of it, I don't remember anyone fitting that description."

Elson glanced at the door. It had a thumb lock. "Okay, maybe I'll just call her on her cell phone to see where she is."

Elson stepped away from the counter. When he got to the door, he
flicked the lock into place. He pulled out his Glock and turned back to

the clerk. He could tell the idiot had leaned over to hit some kind of alarm under the counter.

With the Glock held firm at his side, he walked up to and around the counter. The clerk backed against the wall.

"I'm sorry." The clerk looked ready to cry. "I said I can't—"

"Tell me what room she's in."

The gun found its way to the clerk's chin. His eyes widened.

"Okay, okay, I put her in room 104. She's in room 104. Just take it easy."

Elson lowered the gun and stepped back. "That wasn't too hard, now was it?" He glanced under the counter, where he saw a panic button. "You pushed this?"

The clerk started to shake. "She said you beat her up."

"She says a lot, doesn't she?" Elson moved in quick. The gun dropped into his shoulder holster as his other hand yanked the knife out in a fluid motion. The blade opened slash marks on the clerk's arms. Four quick gashes would render the clerk less effective for the time it would take to deal with Sarah.

The clerk dropped to the floor on his back, writhing in pain. Elson watched him for a moment, then headed for the door.

He looked at his watch. Ten fifteen p.m. He had three minutes left before the bomb detonated.

He got to the door, unlocked it, and jogged down the line of rooms until he hit the door for 104. There wasn't any time left for subtlety.

With a quick pull on the weapon, he shot two bullets into the door handle and stepped back. He reholstered the weapon and lunged forward, his right foot connecting with the door an inch from the splintered handle.

After a crack of protest, the motel room door burst open. Elson ran in and hit the lights.

The room was empty.

There's no way that little punk lied to me.

Elson ran to the back of the room, but the bathroom was empty, too.

He bolted from the room and raced back to the lobby. No doubt someone would've heard the shots. The Tahoe was going to blow up any second, and now the lobby door was locked.

Frustrated at how fast this job was going wrong, Elson used another bullet to shoot out the door's glass. It crashed down in a cascade.

He reached in and, mindful not to touch any shards of glass, unlocked the thumb bolt.

Swinging the door open, he ran to the counter.

The clerk was nowhere in sight, but there was the registry. He scanned the names and saw that a notation was made by Sarah's name along with room 104. The same little pen mark was ticked by room 107, but there was no name attached.

As he passed room 104's open door, a huge blast shook the night. Glass shattered and a woman screamed somewhere.

He reached room 107 and pulled out his Glock. He would make it quick and then get the hell out.

The cops wouldn't be more than a few minutes away by now.

108

A LOUD NOISE jolted her out of a heavy sleep. Sarah leaned up on the bed, rubbed her eyes, and looked at the alarm clock: 10:19 p.m.

She sat up and swung her legs over the side of the bed. Vivian said to go for a drink at 10:18 p.m., and now, a minute later, she was awakened by something outside. Sarah grabbed her gun, jumped from the bed, and ran for the bathroom.

She was sure the explosion came from the back. The bathroom window now had a crack in it. She stood on the edge of the tub, unlocked the window, and slid it open carefully.

Her Tahoe was completely engulfed in flames.

They had found her.

She hopped off the edge of the tub, turned on the bathroom light to make it look like she was using it, splashed water in her face, and stepped back into the motel room, her gun ready. The lamp cast an ominous feel on an area that once felt safe but now had become another prison. She was trapped, without any idea of what was going on outside.

Two shots were fired outside her door. She saw the doorknob bend and parts of it shatter.

Shit.

The door buckled.

How the fuck did they find me so fast?

The chair she had placed under the door handle held up. Hopefully it would give her enough time. Sarah fixed the wrinkles in the bed to make it look untouched. Next, she squeezed herself underneath the desk to hide in the recessed area, her gun resting on top of her knees to steady her aim.

Another kick and still the motel room door held.

She breathed in and out as quietly as she could to calm her waking nerves.

Seconds later, the door burst open. She heard a distant siren, prob-ably heading their way.

"I see you," the intruder said. "Come on out."

She considered it, but fought the urge. He had to be bluffing. He couldn't see her.

She moved the gun on an angle to make sure the safety was off. Funny how life hung in the balance on the smallest deeds.

"I said come out!" he shouted.

He moved deeper into the room. She saw a cowboy boot first, then a pant leg.

He probably assumed she was in the bathroom, as she had hoped he would. Could she crawl out of her hiding spot and leave while his back was turned? She wanted to avoid killing him, if possible. Had she listened to Vivian, the man standing in her room wouldn't be a risk. She'd be long gone.

Still, he had broken into her room to do her harm. Who else had he killed? Who would be next? If left alive, would he try to kill Sarah again tomorrow or the day after?

He stood right in front of her now. The sirens grew louder. There wasn't much time left. He had to know that.

He stepped away and in a crouched position brought his gun around on the empty bathroom. He would probably check the open window.

As he moved into the bathroom she rolled out of hiding and hur-ried to the wall by the bed. In her rush to get into position she almost tripped on the bedspread sticking out by the corner of the mattress. She caught herself from falling at the last second and stopped short of the wall.

He came out of the bathroom, put his weapon away, and started for the door. With the precision she'd learned over many months at the firing range, she aimed for the back of his moving right knee and squeezed the trigger gently.

As soon as her weapon spit out a bullet, the man shouted and fell to the motel room floor. In mid-fall, he was already reaching for his weapon. She aimed for his gun arm and fired. The carpet beside him puffed up where the bullet hit.

She had missed.

His weapon was out now. She fired again, and missed. Her damn nerves.

She jumped over the edge of the bed and closed the five-foot gap to stand over him, firing into his right arm before his weapon was properly aimed.

He screamed as his gun flipped out of his hand.

Tires screeched to a stop outside as police cars pulled up to the lobby of the motel.

There was no fear on his face, only pain mixed with anger.

With the grace of an expert, Sarah brought her weapon down in line with his other knee and said, "Give me your car keys or you will never walk again."

"Fuck you," he said, and turned from her to spit on the carpet.

She fired point-blank into the top of his other kneecap, on an angle that went down and into the femur. She did this with a sense of peace, knowing that, in the end, she had saved lives by making this man a cripple.

She shoved her gun in the back of her pants and bent to rummage in his pockets as he thrashed around on the floor. She pulled out the keys and was surprised at the fight left in him.

His only good limb, the left arm, had come up with some kind of hunting knife. The lazy jab missed by a foot. She got up with one swift movement and kicked the knife out of his hand.

She ran to the door and looked out. Three cruisers sat in front of the office. Maybe he had hurt or killed the clerk. She hoped the clerk wasn't dead, but it explained why the cops weren't going door-to-door yet.

She left the room and started toward the back of the motel. The car keys had no markings on them, but they had a fob.

She pushed the button to unlock it, and at the back corner, beside the exit ramp, a Nissan Altima's lights flicked on.

In under two minutes Sarah was heading south toward Fredonia.

109

WHAT A MESS. It sure made the cops look inept. They always seemed to be doing cleanup.

His cell phone rang.

"Hello. Parkman here."

"I'm coming down there to get a handle on everything."

"Hanover, Sarah's gone. The Tahoe is destroyed, and some hit man that was sent after Sarah is undergoing emergency surgery at a hospital in Salt Lake City. The motel clerk is being treated for knife wounds to his arms. All he said was that Sarah was on the run from an abusive boyfriend."

"I'm coming anyway. Gather anything you can from the other motel guests. Did they see Sarah? Did they witness—"

"I know how to do my job, Hanover. I'll find out whatever I can before you get here."

Parkman stepped out of room 107 and stared up at the darkened sky.

Hanover paused. "Is there something you haven't told me, Parkman?"

"I'm pissed off. I'm sick and tired of showing up after the fact. Sarah is out there alone, and all we're doing is making a pathetic attempt to follow? What exactly are we doing?"

"Our jobs," Hanover said. "That's what the police do. Come on, Parkman, you know how this works. Just . . ." She paused.

"Just what?"

"Just don't do anything until I get there. Ask around and see what you can find out."

"Hanover, it's almost three in the morning. This all went down over four hours ago. Everyone's asleep."

"I'm on my way," she said, and disconnected.

Parkman dropped his phone back in his breast pocket and looked toward the front desk. One cruiser was still parked out front. He turned back and stared at room 107.

"What happened here?" he said out loud. "Where have you gone?"

He walked the scene out again and stood where Sarah would have as she shot one more bullet into the guy's leg from the front.

Down on bended knee, Parkman scanned the area beside the bed but couldn't tell if Sarah had crouched there. Wouldn't the intruder have seen her before he got to the bathroom? Maybe she hadn't hidden beside the bed. Maybe she'd been under the desk.

He hobbled over on his knees, knowing Sarah was a lot smaller than he was.

It would work. She could fit in there and stay relatively hidden.

He crawled back out and pulled the worn toothpick from his mouth. When he turned to throw it in the garbage he saw a crumpled-up piece of paper in the can.

Why didn't he think to look in the wastebasket before? He grabbed the paper and instantly recognized Sarah's handwriting.

Fredonia, Arizona.

10:18 p.m., get a drink.

"That's it," he said aloud, clutching the paper tight.

He needed to find her and sort everything out before anyone else got to her. Now he knew he would find her in Fredonia, Arizona.

He dialed Hanover. Then, before the first ring, he ended the call.

This time it'll be on my terms.

Hanover could get to the motel and ask the tenants all the questions she wanted. She and her *special agents* could do the cleanup.

Parkman was going after Sarah. He wouldn't answer his phone. Let them think his battery had died.

He stepped outside and realized he was still holding the toothpick in his hand. He flipped his wrist and tossed it to the ground.

Minutes later he was in his cruiser heading toward Fredonia, a new toothpick swishing back and forth, calming his nerves.

110

SARAH PULLED OVER at a truck stop on the outskirts of Fredonia around four in the morning and slept for two hours. She woke feeling like she could sleep another full day.

The bruise on her face had turned a jaundiced yellow. Luckily, the bullet wounds were showing no signs of infection.

She eased out of the cramped driver's seat and stood beside the car to stretch. Sometimes a good stretch wasn't enough. Her injured arm felt stiffer. She shut the car door and walked over to the all-night truck stop. Inside, two men were eating breakfast and another was buying a coffee to go.

After using the toilet, she washed her face with cold water. Voices from the restaurant drifted in through the bathroom door. She stepped out and almost walked right into a state trooper.

"Excuse me, I'm sorry," she said, and moved around him, careful to keep her head down in case her picture had been circulated.

"Ma'am?"

Sarah stopped.

"Ma'am, are you okay? Let me look at your face."

Sarah lifted her head and looked into the intense blue eyes of a cop in his mid-twenties.

"I'm fine. Basketball accident. My girlfriends and I get a little rough during twenty-one."

He stared at her a moment longer. "Are you sure?"

Sarah nodded and turned to leave. He let her go.

The cop would be perfect. She was ready to change cars, and as she had learned four years ago, a cop car was ideal for what she had in mind.

She climbed into the driver's seat of the Nissan and waited for the cop to return to his car.

The Nissan had a pad of paper on the dash with handwriting on it. When she grabbed it she realized why her arm was so cramped. She must have written the new note when asleep. There were three pages of text.

Why had Vivian waited this long to explain things to her?

As she read, she kept glancing up to make sure she didn't miss the cop.

Alex Stuart wasn't Armond Stuart's son, the note said. They were brothers. This had nothing to do with Armond's talk of voodoo and everything to do with human smuggling. It always had been, only on a smaller scale years ago. She learned that Jack Tate, as she suspected, was Armond. All that time, she had the leader of a smuggling ring beside her.

She checked the mirrors. The state trooper was still inside.

She continued on with the notes. All that was left was an address, and a warning that it was meant for the police. Sarah was supposed to let them deal with Armond. He had the victims in some kind of fundamentalist Mormon compound, where he was hiding out with a few of his mercenaries. Vivian called it *FLDS*.

"I'm just supposed to hand this information over to the police, after all I've gone through?" she asked the empty car. "Then why do this at all? Vivian, I want an answer. Why?"

Sarah hit the passenger seat beside her with the back of her hand.

"Is it not enough that I almost died? They kidnapped our parents. This is not some kind of joke. I will not just hand this over to the police. I have the address. I'm going to break down the compound's doors and make them pay for what they did. Do you hear me?"

She caught a glimpse of her tear-streaked face in the mirror. The hurt and the anger had finally overwhelmed her. It was okay to break down. She had a right to be pissed off.

"I listen to your messages because I want to help others. But when you intentionally lead me into harm's way, I need to know why or I won't be able to trust you. Do you hear me?" Sarah raised a fist. "I will finish this on my own. Or was that your plan? If this kills me, then we'll be together. Is that what you want?" She stopped and looked down at the written warning: *Attempt on your own at great personal risk. Don't do it. Chances of survival are slim.* "We'll see about that."

Sarah tossed the papers on the passenger seat and wiped her face. She shuddered and took a deep breath to collect herself.

When she looked in the mirror, the cruiser was gone.

She started the Nissan and squealed out to the highway.

She had no way of knowing which way he went. She chose south. The state trooper was from Arizona. He'd be patrolling the highway and not heading toward Utah.

Passing car after car, Sarah chased the trooper. Ten minutes later she saw him ahead and whispered a soft thank-you.

Traffic was sparse. She would wait until the road was visibly clear before she made her move.

A sign said they were entering the Kaibab National Forest area. Another sign said that a sharp right turn was coming up and to slow down.

She looked in her mirror. The road was clear behind her. The corner coming up had small shrubs that would aid in cover, as the land in this area seemed pretty flat and barren.

She gunned the Nissan as hard as she could. In seconds, she was gaining on the trooper. She swung out and passed the cruiser doing ninety. To handle the turn she had to drop her speed fast. With a gentle hand, she pulled back into her lane and hit the brakes as she maneuvered through the beginning of the turn, waiting for the right moment.

The police siren came on behind her. His lights flashed.

He was taking her bait. All she needed now was the right spot.

Then she saw it. The shoulder led into a grassy area that was a foot lower than the road. Behind that were small trees and shrubs.

Sarah jerked the car off Highway 89 and hit the grass. She aimed for the shrubs, careful to drive the Nissan deep enough that it wouldn't be spotted from the highway. The trooper didn't follow with his car, giving her time to prepare.

The Nissan slid to a stop in front of a rock formation, bumping it softly. She killed the engine and turned around. With her gun in hand, Sarah lowered the window and hopped out of the car. She ducked into the brush and waited, hidden from view.

It didn't take long. The siren turned off but not the cruiser's engine. It was so quiet out here she even heard his dispatcher talking through the open window of the cruiser. There was no line of sight, but she

knew he would come and have a look. The only question was how long
before backup arrived.

Seconds ticked by.

Then, from the corner of her eye, she saw the trooper approaching.
He moved slowly, until he was three feet away. Two feet.

Sarah stepped from cover as he passed her.

"Don't," she said as he dropped his hand to the butt of his weapon
and crouched in a spin. "Just don't. Easy now. Raise those hands."

He did as instructed. The holster unclicked without trouble,
and Sarah lifted his gun out while placing her own against the side
of his neck.

"Easy, take it easy. You can walk away from this."

"You may not, missus. I'm a state trooper. You're in a lot of trouble."

"If you only knew," she said as she shoved his gun into the back of her
pants. She stepped around to face him. "Take off your jacket, slowly. No
sudden moves. I'm jittery and this gun could go off by accident."

The cop removed his jacket cautiously. Small beads of sweat formed
on his forehead. "You're that girl from the truck stop. Clearly something has happened to you. Let me help."

"You are helping. Toss the jacket away and remove your handcuffs.
Then put them on your wrists in the front."

He threw his jacket aside and paused. "Are you sure about this? Put
the gun down and I'll tell them you had an accident."

"I told you, you are helping. Now, the cuffs."

He shook his head. "I won't cuff myself. You're going to have to
do it."

Sarah dropped her weapon a few inches and fired. The report was
deafening in the early morning silence. The young officer crouched
down with both hands up.

"Okay, okay, don't shoot. I'll do it, I'll do it."

The trooper cuffed himself and stood back up to his full height of
six feet. He wasn't hard to look at, that was for sure.

"Now what?" he asked.

Sarah reached into her pocket and pulled out the Nissan's key fob.
She popped the lid. Never taking her eyes off the trooper, she lifted
the trunk lid.

"Get in."

"Are you serious? It's going to get very hot later today. I could die."

"I will tell someone you're here, but not for a few hours. In the meantime, I parked it among these little trees. The car will be in the shade until at least late afternoon. Now get in or I'll have to shoot you and drag you in."

A large vehicle passed on the highway, going slowly through the long curve in the road. The officer hesitated.

"Get in," Sarah shouted. "Now!"

He did as he was told.

"Scrunch down."

He lowered his head and Sarah brought the gun up. She blew out holes in the lid of the trunk. Then she tossed the empty gun into the trunk with the cop and pulled his revolver out of the back of her pants.

"What did you do that for?" he asked.

"I know what it's like, being in a trunk for a long period of time. I gave you breathing holes for when it gets a bit nasty."

Before shutting the lid, she snatched the pepper spray off his belt loop.

"Thanks."

Sarah shut the lid and tossed the car keys into the bush. She picked his jacket up off the ground, put it on, and ran out to the waiting cruiser.

The engine was still running as the dispatcher asked for an update. Another truck came up from behind, slowing to take the corner. Sarah ducked down and waited until it passed.

When it was gone, she turned on the lights and siren and did a U-turn on Highway 89, heading back toward Fredonia. Stealing a police car got you where you wanted to go, and fast.

A little more preparation and she'd be ready to enter the FLDS compound.

111

PARKMAN WAS STILL an hour out of Fredonia, and he was lost. He had no idea where Sarah was going or what she planned to do. All he had was a handwritten note.

He called up his own department and was put through to Winnfield.

"Yup," Winnfield answered.

"It's Parkman. I need your help."

"My help." Winnfield yawned. "Why? You're still working with the FBI, aren't you?"

"Was I ever really working *with* them?"

"What can I do for you?"

"I'm about to enter a town called Fredonia in the next forty-five minutes or so. It's in northern Arizona—"

"What are you doing way down there?"

"Never mind that. I need you to find out what police calls they've had in the last three to four hours. I'm looking for something strange, not the usual domestic issues. I'm trying to find Sarah Roberts. Can you do that for me?"

"I might have to go upstairs for this."

"Don't. I need you to do this without anyone knowing. Make up some bogus reason and get the list of calls. There shouldn't be too many. It's only just after seven in the morning. Winnfield, I'm counting on you. Tell me you got this."

"I'll do it, but you'll owe me."

"Call me as soon as you have something."

Parkman drove on. It took twenty minutes to hear back. In that time, he had ground through two toothpicks. He popped a third in his mouth and answered the phone.

"What do you have?"

"Before I tell you, you should know the dispatcher down there gave me the runaround when I called. I had to tell her you were there working for the FBI. I dropped Hanover's name. Then the woman hung up on me. I called back and on the third try she answered the phone saying she had to verify my story."

"Shit. Did you get anything?" Parkman asked as he heard the other line beep in his ear.

"There were two calls around Fredonia itself. Nothing stood out. A rig had blown a tire about two miles north of the city. The other call was a couple of kids sleeping off too much booze. That was it."

"Damn." He smacked the steering wheel.

He glanced at the papers beside him. "Are you sure there was nothing else?"

"Well, there was a call that came in from a state trooper who was pulling a car over about forty to fifty miles south of Fredonia. Something about a car losing control. But that couldn't be Sarah."

He had nothing else to go on. In his gut, something was telling him to play this one out.

"Anything else from that trooper?"

"Let me look." Winnfield paused. Parkman heard him tapping a pen. "Lone female driver. Saw her at the truck stop near Fredonia. Bruised face. Passed the cop going eighty. Lost control on the big curve on Highway 89 as she entered Kaibab National Forest area."

"Winnfield, what part of *locate Sarah Roberts* didn't register for you? Lone female driver? Bruised face?"

"Yeah, but you said—"

"Forget it. Dump the information you have. I'm going to call Hanover now and let her know. I'll see you when this is over."

Fredonia was at least fifteen minutes away, and then he had forty more miles to go on the south side of town. He hit the gas and turned on the dash light. He decided to wait on calling Hanover. After he checked on this lead, he would call her and explain.

Or he would apologize, get brought up on obstruction charges, and lose his job.

112

SARAH REACHED SIX Mile Road and turned. She drove slowly to avoid kicking up dust.

A rudimentary plan had formed in her mind. But the execution had to be precise.

Within ten miles she passed a driveway with a locked iron gate. Beyond the gate was a long driveway, heading at least half a mile in. Without slowing, Sarah continued down Six Mile Road for another minute, until she found an old landfill company that had closed. The building at the back of the lot had boarded-up windows. A chain-link fence surrounded the parking area with a "No Trespassing" sign.

She pulled in and stopped. She recalled a Mormon compound in Texas had been invaded by the FBI in 2008. They had removed over four hundred children of polygamist families.

Maybe that was why this compound was such a good cover for human trafficking. It allowed Armond to manage his prisoners without the scrutiny of outsiders.

Beside her on the passenger seat was the cop's iPhone. He'd left it plugged into the car charger when he got out to investigate her car. Accessing the recording feature, she pressed the button, let three minutes pass, and then recorded her message.

After that, she gathered everything she would need, placed the iPhone beside her, and turned the cruiser around to start heading back toward the compound.

When she was about thirty feet from the iron gate she hit the gas and aimed for the center. The black bars over the grill of the cruiser smacked the gate hard enough to break it open. The vehicle swerved left and then right before she got the car under control and sped down the long driveway.

Their defenses would be low due to the early hour. Hopefully they weren't so unwelcoming that they'd open fire on a police car.

The guard shack came into view. There was nowhere to turn. She would have to continue forward, aimed directly at the shack.

A large white building came into view off to her right. It had to be their temple. Smaller structures were scattered around. As she got closer to the guard shack she saw those smaller structures were more like little schoolhouses.

The cruiser caught the attention of two women in long blue dresses, their hair in buns. It also caught the attention of the man stepping out of the guard shack.

Sarah grabbed the state trooper's hat, placed it on her head, and ducked down as low as she could in the driver's seat.

He waved his arms to get her attention, but let her pass.

In the rearview mirror, Sarah watched him run into his shack, likely to alert someone.

She drove down the line of blue houses, watching for any sign of resistance. At the end of the row of houses, she turned the vehicle down another road that appeared to run along a fence line. It took mere seconds for Sarah to exit the cruiser, dump everything she needed into the trooper's hat, put the car in gear, and shut the door.

The cruiser moved away slowly. It went straight for at least twenty feet, then started to angle off the road. Sarah clutched the hat and ran for the nearest house.

Just before reaching the edge of the building and cover, Sarah looked down the stretch of road and saw no one in pursuit. Other than the guard and the two women at the entrance, the place looked deserted.

As she ran in the open door of the first building, she saw a couple of chairs and beds lining one wall. A door at the back led to another room. Sarah pulled the cop's gun out in case she needed it. The back room was also empty, but the closet was full of blue dresses.

In a frantic rush, Sarah found a dress that would fit, threw it on, and ran to the bathroom to fix her hair. One peek out the window told her no one was outside yet. It wouldn't be long. The guard had to be rallying help.

Using pins, she tried to mimic the loose bun she'd seen on the two women. After a moment, she looked at herself in the mirror and nodded. It wouldn't pass close scrutiny, but it would get her to where she needed to go.

Now she had to find a way to conceal the gun.

Out in the main room she found a wicker basket. She dropped the gun in the bottom and covered it with a shawl, along with the pepper spray.

Before leaving the building, she took a sidelong look out the window. The guard from the shack was jogging up the road, accompanied by two other men. They were coming fast. Sarah waited until they passed the building and watched all three of them start down the road toward the fence where the cruiser had come to a stop.

She gently opened the window in front of her. Then she ran to every other window in the small building and opened them, too. Back at the front, Sarah saw the three men standing by the cruiser. The rest of the street was empty.

She set the cop's bullhorn on a little table by the front window and placed the iPhone behind it. With one last look outside, she accessed the iPhone's voice recorder and pressed "play" on the file she'd recorded. That gave her three minutes to run for the temple.

Basket in hand, Sarah left the building and walked as fast as she dared up the road toward the temple. She got to the end of the line of little houses before she encountered her first person. They passed each other with the barest of nods. Her rudimentary disguise worked. For now. They thought she was one of them.

The three minutes were up. Her voice boomed from the end house. It traveled through the crisp morning air.

"We have you surrounded. This is the FBI."

Listening to it from afar, she thought it sounded ridiculous.

A turn to the left took her down a narrow road. She stopped. People were streaming out the back of the main temple. Dozens and dozens of women were running for the road, heading for a smaller building that resembled an office complex.

Sarah turned into the nearest house, her basket swinging in her arms. Again, this residence was empty. She needed time to think. Why was everyone herding out of the temple? She stepped back out onto the porch. One of Armond's men, a large gun in hand, wearing a black leather jacket, ran toward her.

She hesitated, then ducked back inside. Easing out her weapon, she flipped off the safety. In a crouch, Sarah bent below the front window, peering out at the road.

Armond's man stopped in front of the house.

"Hello in there?" he shouted.

"Yes," Sarah called.

"We're gathering everyone in the basement opposite the temple. We think the police are attempting some kind of inspection."

"I'll be along in a minute," she replied.

Armond's man turned and ran down the road toward the cop car.

With her gun back in the basket and the shawl neatly in place, Sarah left the building and started up the road toward the temple. The women were still streaming out, now followed by dozens of small children.

When she got close, she saw another of Armond's men standing at the entrance to the office complex. If it hadn't been for the sun in her eyes, she would've seen him earlier. She felt like she was losing the element of surprise. These people were hired killers, and she was trying to liberate their captives. As much as she wanted to do this on her own, it was starting to feel overwhelming.

The guy at the door watched every face as the women and children entered the office building. She turned away from him and headed toward the temple. A couple of the women said things like "No, this way" and "To the basement," but Sarah only nodded and kept moving against the current.

Without looking, she almost bumped into the back of a third man in a black leather jacket.

She made to walk past him, but he grabbed her arm.

"No, it's the other way. We need everyone to get to the—" He stopped.

A bullet from Sarah's gun went through his stomach. His grip tightened on her arm in a spasm and then he let go. Slowly, he slipped down the wall, eyes wide.

A couple of women ran up and wailed at the man bleeding on the floor as his body went into seizures.

"Get a doctor," Sarah said. "This man needs help."

She followed them to the temple doors and then shut them behind her. She set her basket down and pulled two chairs over to try to hold the doors shut.

When she picked up her basket and turned around, another woman stood staring at her.

"We're a quiet people," the woman said. "Why would you do this in our temple?" Her eyes watered.

"These men have been kidnapping young girls and using them as sex slaves. They're hiding them here, in your compound. I've come to take them home."

"You want to remove our children? Is that what you want?"

"No, not your children—"

The woman cut her off. "We are a peaceful people." She shook her head.

"Yeah, well, so am I. You may be able to avoid the real world in your compound, but when they brought their victims here, then it became my problem."

A high-pitched squeal came from somewhere above.

"I thought everyone was evacuated," Sarah said.

"Everyone was." A stunned look crossed the woman's face.

"What's upstairs?" Sarah asked.

"Rooms."

"Rooms for what?"

"It's where the babies are baptized and new wives consummate their marriages."

"You might want to get to the basement like everyone else."

Sarah grabbed the gun from the basket and held it firmly in her right hand.

The woman didn't look back at Sarah. She pushed the chair away from the door, and then she was gone.

Sarah started for the stairs and climbed them as quietly as she could.

At the top, a small hallway led to three closed doors. She paused and looked back down into the temple below, allowing herself a moment to catch her breath. She stayed close to the wall and moved beside the first door to listen. Hearing nothing, she moved to the next door. A soft thump told her someone was behind door number three.

She knew she had to get their attention, and fast.

With one hard shoulder bump and a quick twist of the door handle, she knocked the door open. It flew around so hard that it hit the other wall with a bang.

Sarah jumped into the room. As soon as she crossed the threshold, a wooden club dropped down onto her right wrist, snapping it with a loud crack. The gun flew from her grip. Her wrist was instantly on fire. She found herself on her knees, leaning into the doorframe, clutching at it.

She had to blink back tears to see the five teenage girls staring back at her. With forlorn eyes, they studied the one person who might have helped them leave this nightmare behind. But she was just a beat-up girl with her own nightmares, wounded now to the point of immobility.

Sarah held her wrist, rocking back and forth as the swelling set in.

Jack Tate—or Armond Stuart, as she had come to know him—stepped out from behind the door, grinning.

"Glad you could join us. Now I finally get to kill you and end this little distraction."

113

THE NISSAN HADN'T been hard to find. Parkman easily saw the tire treads careening into the shrubs. He pulled over and got out. The sun was high now, the heat rising with it. By the time he got off the shoulder, his shirt was pasted to his back. ·

The rear of the Nissan came into view. He pulled out his piece and approached with caution.

"Hello? Anybody there?"

The voice came from the Nissan. What looked like two bullet holes were in the trunk's lid. A quick sweep of the area confirmed no one was waiting to ambush him.

"This is the police. Identify yourself," Parkman said.

"I'm Andre Wilson, an Arizona state trooper," came a muffled voice from inside the trunk. "Some girl got the jump on me. She tricked me and stuffed me in the trunk."

Sarah Roberts—that's my girl.

"Did this girl have a bruise on her cheek?"

"Yes, yes. Now get me out of here."

Parkman holstered his weapon. "Okay, hold on. If the car is unlocked, I'll pop the trunk."

He walked around and opened the driver's side door. Beside the driver's seat, he flipped the trunk button. Scattered papers were strewn across the passenger seat. Parkman picked them up and pocketed them.

He walked around to the back and saw the trooper crawling out, his hands cuffed in front.

"You doing okay?" Parkman asked. "How long were you in there?"

The trooper got to the ground and stood. "I don't know, probably an hour and a half, maybe two hours. Hard to tell. Where are you from?"

Parkman had grabbed his cuff keys and began working on releasing the trooper's wrists. "Long way from here. I've been trailing that girl for hundreds of miles. Did she say anything about where she was going?"

Andre shook his head. "No, nothing. I should have seen it coming. She's good, but it pisses me off that she got the jump on me."

Parkman nodded. The cuffs flipped open. "Trust me, she pisses off a lot of people. Let me call this in and get one of your colleagues to pick you up."

Andre was already walking away from him, but he was heading toward the trees, away from the highway. "Go ahead, call it in. I gotta take a piss. Didn't want to soil my uniform."

Parkman turned around and dialed Hanover while skimming the papers. By the time Hanover answered, he knew what needed to be done.

"Where the hell are you?"

"Fredonia, Arizona."

"Fredonia? Why is she in Fredonia?"

"Look, how fast can you get down here?"

"Why?" Hanover asked.

"Something big is going down on Six Mile Road. I don't know what yet, but I can tell you, we need to be there."

Andre walked up beside him. "What's this I hear about Six Mile Road?"

"Hanover, hold on a sec." Parkman lowered the phone. He lifted the paper up. "Do you know this address?"

"Sure, it's a huge fundamentalist Mormon compound. Super-secure facility."

Parkman lifted a finger to get Andre to wait.

"Hanover, I think Sarah's in trouble. She stole a police car and will probably use it to break into a gated Mormon compound."

"Why would she do that?"

"That's where the perps have taken their captives." He motioned for Andre to follow and started for the car. "I'm afraid she may be in over her head. How long before you can get here?"

"I have a chopper. It shouldn't be more than an hour."

Parkman clicked off the call and jumped in his car. Andre got in the other side.

"Direct me to this compound," Parkman said. "We need to get there quick." He performed a U-turn, hit the lights, and dropped the accelerator.

"We can't just walk in," Andre said. "That's one of the most heavily guarded compounds in the area. Remember what happened in Texas back in 2008?"

"I have a feeling the front gate will be wide open."

114

"GET OVER THERE with the others where I can see you," Armond said.

Sarah stumbled across to sit with the other girls against the wall. The raw edge of the pain had abated. She had to stay focused.

"I've waited years for this," Armond said as he picked up her weapon and put it in his waistband. He'd closed the door and called to tell someone to let him know when they had the all clear. The all clear would come shortly, because Sarah was alone. When Armond's associates showed up, it would all be over.

"The girl's body was planted by my house to throw the Feds off," Armond said. "I was supposed to be a hero. They've been tracking me for too long. But fuck if they didn't screw that up."

He walked to the door and placed an ear against it. Then he turned back to her. "Ever since you killed Alex, I have wanted my revenge. But you've been on the move. And I have a business to run." He gestured at the girls sitting alongside her, several of them crying.

"It was all planned." He paced in front of her. "I would let myself into your parents' house, lure you over, and kill them off in front of you."

He glared at her. She didn't flinch.

"Then I would take my time with you. But you fucked it all up. If you hadn't shown up at my house that night, you and your parents would be dead. How did you know to be there at that precise moment?"

Sarah drew a sharp breath. Her sister had saved her life by sending her into this madness. Sarah had been spared because she wasn't taken by surprise at her parents' house.

"It doesn't matter now," Armond continued. "You walked straight into my hands."

"Why involve . . . my parents?" Sarah asked, the pain in her wrist lessening as the swelling came on.

"I wanted to hurt you. When you escaped, I traded them for Sam so I could stay on top of police efforts."

"I will kill you before this is done," Sarah said.

Armond stepped back.

"That's a tall order for a little girl with a broken wrist and no *fucking gun!*"

"The police are on their way. You're through, Armond. Now, give me your gun so I can make sure you never see the inside of a prison cell."

Armond laughed. "You are some piece of work. I should shoot you right now."

"You know that if the police are on their way, you need me as a bargaining chip."

"No." Armond waved the weapon in the air. "I've got these beauties for negotiations. I *have* to kill you. You murdered my brother."

He aimed at Sarah. The girls shifted away from her.

Sarah turned away and, using her good hand, balanced herself to her feet. When she turned back around, the gun was level with her forehead from five feet away.

Armond's cell phone rang. Without missing a beat, he answered it. A moment later he lowered his weapon.

"You have won a five-minute reprieve. Chatter on the scanner has a possible police presence on the way. Don't move."

Armond backed up to the door, then stepped into the hallway.

She took a deep breath and leaned into the wall to collect herself.

Maybe someone found the Nissan with the cop in the trunk. Vivian's note was on the seat, and would lead them here. But they would certainly not come armed and ready to attack a compound. She still needed to do this on her own.

She turned to the girls. "It's okay. This is almost over."

Footsteps pounded up the hall. It was the man who told her to head to the basement.

"Okay, girls," he said. "Everyone up. You're leaving with Armond. Everyone except Sarah."

The girls got up and filed out of the room, some crying. The last girl at the door turned and said, "My name is Jennifer. I just wanted you to know."

"How sweet," Armond said, and pushed the girl out. "Sarah, my friend here is going to make you uncomfortable for five minutes, until I return. Please enjoy his company." Armond turned to his man. "Watch yourself with this one. She's a tough bitch."

"I didn't survive Desert Storm to be taken out by this tiny bitch," the guy said, looking Sarah up and down.

The door shut hard, leaving them alone.

He stepped close with surprising speed, and elbowed her in the face. The blow knocked her back into the wall, where she slid to the floor.

Blackness hovered around her eyes. She couldn't pass out. Not now.

The guy removed his jacket. He pulled his arms out of the shoulder holster. "I understand your family knows Armond intimately."

What did that mean?

He was removing his shirt now. Blood seeped out of her mouth.

"Did you know that these crazy fundamentalists consummate their marriages to young girls up here? It was a room just like this where Armond raped your sister almost twenty years ago."

A fire raged inside her. It was a hatred so deep that no pain could subdue it. Sarah reached up to the back of her neck and pulled out a small clump of hair.

"Hey, what're you doing? That's fucking gross." He stopped undressing.

Her scalp ached. Sarah felt a power and strength like never before. She grabbed another patch and ripped it out. The pain felt sweet, delicious. It all came rushing back. On her third pull, she saw the guy's face distort.

"You are seriously *fucked*," he said.

She leaned hard against the wall and pushed herself up. "I haven't survived everything *I've* lived through to be taken down by a piece of shit like you."

"You're fucking crazy."

He moved toward her. She reached back again, her head clear now. Under the pins that she'd placed carefully in her hair, she found the small pepper spray bottle. With her thumb, she unclasped the safety. He was right in front of her now, his arm pulling back to hit her.

Sarah tore at the bottle, ripped it out, and sprayed it directly into his eyes and mouth.

He staggered back, clutching at his eyes, his breathing coming in ragged pants. Sarah ducked down to escape the lingering spray, grabbed his gun out of the holster on the floor, and aimed it at his crotch. Then she flipped the safety and fired.

Blood shot out of his groin. He dropped to the floor, screaming.

Sarah reached the door just as Armond swung it open, his face dripping blood.

His weapon spat loud and clear.

The bullet caught her on the left side of her chest, knocking her off-balance and spinning her down to the floor.

115

THE SUN SHONE through the window across her body, warming her under the covers. She wondered where she was and how she got there. The pain had subsided to something bearable.

"Sarah, you're awake. Oh, baby, it's so good to have you back."

Her mother hugged her arm, no doubt afraid to touch her anywhere else. She sobbed, tears running along Sarah's forearm.

"Don't . . . cry, Mom."

She let go and wiped her eyes. "Tell me, Sarah. Talk to me. What happened this time? Why didn't Vivian help?"

"Vivian did. She . . . saved us . . . all. Without . . . her, we would . . . be dead."

"I don't understand," Amelia said, raising a hand to her mouth.

A man in a white coat entered the room.

"Glad to see you're awake. My name is Dr. Rosenberg. How are you feeling?"

"Not good. I hate . . . being shot."

"You have a sense of humor. It's a good sign."

"Can I . . . go home now?"

"Not yet. More bed rest for you, young lady. You've been through a lot." The doctor reached for a clipboard at the end of the bed.

"You can agree to let me go or I can walk out," Sarah said.

The doctor smiled. "They told me you were a feisty one. You were hit so hard in the face that the orbital bone around your eye is bruised. You've been shot several times. Lucky for you, two of the bullet wounds only needed stitches. The worst was the bullet that lodged just left of your heart. When you were brought in for surgery, we were able to remove it successfully. I'd say you're lucky to be alive."

Sarah nodded. "That's great. But I'm still . . . leaving."

The doctor smiled. "Tell me, do you get this strength from your mother or your father?"

"My sister."

"Your sister?"

"She died . . . when I was young. We still chat . . . once in a while."

The doctor, unsettled, stepped back.

"I'll leave you two alone to catch up," he said.

She felt a wave of tiredness. She didn't want to sleep. She needed to know what had happened.

"Tell me how I got . . . here."

"I can help with that," a man said. Parkman walked into view. "Sarah, you might want to try trusting me. One of these days you're going to get yourself killed."

He stepped closer. Sarah could smell his cologne.

"Tell me . . . "

Parkman grabbed a chair beside the bed, turned it backward, and straddled it. Her mother walked to the door, closed it, and then stood at the foot of the bed.

"When I got to the compound," Parkman started, "the gates were broken, so I drove right in, knowing you might be in trouble. I'd already called the FBI. You might remember Agent Jill Hanover? She had an FBI team en route. Within ten minutes of their security giving me the runaround, the FBI showed up and we saw Armond. He fired on us; we fired back."

"Is that . . . why I saw blood on his face?"

"Yes. But Sarah, you're a hero. Did you know that he had eighteen girls on-site? All of them were hospitalized and released. Two of them were runaways. I also want you to know that no formal charges have been filed against you."

"Where is . . . Armond Stuart now?"

Parkman glanced at her mother. Then he looked down at his shoes. "We don't know."

She moved her left shoulder on purpose. The pain was sharp, but it woke her enough to glare at him.

"What?" she asked, her teeth clenched.

Parkman returned her stare. "When we got upstairs, he'd disappeared. You were bleeding heavily. An FBI helicopter was outside. I had help carrying you downstairs and ordered the chopper to bring you here. By the time we rejoined the search, he had gotten away.

The temple has hidden crawl spaces behind the wall panels. We didn't know about them until it was too late."

IT WAS A warm, sunny day in late August when her father wheeled her out of the hospital, to the doctor's chagrin.

Now a month later, in her old bedroom, Sarah wrote furiously.

Vivian gave her instructions. Together they plotted. Within forty-eight hours she would be on Armond's trail again. The next time they met, she would shoot, twice. Once for Vivian and once for her.

As close as they could be, on earth and in heaven, Sarah and Vivian were hunting.

Armond Stuart was their prey.

PART THREE

PART THREE

116

SARAH ROBERTS STOOD on a dark street in Budapest's Eighth District and waited. This was her third night venturing out in search of a would-be attacker.

She'd been in Budapest for over four weeks, and her sister, Vivian, had been silent since her arrival. It was just after two in the morning. She hoped that the dress she wore would attract the wrong kind of attention. The knee-length dress was decorated with a pretty floral pattern. It was the shortest dress she would ever wear.

Sarah needed a gun.

A soft scuffling interrupted her thoughts. She leaned back against the wall and closed her eyes. She had come to Hungary at the behest of Vivian. She took the money from her father for the plane ticket. Her parents believed in her. And now, after a month, she was no further ahead, despite taking a crash course in Hungarian, which seemed to be the hardest language in the world to understand.

But that introduced another problem. She could be found here. In the States she could use motels that took cash. Here, she had to use her credit card and show her passport routinely. Anyone who wanted to find her easily could. She felt exposed. Maybe Armond was watching her right now.

Sarah stepped from the shadows and shuffled closer to the street. She had read online that the Eighth District was the most dangerous part of Budapest. She was sadly disappointed. Nothing had happened. Beggars lined the streets; prostitutes hung around in the underground areas that led to the subways. Their pimps stayed close, watching everything. Sarah saw it all, took it in, and waited.

She brought no weapons. Her hands were fast enough. She knew the pressure points on the human body. With her thumb alone she could have a man on the ground choking.

Yet no one challenged her.

A four-door Lada drove by. She watched its taillights disappear down the road.

She started the quiet walk back to the Best Western hotel, deflated. The stupid heels she wore kept getting caught on the cobblestones. She leaned against a wall to take them off. Barefoot, she continued walking the empty streets of Budapest.

Something had changed. Receiving messages from the Other Side was different now. There was no way for Sarah to know why. She would just have to wait. Eventually Vivian would make contact or Sarah would be forced to fly back to the States.

She turned a corner and slowed. Three men were whispering to one another on the opposite side of the street. They stood in the shadows under an awning.

She stayed on her side of the street as she continued walking and added some urgency to her step, as if she were afraid to be out at this hour. As she passed the three men, they turned as one and began walking parallel to her on their side of the street.

She kept up her pace, moving so fast now that she was almost doing a slow jog. Up ahead, cars drove by on a busier street. With the aid of a window to her right, Sarah saw the threesome crossing the street behind her. They were closing the distance, moving in.

Another man caught her eye. He leaned against a light post near the corner as she approached. He appeared to be watching her.

It was too dark to see his face. He wore a hat with a small brim. After a moment, he lowered his head and raised his right hand to tip the corner of his hat.

The three men were almost upon her.

"Hey, baby," one of the men yelled.

She glanced over her shoulder to look at them. They were ten feet back. Two of them were of a darker skin color.

Sarah spun around and continued to walk backward. The busier street was just over a block away now.

"Who speaks English?" she asked.

The white guy in the middle nodded. "What are you doing in a neighborhood like this, dressed like that? Are you for hire?"

"Fuck you."

"Oh, feisty. I like that."

She looked for the man in the hat, but he'd disappeared. Sarah hopped off the sidewalk, onto the street. The trio moved as one to close the gap. Now they were five feet from her.

"You wanna have some fun with us?" White Guy asked.

"Not tonight."

"You don't come down here dressed like that and expect us not to notice. You came looking for some action. We've seen you around a couple nights in a row."

Her outfit was not an open invitation. Any man who thought that way needed to learn respect. And it just so happened Sarah was a wonderful teacher.

"Hey, asshole," she said, her eyes narrowed. "No means no."

The man on the right smirked.

She still held her shoes in her left hand. Without looking down, she adjusted the heel of one of the shoes to angle outward and the strap of the other to dangle loosely off her last two fingers. The busy street got closer as she continued to walk backward toward it.

The leader snickered. He had to play the part for his boys. She'd seen this all too often.

Sarah stopped walking ten feet from the corner of the next block. There was no way they were packing guns. They weren't tough enough. It was time to end this.

She needed a shot of whiskey and her bed.

"Okay, here's what we'll do," Sarah said. "You three turn around and go back to wherever it is you crawled out of. I'm going to my hotel. That way, no one gets hurt."

The man smirked again.

A challenge.

Sarah stepped forward and raised her right foot into the guy's stomach. The blow caused him to double over. In that brief second, Sarah was already lifting her right elbow. His face came forward as he folded at the waist and made contact with her elbow, snapping his nose audibly. Then she extended her arm fully, using the back of her fist to smack the side of his head.

The smirking man fell to the ground, moaning through his broken nose. Blood oozed down his face as he rolled on the ground.

Sarah raised her left hand and presented the English guy with the heel.

"Step closer and this heel goes in your eye," she said.

He paused a second, then edged backward, his hands out in front of him.

"I warned him," Sarah said. "Now I'm warning you. Are any of you carrying weapons?" she asked.

English shook his head. She recognized a knowing look, like he suddenly realized who she was. After the Mormon compound was raided, Sarah's face had been plastered on the front pages of hundreds of newspapers across North America. Maybe parts of Europe covered the story as well.

The man on the ground had grown quieter.

Her mind registered the cell phone in his hand. In the distance, a police siren wailed. She guessed it was at least five to ten blocks away.

English whispered something to his friend.

"What was that?" Sarah asked.

He looked back at her. "I told him to help me hold you down if you try to run. The police are coming."

She scanned the immediate area. Where was the man from earlier?

"I won't run," Sarah said.

"You'll be arrested," English stated matter-of-factly. "You attacked our friend without provocation."

Without provocation? Yeah, right.

Sarah shrugged. "Maybe you're right. We'll have to wait and see."

The sirens were a block away now.

The rotating lights on top of the police cars bounced off the walls of the building up ahead.

It was time. Sarah raised her right hand and struck herself across the face, hard enough to leave a serious red mark.

"What the hell was that?" English asked.

Sarah shook her head. "I've been doing this too long."

The police car rounded the corner and slowed as soon as the driver saw them all in the middle of the road. The car stopped behind Sarah, and the driver stepped out.

He addressed everyone in Hungarian. Sarah waited until they were finished.

The guy on the ground moaned louder for show, rolling around and holding his face with his hands.

The officer turned to her and said in English, "What is your story?"

"I was out for a walk when I noticed these three following me." One of the men grunted. "I tried to get to this busier street." She turned and gestured behind her. "But they got really close. I don't have anything to defend myself with, Officer, so I removed my shoes. This guy"—she pointed at the man on the ground—"slapped me hard across the face."

"That's not true!" English shouted.

The officer turned toward him and spewed something in Hungarian. English dropped his head.

"Continue," the cop said to her.

"In my defense, I elbowed his face. I think I broke his nose. I'm sorry, Officer. I just want to go back to my hotel. I'm scared."

English spoke first. "All lies. We were following her, but that's because it's our job—"

"Hey!" the cop yelled. "Enough out of you."

Job? What the hell's he talking about?

"Look," the officer said. "You're going to have to come with me. I will take your official statement at the police station."

"I'm not going anywhere with you," Sarah said. "How do I know you aren't all in this together?"

The officer stared at her. "In what together?" he asked drily.

"He just said that it was his *job* to follow me."

English turned away to avoid her eyes.

"In America you may have crooked cops, but over here I am a member of the *rendőrség*, the Hungarian police. I do not consort with the likes of these men."

"Bullshit," Sarah whispered under her breath.

The cop looked surprised. "Okay, you're coming with me."

"Try it."

"Try what?" he asked.

She could tell her confidence was keeping him at bay. But how far did she want to push this? She was in a foreign country, after all.

The standoff didn't last a second. The officer stepped toward her. He reached for his belt. His chest and face were unprotected.

Without considering the consequences, she lunged forward and jammed her thumb into the base of the officer's throat, where the collarbones met.

He staggered back, clutched his throat, and made a gagging sound.

She dropped her shoes to the pavement, leaned in, and snapped the clip on the holster holding his gun. With deft hands, she had the weapon lifted out of its holster and in her palm in seconds.

"Stay back," Sarah said as she aimed her new weapon in their general direction. In the same movement she flipped off the safety and slid her index finger inside the trigger guard.

The officer was already breathing better. A wheezing sound emitted from his mouth as color returned to his face.

"If anyone tries to follow me I will take it as a personal threat," Sarah said. "Are we clear?"

The officer nodded. English glared at her.

"I asked, are we clear?"

She adjusted the gun to focus on English's face.

He waited another moment, then said, "Yes. No one will follow you. But I will be watching."

"No one *watches* me." She stepped forward into his space, placing the gun at his belt line. "Threaten me again and you will be eating your next meal with no teeth." She dropped her forehead hard. It connected with English's nose. He staggered back and grabbed his face.

"Threats piss me off. Don't forget that."

She didn't lower the gun until she was twenty feet from the men.

She had wanted a gun, but not from a police officer. A *Hungarian* police officer. She couldn't remain in Hungary now.

"Damn."

Nothing was going as planned. Who was the guy in the hat? Why had he been watching her?

Only the gun stashed in her waistband offered comfort on the walk back to her hotel.

117

SARAH FINISHED PACKING her single suitcase and set it by the door of her room.

She'd stayed at the Best Western since her arrival. A "Do Not Disturb" sign had remained on her door the entire time. Sarah made her own bed, and once every three days, grabbed new towels and disposed of the garbage with one of the maids working in the other rooms.

When she returned to the room last night she had been too tired to consider checking out and leaving right away. The police officer would report his weapon stolen. Forms would be filled out, paperwork filed, and her description sent out to other officers. By the time the day shift started, Sarah's face would be on all of their computer screens.

Her plan was to take a cab to the Budapest Ferenc Liszt International Airport, buy a ticket to somewhere in Canada, and board that flight. She'd decided on Canada to avoid the American authorities.

She entered the bathroom, balled her hair into a bun, and tucked it up under a pink baseball hat. No makeup, a baseball cap, and a stupid T-shirt that only a tourist would wear.

She checked the weapon nestled in the waistband of her jeans at the small of her back. The slight bulge was covered by a backpack she had slipped on. At the door, she checked the peephole. No one lingered close to the door. She stepped from the room, let the door close gently, and started for the elevator.

At the lobby, she headed toward the counter to hand in her key and have a taxi called.

Sarah scanned the large room as she waited behind an older couple checking out.

She was happy to be leaving. This had been her first trip to Europe, and it had come as a shock. She missed home. She missed the familiarity.

The couple ahead of her moved to the side. She glanced out the front doors of the hotel lobby. Two police cruisers were parked by the entrance.

"Just a sec." Sarah motioned to the clerk who had been waiting patiently for her to respond.

Sarah nudged her luggage up against the counter, grabbed a hotel brochure, and headed for the back couches. She would leave when the police cars were gone.

A man in an expensive suit sat reading a newspaper along one wall, but otherwise the lobby was empty. Even the clerk had stepped away from the counter.

Walking slowly toward the rear of the lobby, she removed the gun from her waistband and hid it behind her thigh. A burgundy couch sat facing the rear of the lobby. As she passed it, she quickly dropped down to one knee and shoved the weapon behind a cushion as far as it would go.

Getting back to her feet, Sarah continued to the rear of the lobby. After removing her backpack, she unzipped it and withdrew the novel she'd been reading. Seconds later, five men entered the lobby single file. Two wore suits, two were uniformed police, and one wore jeans and a T-shirt.

She recognized the man she called English immediately. Her stomach dropped, and a wave of adrenaline rushed through her.

Where are you, Vivian?

English scanned the lobby until he spotted her. He tapped the shoulder of one of the suited men and pointed. The group of five started her way.

She leaned forward and slowly placed the novel in her backpack.

"Sarah Roberts?" one of the suits asked.

"And you are?" she replied.

"My name is Imre Mátyás. I'm with the Budapest police. This man here"—he pointed to the man behind him, who was also wearing a suit—"is with our immigration office, and you can tell the other two are police officers, as they are in uniform. Finally, the man in the back there is János Csaba."

"How can I help you?" she asked.

"I need to confirm that you are Sarah Roberts."

She nodded. "I am."

"Please stand," he ordered.

"Why?"

"You will need to come with us to police headquarters."

"I'm not going anywhere with anyone until I see some identification."

Her stomach rolled. Even if she got away from them somehow, where would she go?

Both suits had flipped out their wallets. Their IDs looked genuine, but she wasn't an expert.

"What district is your police department in?" she asked.

"District Thirteen. Now please, stand up. We can continue our conversation in a more private setting."

"One more question. What is the common name of your police department?"

The suit turned to his men, exasperation evident in his features.

"It is nicknamed the Police Palace. Now, are you going to come with us willingly or not?"

"Am I being arrested?"

"Not right now, but that can be arranged. Will you force me to detain you?"

Sarah dropped her hands to the armrests of the chair. "I'll come willingly."

She stood slowly, so as not to alarm them. Each man stepped back anyway.

Good. English must've warned them about our skirmish last night.

"Turn and face the wall."

Sarah looked him in the eye. "I said I would come willingly. That means no restraints."

The suit sized her up. "I simply need to pat you down. An officer has reported his weapon as missing."

Sarah waited another moment, then turned and spread her hands high on the wall.

By now a small group of people had gathered by the front counter to watch.

The suit was quick about it, finding nothing. He grunted and told her to turn back around.

One of the uniformed police picked up her backpack, and the group walked through the lobby toward the front doors.

The lone man in the expensive suit had set his newspaper down to watch.

As they reached the lobby's front door the other uniformed police officer grabbed her luggage and rolled it out behind them.

Sarah got in the backseat of one of the cruisers. The gun was hidden and safe in the lobby couch. She had only defended herself last night. That would be her story. Whatever English had told them she would refute. The American Embassy might help her.

Sarah Roberts was something of a celebrity back home.

Wouldn't that count for something in a Hungarian jail?

118

THE HUNGARIAN POLICE were no better than the criminals on the street. It had been over four hours since she had last seen an officer. Were they attempting to sweat her out? At twenty-three years of age, Sarah had already been interrogated several times.

She leaned back in her chair, her bladder about to burst. They'd let her out when they were ready. She would just have to wait.

There were noises outside the interrogation room. Someone was coming.

She sat facing away from the two-way glass. A pad of paper and a pen rested on the metal table in front of her. Maybe they thought she would write some kind of confession.

The door opened. The man in the suit stepped inside.

He held two steaming glasses in his hand.

"Coffee?"

"Sure. But before I add more liquid into this little body, I need to use a toilet. Or in ten more minutes you'll have a mess on your floor."

The cop cast her a strained look. "Are all Americans so crass?"

"It's my way of saying thanks for not offering me a bathroom break for however fucking long I've been stuck in this metal hole."

"That kind of attitude won't get you far in Hungary."

"Will it be a toilet or the floor?"

He turned and gestured at the door. "Let's go."

He walked her down a hall and punched in a code at a square panel on the wall. A door opened, and he ushered Sarah through it. A bathroom door was on the right.

Minutes later they were walking back to the interrogation room in silence.

She sat in her chair after spinning it back around and sipped the coffee.

"Where's my luggage?" she asked.

He appeared flustered. "I ask the questions. But first we wait."

Sarah set her cup down. "Wait for what?"

"My colleague."

Sarah grinned. "I just got you to answer a question."

He stared a hole through her.

This guy is too serious.

"We have plenty of questions for you, Miss Roberts. But don't assume we're stupid. I already know much about you."

Sarah didn't allow the surprise to show on her face. Like a hammer falling, it hit her. English had said something about doing his job last night. He was with the officers at the hotel. He was there in an official capacity. The Hungarian police had been onto her for weeks now, watching, researching, and keeping tabs on her. That had to be it.

But why? What had she done to invite such scrutiny?

Her head shot up. The cop frowned.

Vivian is quiet because I'm being watched.

"You know a lot about me," Sarah said.

"It was a simple matter of running your passport. Although we did find something quite unusual."

Sarah sipped her coffee. She didn't know when she'd get another one that tasted this good.

"You're something of a hero back in the States. Do you want to tell me why?"

"Nope."

"Why not? It may help you here."

"We have nothing to discuss. When you're done here, you will either drive me to the airport so I can continue on my journey home or you will deliver me to my embassy. Either way, I'm leaving."

She sat back and took a couple of deep gulps of her coffee, draining half of it. The warmth soothed her. She felt better when in control. Much better.

The cop stood and left the room without another word. She could only assume he was now watching her from the other side of the two-way glass.

She drained the rest of the coffee. It tasted great. It was probably three or four in the afternoon, and she hadn't eaten anything since the continental breakfast at the hotel.

The door burst open after a five-minute wait.

She jumped back.

The immigration officer from the hotel lobby stepped in.

The cop from earlier stood behind him.

"Is this the good cop, bad cop routine?" Sarah asked. For a second Sarah actually thought she was getting to them.

The immigration officer adjusted his suit jacket and said, "Arrest her."

Sarah set her cup down too hard. "On what charge?"

"Conspiracy to commit murder and attempted murder."

"That's ridiculous. You can't prove any of that."

"Oh, yes, I can. We have everything we need to prove that you are hunting a man by the name of Armond Stuart. I know all about you, Sarah Roberts." He stood to his full height. "You will be in a Hungarian prison doing hard labor for dozens of years before I'm done with you."

119

THE PRISON CELL was cold and damp. The stained mattress smelled of urine, but it was softer than the damp stone floor. She lay back on it and tried not to inhale the acidic odor.

She lifted her shirt up over her nose. Breathing got easier as air filtered through her own clean smell.

If there was one thing Sarah had learned in the past, it was that things were not always as bad as they seemed. But something was going on with that immigration officer; for him it was personal. And really, he was the least of her worries. The problem was, she actually *had* come all this way to find and kill Armond Stuart. She just didn't know how they could possibly know that.

A door opened somewhere in the corridor. Shoes clicked down the chamber.

As the footfalls neared, she got off the bed and edged back into the corner, where a small amount of moisture had pooled to form a puddle.

A trio of men stepped into view. She recognized all three. Imre, the arresting detective; the devious immigration officer; and her personal stalker from the States, Officer Parkman.

He stood there with a half smile and a toothpick in his mouth.

"All this way?" Sarah asked.

Parkman shrugged and tilted his head. "I know, I know."

After trying two keys, Imre got the cell door open and beckoned for Sarah. They left the dank basement cells behind, processed her paperwork, and gave her luggage to Parkman.

"Where will you be staying before your plane leaves?" Imre asked.

"Back to the Best Western for another night, and then we're gone," Parkman said.

"Don't deviate," Imre warned.

The immigration officer remained strangely quiet. When Sarah got to the exit doors she turned back and looked directly at him for a moment. She saw absolute fury in his eyes.

Outside in Parkman's rental car, he turned to her and asked, "You hungry?"

He put the small rental car in gear and pulled away from the curb.

"You know how hard it was for me to get you out of there?" Parkman asked.

Sarah shook her head.

"Hard," he said. "Very hard."

Sarah leaned forward and pulled down the visor against the setting summer sun.

Parkman looked over. "What's that smell?"

"The prison cell."

"Oh. Great."

He lowered his window, spit the toothpick out, then looked at her again. "It started to taste like piss."

"You know what piss tastes like?" She smiled.

"Glad to see you kept your sense of humor."

"How did you get here so fast? It's more than a ten-hour flight. They put me in that cell two hours ago."

"After I talked to your parents I flew out to see what you were up to. I took a leave of absence. I've been in Budapest for about two weeks. It wasn't until today that I found out where you were."

"You serious?"

"Yes."

"The Hungarian authorities knew where I was the whole time."

"This isn't my jurisdiction." He paused and looked sideways at her again. "Wait, what do you mean, they knew where you were?"

"They've been watching me."

"Why?"

"That's what I need to find out."

"Oh, no." He was shaking his head. "We have to leave Budapest. Every day you stay here is ammunition for them."

Parkman turned onto a busy street, dropped the Opel into a lower gear, ground the gear, and then hit the gas, shooting them forward. He eased it back into third and cruised again.

"Sorry, not used to the stick shift."

A few blocks from the hotel, Parkman pulled up at a pizza place. Hungarian pizza took some getting used to, but Sarah devoured her slices.

"Thanks," she said.

He nodded while he chewed.

"No, I mean thanks for everything. You know I appreciate it. I'm just not good at expressing it."

He slowed his chewing and, with a mouthful, mumbled, "You're welcome."

Back in the car, Parkman turned away from the Best Western and drove deeper toward the city center.

"Where are we going?" Sarah asked.

"To the Hotel Erzsébet. It's near the center of town, close to the popular Váci Street. It's also near the Great Market Hall."

"What? We're tourists now?"

"Sarah, we have to show them that you were here for fun. After a day or so we'll grab a flight back to the States and everything will be over."

"It won't be over for me."

"I know. If they're monitoring you, they'll have the Best Western bugged better than a Mafia stakeout."

"Two rooms?"

"I'd have it no other way."

With no toothpick in his mouth he gave her a rare, full smile.

Once at the hotel, they checked into their rooms and said good night quickly. Both of them had agreed to leave the door adjoining their rooms unlocked, just in case.

Exhausted, Sarah sat on the edge of her bed and stared at the television.

A shower was first. Then new clothes. Maybe a drink from the minibar and then sleep. Who knew when she'd get another chance.

That immigration officer was coming after her. She could feel it.

Her hand twitched, then numbed. Elated Vivian was back, she grabbed the little pad of paper and a pen on the desk, then sat on the floor. A dark mist enveloped her vision before she blacked out.

Parkman's voice woke her.

She opened her eyes and looked around. He was on the edge of her bed, with the pad in his hand. She got up on one elbow.

"Wow," she said. "It's been over a month since that happened. I almost forgot how much it knocks me out."

"I knocked a few times. You didn't answer. When I came in, you were just dropping this from your hand." He looked back at the paper he held. "I think you better read it."

She got up off the floor and sat on the bed beside him. He handed her the pad.

I should've made contact sooner, but they had a camera on you and parabolic listening devices. They were watching for contact. Someone wants you for a government project of some kind.

Armond Stuart is in Budapest.

Tomorrow, 2:12 p.m., at the Great Market Hall you will see his new face by the red Ape.

Warning: It all ends at the crypt. Only nine days left.

I'm so sorry, Sarah. Talk to you soon.

120

THE SKY WAS a bright purplish color as it rose on another summer morning in Budapest. Sarah had left the hotel at five in the morning while Parkman slept in his room.

They had talked for over an hour about the message from Vivian. Their best course of action was to give the information of Armond's whereabouts to the police so they could arrest him. Killing Armond was cold-blooded murder. There was no way Sarah could get away with it.

She'd listened to Parkman, then come up with an altogether different plan.

It was close to five thirty in the morning, and she was just approaching the Best Western, a newspaper tucked under her arm. She waited fifteen minutes, watching a few vehicles pass. She checked the parked cars in the area for occupants, but they were all empty.

She crossed the street, entered the hotel, and made her way through the lobby, toward the couch where she had stashed the gun. The night staff behind the counter nodded at her and then turned away. The rest of the lobby was empty.

Sarah eased herself down onto the couch and pulled the newspaper out from under her arm. She opened the paper and began scanning the Hungarian news, even though she couldn't read a word.

With her right hand she reached down beside the cushion and into the back of the couch. She wrapped her hand around the butt of the weapon and pulled upward. With her left hand she folded the newspaper in half to use it to cover the gun.

In one quick movement she slid the weapon out into the open and under the paper. In that same moment a man entered the lobby from the outside. She watched him, waiting. After a few seconds, she got to her feet and then stopped. There was something about the man. She sat back down as it dawned on her. She was sure he was the same man in the hat who had watched her deal with the three attackers.

She got up again and moved to another couch where she could watch him better. He dressed like a 1950s FBI agent.

At the front desk, the woman stepped out from a room behind the counter with a coffee mug in her hand and said something in Hungarian. Fedora Man reached in his pocket and produced a wallet. He showed it to the clerk. The woman turned from him and walked back into the room behind the counter.

Then he pivoted on his heels and stared directly at Sarah. Her breathing slowed. Was he here to talk to her? He walked toward her. Sarah stayed perfectly still.

Fedora Man stopped six feet away and tipped his hat.

"Good morning," he said.

Sarah nodded.

"May I have a seat?"

Sarah nodded again. He sat across from her, adjusted his jacket, and leaned back into the leather couch. Sarah was intrigued. There was something dangerous about him.

"What are you planning?" he asked.

"Excuse me?" He was American. She could tell when he spoke.

"I'm a friend."

"Then explain something to me," she said.

He tilted his head. "Explain what?"

"How come I don't know you?"

He brought his hands together and tented them in front of his chest.

"My name is Rod Howley. I'm with the Sophia Project out of the University of Arizona."

"That tells me nothing."

"One of our main goals is to investigate the experiences of people who claim to channel or communicate with deceased loved ones and find out if these communications can be validated under controlled conditions."

Sarah had never heard of them before. She leaned forward. "Why tell me? Who am I to you?"

It was clear they saw her as a guinea pig. But their timing couldn't be worse. Armond was on the loose, and she wasn't going to be someone's circus act.

"Sarah, we both know why I'm sitting here. You're a very active girl. As I understand it, Vivian gives you messages and you act on them." He raised his index finger. "Very noble of you. But this latest job has crossed the line. We need to continue your mission with more control involved."

This guy talked about her dead sister like she was a pawn being played in his game of chess.

"I am going to stand up and walk out of here now."

He showed her his palms. "I'm sorry. I can see I'm upsetting you. That wasn't my goal."

He removed his hat. Sarah took the opportunity to scan the lobby. It remained empty. The clock behind the main desk said it was coming up on six in the morning. The female hotel clerk had not returned to the counter yet.

"Sarah, parapsychology research—"

"Stop using my name." The hand holding the gun tightened. "I don't know you. You don't know me. We're strangers. It will remain that way."

"I only have a few more things to say, and then you can decide."

"Decide what?"

"Decide whether or not you will accompany me back to America to do some real good."

She leaned forward again. "Are you saying that I'm not doing good on my own?"

"Will you allow me to continue? I need one more minute."

Sarah eased back in her seat. He was American. He had no authority in Hungary. She had the gun. He only wanted to talk. She nodded for him to go ahead and then scanned the empty lobby again. Not a single person had entered the building.

"The Society for Psychical Research was founded in London in 1882. The American Society for Psychical Research followed suit and opened its doors in New York City in 1885. By 1911, Stanford University became the first academic institution in the United States to study extrasensory perception, better known as ESP. Finally, in 1930, Duke University followed."

He stopped. She did not react.

"My organization usually has volunteers, but sometimes we search out people who display a talent far beyond usual parameters."

"Your organization? At the university?" Sarah glanced behind him. The lobby was still empty. Something was wrong.

"Sort of."

"You might want to clarify that comment. Your minute's almost up."

"I'm actually employed by the United States government. My organization works in conjunction with the people at the Sophia Project. Let's just say I'm their recruiter."

"Stand up," she said.

"You're making a mistake. I'm the only friend you've got."

"Stand up." She barked it this time.

He obeyed.

"Now step away from me."

She didn't even need to show him her weapon. He complied without protest.

Once he was over ten feet away, Sarah stood and folded the newspaper and its concealed weapon under her left arm, where it was easy to grab if needed.

"You are making a mistake," he said. "I would find it increasingly difficult to get you back to the States once incarcerated here."

She dropped the newspaper and raised the gun, flicking the safety off simultaneously. It was so fast that Howley stepped back reflexively.

"You want to threaten me? Don't make me angry, Mr. Howley. This conversation could turn ugly fast."

He raised his hands to chest height, keeping his eyes on the weapon.

"Sarah, I'm here to recruit you with or without your consent. I thought we could be civil about it."

Her peripheral vision caught movement in the lobby. She took a step to the right and angled herself to be able to see the front desk without taking her eyes off Mr. Howley.

Seven men with slicked-back hair, all dressed in suits, had emerged from numerous parts of the lobby. They stood with their arms crossed, eyes on her.

"What the hell is this?" she asked.

Everything made sense now. Rod Howley had come with backup. Without waiting for his response, Sarah stepped toward Rod.

"We'll see how well you follow me after I shoot you."

"Do it and more like me will come. You can't continue on your own. It's too dangerous."

She got close enough to place the tip of the weapon under his chin.

"Tell that to the people I've saved over the years. Tell them it's too dangerous that I'm out there helping people. Who are you to decide what's too dangerous?"

"Examine your current behavior."

She lowered the weapon and leaned in with her elbow. It slammed into his left ear with enough power to double him over. As she righted her arm, she brought the weapon up to aim in the general direction of the men standing near the main desk of the lobby.

"Please, someone, pull out a weapon. Do it! Let's all show Mr. Howley here how dangerous people can be when they're cornered." Spittle shot out as she talked.

All seven men stood statue still.

Rod righted himself beside her, holding his ear. "Okay, Sarah, you win. Today you get a free pass."

She edged around him and started for the front. As she neared the seven men, they moved away from her, their backs to the elevator bank. When she got to the lobby exit she looked outside. Another man in a suit stood with his arms crossed, holding back six people with luggage.

How powerful were these people? Better yet, *who* were they, really?

She looked back at Rod and lowered her weapon into the back of her pants.

"This doesn't end here," she said.

"You're wrong, Sarah."

She touched the door handle and cracked the door open a notch.

"How's that?" she asked.

"You cannot hide from us. I was supposed to persuade you to come willingly, but now I can see that will never happen. Our next directive is to take you by force. But not today. We'll wait. We'll watch. You are now the property of the United States government."

She almost pulled her gun out and shot him for that alone. Instead she lowered her head. "I will bury you first."

She eased the door open, slipped through, and walked past the man holding people back. She ran down the street and turned a corner. A small park came up on the right. She headed for the open gates, stepped inside, and sat on one of the benches, where she put her face in her palms. Tears seeped from her eyes.

Those men meant what they said. Hungary had just become even more dangerous.

121

AT NINE IN the morning Sarah entered a pharmacy that was just opening its doors. In less than ten minutes she'd accumulated everything she needed.

By nine thirty she had found a hostel-like hotel that would allow her to rent a room for the night. She settled in right away. In the bathroom she applied the brown hair color she'd bought and began the task of dying her blond hair.

After rinsing in the shower she tied her hair into two braids that hung over each shoulder, then studied the new look in the mirror. She resembled a young Laura Ingalls from *Little House on the Prairie*. Sarah was confident that no one would recognize her easily.

She applied eyeliner and eye shadow to her eyes. After the mascara, she stood back and stared again.

Perfect.

She checked the time. It was just after twelve noon. She grabbed her passport and the gun, checked that its safety was on, and left the room. A few doors down, she stopped at the fire extinguisher embedded in a recess in the wall. With a glance both ways to make sure no one was watching, Sarah reached in behind the extinguisher and placed her passport completely out of sight. Unless there was a fire in the building in the next twenty-four hours, no one would find it.

After a lunch of french fries and a Coke—they'd offered mayonnaise for the fries, but she declined—Sarah started for the Great Market Hall to meet Armond Stuart by *the red Ape*.

She'd been there before. In the first few weeks of living in downtown Budapest, with nothing to do, she had explored the city. She'd been to the Castle District and the Citadel. She'd learned that Saint Stephen I founded the Kingdom of Hungary in the year 1000 AD and that the Hungarian Parliament Building was one of the prettiest structures made by mankind.

She had also ridden the tram to the Great Market Hall a couple of times. The market hosted over two hundred stalls. She'd walked through most of them and had lunch, enjoying goulash the way it was supposed to be prepared. It made her feel normal for once.

But today was different.

Today she was armed. Armond Stuart would be there. She would find him by *the red Ape*, whatever that meant. No doubt Parkman would show. He'd read the note, too. Would the Sophia Project men be there?

She shook the questions off. She needed to concentrate. They'd come when they came, and she would deal with it then.

The sun beat down on her as she walked. Another cloudless day.

Armond Stuart, I'm coming for you.

She got close to the market's main doors, looked behind her in the reflection of a large window, saw nothing of interest, then entered the hall.

For a Thursday, the market bustled. She edged to the side of the hall and walked the length of the tables. People shouted back and forth in Hungarian.

The hall was definitely too busy for murder. Too many witnesses. She would have to follow Armond outside and wait for the right opportunity.

In the meantime she had to find a red gorilla by 2:12 p.m. She also had to watch for Parkman. He would be the only one who could easily see through her new look. He would try to stop her if she got the chance to kill Armond. Keeping him at a distance today was better for the both of them.

A clock on the wall said it was getting close to two o'clock.

In under five minutes she had reached the end of the hall. There had been no ape, red or otherwise. She turned around and began jogging up and down the side aisles, looking at the signs on the various stalls, searching for anything resembling an ape.

Nothing.

Maybe it's upstairs.

She took the closest staircase two steps at a time. A quick, three-minute scan revealed no apes. She had run out of time. She ran

back downstairs and looked for a clock. She found one by the exit to
Pipa Utca Street.

Two fourteen p.m.

Armond was gone.

I screwed up. Somehow I missed the red ape.

"Damn!" She slapped the wall beside the exit door.

A red, three-wheeled vehicle sat parked at an odd angle on the sidewalk just outside the door. On the side of the vehicle it said in English,
"Street Coffee." It looked like a miniature UPS truck, but the back door
lifted straight up to display the menu and prices of the mobile coffee shop.
There was one wheel in the front of the vehicle and two in the rear. It was
an Italian model—an automobile they called an Ape—and it was red.

She couldn't believe she had found it. At times, she wished Vivian
would be more specific.

Four men stood around the Ape with coffee cups in their hands.
The seller of the coffee, donning an apron, stood off to the side, tending
to a machine of some kind.

The doors slowly closed in front of her. Three of the men turned
away and began talking to one another again, while the fourth man
stood rigid, his eyes never leaving Sarah.

Sarah's attention didn't waver. She was staring into the eyes of
Armond Stuart.

There could be no doubt. He was the same height, about the same
weight and build, but his face was different and his hair had been
chopped to a military buzz cut. There was a new scar that traversed
the side of his jaw. She knew those eyes.

The moment had come. Her hand still rested on the wall. She
leaned in closer, resting her shoulder against the brick. Her right hand
had to remain free and clear. The gun was close. In seconds, Armond
would have a bullet in either eye.

The three men around him were dressed in suits. They looked like
expensive bodyguards. Armond wasn't playing games. He whispered
something to his men. In an almost comical slow-motion scene, all
three men turned toward her very slowly.

Hungarians hustled by, bags in their arms, opening and closing the
doors as Sarah and the four men watched one another, no one making
a move.

In the half minute they stared at each other Sarah realized that today was not the day.

She eased off the wall and slowly stepped through the door toward them. Two of the guards reached inside their jackets.

She stopped in front of the foursome, staring at Armond, memorizing every facial expression, every dimple, every eye movement.

"You look well, Sarah," Armond said.

His bodyguards lifted their arms out in unison, each one holding a small, compact piece.

"Can't fight your own battles?" Sarah asked.

"Sarah, Sarah, Sarah," he said, shaking his head. "You are a hard person to kill. You're like a cockroach. But now things have changed."

"How so?"

"You've seen my face. The time and money I spent on it have now been wasted. And you're in Hungary. You've traveled a long way to hunt me down. You're becoming a nuisance. And I've now realized something."

"What's that?"

She stood in the mid-afternoon sun, listening to her sister's murderer.

"I've realized that nothing will ever stop you. How did you know where to find me? Vivian, of course. *How* could you know without her? I already killed her. But we both know that."

He was goading her to make a move. Her fingers twitched. One bullet. It would be done. She was tough. She could handle prison.

One bullet. She reached back for her weapon. Her hand gripped the butt of the stolen police gun.

She didn't care anymore. This was it. Her one chance to kill her sister's murderer.

Then her hand went numb. A blackout was coming.

"No!" she shouted.

The numbness crawled up her arm. The gun fell from her grasp and hit the pavement. She met the concrete a second later.

It was over as fast as it happened.

The guards had lowered their weapons, perceiving no threat.

"Well done, Sarah," Armond said. "What a show."

She grabbed the gun on the ground beside her and clambered back

to her feet, jamming the weapon back in her pants. It was obvious that
Vivian didn't want her to shoot anyone today. There was no written
message to receive, but she got the message nonetheless.

"There will be another day," Sarah said. "You and I will have our
moment."

"I'm sure we will."

Someone grabbed her arm from behind.

Sarah spun and let her reflexes go to work. She clamped a hand on
the person's wrist and used her other hand to grab the person's elbow.
In the second before she rammed the person's elbow upward, intent
on breaking it, she realized it was Parkman.

"Let's go," Parkman said as he pulled his arm back. "We're finished here."

She went willingly.

"What was that?" he asked. "I saw you from thirty feet away. You
reached for your gun and then fell down. I thought they'd shot you.
What the hell were you doing?"

"Vivian interrupted me."

"To stop you?"

Sarah nodded as she turned around and looked behind her. Armond
and his bodyguards had disappeared.

"Who were all those men in suits?" Parkman asked.

"They're probably his bodyguards."

"No, I don't mean the ones standing with Armond. I was talking
about the ten men standing across the street beside three black SUVs.
When you reached for your weapon and fell, all ten of those men
pulled out some kind of weapon of their own and took up position
around Armond. Before the bodyguards even lifted their guns, these
men had them in their sights. I thought I was about to witness a major
gun battle. It all stopped when Armond's guys lowered their weapons."

Sarah was stunned. She turned around, scanning the area. No men
in suits. No Armond. No bodyguards. No SUVs. Only regular people
shopping for fruits and vegetables.

"Do you know who the men were?" Parkman prodded.

"Yeah, they're with the government. The American government."

122

PARKMAN TOOK SARAH back to the Hotel Erzsébet, where he'd rented the room for another night. Once they were inside, Sarah said, "We can't stay here."

"Why not?" Parkman asked. He was in the act of unpacking his suitcase, a toothpick already in his mouth. "This evening both of us can give Imre and the police a statement of what happened at the Market Hall. Let him and his men hunt Armond down. Imre's connected. He can get our description of Armond out to other agencies. Then in the morning we can go to the airport."

Sarah rubbed the back of her neck. "There are too many players in this game. You've used a credit card to reserve this room. In order to stay under the radar, we need to leave this hotel."

"Okay, where do you suggest we go?"

"I've rented a room several blocks from here. Paid cash."

Parkman looked at her. "When did you do that?"

"This morning. So I could do this," she said as she lifted the braids in her hair and let them flop back to her shoulders.

Parkman turned back to his suitcase. "Okay. You're right. We should go out the back door and catch a cab behind the building. No doubt someone's watching the front."

Sarah used the adjoining door to access her room.

"There's something else that disturbs me about this morning," she called through the open door.

"What's that?"

"If those American men found me so easily today, where were the Hungarian authorities? Only the Sophia Project people. Why no cops?"

Parkman stepped into the doorframe. "Sophia Project?"

"We'll talk more about it on the way. But it's strange. Is there an American government agency that could supersede another country's police force? Or are these government men just that good?"

Parkman stepped closer. "We'll look into it and find out what their mandate is. America's a free country."

Sarah grabbed her bag and set it on the floor by the door. "I think you're wrong here. That man said I was property of the United States government. I think they want to do tests on me or something."

Parkman met her gaze. "I trust your instincts. But are you okay with leaving Armond behind, alive?"

"What are you talking about?"

"Leaving him for the authorities to pick up. Walking away. Going home, back to the States. Are you okay with that?"

Sarah inhaled deeply, held it a moment, then exhaled slowly. "I almost shot him in broad daylight today, right beside a shopping area. People were coming and going. If it wasn't for Vivian I would've shot him and he would've killed another girl: me." She grabbed her bag. "I'm ready to leave it behind. He'll be caught soon enough. My goal is to help people, not be lured into cold-blooded murder. I'm not like him. I don't want to be."

"Are you trying to convince me or yourself?"

Sarah ignored the question, opened the door, and stepped into the outer corridor. Two burly men in suits grabbed her on each side, then shoved her back into the room with such force she landed by the foot of the bed six feet away.

Parkman yelled something. Dazed, she shook her head and tried to stand.

Parkman was being dragged from the room, chin resting on his chest. More men than she could count stood in the doorway now.

The hotel room door slammed shut. She was alone. Her neck ached. Her chest ached.

She tried to feel the back of her neck, but her arm was too heavy. She finally touched her neck and felt the handle of a needle.

Her arm dropped at an odd angle as she passed out on the floor of the hotel room.

123

SHE SAT UP too fast and gasped for breath. Her head spun; the room tilted.

"Parkman?" she mumbled. "You here?"

She eased up off the floor and sat on the edge of the bed, her head in her hands. Her right arm was sore.

She hadn't gotten a good look at the men. They wore suits. Strong, too.

She twisted her upper body back and forth to loosen her cramped muscles. She gingerly felt around her neck. The needle was still there. She eased it out slowly, then tossed it into a corner and got to her feet. She looked into Parkman's room. His suitcase still sat on the end of his bed.

"Parkman?"

The early evening sun beat in through the window.

She started for the open adjoining door and glanced at the alarm clock on the side of her bed: 7:15 p.m.

Shit, I've been out all day.

She turned away from Parkman's room and spoke out loud. "Vivian. You gotta help me here. What happened to Parkman? What's my next step?"

Nothing.

Her arm didn't go numb. Could someone have bugged the room? She had to get to the hostel she'd rented earlier. Maybe then Vivian would talk to her.

Sarah grabbed her gun, slid it into the back of her jeans, and headed for the door, still feeling a little woozy on her feet. She decided to leave everything behind. Parkman had said the room was paid for.

She eased the door open slowly. No one was in the hallway. She stepped out and walked past the elevators to the stairwell.

Sarah got downstairs and out the side door without interference. She walked around the building and started for the hostel. As often as she could, she stopped and looked in shop windows, watching for a follower in the reflection.

Her muscles felt better. Everything felt normal again and her head had cleared, but her stomach growled.

When was the last time I ate anything?

She stopped at a street vendor and bought a small container of french fries and a Coke for energy.

The fifteen minutes it took to order the fries and eat them gave her another chance to watch people passing by. No one appeared interested in her whatsoever.

Yet she still felt watched.

Twenty minutes later she walked into the hostel and lay out on the bed. In the night table beside the bed she found a pen and paper. Sarah pulled them out and placed them by her hand.

"Come on, Vivian. Give me something."

It was around eight in the evening. As far as she could tell, no one knew where she was or where she would turn up next.

As if on cue her hand numbed.

Vivian, she thought.

Moments later, Sarah sat up fast and grabbed the piece of paper. It was riddled with her handwriting this time, the message scrolled across two full pages.

There was nothing about Parkman. Most of the note was about the immigration officer that worked with Imre. She'd never forget his knowing smile. He was the one who had ordered her arrest. According to Vivian he was also the one who facilitated Armond's entry into Hungary. He was a crook. Vivian explained how she had to deal with him if she was going to get to Armond. The note also went into detail about one of his neighbors. Sarah had to read that part twice.

At the bottom of the second page, the note talked about a final date for Sarah.

The crypt. Eight days left. I'm sorry, but there's nothing we can do to avoid it. You only have eight days. It has to do with vampires.

Was Vivian saying Sarah would die in eight days?

Vivian had said that dealing with the immigration officer would get her one step closer to Armond. If there was nothing she could do to avoid the crypt, then so be it. Armond Stuart was her priority.

But what the hell was this *vampire* business?

124

PER VIVIAN'S DIRECTIONS, Sarah stood outside the immigration officer's apartment building in the Fifth District. It was close to midnight, and the streets were mostly empty.

She circled the building twice, looking for a way in.

She had tied her hair into a ponytail to keep it out of the way. After a short wait, a man approached the door, unsure of his step. He appeared to be quite intoxicated. Sarah was surprised he could even stay on his feet.

"How was your evening?" she asked as he drew near.

He stopped and looked at her. "Who wants to know?"

"You look like you had a great time." She was grateful the man spoke English.

"*Kurva életbe.* A fine night."

Sarah knew he'd said something like *fucking good* or *bitching good* in Hungarian.

The man walked past her and took out his keys. He glanced over his shoulder and then opened the door.

"You want in?" he asked.

Sarah stood. "Yeah, forgot my key."

"Bullshit. You don't live here." He looked her up and down. Then he smiled a crooked smile and said, "Gonna cost you."

It would be nice if some things in life were free. "What do you want? Money? Booze?"

"No. Just a half hour of your time." He stepped into the lobby and held the door for her. "How about it, Miss America?"

"I don't think so."

Sarah barged past him.

"Hey!" he shouted.

She pulled out her gun and held it up under his chin.

"Stay quiet."

He stumbled back and leaned against the wall, his eyes wide, as a wet spot formed on the front of his jeans.

"I was only kidding," he stammered.

"Me too. But now you can do me a favor."

She lowered the weapon and gently eased it into the back of her pants.

"Anything," he said, suddenly sober.

"Call the police. Tell them you were threatened by a girl with a gun in the lobby of your apartment building. Also, tell them that I will be on the third floor."

"What? You want me to call the police on you?"

In the dim light of the lobby, she could tell he was thinking it over.

"Well?" she prodded.

"Should I let them know what apartment?"

"There will be gunfire by then." She walked away and headed for the stairs. "The whole building will know."

Sarah reached the third floor and scouted out apartment 303. She wanted to know where the neighbor's apartment was—the one Vivian spoke of in her note—before knocking on the immigration guy's door. She continued down to 306 and stopped in front.

Gently, she placed an ear against the door. According to Vivian, he would be home.

Her stomach didn't protest. Her nerves were firing in time. She marveled at how acclimated her body had grown over the years to this kind of stress.

She tried the doorknob. Locked. She knocked.

A soft, subtle sound came from behind the door. Then a voice asked, "*Ki az?*"

Who is it?

Your judge and jury, asshole.

She knocked again, hoping this time he would crack the door a little.

As soon as she heard the bolt click open and saw the knob turn, Sarah charged the door. It shot open hard, breaking the cheap chain it was connected to and smacking into the immigration officer's shoulder. He stumbled back, hit the wall, and slumped to the floor as the door finished its arc.

Sarah pulled out her weapon. She aimed it at the corrupt officer and motioned for him to get up.

"What are you doing here?" he rasped in his harsh accent.

"What's your name?" she asked.

"István."

He rolled to his side and got up slowly, using the wall for support.

"Take a seat at the kitchen table."

They moved deeper into his apartment. Sarah kept her weapon trained on his midsection.

"What is this all about?" he asked.

Sarah didn't respond. Had the drunk already called the police? How much longer before they arrived?

István sat down. "I asked you a question," he said.

His voice grew defiant. She needed to unsettle him.

Sarah lifted the gun and flicked off the safety.

István leaned back and raised his hands in protest.

She fired her weapon. The recoil was minimal, but the sound was quite loud in the small apartment. The bullet zinged by István's head and embedded itself in his microwave oven.

"Are you crazy?" he shouted. "Someone will hear that. The police will be called."

For the second time that night she had made a grown man soil himself. István urinated where he sat, a small puddle forming around his feet.

"We need to talk, and we don't have a lot of time."

He dropped his hands from the side of his head and set them on the table.

"Where is Parkman?"

"What happened to Park—"

Sarah shot forward, flipped the gun in her hand, and swung it. The handle connected perfectly with his left cheek. He reared back and held his face, groaning.

"It wasn't your people who took Parkman?"

He shook his head.

"Do you know a man named Armond Stuart?"

He lifted a finger and whispered, "Not here. These walls have ears."

Sarah nodded.

She grabbed his lapel and helped him to his feet. She guessed she only had five minutes left, or maybe ten.

With the gun firmly planted in his side, she half shoved, half guided István to his apartment door.

"Where are we going?" he asked.

"Don't speak," she said. "The walls have ears."

They exited István's apartment and entered the hallway. The corridor was deserted. She looked left and then right to make it look like she was being indecisive. Then she turned toward apartment 303.

When they got to the door, Sarah knocked. After a moment someone asked who it was.

"Tell him it's you, from apartment 306," she whispered.

"It's me, István from 306. I need to borrow some sugar."

"Sugar? Bit late to be knocking on doors, isn't it, István?"

István looked at Sarah.

"Think of something," she said as she pushed the gun into his side.

"I ahh . . . got this lady coming over in twenty minutes. Her favorite drink is a margarita, and I have to dip the glass. There's no way around it."

A distant police siren reached her ears. If they were coming to this building, then she was down to minutes. She stepped away from István and raised her gun to shoot out the lock, but as she moved, the lock clicked.

Gun still raised, Sarah stayed in position. The door opened slowly.

"Come on in," a heavyset man said.

When he laid his eyes upon Sarah, they widened.

"Step away from the door," she ordered.

The guy was smart. He stepped back.

Sarah pushed István inside and followed close behind. The television was on, but no sound came from it. The guy wore pajama bottoms and a T-shirt.

"Step away," Sarah said.

The tenant moved back.

"Pick up the phone," Sarah instructed.

István stood beside her. He remained still while Sarah set the scene.

"I want you to call the police and have them come to this apartment."

"What do I tell them?" the tenant asked.

"Just tell them that you've been shot."

"What? I haven't been . . . " He paused.

Sarah lowered her outstretched arm and aimed her weapon at his lower leg.

"Wait. What is this about?"

Sarah fired two shots. Two holes formed, one in each foot.

The man screamed and stumbled to the floor.

"What the hell are you doing?" István shouted at her.

"You're not supposed to be asking questions," she reminded him.

Sarah grabbed a clump of his hair and placed the gun at the base of his neck.

"Walk."

He started moving. She guided him down a small hallway and into the apartment's main bathroom. She turned him around and shoved him down on the closed toilet seat.

The bathroom had been decorated by a woman. Flowers sat on the back of the toilet. The shower curtain had a floral pattern, and the counter contained feminine sprays and soaps.

She refocused and turned to István.

"Now, talk."

"I know of no one who has kidnapped Officer Parkman. The Americans are our allies, after all. And of course I've heard of Armond Stuart. As far as we know, that's why you're here. To execute him."

"You're protecting Armond."

Sarah raised her weapon and shot a bullet into his right thigh.

"You're crazy," he screamed, grabbing at his new wound.

Sarah snatched a towel from the rack beside her and tossed it at him.

He raised his right hand in surrender as he covered the wound with the towel and applied pressure. "Okay, okay, no more. Please, I'll tell you everything." His face had reddened and was covered in sweat.

"We've got minutes before the police come, so hurry up."

Blood soaked through the towel and dripped to the floor.

"It started in the nineteen fifties," István said. "During the Hungarian Revolution some of the Hungarian officials in the Immigration Department set up a ghost branch that helped people to move in and out of the country without official papers." He stopped to adjust the towel. "When the individual got to their final destination, all papers were to be burned. At our end, we'd monitor their progress and burn our papers, too. Many thousands of people were able to escape. Now the organization has turned profitable. People like Armond Stuart pay for a free pass to Hungary. From here, he can travel to any other Schengen Area country without a stamp on his passport."

"So you admit to helping Armond get into Hungary illegally?"

"Of course. We're the best at what we do. Only rarely do problems arise."

"Like what?"

"A few months ago in Toronto, a Hungarian woman and her brothers were after this guy, Drake Bellamy. She didn't understand that all our documents are fakes. They're designed to move people from country to country, but that's it. Once in Canada they were supposed to burn their documents. They didn't, and now there's an investigation. It's bullshit."

"Tell me about Armond. Where is he now? Who heads this group?"

Sirens pulled up outside the building. She had to leave.

"You're going to burn for this. You can't walk around Budapest shooting people at will."

"You have no idea what I'm capable of. Who heads this group?"

"You think I'm going to tell you that?"

Sarah raised her weapon and emptied the bullets into the wall behind the toilet in a triangle formation. The gun was so loud she couldn't hear István's screams as he ducked.

She reached past his head and punched a piece of drywall away. Behind it was a camera, exactly where Vivian had told her it would be. A motion-detection camera set up by the pervert tenant. It was set up to videotape his teenage daughter's girlfriends when they changed in the bathroom.

Now the perverted pig lay half in and half out of his kitchen entrance with a bullet in each foot. The police would get two criminals with one camera.

"Your confession is on here." Sarah held the camera up for István to see. "I will give you this camera if you tell me who runs everything."

István was shaking his head back and forth.

"Tell me!" Sarah screamed.

"A guy named Little Tony."

Only seconds left. "Where can I find him?"

"Montone, Italy. He works in a crypt."

A crypt?

István slumped off the seat, hitting the floor beside the bathtub. His confession would finish him and his little group.

Sarah stumbled from the bathroom and ran for the hallway.

"Wait!" István shouted. "You said you'd give me the camera."

"You just confessed on camera your role in aiding Armond Stuart's entry into this country. On here, there's everything I need to lock up that pig lying out in the hallway. This little device will go to the proper authorities." Sarah pivoted away and ran down the short hall to the apartment door. The pervert from apartment 303 still lay on the floor, the phone near his ear.

"That's right," Sarah said. "Good boy." She held up the camera. His eyes widened. He knew he was caught. She watched as he ended the call. "Too late. The police are already here."

Before stepping from the apartment, she checked the hallway. It was empty.

She edged out and down to István's apartment. She eased in and closed the door, locking it behind her.

In under a minute she had the camera hooked up to his DVD player. She turned the television on, rewound the recorder, and then pressed "play."

She recognized the bathroom she was just in. Young girls showed up on the screen in various states of undress. Sarah turned up the volume and looked away. She walked back out to the apartment door and opened it wide. Someone ran by, but they didn't look in.

Leaving the door open, she headed for István's small balcony. Someone shouted from the hallway: "In here."

She stepped outside.

Third floor. Couldn't be more than thirty feet down.

She jumped onto the other side of the balcony's railing and slowly slid down a side bar until she was dangling above the balcony on the second floor.

She calculated the distance and waited for the right moment. After her body swung enough to the inside, she let go and dropped a foot to the top of the railing on the second floor. Balancing perfectly for a brief second, she hopped off and onto the balcony itself.

Then she hopped to the first-floor balcony and down to a bed of moist grass. Luckily for her, István's apartment faced the rear of the building. The authorities had arrived at the front.

Sarah released her hair from the bun and let it fall in waves down her back.

Just as she started to turn away, two guns emerged from the shadowy underside of the balcony on the first floor. One was placed against her forehead, and the other was leveled at her chest.

"We need to talk," said the owner of the gun.

125

SARAH FROZE, HER heart tripping in her chest. The voice was faintly familiar, but she couldn't make out the face.

"If I pull back my weapons, can I trust that you won't run or attack me?"

"Depends on who you are."

"Imre Mátyás. I was the officer who detained you at the Best Western." His weapons eased back an inch as he spoke.

"I won't attack," Sarah said.

Both guns lowered.

"We need to move," he said. "We're not safe here. Sorry about the guns, but I thought if I surprised you . . . well, let's just agree that you're unpredictable."

"What would make you say that?" she asked, her tone sarcastic.

"I heard everything that happened upstairs."

Sarah slowed her step. "How?"

Imre slowed, too. "Come on, keep moving. We can't stop. We're probably being watched."

Her curiosity spiked, Sarah followed as he talked.

"István has been under investigation for some time. I was in a van across the street listening in when you showed up."

"Is there a reason you guys didn't storm the apartment yourselves and keep the other cops from stealing your arrest?"

Imre ran a hand through his hair. He scanned the area around them.

"I was in the van because of an anonymous tip. We were told you'd be there with the evidence we needed to lock you up. We waited in case you actually got a confession out of István. But our instructions were to get both of you."

"What's this then? You letting me go or taking me in?"

"Look, I know the authorities want you on a theft charge. From what I just heard, you deserve to keep that gun."

"So where are we going?"

"I need more information. I thought we could talk. Do an exchange."

"What kind of exchange?"

They were a block from the apartment building. Imre turned right onto a long street, then toward a small park coming up on the left. Sarah followed, watching behind her.

"Why do you look so afraid?" Sarah asked.

"Because they're everywhere."

"Who?"

"The Americans."

They entered the darkened park and found a secluded bench.

"All I know," Imre started in a whisper, "is that these American guys showed up about three weeks ago. They come with a lot of clout. I have a friend at the FBI. He had never heard of them. After he looked into it, he learned they might be from your National Security Agency, in an unknown branch that oversees some kind of ESP thing."

Sarah scanned the park. "How powerful could they be?"

"A dozen of them came to Hungary. They operate like a military unit and come with full diplomatic immunity. We're supposed to co-operate fully. They have only one task: you."

"I don't understand. This doesn't make sense."

"Come on, Sarah. You're aware of your special abilities."

"They'd get tired of me quick," Sarah said, knowing that Vivian wouldn't send her a message if someone were watching. "How do I know you're not one of them?"

"You don't. But if I was, wouldn't they just grab you right now?"

Sarah considered that and then asked, "Where's Parkman?"

Imre looked away. "We don't have him. They do."

"What do they want with Parkman?"

"I don't know, but I think they want information about you. You should leave Hungary while you're still free. Disappear."

"Earlier you said something about an information exchange."

Her hand went numb. *No,* she screamed in her head. *Not here, not now.*

Her arm followed, and a second later she slumped to the ground.

The blackout felt like it lasted one second. Just long enough for Vivian to make her fall from the bench.

Sarah opened her eyes. Imre was also on the ground in front of her.

She reached forward and touched his shoulder.

"Imre?" she whispered.

A feather was attached to a steel pin that protruded from Imre's skin. *A tranquilizer.*

Something rustled beside her as footsteps pounded over grass. A flashlight switched on.

"I got both of them, sir," a man close by said.

Vivian had saved her again by knocking her out for that brief second. She leaned forward and reached inside Imre's jacket. Feeling her way around as fast as she could, Sarah grabbed both his guns and eased them out of their holsters.

She rolled under the bench. As the shooter stepped closer, he lowered his flashlight. Sarah edged behind the bushes. It was enough to avoid being caught in the flashlight's beam. The shooter turned away and scanned the area while reaching for a radio clipped to his belt. Sarah got to her feet and crept to a tree about seven feet from the bench.

"Come in, sir."

With the stealth of a predator she twisted to get a glimpse of his face. His flashlight cast him in silhouette.

"Yes, sir, I understand. I shot two darts. Both parties went down. The girl first. These darts would take down a horse. There's no way she's awake."

There was a pause.

"When the girl—wait, sir, I see the problem. There's a dart on the bench. Sarah must have ducked at the exact moment I fired." Another pause. "Yes, sir, copy that. The girl's the priority. Yes, sir. I'll have my team scour the area. We'll get her, sir. Over."

Sarah moved away from the man as quietly as she could. At twenty feet, she climbed a small fence to exit the park.

After clearing a full city block, she ran for her life.

126

SARAH MADE IT to her hotel without stopping. She leaned out of an alley around the corner and scanned the street. Nothing moved. The front doors to the little hotel were propped open. Light spilled out and lit up the sidewalk in front like a welcoming carpet.

Halfway there and no tranquilizer yet. Things were looking up.

A lone car turned onto the street up ahead. Sarah slowed and stepped into a recessed doorway. The car approached and then shot past her without pause.

She waited for a breath and then stepped back out onto the sidewalk. These government guys were getting under her skin.

"Come on, Vivian," she whispered. "Where are you when I need you?"

Sarah crossed the street and strode with purpose to the lobby. When she entered, she saw the clerk behind the counter. He nodded and continued to shuffle a stack of papers on his desk.

A janitor working the night shift was moving his mop back and forth across the tile floor in the side corner. He had placed a "Caution: Wet Floor" sign out in Hungarian, English, and German.

Sarah headed for the stairs and hopped up the first two as fast as she could. She continued slapping the steps with her feet as if she were continuing higher, each step tapping softer, making ascending sounds.

Then she waited.

The mop hit the floor outside her sight line. The janitor whispered something. She leaned out enough to watch the guy behind the counter. His head turned slowly as he tracked the janitor toward the staircase.

In absolute silence she eased one of Imre's guns out of the back of her pants and placed it in her left hand. The janitor stepped into view and half ran, half jumped up the first two stairs, almost colliding with Sarah.

She set the gun tip on his right eye and reached down to his crotch. Caught by surprise, he almost fell back down the stairs, but her hand was firmly in place.

She clamped onto his scrotum and squeezed. Then she leaned in close and whispered in his ear. "Don't move."

He nodded, a vein bulging on his forehead.

Barely audible, she whispered, "Kill the connection to the outside."

He brought his left hand to his ear and yanked the wire out. Then he reached down and pushed a button on a small device clipped to his breast pocket. A red light blinked out.

"We're alone," he managed to say.

"Since we're alone," Sarah said. "Let's head up to my room."

He nodded.

"Move," she ordered.

He started up the stairs on wobbly legs. They made it to the third floor. The fire extinguisher was exactly where it sat earlier. She reached behind it and snatched her passport, placing it in her front pocket. It might get bent, but at least she knew she wouldn't lose it.

He knew what room was hers.

"We going in?" he asked.

"Open the door."

Her door was unlocked. They stepped in and Sarah ordered him to go stand in the corner. The room had been ransacked. She took quick glances around. Someone had been looking for something.

"Where's Parkman?" she asked.

He shrugged.

Sarah flipped the gun to her right hand and clicked off the safety. Then she aimed the weapon down to his right leg below the knee and fired.

He fell to the floor and curled up in the fetal position, grabbing at his wound. She pointed the weapon at his other leg.

"Wait, wait," he spat. "We have Parkman."

"Tell me something I don't know."

"We don't have offices here in Hungary. We use Escalades as a mobile unit. Anyone we take in to question is usually placed in the middle Escalade. Find the vehicles, you find Parkman."

"Why did you take him in the first place?"

"He told us what we needed to know about you. Kill me if you want, but they will never stop."

She pushed on the barrel of the gun, shoving it deep into the flesh of the guy's nose. His head pushed back to avoid the pressure.

"What did your people do to get Parkman to talk?"

"That wasn't my doing. I'm part of the surveillance team, that's it."

His face had gone a pasty white. His leg wound bled profusely.

"Before you lose too much blood and die in this shitty hotel, tell me, where can I find these Escalades?"

"They're always on the move. We're a roving force."

Sarah snatched the device out of his breast pocket, the earpiece cord coming with it.

She paused at the door and looked into the hallway. No one seemed to have been bothered by the gun going off.

"You made a mistake coming after me," Sarah said, then slipped out of the room. She reached the lobby without incident. The front desk guy was gone.

She jumped over the desk, raised her weapon, and opened the door to the back room. The desk clerk sat in a chair with a coffee in his hand, a television on in front of him.

"That wasn't cool."

The clerk raised his hands at the sight of the gun, the coffee cup balanced perfectly. "*Bocsánat*, I'm sorry, I'm sorry."

"How much did they pay you?"

"Five hundred American dollars. That's good money for me."

"Okay, but now I need something from you."

His hands still raised, no coffee spilling yet, he said, "Take what you want."

"I need a knife. A good knife. Nothing dull."

He pointed to the side bureau. "In the drawer over there. I have a fork and knife for when I eat on duty."

Sarah moved a few steps to the side and pulled open the top drawer. It was filled with random papers and notepads.

"The other one, to the right."

She shut the drawer and moved to the right. Inside, she grabbed a steak knife, and then she stepped back to the door.

"I'm checking out now. You won't see me again. Actually, it would be better if you didn't see me at all. Do you understand?"

He nodded. "I understand." A little coffee slipped over the edge of the raised cup.

Sarah walked out of the back room, hopped over the counter again, and then hustled to the front windows. The Escalades hadn't shown up to rescue their man. She ran around to the back of the building.

She had two guns and a knife.

And she had a plan.

127

SARAH EXITED THE side door and stepped out into the warm Budapest night. She started around the hotel until she had a clear view of the front, then hung back in the shadows and waited for the three SUVs to arrive, as she suspected they would. She didn't have to wait long. Ten minutes later, three Cadillac Escalades slowed half a block from the hotel, then pulled to the curb. Sarah leaned out of the shadows and watched as the passenger doors of the first and third Escalades opened and a man from each vehicle got out. No one moved from the center vehicle.

The two men marched to the front of the hotel and disappeared inside. Staying close to the wall of the building to keep out of the streetlight, she made her way toward the three vehicles. Five feet from the lead SUV, she dropped to one knee, aimed carefully, and fired a shot into its tire. A loud *poof* from the wheel accompanied the weapon's discharge. She pivoted and repeated the action on the rear SUV. The doors opened on both vehicles, their drivers walking around to inspect the damage.

"Hands where I can see them," Sarah ordered.

It startled the men enough that they stepped back several feet.

"Take it easy," one of them said.

She recalled that this group of men didn't want to kill her. She was valuable to them.

The two men who had entered the hotel moments before were coming back across the street. They had their injured friend between them.

"Hold up," she shouted at them.

The threesome slowed at her command.

Sarah motioned with a flick of her wrist for the driver of the second SUV to open the door. He shook his head, mouthing the words *no way*.

"Bulletproof?" Sarah fired at the window. Nothing happened. The driver shrugged, showing his hands.

"How about the gas tanks?" she shouted.

Sarah dropped her gun arm and emptied her gun into the rear of the lead SUV. When that weapon clicked empty, she tossed it into the street, aimed her other weapon, and held the trigger tight. Things were going downhill fast. She was surrounded by Howley's men. If she ran out of ammo, she'd have no way to defend herself.

While she still had the gun aimed at the lead SUV, the driver of the second SUV opened his door a crack.

"Okay," he shouted. "I'm getting out. Stop shooting like a crazy lady."

"Go join the others on the sidewalk," she told the driver, then peeked inside the vehicle. "You too," she said to the man in the passenger seat.

When the front seats had been emptied she jumped up behind the wheel, closed the door, and leaned across to close the passenger door. Now secure in their armored vehicle, Sarah looked into the back of the SUV. Parkman sat beside Howley.

"Good to see you, Sarah," Howley said. "I wasn't sure we'd meet again so soon. Parkman here and I have been enjoying a little chat."

"Chat's over. Get out." She motioned sideways with her head.

"I don't think so," Howley said, his voice calm.

Sarah turned enough in her seat to show him her weapon.

"Go ahead, Sarah," he said. "Shoot me. Get it over with. All these threats. All this violence. Where will it get you?"

Sarah held the weapon tight, adjusting the aim toward his face.

"I know who you are, Sarah," he continued. "You help people; you don't kill them unless they're trying to kill you. That's the distinction between you and a murderer. You're not a murderer, Sarah."

"Chat's over," Sarah said as she shifted forward in her seat. The engine hadn't been turned off. She dropped it into gear and hit the gas. After clearing the lead Escalade, she gunned it down the street.

"If Parkman has any restraints on, remove them," she said.

"He's unrestrained."

"Good. If there are any restraints back there, Parkman, use them on this guy."

In the mirror she saw Parkman shake his head.

"Where are you taking us?" Rod asked.

"To the airport."

"And why is that?"

"So Parkman and I can go home."

"Do you really think you can get through customs without me?"

Sarah looked back in the mirror. Parkman remained strangely quiet. Something was wrong with him.

Just before the airport, Sarah pulled into long-term parking. She drove to the back corner and turned off the SUV.

She swiveled in her seat, her gun hand loosely aimed at Howley. Then Sarah saw why Parkman had been so quiet. The American government man was holding a syringe against Parkman's leg.

"Shoot me, and I will plunge this into his leg. If your aim is true and I die instantly, my nervous system will contract my hands enough to plunge the needle into Parkman's leg."

"And what's in the needle?"

"Death takes place in less than five minutes."

"What do you want?" she asked.

"You."

"You can't have me."

"We need you. Come back to the States with us. I will personally make sure your stay there is quite comfortable. After a few months of tests you can go home."

He held the needle firm, his gaze unwavering. Parkman seemed tense.

Sarah aimed at Howley's heart. She added pressure to the trigger. With only a couple of pounds per square inch to spare, Howley moved the needle away from Parkman and held his hands in the air. Parkman breathed an audible sigh of relief.

He tossed the needle into the back of the vehicle and addressed Sarah. "What now?"

"Parkman, get out," Sarah said.

Alone with Howley, she asked, "Are you wearing a belt?"

He cocked his head sideways. "Why do you ask?"

"I won't ask again."

"Yes."

"Good. Pull it off."

Parkman knocked on the driver's side window and said "Let's go" through the door. Sarah held up a finger for him to wait. Howley pulled off his belt and held it up for her to see.

"Okay, you'll need that as a tourniquet for your wound."

"What wound?" he asked. Realization flashed across his face.

"This one," Sarah replied as she shot him in the right shin. The bullet entered a little to the right of center. He gasped and reached for his cell phone, his forehead glistening in the dim light.

Sarah snatched the phone away before he could dial out. Then she emptied the rest of the bullets into the dash, rendering the vehicle useless. There was no way he could follow her or contact his friends.

"Stop following me," she said as she closed the vehicle's door. "Or the next one will be fatal."

She placed the empty gun under a back tire, grabbed Parkman's hand, and ran for the airport terminal.

128

"YOU KNOW THEY will be there when we land," Parkman said. "And they'll have an even larger team waiting. And that's even *if* we can board."

"We aren't flying anywhere," Sarah said.

They entered the sliding doors to the main terminal. Sarah veered to the right, toward the ticket counters.

"Then what are we doing at the airport?"

"We're buying two tickets to the cheapest American destination. Then we leave the airport." She glanced at him. "On foot."

"Where are we going?"

"Montone. Italy."

"Italy!" He stopped walking.

"We'll buy the tickets first. Then I'll bring you up to speed."

Twenty minutes later they had two tickets to New York, for a flight leaving in forty-five minutes. They headed for the security gates. Once they were out of sight of the ticket booth, they turned and exited the airport through another set of sliding doors.

When they reached the outside, Parkman grabbed her arm and spun her around.

"Bring me up to speed, Sarah. You're in a foreign country shooting American government agents, or whoever the fuck they are. We're in a lot of trouble here." He released her arm.

"I'm going to expose a human trafficking ring. These are the people that allow Armond to go from country to country undetected. My suspicion is that it's the same group he uses to locate girls to bring to America for the highest bidder. The way to Armond Stuart is through these people in Italy. The man in charge is called Little Tony."

"Really?" Parkman asked.

Sarah walked away. Parkman followed.

"We need a car," she said. "We have to get into Germany or the Czech Republic and then use the train from there to get to Rome. After that, we can catch a train to Montone."

"You aren't screwing around here? We're really going to this Montone place to look for a guy named Little Tony?"

"When have I ever screwed around? Now focus—we need a car."

Sarah headed for the short-term parking area of the terminal.

"Sarah?"

She kept walking.

"Sarah?" Parkman said louder.

She spun around.

"We can't steal a car."

She sighed, waiting for the lecture.

"But we *can* take the train."

"The train?"

Parkman nodded.

Sarah crossed her arms. "What about border crossings? Passports too?"

"Follow me," he said, and headed toward a taxi. "You had your passport checked and stamped when you landed in Budapest. You have three months in the Schengen area, including Germany and Italy. There's nothing to worry about."

AT THE RAIL Europe ticket counter, Parkman paid cash for two tickets to Bologna, Italy. There was a brief stopover in Germany, but they'd be in Bologna in fourteen hours. They bought a quick breakfast and jumped on the train an hour later. Sarah tied up her hair and leaned back in her seat, legs crossed, watching the platform. Parkman sat beside her, his eyes on the interior of the train.

Eventually the train started crawling down the track. Ten minutes later, Sarah was fast asleep. They exited the train in Bologna just after ten that evening.

Parkman checked the schedule and determined they would take a morning train to a place called Umbertide, Italy. Sarah watched him handle all the details. It was actually comforting to have someone help take care of things. She had been on her own for a long time.

So far, the trip had been just as Parkman had predicted. No one asked to see their passports, and there had been no customs or border control.

Parkman had located a hotel for them for the night. He hailed a taxi and got them to the Pensione Marconi. Sarah marveled at the stone architecture of the buildings. Ever since they'd entered Italy, she'd seen hilltop houses and buildings that had turrets and large walls built into the sides of hills. Italy was aesthetically stunning. She entertained the idea of returning one day as a vacationer to enjoy the sights.

The hotel room was basic, with two single beds. Even though she'd slept on the first train, an entire day of traveling had exhausted her. She flopped on her bed and closed her eyes.

"What are we going to do once we get to Montone?" Parkman asked.

"Find Little Tony."

"Any plan on how to do that?"

"Nope."

"Sarah, look, I'm tired, too, but we need a plan. We can talk about it in the morning if you want, but I don't want to show up in Montone and just walk around asking for Little Tony."

"I suspect they'll know we're there." She felt his eyes on her.

"And how's that?" he asked.

"Someone as big and powerful as this Tony guy will have sentries posted. For all we know, they'll be waiting for us at the front doors of the city. This guy is their leader. He's the money man. No one gets close to the boss without the boss knowing about it."

"We don't have any weapons. We don't have any backup. No disguise and no plan."

"Unless we're going in with an army we'll never get close to this guy," she said. "We need *his* men to lead us to him. Then we make our move."

"And what move would that be?"

"We'll know it when we see it."

"Great." She heard Parkman flop down on the bed.

"And I need an Internet café tomorrow."

"Why?"

"To do a few minutes of research."

"Do I have to pry everything out of you? Research on what?"

"Vampires."

Parkman paused. "Okay, great. No response needed on that one. I'm going to find some food. We haven't eaten all day. Do you want anything?"

"I'll have whatever you're having, and get me some underwear, too."

"What? Underwear?"

Sarah sat up on her elbows and opened her eyes. "We traveled all day with the same clothes, and we didn't bring our luggage. I will want a change of underwear after my shower, before we travel more tomorrow."

Parkman nodded and stepped from the room, closing the door softly behind him.

Sarah lay back on the hard mattress and stared at the ceiling. "Vivian, I need you more than ever. Am I on the right path here?"

Sarah didn't have to wait long. She reached for the hotel pen and paper on the desk as her arm numbed.

129

SARAH HELD THE note in her hand. Who was Drake Bellamy? Where had she heard that name before?

She reread the note: Tell them that Drake Bellamy has retrieved the original documents and you have a copy. Tell them you know about the baseball game in two weeks. You also know about Armond and how he gets his girls through customs. And Sarah, use the fire. Remember to use the fire. The crypt: less than six days left.

"Drake Bellamy?" she said out loud. "Baseball game? Use the fire? What the hell?"

She fell back on the bed, exhausted. Whatever was supposed to happen in the crypt would happen in six days, on Friday. Where in Europe was she supposed to be on Friday? There were crypts all over the continent. And vampires—did that mean Hungary or Romania? After she finished in Italy, she would deal with that part of her sister's riddle. Until then, she needed sleep.

Sarah was out before Parkman got back with food.

THE SOUND OF the shower woke her. She rubbed her eyes and rolled over. The shower turned off.

"Morning," she called out.

"Morning." His muffled voice came through the bathroom door. "Coffee's on the bureau, and there's some leftovers of last night's pizza if you want some."

"Thanks." Sarah kicked her legs off the bed and sat on the edge. She poured herself a black coffee. It was half gone before Parkman came out of the bathroom. He was already dressed and messing with his hair.

"Where's my underwear?" she asked.

"In that bag. There was nothing available last night. I ran down this morning and found a market two blocks up. I hope the size is right."

Sarah pulled out a small pink piece of cloth. "You have got to be kidding me."

"What?"

"This is a thong. I don't wear thongs."

"All the kids wear thongs."

"I'm not a kid."

"Sarah. Give me a break."

"Because I have no other option, I will wear these."

She entered the bathroom and started the shower.

Forty-five minutes later they were on the train headed to Umbertide. After a large number of stops and a few train changes, they got off in Umbertide and started toward the main piazza, the center of town.

"Any real plan?" Parkman asked.

"I still don't know what we're walking into."

"Have you heard from Vivian?"

She snuck a glance at him. "Yes. Last night."

"You going to tell me about it?"

"She said to use the fire, but I don't know what that means yet."

"Anything else?"

They hit a roundabout and crossed through its center as they left the city limits of Umbertide. The road started on a slight incline as it rose toward the hilltop town of Montone.

"She said to tell these people that Drake Bellamy has the original documents and that I do, too. If anything happens to me these documents go public. I'm also supposed to say that I know about the baseball game coming up in two weeks. Something like that."

"Who is Drake Bellamy?"

"That immigration officer, István, in Budapest, said something about Bellamy being in Toronto and how people died because of a failed operation. Vivian just added several details."

They hit a switchback in the road and continued climbing. Sarah was starting to feel seriously drained. As soon as they got to Montone a large bottle of water was first on the agenda.

"Well, Sarah, I have a plan," Parkman said.

He was breathing as hard as she was. "What's your plan, Parkman?"

"Once we get there, we separate to cover more ground."

"I usually work alone anyway," she said.

They walked on in silence until the walled city of Montone came into view. Before entering the *centro storico*, Sarah slowed by a pizzeria on the right. Inside, she located two bottles of water. Parkman waited outside.

Two customers sat eating at a table in the corner. A lone man dressed in funeral black stood at the counter, sipping from a very small cup. The large man behind the counter wore a stained white apron. She paid with American currency. They didn't plan on staying in Italy for long, so she hadn't changed any money over to euros.

"*Buongiorno,*" the heavy man said.

Sarah nodded and handed him the money. He accepted the bills with a smile. Once outside, she saw Parkman waiting across the street, surveying the hills below. She handed him a water, then chugged half of hers in one pull.

"Any problems in there?" he asked.

"Some guy was staring at me. Probably nothing."

"If it was one of Little Tony's men he wouldn't have made it so obvious."

They headed up the cobblestone ramp that led into Montone, passing through an ancient gate. The town was vast, the fieldstone walls high. Tourists walked by, speaking in a distinctive British accent.

Parkman touched Sarah's arm and pulled her to the side. "Okay, here's where I go my way and you go yours."

"Where do we meet?"

"Out here at the gates. We'll walk back to Umbertide. When we came in on the train I saw another hotel called Hotel Rio. We'll stay there tonight. Deal?"

She offered a slight nod. "Be careful."

Parkman started up a different ramp to the right. Sarah continued straight to an open square. Two different restaurants had tables outside with umbrellas. One of them served gelato. She scanned the crowd, but nothing seemed off.

Four cobblestone paths led away from the piazza in different directions. She decided on the one on the right, just past the *gelateria*. When she turned a corner, two men were sitting on a bench talking to each other. They appeared to be in their fifties or sixties, idly watching as people walked by.

As she passed, she kept them in her peripheral vision. They had glanced at her but paid no extra attention. When she reached the top of the little road, she saw a group of seven men setting up some kind of concert apparatus. It appeared to be for a show or festival of some kind. Two black vans were parked with their back doors open as the men worked hard to set everything up.

An old man with a cane headed toward her. She smiled and moved to step past him.

"Another funeral," he said, shaking his head.

Sarah stopped. "You speak English."

The old man leaned heavily on his cane. "My son went to school in America. I learned English many years ago."

Sarah couldn't place his accent. "What's your accent? It doesn't sound Italian."

"That's what happens when you have an American-educated son and a British wife. My Italian is fine, but my English has been confused."

Sarah smiled. Cute old man. She studied the people in the area in case the old man was a decoy. The men setting up the stage continued to do so, paying them no attention. Maybe there was nothing in Montone after all? Maybe Little Tony was a fable and this was a huge waste of time.

Sarah turned her attention back to the old man. "Your English sounds great to me. I don't know any Italian, so it's a pleasure to talk to you. What was that you said about another funeral?"

"They're setting up for a funeral. The mayor does this big speech, and everyone comes to pay their respects."

"Who died? Was it someone you knew?"

A soft breeze cooled the sweat on her forehead. She drained the rest of the water bottle.

"A Hungarian man."

Alarm bells rang in her head. "Hungarian? Why is there a funeral all the way out here in Montone?"

"This is more of a ceremonial funeral. The man died in Hungary yesterday. People here in Montone worked with him. They set all this up as a way to send a message."

A message? What kind of message?

"I'm not sure I'm following." Sarah paused. "Do you know a man named Drake Bellamy?"

The old man started away from her, using his cane to guide him.

"Come back in an hour and watch the funeral. Then you'll see."

"You didn't answer my question." The old man just waved his hand in good-bye.

Sarah moved from the area quickly, intent on finding Parkman.

130

AN HOUR LATER, Sarah leaned against a stone wall and watched as people assembled in the area in front of the stage, speaking in hushed tones. At least 80 percent of them were dressed in black. A congregation of men surrounded the podium. Three vehicles had made it up the narrow cobblestone roads. Whatever this was, it was big for this little town.

She worried for Parkman, though. He hadn't turned up anywhere yet. The surrounding buildings appeared shut down. Windows as high as three stories up were shuttered.

"Sarah, ready for the show?" The old man ambled toward her.

She started at his voice. "Yeah. Does your town do this for all of its citizens?"

"Every time." The old man passed her and kept walking.

"Wait. Any chance I could get your help as a translator?"

He slowed and turned back to face her. "I'm performing the ceremony. I'll translate what you need to hear."

He continued toward the stage. As the old man reached the platform, he tossed his cane to the side, righted himself, and walked up the steps two at a time, able-bodied. The hair rose at the back of her neck.

The old man had reached the microphone and began speaking in Italian to the crowd. Some people responded verbally, speaking in soft voices. Some shook their heads, while others nodded and clapped.

Then the old man spoke her name.

"Sarah Roberts," he said. "She's over there." The old man pointed. She felt the eyes of everyone as they turned to stare.

When did I tell him my name?

She kept her feet rooted to the ground.

"Sarah has been the cause of all this turmoil," the old man continued in English. "She comes speaking the name Drake Bellamy.

And look who she brought with her."

The old man pointed to the roof of a building on Sarah's right. She followed his finger. Five men dressed in black held Parkman, his hands behind him, a cloth gag in his mouth.

When Sarah turned back to the podium, two men materialized out of the crowd a few feet from her. The townspeople slowly dispersed.

When she looked back up to the roof, it was empty. The old man stepped from the podium and started toward her. She waited until he stopped in front of her. There seemed to be no other play. "Let's walk."

"What is this? Where's Parkman?"

"Your reputation precedes you," he said. "We were waiting. We were prepared. But I don't fear you, Sarah Roberts."

"Armond Stuart?" she said. "Is he here, too?" Sarah breathed in deep to calm her nerves.

"He is one of my best customers. There's no way I could ever allow any harm to come to him." He leaned in conspiratorially. "Sarah, you have been quite a nuisance."

An image of István filled her mind. "The Hungarian man who died was István, wasn't it? The man who told me where to find you, Little Tony."

The old man didn't respond.

Something banged above them. Sarah ducked. The shutters of several windows had been slammed open. She counted seven men holding rifles with scopes on them.

"You've been watched since the moment you entered Montone," the old man said. "Did you think you could just walk in?" He turned to his men in the windows. "Shoot her like a rabid dog if she doesn't follow me." He spit on the ground as he shuffled along.

Sarah waited an extra moment, then started forward, unwilling to see if he was bluffing.

Two men dressed in black moved in to flank her on either side. As she followed the old man, new shutters opened as others closed.

They guided her down a sloping cobblestone road and onto the front steps of a church. She could no longer see the old man, as he had already passed through the large wooden doors.

Sarah entered the ancient church and took in her surroundings. Long wooden pews sat facing the front. The roof was made of stone, with huge paintings on all four walls.

She was shoved forward by one of the men. The altar at the front of the church became clear. A large wooden crucifix hung on the wall.

Parkman had been tied to the cross, bound there by his wrists and ankles, his head fallen, his chin resting on his chest.

131

"HOW SICK ARE you people?" She started toward Parkman. Footsteps sped up behind her. She dodged to the right, anticipating them, and slipped in between two pews. One of her escorts had lunged for her, and he lost his balance, careened off a pew, and dropped to the stone floor.

Sarah jumped out and planted a foot in his stomach, her rage overwhelming her. She grabbed for his weapon, yanked it out of his belt, then aimed it at the other man in black.

"Back away!" Sarah shouted.

The man raised his hands, then eased one step back. Other men were filing in through the front doors of the church. There was no escape. Nothing she could do except fight until she couldn't continue.

Sarah walked backward, heading for the crucifix at the front. She turned at the last pew and ran up a couple of steps.

A ladder sat to her right. She tucked the weapon into her waistband and grabbed the ladder, placing it beside Parkman. She climbed until she was face-to-face with him.

"Parkman," she whispered, touching his cheek softly. "You still with us?"

He nodded, but it was almost imperceptible. Then he whispered something.

"What's that?" she asked, leaning closer.

"Talk to these people. Keep them busy. I have a way out. Trust me."

"How am I going to get you down?" she asked. "Oh, Parkman, what have they done to you?" She lowered her voice, said "Good luck," then descended the ladder.

At the bottom, she turned to face her enemies. "This will cost you."

Little Tony, the old man with the cane, emerged from a side door of the church.

"Bring the girl to me," he said, and then disappeared behind the door again.

Sarah raised her hands. "I'll go willingly."

She started toward the side door as she eased out the weapon she'd taken from the escort, holding it by the grip, and handed it to its owner. He snatched it from her hand and pushed her toward the door.

At the opening, a set of stairs led down into darkness.

The crypt of the church.

Is this the crypt from the note, Vivian?

She took one step at a time, descending below the stone floor of the church. The tight stone corridor angled to the right. She walked no more than four feet before a vast room opened in front of her. The walls held large, square tombs. To the side, another door sat open. Soft amber light filtered through.

She took a deep breath, moved across the crypt floor, and entered Little Tony's office. Tony sat behind a large metal desk littered with weapons and ammunition. She scanned the room, surprised they were alone. A red couch ran along the back wall. Two chairs faced the desk. To the right of the desk a fire licked away at fresh logs.

Vivian said to use the fire. But how?

"You approve of my office?" Tony asked.

"A fireplace in a crypt?"

"This room sits directly below the old leper's hole. The smoke funnels through there and then outside."

"What's a leper's hole?" Sarah asked.

"Years ago the church would feed the lepers through a hole in the wall so the people inside the church wouldn't catch the disease."

He pointed at one of the two chairs facing the desk. When Sarah sat down, shoes scuffed the stone floor behind her. She turned to see two men enter the office and move to the couch along the back wall. They both sat, the guns in their hands resting on their thighs.

"What do you know about our little group?" Tony asked.

Sarah faced him. "I know about Drake Bellamy. He has the original documents, and he gave me a copy. What you're planning in two weeks at the baseball game will fail. If I don't leave here alive, the authorities will get everything. I came to tell you it's over." Inside, she knew she nailed it. Word for word.

"You're a stupid little girl, Sarah Roberts. Do you think I actually believe you?"

"I don't bluff."

"Our organization is too big to be brought down. Too connected. We have employees in almost every government worldwide."

"If I don't have the documents, why would I come to Montone unarmed?"

Tony looked down at the weapons on his desk. "I'm a collector of weapons and ammunition," he said.

"I can see that."

"I like guns, but I love bullets. Guns don't kill people; bullets do."

"If you say so."

Something crashed above them.

"Vincenzo," Tony said. "Go upstairs and see what that is."

One of the men on the couch rose and ran from the room.

That had to be Parkman.

He set the gun in his hand down and picked up another. She watched as he dropped the magazine out of the handle and began loading bullets into it from an open carton on the corner of his desk. The fire crackled beside her.

Use the fire. Sarah adjusted herself in her seat. "You're not above the law."

Tony raised the weapon until it was aimed at her. "That is where you're wrong. You will never leave Montone. But before I kill you, tell me one more thing."

Gunfire erupted upstairs. Tony cocked his head. "What was that?"

"My backup," Sarah said, hoping he'd buy it.

"Bullshit."

The gun moved to her left a notch and then jolted. The report made Sarah drop to the floor, her chair toppling over. The guard behind her on the couch gasped for breath. A neat hole had formed in his chest, blood already oozing from it.

"My men do not get disarmed by their captives," Tony said. He motioned with his gun for Sarah to retake her seat. "Sit," Tony ordered.

She righted the chair, placing it in the most opportune location. Her heart raced, pulse pounding in her ear.

"Tell me about Vivian," he said.

She calmed herself, breathing in and out through her mouth, mentally preparing for what she had to do. "My sister talks to me. She tells me how to stop criminals, how to kill them if I have to. Ever since

Armond murdered her, she has been haunting him through me." She leaned forward and took another deep breath. "She told me how to kill you."

"Oh, really?" Tony smiled. "What did Vivian say about me?"

"She told me about Drake Bellamy."

"Is that all?" He rubbed his chin.

"No, it wasn't."

Sarah lunged forward and knocked three full boxes of bullets into the crackling fire and then dove behind the desk on her side, covering her head.

Nothing happened at first. The fire continued to burn. Tony's chair slammed back on the other side of the desk.

A bullet fired somewhere in the room. He ducked at the sound as more bullets discharged and ricocheted around the room.

Sarah dropped her head and curled into a ball behind the desk. Bullets continued to discharge. The desk vibrated several times as some lodged into its front and sides. She prayed none would strike her. When things quieted down and she thought it was safe, she opened her eyes and saw Tony on the floor beside her, blood coming from a wound in his eye. His other eye stared into space.

Vivian, you are a genius.

She grabbed Tony's gun from his hand. On the desk sat three other guns and six more boxes of ammunition. She loaded as many bullets as she could, stored a couple of guns in her waistband, then moved to the door.

It was time to get Parkman.

She kissed her palm and touched the wall beside her as a gesture of respect to Vivian. Then she left the crypt, intent on murder.

132

SARAH EDGED OVER the top of the stairs leading from the crypt. Two men and one woman—fully armed—were looking outside through square windows. Sarah aimed at one of the men and considered firing. The stairwell could act as a trench to protect her from return fire. She waited a heartbeat and then lowered her weapon. She couldn't just shoot someone in the back.

When she spun around to look for Parkman, the tall wooden cross at the front of the church was empty. Whatever he did seemed to have worked.

When she looked back at the three people, the woman was staring at her. Sarah raised her weapon. The woman lowered hers to the floor and left it there by her foot as she stood back up to face Sarah, hands raised.

"I'm unarmed," the woman said. "Don't shoot."

The men turned to see who their companion was talking to, then looked away. Evidently, whatever was happening outside was much more important to them.

"We are your friends," the woman said.

"Bullshit," Sarah yelled.

"Can I lower my hands?"

Sarah nodded.

"Tony was the head of a large organization that goes deeper than one man," the woman said. "They traffic people every day throughout the world. We've been hunting them for years. Only in the last six months have we been able to get this close to Mr. Tony."

"Who are you?"

"My name is Rosalie Wardill. I'm leading the task force handling Operation Border Control."

"You're what?" Sarah lowered her weapon.

"We are a task force set up by multiple police and law enforcement agencies around the world. Our objective is to stop Mr. Tony and his international group of thugs. It has been over three years, and today we have made great progress because of you."

"Can you prove any of this?"

Rosalie reached inside her black suit and came out with what looked like a leather wallet.

Sarah ascended the last few steps, and after a quick check behind her, she walked across the stone floor of the church until she was close enough to read Rosalie's identification.

"Okay. The gun stays in my hand. I don't exactly feel safe yet."

"Understood. Come, we need to talk."

Rosalie gestured to a nearby pew. Sarah sat facing the two men by the windows.

"Where's Parkman?" she asked.

Rosalie sat opposite her. "He's outside. We invaded the city when you were down with Tony in his office. Parkman said you would use the fire, whatever that means. We assumed you would use our cover fire to make whatever move you needed to make. It's a relief to see you come up those stairs and not Mr. Tony."

"I used the fire, but it wasn't yours."

Rosalie frowned, puzzled. "Your file is quite something."

"How do you know me?"

"Your name crossed my desk a few months ago—that compound bust in Arizona where you almost stopped Armond. He's one of the most cunning perps we've ever come across."

"He's clever. I won't rest until he's dealt with."

"That's why we need you. We organized our team and planned the attack to match your arrival."

"How did you know I was coming?"

"A man named Rod Howley, an American, said you would be in Montone to meet Little Tony today. He's involved in some kind of paranormal research. This man said you were to be taken care of, kept safe. His message came to me directly from my superiors. They took a risk contacting me like they did."

Sarah exhaled a breath she'd been holding. How powerful was this guy Howley?

"I couldn't believe it either," Rosalie continued. "Anyway, once you went downstairs, we took out the few men Tony had in the church, got Parkman down, and tossed him a weapon. The three of us were left behind to debrief you."

Rosalie continued. "The city of Montone will be ours in the next few minutes. After that, we have months of paperwork to sift through. That paperwork will effectively bring down all the people in each government around the world that are on the take." Rosalie rested her hands on her lap. "Sarah, we need you to accompany us back to Budapest. Only you and Parkman can positively identify Armond Stuart's new face."

"Then what?"

"Mr. Howley said he would meet up with you after that. The two of you are heading back to the States."

Sarah shook her head. "No way."

Rosalie frowned. "What?"

"It's a long story. If you've got Montone locked down, I need to meet up with Parkman and get something to eat. Kinda shaky."

"Absolutely. By the way, taking out Little Tony was like taking out the master vampire. All his minions will soon follow."

"Vampire?" Sarah asked. "Funny choice of words."

"What?" Rosalie raised an eyebrow.

"Nothing." Sarah brushed her off.

"Tell me, how did you do it?"

"I didn't. Tony shot himself. He had bullets in boxes on his desk. I just knocked them into the fireplace. When they began discharging, he was in the way. I wasn't."

"That's risky. You could have been shot, too," Rosalie said, leaning back in surprise.

"I had a feeling I'd be okay," Sarah said, thinking about her sister's note. Vivian wouldn't have told her to do it if she knew Sarah would be fatally injured.

Rosalie got up from the pew. She addressed her men and then talked into a lapel mic. She looked at Sarah and waved her over.

"It's done. As far as we can tell, the streets are safe. My team has the last four of Tony's men locked down. Everyone else is accounted for."

"Parkman?"

"Other than some bruising on his wrists, he's fine. He saved the lives of a couple of my men today."

The four of them stepped from the church into the late afternoon sun and watched as people ran left and right, cleaning up shell casings and bodies as they went. Blood stained the ancient stones at Sarah's feet.

Something still nagged at her conscience. It felt like the woman was telling the truth. A gun battle had taken place. The enemy was dealt with. Rosalie greeted her team. Everyone recognized her authority. Some even stopped what they were doing to salute her. Most stared at Sarah.

But Rosalie had known Sarah was coming for Tony. She had been ordered to take care of Sarah like a babysitter, then deliver her afterward. They had waited years to advance on Little Tony, but the day they decided to move forward was the day Sarah was coming—Sarah, an unproven professional, untrained, unattached to any legal agency in law enforcement.

Was it a test? Any way she sliced it, Sarah wasn't comfortable with how it had been handled. A full assault on Montone with a professional task force would've been a better option. It would've been safer for her and Parkman. What if Tony had an itchy finger? They had taken a big chance with her life.

Walking the tilting streets of Montone, she realized that ultimately she was a prisoner. This task force had its directive and that was to deliver Sarah to Budapest and then hand her over to Rod Howley.

The handover to Howley would never take place. But she'd allow them to take her to Budapest, because taking down Armond was her first priority.

Once Armond was dead, Sarah would disappear—maybe go to Canada and meet that Drake Bellamy guy who kept popping up. The paperwork these people had to go through would keep them from stopping the hit on Drake at that baseball game in two weeks.

Decision made. She would deal with Armond and then flee to Toronto to save a life. Pulling her thoughts together, she looked past a small crowd of Rosalie's men and spotted Parkman.

The gun was still in her hand. She stashed it in her jeans.

Parkman looked up at her. Their eyes locked and she felt safe again, but only for a moment. They needed to talk. Parkman was the only one she trusted to help her escape Howley once Armond was dealt with.

133

OSALIE'S TEAM REMOVED Parkman and Sarah from Montone and put them up in Hotel Rio for the night, with Rosalie's men guarding their room.

"What are we going to do?" Sarah asked Parkman when they were alone."

Parkman was trying to get the television to work. He smacked the top. "I don't know. Maybe they can bring us another one."

"I'm talking about these people guarding us. You're aware we're prisoners?"

Parkman turned from the TV. "There's nothing we can do right now. They're feeding us and flying us back to Budapest. Our luggage has been picked up, and we're lucky to be alive. And now we have a major task force on *our* side hunting Armond. In my opinion, everything's coming up roses."

Sarah plopped down on her bed. It was hard as a board—like every other European mattress she'd slept on. "Parkman, after they're done with us, they're handing me over to the people who kidnapped you in Budapest."

Parkman stepped to the window. "You know, I could really go for a toothpick right now."

"Parkman!"

He raised his hands. "I'm listening, I swear."

Sarah looked down at her hands. "This is the first time I've had to cooperate with so many law enforcement types. You know me better than anyone, my parents included. I could use your help."

Parkman glanced back at her. "You're right. We'll do it together."

Sarah raised her eyes. "Do what together?"

Parkman sat beside her on the bed. "I paid attention when I was taken by those Sophia Project men. They use the university as a cover. They're actually working a black operation. Something seriously top secret. It's given them massive power. It's almost like this guy Howley has direct access to the president."

Sarah frowned. "That's not very comforting."

Parkman continued. "Howley and his team are military contractors—mercenary types."

"How is that possible?"

"Think of the first atom bomb."

Sarah shook her head and frowned. "What?"

"When the United States dropped the bombs on Japan, twice during August of 1945, people were shocked. A bomb that could destroy a city. No one else had that technology yet. Japan surrendered and the war ended a few months later. This Howley guy is charged with developing the next atom bomb. Something no other country would have in their possession."

"Are you trying to say people like me are a weapon?"

"You've saved lives with your gift. You're using it at the risk of your own life. If someone like Howley could leverage that power, America could destroy any enemy in their path. It would begin a new era of warfare. You could tell them enemy weaknesses. You could have insight into any country's defenses and strengths."

"Vivian decides to send messages when she feels like it. It's out of my control."

"Howley suggested that he had other psychics in his care already. He wanted to assure me of your well-being. He felt getting to me was important."

Sarah got up from the bed to pace the floor. "He contacted Rosalie and told her we were coming today. He said to take care of us. Rosalie planned her attack to coincide with our arrival. Why would they do that when they know I'm not law enforcement?"

Parkman leaned back on his elbows and offered her a wry smile. "Ah, but you are. You're better than most, and they know that. It was an honor to work with the great Sarah Roberts, I was told. You've been doing this for almost five years now. Everyone knows your name, and has heard about what you can do." Sarah dropped into the chair in the corner, emotionally spent. "See, that's what I'm talking about. I don't want to be *known*."

"Too late. You can't save countless lives over almost five years and not get noticed. You've been on the front cover of newspapers around the globe. You're being hailed as a hero more often than not. People want to meet you. People want to understand you. It's human nature."

"Shit," Sarah said, and slapped her hands together. "Shit," she said again. "Okay, first things first. Let's go to Budapest and deal with Armond. Then I disappear for a while."

"It won't be that simple, but I agree. Deal with Armond and then drop out of sight."

Sarah nodded. "But how?"

"You'll find a way. You always do. Ask Vivian what to do. She'll tell you what's best. After all you two have been through together, I have faith. You'll figure this out."

Parkman lay back on the bed and closed his eyes.

"That's a lot of faith, Parkman."

"I believe in you, Sarah. When this is done you'll get us both out of trouble and back to the States."

"Canada."

"Wherever," Parkman said, his voice sleepy.

"Hey, get up. That's my bed."

"What? Why is it your bed?"

"Because I said so."

"Okay, okay. See what I mean? Sarah has it her way."

She rose from her chair. "You're patronizing me."

"I'm not. I'm here for you. I didn't come to Europe for a vacation."

Parkman moved to the other bed and promptly fell down. She waited a few moments, then lay on hers.

"Why did you say Canada?" Parkman mumbled.

"We'll talk later."

In minutes, Parkman's breathing was slow and deep. It took her an hour to fall asleep. She couldn't get Howley out of her mind. Things would be different when they met again. There would be no *taking care* of her. She would take care of him. He was leaving her without any other options.

134

A KNOCK ON their door startled her awake. Sarah opened her eyes and leaned up on her elbows. The sun blazed in through Hotel Rio's thin curtains.

She rolled off the bed and shuffled to the door just as it opened an inch. Sarah bodychecked it with her shoulder, slamming it shut.

"What do you want?"

"Orders from Rosalie. Truck out front taking us to Rome. You have fifteen minutes."

"We'll be ready. Don't open the door again."

After using the bathroom, she came out to see Parkman standing at the end of his bed, fully dressed. He gathered up his meager things. "I've been thinking. What will happen when we deal with Armond?"

"I told you. Disappear for a while. Canada. Maybe I'll go back to helping strangers like I used to before this whole mess started."

Parkman looked at her. "There's something you haven't considered."

Sarah shook out her hair and played with the ends. It needed a wash, but there was no time. "What?"

"Vivian."

"What's there to consider?"

"Will she continue sending messages?"

The idea that her sister would stop communicating hadn't crossed her mind. What *if* Vivian stopped? What would she do? Get a job? Get married? Have kids one day? This was her life now. She'd killed people. She couldn't pretend it never happened.

"Sorry, I didn't mean anything by it." Parkman touched her arm.

"You have a point. I'll deal with that if I have to."

"Let's find me some toothpicks or I'm going to lose my mind."

Someone knocked on their door again, and shouted, "One minute!"

"Coming," Sarah shouted back.

Three black sedans were waiting out front. Sarah and Parkman
were directed into the second one. Rosalie sat in the back, waiting.

She signaled the driver, and then all three vehicles pulled out of Hotel Rio. In minutes they were on the E45, heading south toward Rome.

An hour into the ride, Sarah watched the countryside race by the windows. Without turning, she asked, "Rosalie, how will you handle Little Tony's people? The ones who are still out there?"

"I'm not sure what you mean."

Sarah yawned, covered her mouth, then stretched. "A man will be killed in Toronto in two weeks. If that order isn't rescinded, then the men directed to take out the subject will go ahead. While your team sifts through paperwork, there will be people out there still in trouble."

"What could I possibly do? If you're privy to specific information, then you should bring us up to speed and we'll attempt to deal with it. But until I learn everything Tony was into, I couldn't possibly save everyone."

"Hmph," Sarah grunted. "I'll deal with it. I was planning on visiting Canada next anyway."

"What was that?" Rosalie asked, her tone curt.

Sarah suppressed another yawn. "I said I will deal with it."

"It's our job to handle that sort of thing. You can't act like a vigilante out here, with no accountability."

Sarah leaned forward. "I've been through things that would make the best-trained operatives sick. But I persevered and did what I could to stay alive. Look what it's gotten me. Rod Howley wants to turn me into his lab rat. I'm still here because I have to be. I have no choice. It comes from in here." She tapped the center of her chest. "This isn't about being a vigilante. This is about dealing with a criminal element that works outside the reach of the authorities." Sarah stole a glance at Parkman. "I'm sorry. You know that doesn't include you."

Rosalie turned away and stared out her window.

After five minutes of silence, Sarah said, "If you think of me as a vigilante and not capable of handling the situation in Toronto, then why did you wait to infiltrate Montone until I arrived? Why leave me alone, unarmed, in the crypt with the head of the organization?"

"I don't have the information you're looking for. I'm a soldier. I follow orders. Currently my orders are to deliver you to Budapest and use you to locate Armond Stuart and identify him. That's all you'll get from me."

Sarah nodded. "Now we understand each other. You've got orders. I don't."

"What does that mean?"

"That's all you'll get from me."

Sarah looked back out her side window. A sign went by, saying they were just over a hundred kilometers from Rome. The rest of the ride was quiet. At the airport, the driver passed through security and drove onto the tarmac, where a private jet waited.

Several hours later, they made a quick descent into Budapest and then filed into two waiting SUVs. Sarah could've sworn they were Howley's. The last twenty-four hours gnawed at her. Essentially she was still a prisoner, a captive. The only reason she'd allowed it to get this far was because they had the same goal. This was the best way to hunt Armond because it wasn't just her anymore.

The SUVs drove through Budapest. They pulled up to the Best Western and stopped.

"This is a joke, right?" Sarah asked.

"No," Rosalie answered. "We have two rooms booked for you and Parkman here. Your luggage is already in your rooms. You're to wait for my contact. Once we have something, we'll be in touch."

"That's it?" Sarah asked. Parkman had been mute the whole trip.

"That's it," Rosalie said.

"What's to stop us from walking away?"

"As far as I understand it, Mr. Howley and his team won't let you stray too far. This thing we're doing here, allowing you to help ID Armond, is a favor from Howley. An olive branch. Too many countries want Armond stopped. It would look bad if the Americans jeopardized that."

The SUV idled in front of the hotel.

"So what you're saying is, I'm already Howley's property. Deal with Armond and then he does with me as he sees fit."

"I'm following orders."

Sarah stepped from the SUV and Parkman followed.

"Sarah," Rosalie shouted from the inside of the vehicle.

She turned back to face Rosalie.

"If it means anything, I'm sorry about this whole situation." Rosalie's eyes clouded over.

Sarah closed the door and headed for the lobby. Ten minutes later Parkman was in his room knocking on the dividing door. Sarah opened her side.

"What was all that back there in the SUV?" he asked.

"I wanted to know if I could rely on her when the chips fall. Now I know."

"And? Is she with us?" Parkman asked.

"She's with us. When it comes to the handoff to Howley we may need her."

"You got all that from your conversation?" Parkman looked perplexed.

"I'm going to have to die. That way Rod Howley can't come after me anymore. And Rosalie is going to help kill me to make me disappear."

135

SOMEONE WAS KNOCKING on the hotel room door. The alarm clock beside her read 4:18 a.m. They had eaten in the hotel restaurant and retired early to bed.

The knocker rapped again.

"Coming," she called.

Sarah leaned against the door.

"What do you want?" she asked.

"We've located Armond," Rosalie whispered. "We need you to come with us."

"How much time do I have?"

"Will five minutes be enough?"

"Yeah." Sarah stepped away from the door.

Four minutes later, she exited her room. One of Rosalie's men sat a few doors down on a chair. He escorted Sarah to the lobby and out into a waiting SUV. The wind blew Sarah's hair into her face. She brushed it clear and remembered a very different time, when she didn't have to put it up out of the way.

She eased into the backseat across from Rosalie as the vehicle got moving.

"Where's Parkman?" she asked.

"He's not joining us on this one," Rosalie said.

"Why's that?"

"Only one of you is needed to make an ID. Actually, I think he's heading home to America today."

That's strange. "Does Parkman know he's going home?"

"No. But Howley isn't interested in Parkman. I have my orders."

Sarah stewed for a moment, considering her next words carefully. "Are we truly following a lead on Armond right now, or is this just a way to separate me from Parkman?"

"There's a lead."

"Tell me about it." Sarah leaned against the door while the SUV turned a sharp corner. The driver wasn't wasting time. They were certainly in a hurry.

"The Palace Nightclub, a strip joint, had a complaint called in to the police. A couple of young girls showed up without the proper documentation."

"Management called this in?" Sarah asked. "Doesn't make sense."

"Why not?" Rosalie asked.

"If Armond is running girls, then management is getting a kick-back. They'd be paid off."

"We suspect other dancers called it in. The police are holding the girls until we get there."

"This seems a bit weak."

Rosalie fell silent. The SUV crossed the Danube River. Sarah stared at the glimmering Budapest skyline, wondering where her sister was.

"Okay," Rosalie said, startling Sarah. "Here's the drill. We handle the questioning. We deal with the girls and get them out of there safely. This is the closest we've been to Armond in a long time. We should get a good description of his new face, too."

Sarah had to accept this. This was their gig, and she was just along for the ride.

"Understood?" Rosalie asked, a worried expression on her face.

"How do you know this is tied to Armond? Sounds small-time for him."

"We know. He did this years ago to get fast cash when we were on his tail. After a couple weeks, he fled with his pockets full and another new identity. Now"—Rosalie leaned forward as the vehicle slowed—"I need to know you'll follow directions. You're here in case we get a visual. Clear?"

"Clear. But I'm not waiting in the SUV. And when this is over I want coffee."

Rosalie nodded. The SUV pulled up to a building and stopped. Sarah waited until everyone had left the vehicle, then edged out. She leaned on the open door as she took in her surroundings. This was a part of Budapest she hadn't gotten to in her month's stay. It seemed older, more decrepit. She scanned the horizon as the rising sun colored the sky a light blue.

Three police cars were parked at the front of the strip club. Rosalie's SUV was the only other vehicle. Something bothered her about the situation.

A loud, metallic bang made her jump. She dropped to her knees. A young couple walked the street three blocks up, but other than that the streets were empty.

To her left, a flash of light caught her eye as another bang sounded. This time it was much closer. A bullet hole had formed in the hood.

She moved behind the open back door and focused on the building across the street, staring at its windows. Movement in a second-floor window lined up with where she'd seen the flash. Whoever had shot at her was packing up and leaving.

Sarah bolted across the street to the nearest building and pressed herself flat against the brick wall. Once there, she realized the shooter would probably try to escape out the back. Without a moment's hesitation, she raced down an alley. A small fence had a hole in it just large enough to fit through. Sarah dropped to her hands and knees and crawled through, standing up on the other side.

The sun had gained more ground, illuminating the area enough that she didn't need streetlights for guidance.

She reached for her waistband. Empty. She would have to stop the gunman unarmed.

Footsteps sounded close. Someone was coming.

Shadows covered her as she crouched behind a garbage bin. The smell almost made her gag. She held a hand over her mouth and waited.

The shooter came into view. He wore a black jacket and black pants. He had a long black bag slung over his shoulder. He moved slowly, wary of his surroundings, then edged around the corner of the building. He peeked toward the front. Satisfied that no one was on to him, he turned toward Sarah and jumped over the back fence not six feet from her.

She waited until he had passed, then got up to follow him. She stayed close as he rounded the corner of another brick building. At the corner, she held back and peeked around. He was trotting up the street through a construction area, toward a large black vehicle.

Sarah kept to the shadows as best she could, her running shoes emitting almost no sound off the cement.

The shooter reached the black Cadillac, and fumbled with his keys. Sarah picked up her step as she heard the chirp of the car's alarm deactivating.

The sidewalk was under construction to her right. The public works team had left the area cordoned off with warning signs and sawhorses. An orange and white construction bar suspended a make-shift yield sign in front of the newly laid cement. Sarah grabbed the pole, leaned into it, and tore it free from the sign.

Now she had a weapon. The shooter had disappeared inside the vehicle and was just turning the Cadillac on when the pole crashed into his windshield. The glass cracked. Sarah pulled back and twisted inward to smash the driver's side window.

At any moment the gunman could pull a handgun and shoot at her. Before her next windup, the shooter managed to get the vehicle moving. She swung hard, knowing that it might be her last attempt. When the pipe made contact with the driver's side window again, it broke through.

The car shot forward, pulling the pipe from her grasp. The Cadillac rolled ahead, veered to the side, then jumped the curb. Five feet into the sidewalk, it bumped into a light standard and stopped.

She ran for the vehicle's door, grabbed the handle, and yanked it open, spilling the driver onto the sidewalk. He moaned and reached for a cut on his cheek. His good eye stared up at her, wide and scared.

She dropped to one knee and searched his waistband and pockets for a weapon. The fight had gone out of the man. A small pistol came out of his jacket pocket. After she checked if it was loaded, she flipped off the safety.

"Who hired you?" she asked.

He grunted something.

She brought the gun to his stomach and checked the street. They were alone. She pressed the barrel hard, hoping if she had to use the gun, his clothing would muffle the shot.

"Gut shot by a carjacker," she whispered. "You'll probably live, but a hole in the stomach can mess you up for the rest of your life." She shrugged. "But what do I care?"

"Wait," he mumbled. "I was told . . ." he started, but the pain took his breath away.

She glared down at him. "Tell you what. You get an ambulance as soon as I know who sent you. Now, talk."

"I was told. You might shoo—uh. I was told to make sure you don't get away."

"By who?"

He stared at her with his good eye. "He say you would know him. He say his name is Jack Tate."

"You just saved yourself a bullet."

She eased off him, scrambled backward, and sat on the sidewalk with her back to the building's wall. What was going on here? Draw her out, away from Rosalie? Maybe the strip joint thing was a decoy to expose her?

An old man with a cane stopped to peek in a store window a block away. It was an odd time to be window-shopping. He eventually headed in the other direction without looking toward the Cadillac.

The sun had gotten higher. Her shadow stretched out before her. She sat there, in that moment, feeling a surreal sense of ease, calming her pulse after the adrenaline rush.

Her attempted shooter had curled into a ball on the sidewalk. She crawled over, placed the gun against the back of his skull, and removed his wallet. He didn't put up a fight. Was he waiting for someone to save him?

The man had no identification. There were a few hundred dollars in Hungarian currency and a note on a lined piece of paper in his wallet. She opened the note to see a small grocery list.

What the hell is palichinta?

Her hand numbed.

She frantically searched for a pen. The shooter had one in the same pocket. She grabbed it as a full blackout came upon her.

"Sarah?" someone said. "Sarah, are you okay?"

She snapped awake. Rosalie leaned over her. Two of Rosalie's men were attending to the shooter.

"What happened here?" Rosalie asked. "We came out of the strip club, and you were gone. When we got here, an old man with a cane was approaching you. We got him out of here and tried to wake you up."

Sarah sat up, blinking in the morning sun. "I'm fine. I must've blacked out. This guy tried to shoot me outside the front of the strip club."

Rosalie looked at the man, then back to Sarah.

Sarah explained everything from the first shot until she blacked out, omitting why she passed out.

"We're being played." Rosalie shook her head.

"Armond plays everyone."

Rosalie glared at her. "You don't understand. I put a lot of time into this undercover job. There's no way Armond could know who we were until we raided Montone. In such a short time, how could he know so much?"

Sarah used the wall of the building to stand. Two police cars were arriving. An ambulance brought up the rear.

"Armond hides in plain sight. When my sister sent me to find him, he insinuated himself as a colleague using the name Jack Tate. I barely got away with my life, thanks to Parkman."

"Thanks to me you almost lost your life tonight. I'm lucky he missed."

Sarah grimaced. "*You're* lucky he missed? How about me?"

Rosalie looked sideways at her. "My orders are to keep you safe, protected. I'm to deliver you to Howley when this is over. I don't do that, I'm finished."

Sarah stepped away. "Then quit now."

"What?" Rosalie called after her.

Sarah moved away. She needed to find the note Vivian gave her. To her relief she found it in her back right pocket. It paid to have paper accessible at all times. After unfolding it, she scanned the words.

Rosalie had stepped out from behind the Cadillac, following her. She motioned for Rosalie to join her as she folded the paper and pocketed it again.

"You know that old man with the cane?" Sarah asked.

Rosalie nodded.

"That was Armond Stuart."

"How do you know?"

"Do you know anything about me?"

"Your sister?"

She nodded. "He was about to make his move when you got here. So you did save my life after all." Sarah said this without conviction.

Rosalie spoke into a lapel mic, telling her men to scour the area for the old man with the cane.

"Did your sister tell you anything else?" she asked.

"She told me it all ends in a crypt on Friday."

"A crypt," Rosalie repeated. She turned to watch as her men escorted the attempted shooter to a waiting vehicle. "Most of the men involved in the organization use crypts as a meeting place. It makes it impossible to record them talking. They have other reasons, too." She seemed dazed. "Did your sister tell you what crypt?"

"Just that it has something to do with vampires."

"Vampires?"

One of Rosalie's men called out. The police required a statement from Sarah.

"Stay here," Rosalie said. "I'll deal with the police. And let me think about this crypt thing. I may have an idea what your sister means."

Sarah nodded and sat down on the opposite curb. Vivian knew the gunman would miss, so she'd done nothing. She expressed her love for Sarah. As for the crypt, fate was in charge this time.

A man shouted for Rosalie to come to the SUV. The shooter was convulsing in the backseat.

He'd taken a drug of some kind. It took him just over a minute to die.

Rosalie's men yanked the body from the SUV and laid the corpse out on the sidewalk for the police to handle. In under five minutes, they were on their way back to the hotel, no closer to Armond than they were before.

136

AN HOUR LATER Rosalie sat across from Sarah at a small café.

"Thank you for finding a place that sells American coffee," Sarah said. "Everywhere I go, all I can find are cappuccinos and espressos."

They sat in a corner booth, with Sarah's back to the wall. She watched the windows, her eyes drawn to the random people walking by.

"You seem lost in thought," Sarah said.

"I think I know the crypt."

Sarah set her cup down and leaned in. "Where is it?"

"Esztergom."

"Where's that?"

"Just north of us. About an hour's drive."

"What makes you think it's the one we want?" Sarah asked.

"When you said vampires, it clicked. The place is called the Esztergom Basilica. It's the largest church in Hungary. The crypt is the resting place of many famous people. Bela Lugosi, a Hungarian actor, filmed part of the original *Dracula* there. Your vampire connection."

Sarah sipped her coffee and eased back in her chair. "How did you know that?"

"I toured it five years ago when I was first stationed in Hungary. The Esztergom crypt is quite impressive. The basilica overlooks the Danube, with Slovakia bordering the other side of the river."

A plan formed in Sarah's head. "How close to the river is it?"

"I don't know exactly, but you could hit a golf ball from the main dome of the basilica and make the water. It's a long climb up narrow, winding steps to get to the top of the basilica, but it's a gorgeous view of the city. And the crypt is magnificent."

"You know the place well?"

"It makes sense that this crypt is important to Armond. Much of it is cut off from the public." She tapped furiously at her phone, then studied Sarah intently. "Did you say the event would happen Friday?"

Sarah nodded, gripping her coffee with hands that had suddenly gone cold.

"On the first Friday of each month the church is closed to the public for mass. No tours. Just local churchgoers. This happens in the late afternoon, early evening. Based on what you've said, we think Armond will be there this Friday."

Sarah took a few big swallows of coffee to warm her insides. "So you believe in what I do?"

"What do you mean?"

"That I receive messages from the Other Side."

Rosalie averted her eyes, then fidgeted with a fingernail before looking back up. "I believe now, yes. I didn't believe until I met you."

"Then you'll help me escape."

"Escape?" Rosalie scrunched up her forehead.

Sarah drained the rest of her coffee. "I can't go with Howley."

"So what are you saying? Spell it out for me."

"You'll know when the time comes. Just make sure you do what you think is right."

Rosalie's phone chirped. She read the text.

"Parkman's furious. He wants to see you right away."

"Sure, he's probably worried. He did travel to Europe on my account."

"We'll drive you to the hotel, but only to pick up your things. From here on in you stay with us. I can't let Armond send another sniper after you."

"Gee, thanks," Sarah said as she rose from her chair. "I don't really like the idea of being picked off either."

"Are you always this sarcastic?"

"Only with people I like."

"How do you treat the bad guys?"

"I just try to hurt them."

They made it back to the hotel in good time. On two different occasions Sarah was sure they were being followed. They were using the same vehicle that took a bullet in the hood.

When she jumped from the vehicle, Sarah turned to Rosalie. "Give me a gun. I need to be armed."

"No way. You're here in an advisory capacity only."

Sarah shook her head. "You saw what happened this morning. I was lucky there was a pipe nearby. Don't be difficult. Give me a gun."

Rosalie looked her up and down. "Even if I wanted to, I couldn't. What if you shoot somebody?"

"I plan to."

"You're not helping your case."

"If you won't give me a weapon, I will be forced to take one."

"Sarah, are you always this difficult?"

"Seriously, think about it. Someone like Armond is out there and wants me dead. I have had the damnedest time trying to stay armed in Europe, and I have almost been killed a few times because of it. This is me. This is who I am. I get a gun or screw you and your advisory role bullshit."

Rosalie sighed. The mic on her waist beeped.

"You better get that," Sarah said, then stepped away.

A piece of stone chipped off the wall where she had been standing. She dove for cover as another bullet pinged off the side of the vehicle.

As she landed on the hard cement, Rosalie yelled into her mic, "We're under fire."

Sarah nestled up against the rear tire of the SUV. Rosalie had crouched down by the front tire, opposite her. "Gonna rethink your position on arming me?" Sarah shouted.

"This isn't the time—"

Another ricochet shot past Rosalie's head, cutting her off mid-sentence.

Sarah slapped her thigh. "I knew we were being followed."

"Why didn't you say anything?"

"You guys are the professionals," she screamed. "I mean, how else could Armond keep tabs on me? He's not a god."

Rosalie groaned and reached into an ankle holster. She tossed Sarah a small-caliber weapon.

"I want it back. You Americans and your guns. Just don't kill a citizen or worse."

Sarah looked back at her. "What's worse?"

"Me."

Another shot rang out. A car turned hard, its wheels screeching. It hit the wall of the hotel ten feet in front of the SUV they were hiding behind.

"We have to move," Sarah shouted.

"Why? We're covered here."

"The sniper is shooting random drivers. He's trying to get them to ram into this SUV. We need to move. Now."

Another shot rang out. An engine revved.

"On my count," Rosalie shouted.

"No counting. Go now!" Sarah scrambled to her feet and ran for the hotel doors, head down.

Bullets rained down from some kind of automatic weapon. She made the door and half fell, half dove into the cover of the hotel lobby. Gratefully, Rosalie fell in behind her.

"How did they miss?" Rosalie gasped. "That gun was on rapid-fire."

"I have no idea," Sarah said, patting herself down.

Footsteps pounded down the hotel stairs. A door banged open behind them. The women spun around on the floor and raised their weapons in unison.

Parkman emerged from the stairwell, gun in hand.

"Got him," he said. "Lone gunman across the street. He was sitting in a black car. Dead now. Didn't you hear me unloading on him from our room?"

Sarah looked at Rosalie. Rosalie looked at Sarah. They had both thought the barrage of bullets was coming from their attacker.

"We didn't know," Rosalie said. "We thought—"

He smirked, slightly pleased with himself. "Sorry about that. Didn't mean to scare you."

Sarah got up off the floor. "How many times are you going to save my life, Parkman?"

"Don't know." He shrugged. "As many as I can, I guess. Where'd you get the gun?"

Sarah pointed at Rosalie as she stashed it. Four stunned people were taking cover in the lobby. The desk clerk and what looked like a manager were behind the counter, only their eyes and foreheads showing. A man and a woman crouched behind a sofa in the corner.

"We good now?" the man in the suit asked. "*Minden jó?*"

Sarah nodded. "Yeah, bad guy dead. Everything back to normal."

The man in the suit shook his head and ran his hands through his hair. In his broken English he said, "No, not normal. Please, everyone leave. No stay my hotel. Please leave. Get things and go. Not good for business."

Rosalie glanced out the door and then turned to the manager. "My associates will pick up their bags, and we will leave." She turned to Sarah and pointed at the gun. "I'm gonna need that back."

"Come and get it."

Rosalie glanced at Parkman.

"He isn't going to help you," Sarah said. "I know *he* wants me armed."

Parkman shrugged at Rosalie, who threw up her hands. Sarah started toward the stairs. "Let's get our things."

Fifteen minutes later they had checked out. Rosalie's men were outside dealing with the local police. A tow truck had shown up to remove the car that had careened off the road. Parkman was told he would need to make a statement.

Knowing Rod's men would be close, Sarah peered around for the familiar suits. As predicted, three men stood in the shadows of an office building across the street, observing everything. One of them lifted his hand to his mouth and spoke into it.

As much as she hated them, it was good that they were staying close. She needed them at the crypt on Friday. Unless Vivian said something different, Sarah knew her plan would work. It had to.

Be killed or remain a prisoner.

Although, after surviving two attempts on her life in one day, it was clear that being a prisoner wasn't very good for her health.

137

ROSALIE ARRANGED FOR everyone to leave Budapest. She got Parkman to ride in a separate vehicle from Sarah in case Armond's team launched another assault. She wanted at least one of her witnesses left alive. Comforting thought.

They headed north. Sarah watched the countryside pass by outside her window. After an hour, the vehicle slowed. They pulled into a gas station, angled up to the pumps, and stopped.

The driver was a clean-cut military man who followed Rosalie's orders without batting an eye. He seemed two parts human, three parts robot.

He turned in his seat. "Grab a coffee. We have five minutes."

Sarah opened the door and hopped out. Parkman walked up.

"You going in?" he asked.

"Yeah, could use a coffee. You?"

He flapped his hand in the air, bowed slightly, then gestured toward the gas station as if he were a maître d' at a fancy restaurant. Sarah almost let out a giggle as she grabbed his arm and walked with him to the kiosk.

Inside, she took a quick look around. The only person in the store was the clerk behind the counter reading a magazine.

"Feeling paranoid?" Parkman asked.

"You can tell?"

"Me too." Parkman got to the coffee machine first. "They tried twice today. They'll regroup and try again later. Relax for a bit. They have no idea where we are."

He placed a cup under the spout and hit the button for a coffee with cream. Sarah turned to stare out the gas station's windows. Her driver stood at the back of his vehicle, filling the tank. The SUV Parkman had been in was farther down at the next pump, also being filled.

"Do you know where we're going?" Parkman asked.

Sarah turned to the coffee machine, selected a large cup, and hit the "black" button.

"Esztergom."

"What's that? A city?"

"We think it's the crypt Vivian told me about."

A car tire screeched outside. Sarah spun so fast she knocked the coffee out of Parkman's hand, spilling it across a row of magazines. Three vehicles exited the highway in formation, going too fast for the ramp. The lead vehicle drove around the front of the SUV, where the driver was finishing with the pump. The other two parked in a V formation, blocking Rosalie's SUV. The driver ducked and ran for the passenger side, frantically trying to get in.

"No way," Sarah mumbled. "Can't be." She turned to Parkman. "Regroup and try again later, eh?"

Parkman grunted under his breath, then faced the clerk. "You got a weapon under the counter?" he asked.

"*Mi az?*"

"Gun? Bat? Knife? Anything to—"

Something crashed outside. Sarah was already yanking Rosalie's gun out.

"Shit," Parkman shouted beside her.

The lead SUV had been rammed. Rosalie's driver never made it inside his vehicle. He got knocked into the gas pump as he was reaching for a weapon. The attacker's car reversed and rammed the SUV again. This time the SUV bumped up and into the gas pump. Sarah watched in horror as their driver was crushed.

Gunfire erupted from the vehicle Rosalie was in. Return gunfire came from the car in the back.

"How many times are they going to try to hit us in one day?"

"Until they complete the job," Parkman said, his face dark.

Sarah watched in stunned silence, her mind flipping through options.

"Find a weapon, Parkman, and meet me outside."

"Stay alive, Sarah. I'm serious."

"That's my plan." She ran behind the counter and past the stunned clerk.

She got to the back door and slammed into it, stumbling out at the rear of the building. She spied a line of four large eighteen-wheelers parked side by side, all idling. One of them started moving, edging out and turning toward the ramp that led back onto the highway.

She ran along the wall of the gas station. More gunfire erupted from the front. It sounded like Fourth of July celebrations. At the corner of the building, she risked a look.

Her driver was sprawled on the pavement beside his vehicle, blood on his abdomen. Rosalie was crouched down behind her SUV, adding bullets to her gun.

Sarah counted three vehicles and three shooters.

"Hold them down," she whispered as she turned around and ran toward the back.

She passed the open back door and continued running to the row of long trucks. More shooting came from the front as she made it to the first rig. It was a Peterbilt with a long nose. The cab was empty. She tried the door, and it opened on the first pull. There was no way she could drive anything this big. There were too many gears. She jumped into the driver's seat and turned to rip open the back curtains. The truck driver was asleep.

"Get up!" Sarah yelled, and jabbed him with her gun. "Get up now. I need your truck."

He grunted and opened his bloodshot eyes, lifting slightly from the thin mattress. "Wha . . . what?" he managed.

Sarah gestured to the steering wheel. "Drive this thing."

He leaned toward her and asked her something in Hungarian.

"Drive!" she yelled, and pushed the gun close to his face.

More gunfire erupted in the distance. She was running out of time.

The truck driver had raised his hands. He moved to get off his sleeper bed, and she kept the gun trained on him as she hopped over to the passenger side. The truck driver maneuvered down into his chair.

"Where?" he asked, using a hand to gesture out the front window.

Sarah pointed to the front of the gas station in a hurried fashion. She had to get him to work faster.

Finally, he got the truck in gear and pulled hard on the big steering wheel and turned it toward the front of the building. The truck was slow to get moving. As they got closer to the front, she heard gun-fire again and felt relieved. The fight was still going on. That meant someone on her side was still alive.

They cleared the gas station building and came up behind the SUVs. One of the hit men had crouched behind his car. Sarah leaned across the cab and spun the steering wheel toward him as fast as her hands could manage, even as the truck driver protested.

As the truck hit the vehicle, the cab tilted to the right. Sarah dropped back in her seat. Petrified, both hands on his chest, the driver's body shook all over.

There was no time to console him. She yanked his keys out of the dash, grabbed her weapon from the floor, and ripped open the door. When she hit the ground, she jumped behind the front wheel to cover her feet.

At first glance, all three SUVs were littered with small holes. The one she'd ridden in was tilted on its side.

The man who had fired on the rig was dead, trapped between the trailer and the car he'd been hiding behind, his upper body sprawled out on the back of his car's trunk.

"Rosalie!" Sarah shouted.

"Over here."

"You okay?"

"Yeah."

"Are there any more?"

"There were three of them," she shouted back. "I got two." Rosalie stood from behind her vehicle. "Looks like you got the last one."

Parkman exited the convenience store. "They're all dead," he shouted. He held a chair in his hands.

Sarah dropped her gun into her waistband, trying to calm the shaking in her hands. She pointed at the chair. "Is that supposed to be a weapon?"

"It's all I could find," Parkman shouted back.

"They weren't tigers."

"Well, it was something."

Rosalie headed over. "We need that truck."

She motioned for the driver of the rig to come down and join them.

"What?"

"We have to leave before anyone gets here. I have people who will come and clean this mess. We have to stay on the move." She pointed at the rig. "In something they won't expect."

"They're after me," Sarah said. "Leave Parkman and me to deal with this. You go home."

Rosalie looked at her sideways. "I just lost good men here. Men I went undercover with. Your driver, I've known him for ten years. I'm seeing this through to the end."

"Fine. We go together," Sarah said.

"Hey." Parkman stepped forward. "You two think they'll try again today? I mean, we're not cats. We only have one life to live."

"Yes." Sarah gestured at the rig. "This'll slow them down. Rosalie is right. Let's move."

"There's one thing you're not considering," Rosalie said.

"What's that?" Sarah asked.

"These men entered the lot and engaged me and my drivers. During that time, you and Parkman were in the gas station."

"Your point?"

"If they were truly after you, why engage us? We're trained professionals. Why not just drive up, walk into the gas station, and take you two out?"

"I have no idea."

"I think they're after me as much as you."

"Why?"

"I orchestrated the attack on Montone. Armond is after my head for that."

Sarah mulled it over. "If that's the case, all the more reason to keep moving."

138

THE DRIVER OF the rig glanced at the stray bullet hole in the windshield from time to time. Rosalie spoke passable Hungarian, so communication with him was no longer an issue. Sarah and Parkman sat in the back, on the driver's bed, while Rosalie directed the driver to Esztergom.

Parkman rummaged in his pocket a moment, then produced a small package. Sarah watched as he tore it open and yanked out a toothpick.

"Got those at the gas station?" she asked.

He nodded. "Haven't been using them much lately, but I need one today. By the way, that was good thinking back there."

"Thanks."

"Sarah?" Rosalie turned in her seat.

"Yeah?"

"I'm requesting more men to meet us in Esztergom."

Rosalie got on the phone, stated a series of numbered codes, then spoke in what sounded like German. When she was done she turned to the driver, pointed out the windshield, and gestured at an exit.

"My new team will meet us near the basilica tomorrow afternoon at seventeen hundred hours."

"To do what?" Sarah asked.

"Whatever I need them to do. They're coming in a helicopter that'll land on the Slovakian side of the Danube. No one on the Hungarian side of the river will even notice their arrival."

"Is there evidence that Armond will be in Esztergom?" Sarah asked.

Rosalie shook her head. "Just you, kiddo. Just you."

Sarah leaned back on the bed. The driver exited the highway and gently steered the rig onto a narrow street as he explained something to Rosalie.

"This is it," Rosalie said. "We get out here."

The three of them filed out, and the rig pulled away. They crossed the street and stepped into the shadows of a line of trees.

"I wonder how many men Armond employs," Sarah said. "Or does he hire mercenaries as he goes?"

"We believe it's a consortium, a large group of individuals and companies that pool together to reach their common goal of immigrating whomever they want for a price. That includes trafficking young girls and women. Their document stream is perfect because they actually come from the regular branches of government that produce them."

They continued walking in the shade. After three blocks, Rosalie gestured for them to stop. The Esztergom Basilica sat in the distance, its dome rising high in the air. A stunning masterpiece.

"Wow," Sarah said. "That's gorgeous."

"Yes, it is," Rosalie whispered.

Parkman didn't say anything. He just flicked his toothpick back and forth in his mouth.

"Come on," Rosalie said. "We should take a tour. The place is full. High chance none of Armond's people are in the area yet."

Ten minutes later, the trio entered through the side door. They walked into a vast room filled with majestic art. At the rear of the church sat the largest organ Sarah had ever seen. The interior was jammed with tourists taking pictures.

After some time, they tackled the twisting stairs to the top for a look over the city. After an hour, Rosalie led them down to the crypt. Just as Rosalie had explained, certain areas were blocked off. Sarah memorized the layout. The stairs they descended provided the only access, as far as she could tell.

When they were finished, Rosalie proposed dinner. The women emerged from the church, Sarah raised a hand to shield her eyes from the lowering sun and bumped into Rosalie.

"Hey, what the—"

Seven men stood in a semicircle around the exit doors.

"Come." Rod Howley stepped away. He limped toward the back of the church. Sarah was surprised he was already up and walking.

Without a word, Rosalie, followed by Sarah and Parkman, marched behind him. The rear of the church had two very large doors. Howley stopped there, let his hands rest at his sides, and turned to face them.

"Tell me, Sarah, what has your sister been up to lately?" Howley asked.

Sarah glanced at Howley's men behind her. "You followed us all this way to ask me about my dead sister?" She waved a hand. "You could've just called."

Parkman moved closer to her. She was beginning to love it when he got protective.

Howley's attention turned to Rosalie. "I understand your objective is locating a man named Armond Stuart?"

Rosalie nodded. "That is correct, sir."

"My government has agreed to aid in this investigation. If your mission is not complete by midnight tomorrow, Sarah comes with me."

"Says who?" Sarah asked.

Howley snapped his head toward her. After a moment's pause he looked back at Rosalie. The smile slipped from his face. "Your support team is landing." He turned and pointed at Slovakia on the other side of the river. "I understand you're getting a quality assault team. I would remind you that Sarah cannot be involved in the actual arrest of Mr. Stuart. We need her unharmed."

Howley produced a weapon so fast Rosalie couldn't respond. He pressed the blade of a large knife with a brass knuckle handle against her cheek. Sarah reached for her own weapon but never made it to the gun. Strong hands lifted her off the cement from behind, restraining her arms. Parkman was already on the ground, with two men holding his arms, a knee jammed into the small of his back.

The pain in her shoulders intensified. She took a deep breath, then ducked her head, lifting her feet up like a horse would buck.

The man holding her wasn't prepared. Her feet made contact with his face. He teetered back as he released her wrists. Gravity did the rest. She landed on her right shoulder, pulling her face up just in time to avoid losing teeth. She rolled and hopped up to her feet. This all happened in seconds. One of the men holding Parkman let go and jumped toward her. Sarah gestured for him to come and get it.

"Wait!" Howley yelled.

The man stopped.

"Drop the knife," Sarah said.

"Rosalie, you're a professional," Howley said. "The gas station gunfight could've seen Sarah hurt or worse. You have her on loan. Your orders are to take care of her."

"Hey, asshole," Sarah said. "Don't talk to her. Talk to me. Drop the knife." She edged closer.

"We will eliminate you if anything happens to Sarah," Howley continued. "Do we understand each other?"

Rosalie nodded.

"You have rank in your organization. But to me you are completely dispensable."

Sarah moved in quickly and shot a fist up into his armpit. Then she slammed a foot down on the back of his knee, missing slightly, with her foot landing on the top of his calf muscle. Howley dropped to the ground like a pro. He landed, rolled, and sprang back up, the knife held out in front of him. He didn't waver, even with his wounded shin.

"I actually think I'm beginning to understand you," he said. "We all have to be accountable for our actions. In your eyes I can see that you are going to try to make me pay for upsetting you. Is that right, Sarah?"

"The price I charge is high."

Howley nodded, then started limping toward the front of the basilica. As he passed Rosalie, Sarah heard him whisper, "Don't let anything happen to her."

Howley's men followed him.

Parkman stepped up beside Sarah. "You could've gotten seriously hurt."

"Do I ever consider the consequences?"

"You didn't have to do that," Rosalie said.

"He was threatening you. All the provocation I needed."

"For what it's worth, thanks." She looked down at the ground and then off in the distance.

"What is it?" Sarah asked. "Something bothering you?"

"How does he know where my team is landing? If he knows, could Armond? Those plans were just arranged. They were highly confidential."

"Maybe your phone is bugged?"

"What scares me is, there's above the law, and then there's Howley. No government would admit to knowing him. He could get away with mass murder, and he knows it."

Sarah started toward the front of the church. "I will not go quietly."

139

THEY CHECKED INTO Hotel Esztergom. They rented two rooms and stayed in one together, leaving the other room empty and available if they needed it. Rosalie set a rotating watch, with Parkman on the first shift, Rosalie next, Sarah last. Parkman settled into the corner chair with the lamp turned toward him.

"Wake me at two in the morning," Rosalie said.

"Trust me, I will," Parkman said. "I want some sleep, too."

"Rosalie," Sarah said, her voice already heavy with sleep. "What happens tomorrow?"

"Let my team handle everything. Once they nab Armond and secure the crypt, you come in and ID him. Nice and simple. You don't get hurt. That's my position."

"I like that idea," Parkman chimed in.

Sarah smiled. "What about Howley? How's the handoff supposed to take place?"

"There's nothing set yet. We arrest Armond, and then I'm sure Howley will be around to collect you. I suspect his team will be close."

Sarah crawled out of bed. She walked over to the desk and pulled out the chair. A pen sat beside the hotel pad of paper. She grabbed the pen and held it up.

"Sarah?" Rosalie asked. "You okay?"

In her peripheral she saw Parkman wave Rosalie off. Sarah lowered her head and dropped the pen down. After a moment she lifted her head and gasped. She neatly folded the paper before returning to bed.

"What was that all about?" Rosalie asked.

"Nothing," Sarah said.

"Sarah, what did you write?"

"I didn't write anything. Vivian did."

"Will you read it to us?"

Sarah looked at Parkman and then at Rosalie. "You're not going to like it."

"I don't care."

Sarah unfolded the paper. Parkman looked bemused. He'd seen her in a blackout state before, and she was sure he could tell that she faked it.

"Vivian said Howley and his team are watching us right now. They're listening, too."

"How?"

"He planted a listening device on you when he brought the knife to your throat."

Rosalie jumped from the bed and grabbed her folded jeans from the dresser. After a quick search she came up with a little, buttonlike piece of metal. She held it up for Sarah and Parkman to see and then set it on the floor and stepped on it, grinding it into the floor. At the hotel window, she peeked through the curtains.

"They're across the street in a black van," Rosalie said. "One of them stepped out and looked up at our room. What else does the note say?"

Sarah was dumbfounded. She'd been right. She looked down at her scratchy handwriting, then met Rosalie's eyes. "I don't want to read the next part."

"Why not?" Rosalie said.

She exchanged a glance with Parkman, his face blank now, the toothpick in his mouth unmoving.

Sarah shrugged. "Okay." She cleared her throat. "It says that Howley has ordered Rosalie killed after Armond is neutralized. He doesn't want witnesses when he takes me."

"What?" Rosalie collected herself. She stomped across the room and grabbed her pants, intent on putting them on.

"Rosalie, take it easy." Sarah sat up on the edge of her bed. "Stop what you're doing and come sit down."

Rosalie looked at her for a long moment. She sat on the bed, facing Sarah.

"I'll kill him first." Rosalie fidgeted with her fingers.

"He doesn't want anyone to know that he has me. I think he even has plans for Parkman."

"But why?"

"I think I'm rare. I can talk to the Other Side. He needs me, but he will never get me."

"How can you be so sure?"

"Because you're going to save me, and in doing so, you will save yourself."

Rosalie stopped fidgeting and looked up. "What do you have in mind?"

Sarah explained her plan. Rosalie listened closely.

"Do you really think you can do that?"

Sarah nodded. "Absolutely."

Rosalie turned to Parkman. "Are you on board with this?"

"Of course." He smiled at Sarah. He knew exactly what she was up to.

Rosalie was her wild card.

Sarah leaned back on her pillow, sleepiness weighing her down. Rosalie got up and paced the floor.

"Parkman?" Sarah said.

"Yeah?"

"You can relax. No one is going to hit us tonight."

"Not with Howley's boys out front. They won't move an inch now that they can't hear us."

Rosalie lay back down on her bed. "Sarah, can you really pull this off?"

"Yes," she said.

"Do you know how fucked this is?"

"Yup."

"That my life"—Rosalie caught her breath—"would depend on you faking your death is ridiculous."

"I know," Sarah said. "But we will live, *because* we're dead." She let sleep take over and passed out before she heard a reply.

140

SARAH SQUINTED AT the light coming from the hotel window. To her right, the alarm clock read 10:48 a.m. Rosalie was asleep, and Parkman was sprawled out in the corner chair.

She rolled off the bed and trudged to the hotel window. Above, overcast skies threatened rain. The van was still across the street, and most of the hotel parking lot had emptied. She closed the curtains and turned around. Parkman's eyes were open.

"That was quite something last night," he whispered. "I've never seen you do anything like it."

She moved toward him. "I made a good guess with the listening device and got Rosalie on our side. No harm, no foul."

"Can you trust her?" Parkman asked.

"I have to try." She headed for the bathroom.

"You're not the trusting kind. Why now? Why her?"

"With her, our odds of success increase."

Parkman retrieved a toothpick from his breast pocket and popped it in his mouth as Sarah closed the bathroom door and jumped in the shower.

Before noon, Rosalie had awakened. "There's not much we can do until later," Rosalie was saying. "My team doesn't show until then."

"We could take another crypt tour and disappear behind one of the roped-off areas," Parkman suggested.

Rosalie shook her head. "They monitor everything. Alarms would sound."

Sarah walked over to the window. Rain covered the empty cement of the parking lot, coming down hard.

"Then what's the plan?" Sarah asked.

"Not sure yet." Rosalie rested her chin in her hands. "The only problem with any kind of assault is that the building and any artifacts could be damaged or destroyed. The Hungarian government won't look too kindly on us for shooting up their largest church."

"Why not phone in a bomb threat?" Sarah said. "Wait until we eye-ball Armond, and then we go in armed to the teeth. With the Hun-garian authorities on hand to deal with the public, we stay inside the building and deal with Armond."

Rosalie was staring at her. "Brilliant. I'll propose that."

"Propose it? Aren't you in charge?"

"I am. But this team has its own chain of command. If they feel there's a fault in my idea—scratch that, your idea—they will come up with their own."

Sarah moved over to the bed and sat down on the edge, facing Rosalie. "You have to be accountable; I don't. Whatever happens, Armond doesn't get away this time. He either gets taken into custody or taken out. We're on the same page here, right?"

Rosalie nodded. "Absolutely."

Someone banged on the hotel door, making all three of them jump. Sarah dove across her bed and retrieved her gun. Parkman walked to the wall beside the door while Rosalie fumbled for her weapon.

"Who is it?" Sarah yelled.

"Hotel management. You are past the checkout time."

They breathed a collective sigh.

"Five more minutes."

Footsteps retreated.

"Damn." Sarah rolled over onto her back. "I thought a good night's sleep would have calmed me."

Parkman sat back down. Rosalie put her weapon away.

"We need to be more alert," Rosalie said. "One of us should have heard someone approach."

Parkman nodded at her. "Indeed."

"Let's pack up and go get some food." Sarah rubbed her cheek. "I'm starving, and we have a lot to do tonight."

After their late lunch, the trio crossed the bridge into Slovakia. They drove in two rented cars that Rosalie had picked up, Parkman driving one, Rosalie the other.

They met Rosalie's team and were debriefed on how extraction would work once the target was confirmed. With or without Armond, they would all fall back, cross the bridge, and make it to the helicopter. The plan was to fly to a military airport in Romania.

After that, they would fly Parkman and Sarah back to the States or wherever they wanted to go on a military jet. The team didn't work for Howley's group, nor did they recognize his authority. Sarah would be declared lost in the battle. Probably drowned in the Danube River.

Rosalie stressed that it was vital to get Sarah and Parkman out of Hungary as soon as this was over. Based on that plan, Howley would think she was deceased.

To Sarah's relief, the team of professional soldiers were dressed in civilian clothes. There would be no military assault for one man on Hungarian soil. On the outside, this was simply a group of law enforcement officers arriving to arrest an international criminal.

Back at the basilica, they filed out as a group near the rear of the parking lot. The rain soaked them as they separated and went their different ways. Radio communication had been established between the six-man team and Rosalie. Parkman and Sarah were considered civilians who were only here for positive identification. They were just supposed to stay close.

Sarah's bomb threat idea had been rejected. The team leader said Armond would see past it. "We will go in and attend mass and look around. He'll turn up."

Parkman stayed close to her as they entered the basilica. Rosalie planned to enter after them. People waited patiently for mass to begin.

There was still no sign of Armond Stuart.

Parkman started off toward the rear of the church. Sarah followed. Faking her death would mean her parents would think she was dead, too, but she had to concentrate on her freedom. She hoped that after a few months she could contact her parents to let them know she was okay. She knew what losing her would do to them. After all, they had already lost one daughter.

Over her shoulder, Sarah saw Rosalie enter the church and start for the front. Then more of the team entered. They'd all introduced themselves by name when they met at the helicopter. Sarah only remembered one of their names.

"What are you looking for?" Parkman asked.

"Bennett."

"Why?" He looked at her sideways.

"His name stood out to me. It reminded me of Mary Bennett."

"I'll watch for him and tell you when I see him—"

Parkman was cut off by an alarm. A high-pitched siren sounded throughout the building. Sarah had her hand on her weapon, waiting to draw.

"What the hell is that?" she yelled at Parkman.

He shrugged.

The siren stopped as fast as it started. A voice over a loudspeaker said, "Could everyone please leave the building. Please find the nearest exit and leave the basilica. This is not a drill." The message was repeated in Hungarian.

"What do we do now?" Sarah asked. "I thought the team nixed the idea of a bomb threat."

"Maybe they went ahead anyway."

Everyone in the large church began moving toward the exits. Rosalie stood by a column, watching her and Parkman. She shrugged as if to say she had no idea what was going on. Someone stepped up close behind Sarah. She spun around and drew her weapon as she looked into the eyes of the team leader.

"Put that away," he said. "Did you have anything to do with this alarm?"

"I thought you did."

"We'd better get you outside in case they lock this place down. We'll stay inside and start a room-to-room search in the crypt."

Hungarian police were entering through the main doors and showing people which way to go. The inside of the church was almost empty. Sarah started for the doors, with Parkman following close behind. She saw Bennett again. He stood back behind a pillar, watching her and Parkman advance on the exit. They neared the doors. The police said something in Hungarian. Sarah shook her head and said, *"Angol." English.*

"You appear to be the last two. Please come with us."

"Go with you? Why?"

"We understand. It's this way." The cop gestured and walked away. Sarah and Parkman followed. They reached the outer doors and stepped out into the rain. People had gathered under the overhang. A few others were collecting under a tree to wait it out.

"Come with us," the police officer said again.

"Where are you taking us?" she asked.

Both officers wore thick bulletproof vests. The officer turned to face her. "We'd like to check your passports. We are Hungarian police officers. It will only take a few minutes. Now, follow me."

The officer headed toward the parking area. Sarah saw his police car in the distance. His partner waited behind them. Parkman started after him and Sarah followed.

They got to the cruiser. The officer opened the back door. "Get in."

Sarah waited for a moment as the rain soaked through her hair.

"Please get in," he pleaded.

No way was this routine. Something primal told her to run. She looked around. No one was watching them. Rosalie's team was still in the building.

"We're not getting in," she said.

"Sarah," Parkman whispered.

The officer had pulled out a gun.

"Get in the backseat of my cruiser. Armond is waiting in the crypt to see you."

141

THE HUNGARIAN OFFICER'S partner slipped in beside Sarah in the backseat, a weapon pointed at her side. Parkman was ordered into the front.

They left the basilica's parking area, the wipers trying in vain to keep the windshield clear of the downpour.

"Where are you taking us?" Parkman asked.

"Shut up," the driver shouted at him.

Sarah stared straight ahead. Her thoughts turned to Vivian. She had apologized about tonight. What did that mean?

The police officer steered the car onto the green bridge connecting Hungary to Slovakia and raced across the Danube. After the bridge, they took a hard right. A sign on the side of the road had the number 63 written on it. The driver drove another hundred meters and then turned in between two houses and stopped.

The driver barked at Parkman. "You. Out."

"I'm not leaving Sarah."

"You have no choice," the driver said. "Get out."

Something flashed by her window. Two men walked up beside the police car. They were in uniform: more officers. Neither one of the new cops wore Kevlar.

Parkman's door was ripped open. One of the men grabbed him around the neck. Even though Parkman's hands clung to the door-frame, he was pulled from the vehicle.

"No!" Sarah grabbed her door handle, but it was useless.

Parkman was taking serious blows to his body. The driver eased across the front seat until he was at the passenger door, leaning out to watch.

She felt a shift in the seat beside her. The guy next to her had leaned forward to catch the action, too. She did her best to judge the location of his throat without looking directly at him. The Kevlar he wore came right up to his collar. There would only be one chance.

She raised her left arm to rest on the back of the front seat. She too leaned over to pretend to watch the beating on Parkman. A quick check using her peripheral vision showed that her elbow was about a foot from the guy's exposed throat.

She waited. He edged closer. The driver leaned out even farther.

Sarah shot her elbow backward. When she hit the center of his throat, it drove the cop back in the seat, his head banging the blind spot between the back and side windows. Her right hand went for the gun and was able to wrest it away as the man tried to breathe.

The men outside the car were too preoccupied to notice what Sarah had done.

The cop beside her had started to turn blue. His trachea was damaged and had probably collapsed. She kept her left arm across his chest so he couldn't lean forward to warn the driver.

The men outside stopped hitting Parkman. They started to drag him away from the vehicle. The driver leaned back into the car and slid along the front seat after slamming the passenger door shut.

Luckily, the guy beside her had fallen silent. The driver put the car in gear and was about to reverse when he pivoted in his seat and saw his colleague. The car stopped. She held the gun up on the back of the seat so the driver could see it easily.

"Unlock the back door."

He reached for something. A second later, the audible snick of the door confirmed it was unlocked. Without taking her eyes off the driver, she opened the door.

"Where were you taking us?"

He shook his head.

"That's not an answer. I'll ask one more time. Where were you taking us?"

The driver glanced at his partner. His eyes found Sarah. "Back to the crypt in the basilica."

"So you kidnapped us to bring Parkman here to be beaten?"

"Yes. And to give Armond a chance to neutralize the assault team."

"Why not leave Parkman and neutralize him, too?"

"He would never have left you without a commotion. Our orders were to remove anyone who was with you and bring them here, then return with you. By that time everyone else would be dead."

Nausea threatened her stomach's calm. *Everyone would be dead? Rosalie's team—gone?*

"Is that why you're wearing vests? Because of the assault team at the basilica?"

He nodded. "Everyone has one tonight."

"Tell me your name."

"Why?" he asked.

She gestured with the weapon. "Tell me your name."

"Peter." He frowned. "You can't win. Whether you shoot me or not, Armond will kill you tonight and everyone you brought with you. No one can stop him."

"I'll take my chances," she said.

Sarah squeezed the trigger. The bullet entered Peter's throat at the base. He smacked backward into the door; his hands rose to the wound as he slumped down in his seat. Blood spurted onto his chest.

"That was for Parkman."

The rain pelted the car like hail now. It had helped to mask the sound of the gunshot. She eased out of the backseat, the gun in front of her, as the driver spasmed and dropped lower in the front seat. The lane between the two houses was empty. She started down the alley the way she'd seen the two men take Parkman.

At the corner, she saw the men inside an open garage door. They had the trunk of a car open. Sarah could see the edge of Parkman's elbow.

"Hey!" she yelled, deepening her voice as best she could. When she peeked back around the corner, the men were staring in her direction.

"Peter said to bring the American cop back to their car," she shouted, trying to sound as masculine as she could, hoping the barrage of rain masked her voice further.

They looked at one another. One of them shrugged and reached into the trunk to pull out Parkman.

I'm sorry this happened to you, my friend.

She waited until they were a few feet from the corner before stepping out. Two quick shots from such close range dropped each man.

She ran to Parkman, held his head, and brushed the rainwater from his face. He blinked, then shut his eyes again. Blood covered his face. He was still bleeding around his mouth. His left eye looked like it would swell shut.

"I'm so sorry," she whispered.

He grunted something.

"What?" She leaned in closer.

"Finish this shit. Get Armond."

"I will, but I'm not leaving you here. Can you walk?"

An imperceptible nod of his head.

"Okay, let's get you to your feet. And next time, don't let them hit you so much." She turned him over and wrapped his arm around her neck. "Man, are you heavy. What the hell do you eat?"

When he grunted it almost sounded like laughter. To Sarah it was musical.

"What happened . . . to dem?"

"They're all dead. Every one of dem," she said. He was alive. He would heal. The people that stood for her would make it through to see another day.

Something loosened and moved inside her. It was filled with love and trust. She was *feeling* again. It had been so long that it felt foreign. She knew she would die for Parkman if it came to that.

They shuffled to the police car, arm in arm. Sarah gently placed Parkman back in the passenger seat. When he was seated and secured, she raced around to the driver's side and yanked the dead cop out of the front seat and onto the wet pavement. Then she undressed him. She tossed the Kevlar vest to Parkman and then opened the back door to work on the other cop.

After she'd removed his vest she left him in the backseat, got behind the wheel, and started the car.

"What about . . . im?" Parkman asked, pointing to the guy in the backseat.

"He comes with us."

Parkman moved his head sideways and raised his bloody hands in a questioning gesture.

"I want Armond to see what happens to the people he sends after us."

Sarah dropped the police car into reverse and backed down the alley between the two houses. She eased onto the street and started back the way they had come, hoping Rosalie and some of her team were still alive. As they crossed the bridge back into Hungary she flipped on the police siren.

Parkman muttered something beside her.

"What was that?" she asked over the sound of the siren.

"I could use . . . a tooffpick."

142

SARAH ENTERED THE mostly empty parking lot of the Esztergom Basilica, siren still blaring. Three police cars were stationed near the front entrance. She killed the siren halfway up the lot and pulled to the far right to park in the shadows. After driving onto the lawn, she turned the cruiser off.

"Put that vest on." She nudged the Kevlar vest in Parkman's lap. "I know you're in pain, but I can't leave you here without it." He lifted the vest and slipped one arm into it, only wincing once. "Stay out of sight. I'll come and get you when this is over, and we'll get to the helicopter together."

He nodded and slid his other arm into the vest.

Sarah lifted her T-shirt over her head and then donned her own vest, slipping the T-shirt back on over the top.

"Sure hope these things are effective," she muttered to herself.

"Me oo," Parkman mumbled.

After a moment of silence she leaned in and gently kissed his cheek. She saw his good eye open in surprise.

"I love you, Parkman. You've helped me in more ways than you know."

"I uv oo, too."

She raised a finger. "Just be clear. Love as in a brother. Not creepy shit."

He tried a smile. "Of orse."

A small amount of blood oozed out of his mouth. In the short ride back to the church, his face had darkened with bruises.

"We'll get you to a doctor as soon as this is over."

He nodded.

She jumped from the vehicle. In her right hand she held the cop's gun, and she had a second stashed at her waistline. The rain had eased up, but her shirt was soaked and her pants felt like she'd gone swimming in them.

She headed around to the back of the church to find another way in. After turning the corner, a car door shut behind her. It had to be Parkman moving to a more secure location.

The back of the church was empty. Everyone had to be inside. In the darkness, only a few small security lights were affixed to the side of the church. They didn't give off much light to see by.

She passed the two large back doors of the church, where Howley had grabbed Rosalie earlier. As she came up to the next corner she heard a solid thump behind her and nearly jumped out of her skin.

"Shit," she whispered. "What the fuck was that?"

Faint gurgling sounds came from the darkness ten feet in front of her. Beyond the reach of the lights, she couldn't make anything out in the inky black.

She brought up the cop's gun. "Identify yourself." She stepped closer. "Identify yourself," she repeated.

More gurgling, sputtering.

Her eyes adjusted to the faint shape of a man lying on the ground in front of her. It was one of Rosalie's team members.

She knelt down beside him. "What happened? Where is everyone?"

The man's eyes rolled to her. Then, as a final release of air escaped from his lips, his eyes stopped moving. She checked for a pulse but couldn't find one.

"Shit."

As she got to her feet, another heavy thump vibrated the ground. She ran over and saw another of Rosalie's team. He was still alive.

"What happened?" she asked. "Tell me."

"They——" he gasped, fighting for air.

"Try to tell me."

"Roof . . . throwing——" Two big gasps and then he said, "Off roof." His head rolled to the side; his body stilled.

Sarah looked up at the roof. Flashlights roved around the edge. She ran for the building. Another thump smacked the ground behind her. Rosalie's team were being thrown off the roof of the church as if they were garbage.

A paralyzing anger encompassed her. Another body thumped to the ground. She didn't stop to look. There was no point. The only thing that mattered was stopping this madness.

She ran around the corner and jogged up to the main doors of the church. They were open. She looked down the steps that led into the crypt, then moved forward into the main church. Something moved above her. She ducked. A straw broom swung down, attached to a rope. She stepped sideways, easily avoiding its arc. She must've tripped a wire as she entered. When she looked up to see where the broom had come from, something hit her below the right knee. She screeched in pain and crumpled to the floor. A second later, a heavy black boot stomped on her forearm, and the gun in her hand flew away. Someone tore the other weapon from her waistband.

At least three men grabbed her legs and arms and half lifted, half dragged her toward the line of pews. She gritted her teeth and chastised herself for being so stupid. Armond's men dropped her on the marble floor. She cried out at the pain in her leg despite herself. Something felt broken.

One of the men wrapped wire around her wrists, binding them. Her hands were clammy.

"Pussy," she said. "Beating up on a girl. Your mother know what you do for a living?"

He backhanded her across the face. She instantly tasted blood.

"Don't talk to them," a voice said. "They don't speak English. Only Hungarian."

She glanced upward and into the eyes of Armond Stuart. He stood in a raised pulpit, wearing a priest's vestments. The pulpit was attached to the side of a rounded pillar. Behind the pillar were curved stairs.

"Are you enjoying your evening?" Armond asked.

"Why are you dressed like a priest? Graduating from young girls to young boys now?"

She struggled with her wrists, but the binds were too tight. Armond's men had stepped away, except for the one who had slapped her. He stood at the end of the pew, watching her struggle.

"You know," Armond said, arms out in front of him, "it's too bad you aren't working for me. I could've used someone with your resources."

Her knee felt swollen. "I've still got one more card to play," she shouted.

Armond raised an eyebrow. "Oh, really. What's that?"

She shook her head. "In time, Armond, in time."

"Sarah, I have this church surrounded. The *rendorség* work for me. Rosalie's team has been neutralized. Didn't you see them falling from the sky?" He glanced to the side for a moment, then looked back at her. "How did you like my bomb scare? I stole the idea from you. We've been listening to you since you toured the basilica yesterday. You should've seen Rosalie's face when I popped up out of this pulpit and shot four of her men before she even had a chance to pull her weapon. It was over before it started." He paused to scan the church again. He seemed agitated. "Where's Parkman?"

The basilica was surrounded. He had known she was in the rear of the building when he had Rosalie's men tossed over the edge.

"I see you're working it out," he said. "That's right, your American cop will die in the crypt tonight. After all the shit he pulled at the FLDS compound in the States, he's lucky that I'm just going to kill him. You too, for that matter. But we must hurry this along." Armond turned from her and walked down the steps at the back of the pulpit. He came around the pillar. "The number of people I have killed in my lifetime could fill this room. What's two more?"

He addressed the man at the end of the pew and spoke in Hungarian. After listening to Armond, the man strode briskly to Sarah, grabbed her under the arm, and pulled her from the seat. She staggered along as best she could, trying to stay off her bad leg.

She was dragged toward the stairs that led down to the crypt. Armond moved ten feet ahead of them.

Something outside the doors clicked. A scuffling sound.

The man holding her suddenly let go. Sarah fell to the floor and sprawled out flat, her right shoulder taking the hit.

A gun fired. Bullets zinged above her.

She lifted her head an inch when the guns fell silent. Armond hid behind a door to her left. The man who had been holding her was sprawled out on the stone floor, eyes wide, blood oozing from a wound in his forehead.

"Stay down, Sarah," a man yelled. "It's Bennett."

Armond spoke into a cell phone.

"Watch your back," Sarah shouted. "Armond just called somebody."

Another burst of gunfire erupted from the outside. She looked at Armond again. He eased out from behind the door."

"Got him." He snapped his phone shut and stashed it in his front pocket. "My men just told me the problem has been neutralized."

He walked over to Sarah and yanked her to her feet. She almost fell back down when she put weight on her bad leg. Repulsed by his touch, she reared back, trying hard to dislodge his hand.

"Take it easy," Armond grunted. "Your sister wasn't as much of a fighter. And I'm not even interested in your cunt. I just want you dead."

Armond dragged her to the stairs and tried to push her down. He mumbled something to himself, shoved harder, almost knocking her over the top step, then mumbled something else. She couldn't let him get her over the edge. The stairs would pummel her to death on the way down. She turned on her butt and got her good leg in position. Then, putting some weight into Armond's tight grip, Sarah was able to hop down the stone steps to the bottom. Once there, he dragged her past a gated area and into a darkened chamber.

"Here is where you will lie for eternity," he said.

The air was colder down in the crypt. Thoughts of Vivian's warning flitted through her head. Armond led her into a room where candles burned.

An old wooden table sat in the center of the room. He dragged her a little farther and then tossed her down to the floor. She leaned up against a wall in a sitting position.

"Was that man Bennett your final card?" he asked.

"Not even close."

Armond pulled a gun from his vestments and aimed it at her. "I'm sick of your games."

She struggled to sit up higher. "You know, I was thinking the same thing about you."

He lowered the weapon and touched the wall around one particular square. "I had this stone removed. This will be your new home." He clicked something under the stone and drew it out on wheels. "I even had my men install these wheels so that I could do this alone, without having to lift the slab myself."

More gunfire erupted above them.

"What the hell is going on up there?" Armond shouted.

He flipped open his cell phone and dialed out. He moved to the doorway to get better reception. He spoke in Hungarian on the phone. After a couple of sentences, he flipped the phone shut and swore to himself. "I'm going upstairs. That Bennett fucker is proving to be a real asshole."

"Don't worry about me," Sarah said. She patted the stone beside her. "I'll wait here for you."

"With that bum knee, you wouldn't make it back up those stairs. But I would like to kill you now anyway. Think of it as insurance."

Armond brought his weapon up to bear, then pulled the trigger without hesitation. Each impact jammed her body into the wall and punched air from her lungs. Vivian took over by numbing her arm. Before she lost consciousness, Armond's gun fired four times.

Sarah felt each and every bullet hit her body before she passed out.

143

SARAH SNAPPED AWAKE with a start. She looked down at her chest as she gasped for air. Each intake of breath was accompanied by a burst of searing pain throughout her rib cage. Her eyes watered.

Four small holes dotted her chest where the bullets had made contact with the Kevlar. She wriggled her hands, but they were still tied too tight.

Sarah leaned against the stone wall and forced herself to her feet. As she did so she grunted to suppress a scream. Sweat broke out on her brow. Briefly, light-headedness swept over her. She took a deep breath, then another.

"Don't you faint," she whispered out loud.

The metal gate that closed off this section of the crypt had a hook for a latch. She scrambled over, taking careful steps. She got to the gate and paused.

Gunfire came from above again. Two shots, then silence. Then two more.

She hooked her bound wrists onto the latch and pulled, hoping to loosen the binding as one would take the tine of a fork to a knotted shoelace. The wire dug into her wrists as she pulled. After a couple of pulls, she loosened it enough that her wrists were able to struggle back and forth. They were looser, but it wasn't enough.

Someone ran by upstairs, shouting something in Hungarian.

One more attempt with the latch pulled an edge off the twine. Finally, she pried her hands loose. More pain erupted in her chest as it contracted.

"Shit, that *fucking* hurts."

Her adrenaline pumped, endorphins kicking in. She turned for the stairs and started to climb. With each step she reminded herself she was that much closer to killing Armond. It motivated her through the fog of pain in her leg to take each step, then another.

She made it halfway up the stairs, then stopped. Before climbing any farther, she kissed her right hand and pressed it against the rock wall.

"Thanks, Vivian," she whispered.

Her right knee felt better the more she used it. While climbing, her limp was minimal. She reached the top without encountering anyone. There was a small turn to the right and then a few more steps to enter the corridor that led into the church or left to the outside. With no weapon and nothing to defend herself with, she took the last few steps carefully.

A shot popped somewhere outside the church, making her duck.

Another gunshot outside.

She ascended the rest of the way and stepped into the open. The man who had tied her up was still lying in the hall. After a quick pat down, she was rewarded with both her guns back.

Lucky me.

She limped to the wall, then edged around and peeked into the church. The inner sanctum was vacant. All the action had moved outside. Grunting with the effort, she continued toward the exit, now armed and dangerous.

Outside, Armond Stuart was hiding behind a refreshment kiosk for the tourists. His face was turned away from her, a gun in his hand. Sarah had a clear shot. She brought up her arm and took careful aim.

He swiveled his head and looked straight at her, taking her in through wide eyes. The expression on his face told her everything. He thought she was dead.

She fired.

His gun was thrown from his grip. She had missed his head and hit his hand instead.

Armond screamed as he stared at the hole in his hand. Sarah fired again. Then again. She aimed for the center of his chest. He wavered on his feet.

She moved forward and shot him a fourth time.

He fell to his knees and then onto his back. Sarah limped across the opening between the church and the kiosk. Whoever had been exchanging fire with Armond wasn't her enemy.

"I shot you," Armond stammered. "You were dead."

His Kevlar vest had stopped every one of her bullets, except for the one in the hand. She pulled her good leg back and kicked him in the chest. He shouted out in pain and tried to curl into a ball away from her.

"Sarah!" someone yelled behind her.

She pulled on his arm to right him, then dropped and sat on his stomach, straddling him like a horse. Whoever it was could wait.

"Yes, you shot me," she said. "But there's another matter to clear up first."

"What's that?" he managed to say. His breath was shallow, his face shining in the dim light.

"My sister, Vivian. My trump card."

Sarah withdrew the weapon from her waistband, and placed it against Armond's crotch.

"No!" he managed to shout.

Sarah didn't hesitate. She just pulled the trigger. The bullet tore a hole in his vestments as he bucked at the hips.

"That's for all the girls you've raped. All the lives you've stolen." She raised her voice over his screaming wail. "All the innocence you took from everyone you've ever touched." She placed her right hand on his throat and squeezed. "And this is from me to you!" She set her weapon down and applied her thumb on his eye socket, leaning into it. Armond couldn't shake her off. Even through the pain in her ribs, she applied more pressure.

And then someone tackled her from the side, knocking her into the wall. After landing on her ass, flashes of light sparked in her peripheral vision. Sarah clambered for the second gun. She wrapped her hand around it, moaned at the pain, then aimed at her assailant.

Howley stood over her. "You don't want to do that."

She could barely hear him over Armond's screams.

"Give me"—she sucked in air—"one good reason."

"If you kill me it doesn't end. You have a file now. This does not end with me. It ends with you." His eyes turned to pleading. "Come in with me, Sarah, willingly. I will make sure you are comfortable. Then after six months, you can go back to civilian life. Do we have a deal?"

She pretended to think about it. "I don't go anywhere until he is dead." She gestured with the tip of her gun at Armond.

The pig writhing on the ground turned toward her, following her voice. His one good eye was filled with malevolence. Blood pooled below his crotch. He would soon bleed to death.

Howley brought his gun up—a rather large handgun, the kind of sidearm Sarah hadn't seen before. He fired from two feet away, blowing the top of Armond's head clean off. He fired again, this time at the throat. A hole the size of a cantaloupe opened above Armond's collarbone, half his throat vanishing into the ancient stone as bloody flesh and pulverized bone.

It was over. It was truly over. Armond Stuart was dead. Vivian could rest in peace.

"Get up, Sarah. Come with me. Everyone's dead. There's just you and me. We'll leave together."

"Someone else is still alive," she said. She stared into his eyes. "Who was Armond shooting at?"

"Me." He holstered his weapon. Then he adjusted his hat and looked down his nose at her. "Let's get you out of here before the real police show up. When they find Armond here, they'll know this was about him. If we're still here we will have too much explaining to do."

Howley reached out to help her up as someone moved in behind him. Bennett, Rosalie's man.

"Okay, Howley." Sarah reached for his hand.

Bennett placed the tip of his gun against the back of Howley's neck.

"Everyone's dead, eh?" Sarah asked. "Six months or so and then back to normal life? Who the hell do you think I am?"

"Step away from the girl," Bennett ordered.

Howley raised his hands. The hand cannon he'd killed Armond with had disappeared.

"Now what?" Howley asked.

"He's packing," Sarah said. "A huge handgun."

Bennett found the weapon easily and disarmed him, tossing the gun away.

"In the crypt there's a slab pulled out from the wall," Sarah said. "It's on wheels. Lock him in there for the night. His men can retrieve him in good time."

Bennett nodded. "You heard her. Let's go." Bennett motioned with the gun.

"You haven't heard the last of me," Howley said to Sarah as he walked back into the church.

She waited for what felt like a long time before she saw Bennett coming back up the stairs.

"You okay?" he asked when he got to her.

"Other than the bruising and broken ribs and the sprained right knee, I'd say I'm doing fine. Actually, scratch that, I'm better than fine. Armond is dead."

"Yes, he is. Come on. Let's get you to the chopper."

"What happened to your team?"

"It was chaos. I was the only one they didn't see."

"Rosalie?"

He shook his head. "Dead."

"Shit." Her stomach dropped. "I liked her."

Bennett took the lead, walking her along the wall of the church. His training came through in everything he did. They moved along the wall, Bennett in front of her, going her speed while still keeping an eye on their rear.

"Howley's secure in the crypt?" Sarah asked.

Bennett motioned with his hand to stay quiet. Then he leaned in close to whisper. "Howley may have more men close by. We'll talk in the chopper."

Sarah nodded, then pulled him close and whispered, "Do you know what happened to Parkman?"

"I don't know, but I heard Armond say Parkman was killed. I'm sorry."

Sarah looked down at the ground. Parkman knew they were to fall back to the helicopter. She would get Bennett to delay as long as he could. Maybe Parkman was still alive somewhere. She couldn't bear the thought of losing him.

They were nearing the rear of the basilica. Bennett looked back at her. "Are you crying?" he asked, softly.

"Keep moving. Let's get out of here." She wiped her cheeks.

They got to the lawn at the back, and Sarah hobbled along as fast as she could manage on her bad knee. The rain had stopped, and the moon was out from behind the clouds. Her eyes adjusted quickly.

Within minutes they had reached the edge of the Danube River. Sarah looked back up and saw the massive dome on the hill.

A quick run up the gravel road by the river would take them to the bridge. They could cross it on foot and be at the helipad fifteen minutes after that. Sarah glanced at the river. Streetlights illuminated the area. Boats lined the side, tied up and bumping softly with the current.

They continued up the road, Bennett protecting her as they went.

"I used to know a girl named Mary Bennett," Sarah said.

"I know."

She started in surprise. "You know? How?"

"She's my sister."

Sarah stopped walking.

"Sarah, we have to keep moving. We have to cross the bridge and get into Slovakia before the Hungarian authorities show up."

"Mary is your sister?" She couldn't believe it.

"As I understand it, you saved her life. Now we're even. You saved my sister, and I'm going to save you from Armond and Howley. I do this in honor of who you are and what you do. Also in honor of a brave and courageous woman who died tonight, Rosalie Wardill."

Sarah was moved. "Thank you."

They started walking again. A gun fired somewhere behind them. They ducked and ran to the river side of the road.

"If they're firing at us we can jump in one of these boats for shelter. If they aren't—"

He was cut off as his skull opened up. He spun on his feet, trying to find Sarah, then fell into the boat moored below their feet.

Something punched her in her back as she stared in disbelief at Bennett's body. She stumbled, tried to right herself, then stumbled again. Before she could fall into the shelter of the boat, another punch hit her from behind, shooting her forward off her feet.

She plunged off the edge of the road, hit the front of the boat, and flipped into the Danube River.

144

SARAH OPENED HER eyes under the water but saw nothing. It was cold, chilling her to the marrow. The Kevlar vest had saved her life again, but now its weight threatened to drag her deeper. She didn't have the energy to swim to the surface.

She was able to remove her shirt and let the Kevlar vest fall from her body. The cold stabbed at her exposed skin as her lungs starved for air. In the dark she couldn't tell if she was sinking or rising toward the surface. Or was that just the current? Her lungs protested further. Her chest heaved, the pain immeasurable.

She wanted to scream for Vivian. Something brushed against her. Weeds as she traveled past them. She needed to breathe. A light pierced the water from above. She fought for it, arms pinwheeling, refusing to open her mouth.

A thick weed caressed her arm. She grabbed at it and held on.

Her feet touched mud.

She opened her mouth and let her lungs release the last of their air. On the inhale, her face broke the surface. She pushed with her feet and landed half in, half out of the Danube on the Slovakian side.

145

SOMETHING STUNG HER face.

"Sarah, ake up!"

Parkman?

"Sarah?"

More coughing. She curled into a ball and moaned.

"We need to get to da cho . . . er," Parkman said.

She opened her eyes and saw his face. Everything came back in a painful torrent.

"Parkman, you're alive," she said. She studied his eyes. "Your face is fucked."

"I know, I know. Get up. No more screwing around. We have a cho . . . er to catch. What happened to your shirt? Why are you in your bra?"

She didn't answer. She did her best to get to her feet with Parkman's help. They walked up the embankment. Parkman had brought one of the police cars.

"What happened to you?" Sarah managed to ask.

He helped her into the passenger seat. "After putting on the vest you gave me, I got out and crawled under the car. I was in no position to fight. I waited there until it was quiet. After crawling out, I saw Bennett take you over the hill. I went to follow, but then Howley came running out of the church. He fired his weapon at you two. I saw Bennett hit the boat and you hit the water. I would've killed Howley, but I was unarmed. I ran back for the car and here I am."

He slammed her door shut and ran around to the driver's side. After getting in, he said, "When I saw you fall into the river, I thought you were dead."

"I nearly was."

"Howley thinks he killed you. Let's get you out of here before he confirms otherwise."

Parkman threw the car into gear and drove away from the river. Ten minutes later, they were in the helicopter. Once seated, the pilot lifted off.

No one else was coming.

After fifteen minutes in the air, Parkman leaned forward, reached into his back pocket, and produced a small plastic container. After flipping it open he pulled out a toothpick and placed it in his mouth.

"Cinnamon," he shouted.

Sarah leaned her head back, exhausted. "Man, I love you, Parkman."

"I love you, too, Sarah. I love you, too."

AFTERWORD

Dear reader,

The Sarah Roberts series was inspired by my dead brother.

I miss him.

My brother disappeared while skiing at Sunshine Mountain in Alberta, Canada. He'd taken a Greyhound bus from Calgary and didn't return. The authorities did their best to locate him. An investigation was launched, and search parties were formed. He was found two weeks later by a family out snowshoeing.

My brother had gotten lost on a ski hill, gone out of bounds in a whiteout—snow so thick you can't see more than a few feet in front of you—and been unable to find his way back to the chalet. After removing his skis, he left them behind and started walking. He was found buried in snow, partially undressed. In the final stage of hypothermia, his body had shot heat out to his major organs in a last-ditch attempt to save his life, causing him to feel like he was too hot.

I was fourteen years old.

Four years later I saw him in an extremely vivid dream. He explained that I would need to take an extra pair of pants to work that day. I was working security at a construction site. To take an extra pair of pants to work was unusual for me, as I would normally don my uniform, hop on my bike, and ride to work ten minutes away. But to humor him and his memory, even though I knew it to be a dream and nothing else, I packed an extra pair of work pants.

As I entered the construction site, loose gravel caught the front tire of my bike. It skidded out from under me, and I lost control. I wiped out and slid along the pebble-covered pavement. I had a Kubaton in my pocket, attached to my keys. That Kubaton caught on something in the road while I kept sliding. The result was torn work pants—a slit right up the side. I was unhurt but for a couple of scrapes on my hands. When I got to my feet, though, my pants fell off me.

Standing in the middle of the road at the construction site, with ten more minutes until my shift was to start, I opened my backpack, retrieved my spare pair of pants—as per my brother's instructions—and slipped them on.

I quietly looked upward and thanked my brother for the warning—the premonition.

He's visited me several more times in dreams. I was saddened that he would never get to meet my wife. One night I had a vivid dream of him having dinner with us. That dream is embedded in my mind just like a movie scene I've watched over and over. I didn't recognize the house in the dream whatsoever, though.

It wasn't until six months later, when I was viewing a house to rent, that it appeared familiar: the stairwell, and the banister my brother leaned on. I toured the kitchen and living room of a house in a city I'd never been to with the foreknowledge of what I would find.

It was the house where my brother had met my wife in my dream.

That was where the seed was planted for the idea of Sarah Roberts and her sister, Vivian.

In search of more answers, I visited a traveling psychic fair in 1998, just outside of Toronto, and had a reading done. (Notice the similarities to Sarah's humble beginnings.) As I walked past booths (similar to Esmerelda's), I wondered how much of it was fake and how much could be construed as real.

During the summer of 1999 or 2000 (I can't remember exactly), I saw renowned psychic Sylvia Browne at the Hershey Centre in Toronto and was convinced of her ability. She answered random questions from strangers in the crowd who had been given wristbands with numbers on them. Sylvia would choose numbers and have those attendees come down to a microphone and ask her anything they wanted. One woman chose to give up her question for someone else whose need to speak to Sylvia appeared more dire. The question posed to Sylvia was: could she help locate the woman's mother, who had been missing for several days?

Sylvia lowered her head, shook it back and forth slowly, and then spoke into her microphone for the entire auditorium to hear. "Sometimes I hate this job."

She raised her head and told the woman where her mother could be found and that her disappearance had involved three men, one wearing a red jacket. Sylvia instructed the woman to meet her after the event to learn more personal information.

I watched the newspapers the next day and read an article about a woman who was found dead. The police were searching for three suspects.

I was moved to tears as those real visions had taken place before my very eyes.

By 2002, I realized I needed to write a novel about a pack of "psychics" who were kidnapping young girls and then locating them by using their "ability." They would appear real to the world and sell hundreds, if not thousands, of tickets to their psychic fair.

But what would happen when a real psychic (Sarah Roberts) stumbled upon them? Add to that other problems for the kidnapping ring, and after Part One of the novel, I realized human trafficking needed to be addressed, which led to the book *The Future Is Written*.

It went through quite a lot of drafts. In one draft, Caleb, Sarah's father, was a philandering drunk. In another draft, Caleb is shot and killed by the police in his own home while they're monitoring his phones. I've lost track of how many story ideas and plots have maneuvered in and out of Sarah Roberts's world. Ultimately, this novel came to be what it is after countless hours of rewrites, with the help of so many people.

By 2011, I felt I had a solid manuscript. I began to write Part Two, which takes place when Sarah is twenty-two years old. At the end of that section, I wanted Armond to escape so I could go for a trilogy. Since I'd been to Hungary and toured the crypt at Esztergom, and since I'd lived for a year in Umbertide, Italy, which was located next to the mountain town of Montone, I decided to take Sarah on a journey to Europe for Part Three, and there you have it.

The Future is Written, after all.

This novel originally came out as separate books called *Dark Visions*, *The Warning*, and *The Crypt*. However, my wise and brilliant publisher felt these novels needed to be placed into one book titled *The Future Is Written*. I couldn't agree more. It was a fantastic idea. Sarah's journey will reach so many more readers because of the wonderful team at Adaptive Books. I can't thank them enough for the journey we're taking together. Special thanks go out to Matt Wise for his insight and belief in this project.

I'd also like to thank my agent, Italia Gandolfo, for her leadership and wisdom in knowing where to place the series. She knew the writing, she knew the story, and she knew exactly who would offer the best chance for it to be the best it could be—and she was right. (It seems she always is.)

My wife had a huge role in the success of this novel. Author Brenda Sedore is my first reader and my most critical reviewer. As a ferocious reader herself, it's like she's always looking for something to take apart and break down. In the end, I couldn't have done it without her. (She's also my tech support, as she's a computer guru.) Special thanks go out to my wife for all that she is and then some. (Oh, and for her patience—duly noted.)

Lastly, and most importantly, I want to thank the greatest people in an author's life: the readers. If it weren't for you, I'd be lost. I'm extremely grateful to each of you.

Join me on Facebook, Instagram, Goodreads, and Twitter. Come chat with me, send me questions, and offer feedback. You'll learn quickly that I am very social and love to add readers' names to my novels. I'm also known for sending postcards from wherever I'm traveling; so stay in touch with me on Facebook and watch for destinations.

I hope you've enjoyed the ride and that you're looking forward to many more Sarah Roberts adventures.

In the meantime, keep reading and be well.

—*Jonas Saul*

• ABOUT JONAS SAUL •

JONAS SAUL has been writing for more than two decades and has thirty novels and more than fifty short stories to his credit. At times, he has outranked Stephen King and Dean Koontz on the top one hundred authors list on Amazon.

Jonas has traveled extensively to scout settings for his thrillers. Having spent three years in Greece, one year in Italy, and almost six months in Denmark and Hungary, Jonas offers rich cultural diversity in his novels. Currently, he's living in Canada.